Joseph's Portal

Book 3 of The Swan Knights Trilogy

STEFAN SCHEUERMANN

"Joseph's Portal: Book 3 of The Swan Knights Trilogy," by Stefan Scheuermann. ISBN 978-1-949756-86-9 (softcover); 978-1-949756-87-6 (hardcover); 978-1-949756-88-3 (eBook).

Published 2019 by Virtualbookworm.com Publishing Inc., P.O. Box 9949, College Station, TX 77842, US. ©2019, Stefan Scheuermann.

TABLE OF CONTENTS

Centerfold of Rudolf's Map

Prologue

VERENA ELIZABETH KESSLER, a teenage American girl, developed an obsession with King Ludwig II of Bavaria, who died mysteriously in 1886. She swore that Ludwig had something to say to her from beyond the grave, but she didn't know what. In a visit to the castles and palaces of King Ludwig, Verena got her answers. She discovered a manuscript written by the King and left for the next Swan Knight, the next custodian of the portal to the Sweeter Realm, the hiding place of the Holy Grail.

Verena sat in a boat, on an artificial lake, in an artificial cave, built by King Ludwig outside of his palace, Linderhof, near a mural of the legendary Germanic hero, Tannhäuser, and she read the journal. She learned that Linderhof valley is the home of the Grail Portal, the gateway to the Sweeter Realm, opened by the Grail Knight Parsifal in the sixth century, after he was stabbed with a blade by an enchanted flowermaiden. Parsifal drank from the Grail and his wound closed. Before it did, a single drop of his Grail Blood hit the ground of the Bavarian valley. On the very spot, the portal to the Sweeter Realm opened. Parsifal placed the Grail into the protection of the Queen of the Land and Shallow Waters, in the Sweeter Realm. It has been there ever since, waiting for the day that God recalls it into service.

The portal opened each time Parsifal approached it and closed as he walked away. It did the same for every one of his descendants, all the way to King Ludwig II of Bavaria. From Parsifal to Ludwig, generation after generation, a Swan Knight was sworn into the service of the Queen of the Land and Shallow Waters for the protection of the portal. To assist the Swan Knights, many fantastic creatures came through the portal, into Linderhof valley, first among them was The Ancient One, a giant swan who served every Swan Knight as teacher, friend, and counselor.

But not all creatures of the Sweeter Realm were friendly to the Swan Knights. The Sweeter Realm knew its own share of war. Löwschock, the King of the Deep Waters, wanted the Grail for himself. In 1886, he found his way through the portal and killed King Ludwig II on the banks of Lake Starnberg. After Ludwig's death, there was no Swan Knight, no Grail Blood to protect the portal — until it opened for Verena, opened by her Grail Blood. The portal pulled Verena into the Sweeter Realm, where she found a set of armor. The armor belonged to the third Swan Knight, Elsa, the granddaughter of Parsifal. Verena recognized it from its description in Ludwig's manuscript. She put on the armor. It fit her perfectly.

There, on the shore of the Queen's Lake, in the Sweeter Realm, wearing the armor of Elsa, the greatest Swan Knight, Verena met her first friends in the Sweeter Realm. They too recognized Elsa's armor. And seeing it on a human, on their side of the portal, they declared her the Queen of the Land and Shallow Waters. Verena, who just days earlier was an ordinary American girl, about to enter high school, had no choice but to admit the truths before her. *She* found the manuscript that Ludwig intended for the next Swan Knight. *She* opened the portal with her Grail Blood. She found Elsa's armor and it fit her as if it had been crafted specifically for each contour of her figure. She is the Queen of the Land and Shallow Waters, and she is the Swan Knight.

From the narrative in Ludwig's journal, Verena believed The Ancient One to be dead. Two kind creatures, called Schierers, convinced her otherwise. The Schierers led Verena and a company of kind creatures on an expedition to find good and loyal swimmers of the Shallow Waters to help rescue The Ancient One from his prison, inside of the Queen's Lake, where Löwschock ruled tyrannically. At her side were new friends who fast became as old friends — including a feathered man named Felix.

With great losses, they rescued the swan and Verena began her training. She trained for more than a year in a Brunnen city, with The Ancient One and a Brunnen abbess named Taufe. When Verena's training was complete, she toured the Land and Shallow Waters, followed by a growing army of kind creatures loyal to her. They brought life back to the abandoned, war-ravaged cities and shrines of the Land.

Löwschock did not yield to Verena's momentum. He fought, and lives were lost on both sides. The King of the Deep had one weapon Verena did not want to face. He had the obedience of the Wühlenvogels, the Sweeter Realm's most efficient killers — a breed of flying, burrowing creatures, with hard horns, sharp teeth, and vicious claws. The Wühlenvogels had been loyal to Queen Kandake, and they had been friends of the Swan Knights. But in the absence of a Queen, before Verena's arrival, Löwschock claimed their allegiance.

In Gemeinsam, the ancient Unicorn capital, Verena found the Holy Grail, hidden there by Kandake. With the Grail in hand and an army of loyal creatures, Verena met Löwschock in battle, in the river canyon of the Achima Mountains. She turned the loyalty of the Wühlenvogels back to the Queen of the Land and Shallow Waters. The Wühlenvogels turned the tide of the battle in Verena's favor. The creatures of the Deep were forced to retreat to the Queen's Lake.

The Land was safe. But the Shallow Waters were still under Löwschock's control. With the guidance of Taufe, Verena gained a glimpse into her destiny — to rid the entire Sweeter Realm of evil. Löwschock and his beasts had to be vanquished. Verena entered the lake alone. She fought Löwschock.

With the Holy Grail in hand, and slipping from consciousness, Verena breathed water from the cavity of the Grail. In the fight with the King, Verena's spilled blood opened a Grail Portal. The portal pulled the monsters of the Deep out of the Sweeter Realm. With control of the portal, Verena used the opening to sever Löwschock in half. Having vanquished her enemy, she released herself to the will of the lake.

She awoke on the shore, surrounded by the newly liberated creatures of the Land and Shallow Waters. She married Felix, her feathered man, and they entered a new life together — together with the kind creatures, The Ancient One, Taufe, and the many trusted friends who had fought and bled with her to secure the purity of the Sweeter Realm.

CHAPTER 1
Refocused

IN THE WAKE OF THE BATTLE in the Achima Mountains, after the death of Löwschock, I was blissful. I felt cradled in the palm of the Sweeter Realm, in the embrace of a world that adored me. The love and loyalty of the kind creatures sang a perpetual and intoxicating lullaby directly to my soul.

I had my husband — my Felix. When he strolled through the crowd to meet me on the shore, and we declared our affections, when we held hands and recited our vows in front of The Ancient One, I loved him to the fullest of my ability to love. I swelled to near bursting with admiration and gratitude for him. I could not have known then how my capacity for love would grow, how my love for him each day would be buried under the weight of the following day's love.

The victory over Löwschock, the salvation of the Sweeter Realm, our survival, and my marriage, all happened so suddenly and unexpectedly. Fear and despair turned so quickly to joy. On the very morning of my wedding, I had resigned to my own death, as The Ancient One pulled me to the center of the lake and I plunged and sank. Having been flooded so suddenly with blessings too numerous to tally, blissful contentedness defined my every breath. I had earned it. I had suffered and I had struggled. I felt my losses and deserved my rewards. For the first few weeks of my marriage, I believed this, and I thought that the rest of my life would be the same — a constantly growing, snowballing reward for my efforts.

The Sweeter Realm was clear of all violence, of all hatred and jealousy. I had purified Eden. I fulfilled my duty to God. The Holy Grail sat at the bottom of the Queen's Lake, retired from duty, like me, having served its purpose. Despite the warnings that Taufe and The Ancient One had slipped into my lessons, in various degrees of disguise — that my duties as the Swan Knight would require much more of me — a piece of my subconscious held those thoughts back, preventing any approach toward my active musings. Both of my teachers had warned of great sacrifices required of me in the fulfillment of God's will. God was not yet reunited with his people. My home had not yet come to me, as Taufe had predicted. The Grail had not yet vanquished human suffering. Some deep consciousness inside of me knew that my hardest struggles were ahead. But victory and peace, love and admiration, mixed into a tonic that I sipped daily, inebriating me and dulling my desire for anything but the appreciation of my immediate blessings.

The blessings poured in. Visitors both intimate and strange to me graced each leisure hour with praise, gratitude, and gifts. I consumed exotic foods and exotic tales at a ravenous rate. Colors were bright and vivid, embraces were soft and nurturing, and flavors were vibrant, seeming to tingle every inch of me. Every day was spent pleasing my senses and transfixing my imagination. Every night was spent in the feathered arms of my husband. I was in love with everything and everyone, in love with God, and in love with life.

I had imagined, during points of my training and the battles that followed, that I might find a way home, back to my parents, my school and friends, my previous life. When

2

I awoke on the shore of the lake, and saw Felix part the crowd, I knew that I *was* home. I would have appreciated a portal into my old old living room, just a quick passage to allow me to kiss my parents and brother, tell them I love them, and introduce them to my husband. But no such passage existed. I still loved my family. I loved my best friend. But I did not mourn them. I pitied what pain they felt with my dissappearence. But my life in the Sweeter Realm, my marriage, my queenship brought me such an abundance of love that pensive thoughts of any kind struggled to push their way into my full mind and heart.

My lakeside palace is an open, dreamy place. The walls are rounded. There are no harsh lines. There are no doors or locks. Except for a decent respect for the privacy of our sleeping chamber, the palace was open for visitors, day and night, who roamed freely and gathered in impromptu symposiums and celebrations. A twisting ramp near the back of the main chamber, behind the throne, spiraled upward and held several smaller chambers like fruit on a twisting vine. Our sleeping chamber sat at the end of the ramp, capping the palace interior like a cherry on a sundae. The exterior appears as every color, shimmering with waves of colors both deep and bright that rush across the surface with every shift of the eye. The interior walls are pale-blue, but take many various hues based on lighting, angle, and distance.

The ramp and the rooms bustled constantly in those first few weeks. Pilgrims from across the Sweeter Realm came to offer thanks and gifts, to wish the newlyweds well, and to touch the armor and sword, which had become instant relics. I had not worn the armor since it was removed from me when I immerged from the depths of the lake. I could not have even if I had desired it. It was on display and surrounded by a perpetual shield of creature visitors. I had worn it almost constantly, from when I first put it on until it was stripped from me while I was unconscious on the shore of the lake after killing Löwschock.

I did not care to see it or think much of it. Although it was a relic of the Swan Knights history, it was also an emblem of war. During those first few weeks of my marriage, I wanted no reminders of the many things that brought me to my bliss. I wanted only the bliss, with all of its ignorance. I had no need of the armor's magical properties. I needed no ancient Scherier ore to give me a sense of well-being. No armor could embrace and cradle

4

me like my grateful friends and subjects did. I reduced the armor to nothing more than a palace decoration for the fascination of others.

The Zweigwesens built a stand to hold it upright. It was difficult for anyone to see, let alone reach. It was protected by a constant halo of mesmerized visitors. They ooohed, ahhhed, and gasped as they ran their hands and claws across it. Many reveled in the soothing properties of the ancient Scherier ore. Others had a more cerebral fascination with the armor. They pushed their fingers into the fang-holes, allowing chills to rush their bodies as they imagined me at the bottom of the lake with Löwschock's fangs piercing through the armor and sinking deeply into my body.

I too had become an instant relic. I too was touched and caressed, and my ears were filled with praise and gratitude during virtually every waking moment. My dearest ones, those who sat, ran, fought, ate, and studied by my side during the war, struggled to breach the crowd that surrounded me. They found me when they could, in the rare lulls in palace activity, or in the wee hours, when I should have been sleeping.

My first step out of my palace chamber each morning was greeted by Lina, wrapping herself adoringly around my legs. Cort was an ever-present servant, directing his kind in the fulfillment of my every need. For the first few weeks after our victory, my only queenly duty was to be loved and thanked. In truth, I did not feel that my contribution to the victory was greater than any other's. But the attention I received in those first few weeks told a different story.

From my first step into the Sweeter Realm until the death of Löwschock, I was revered for who I was, for the blood in my body. After the victory in the lake, I was venerated for my accomplishments, for liberating an entire world from a tyrannical presence that had tortured, tormented, and murdered the lovely creatures of my queendom for centuries. Between the anticipation of battle, the relief of victory, the loss of loved ones, my reunification and marriage to Felix, and all of the praise and all of the pleasure thrown upon me, my head and heart were swimming. It was all so overwhelming at first. Yet, I adjusted quickly and allowed myself to believe that such blissful chaos would be my life for the indefinite future.

The Ancient One, ever-dutiful, ever-devout, joined me for breakfast four weeks after I killed Löwschock. He was light-hearted and relished the rare moment alone with Felix and me. Conversation was light, a seamless continuation of the previous weeks — *until* he declared himself ready to resume teaching me. He declared me ready to resume learning. He dropped the declaration so subtly into the flow of conversation that it did not immediately strike me. But it hammered me harshly when, with a degree of austerity I had seen in nobody for several weeks, he turned the mood of the moment, warning me of great challenges ahead and of the intense preparations I must undergo in my commitment as the Swan Knight and Queen. I was dumbfounded — entirely lost for words, and the shock of his announcement stripped me of my ability to pretend otherwise.

Astute as always, my old teacher tamped his eagerness.

He softened his excited features and said, "I have surprised you. Take another week. Savor your victory *without* blindness to the future. Enjoy these celebrations with conscious thoughts of what lies ahead. When it is time, we will begin with whole-hearted commitment."

We ate the rest of our meal in silence. Not a word and hardly a glance passed between the three of us. I had raised my spirits so high above the turmoil of the war, to a perch

6

from which no person can conduct normal life, let alone extraordinary life. The plunge to reality was sudden, deep, and wreckful of all I had constructed in my mind. Every dreadful prognostication, every weighty premonition, every notion of truth that I had stuffed beneath the celebrations exploded to the surface of my mind simultaneously. And the burdensome sense of responsibility that had chained itself to my every step during the war was again shackled to my being, despite the swan's attempt to lessen the shock.

Felix did what Felix does. He softened my burdens with the subtlest of gestures. He leaned his shoulder against mine and laid his palm over my hand. So much of the troubles I had faced and pain I had suffered had occurred without him. With his slight squeeze of my hand, he reminded me that I was *not* without him. His feathers, which touched lightly against my shoulder, silently repeated the vows he proclaimed four weeks earlier, that the strength of his arms, the warmth of his feathers, the very beat of his heart have found their purpose of existence — to be mine in any and every way I may need them. It was enough to return the vibrancy of the scene to my senses. The food was again delicious, heightened still by pleasure's contrast to the pain that The Ancient One had recalled to my mind. The numbing effects of intoxicating bliss had faded, and the ephemeral nature of contentment made the peaceful pleasures of the morning all the more precious and enjoyable.

After breakfast, I went for a long walk alone. I had much to contemplate. It was my first experience of solitude since I dropped from the rim of the boat and sank alone to the bottom of the lake. I had forgotten what my own company felt like, the sound of my private thoughts, finally able to converse with themselves, uninterrupted. I blocked all whose thoughts reached for mine, and I found pleasure in the intimate company of my *own* mind. It was warm, like the arms of my mother at the end of a long day.

I strolled along the edge of the lake, recalling memories both tender and horrid, from my whole life, before and after my passage through Parsifal's Portal. Through my training and through practice, I had become good at digging into the hidden memories of others. I had never tried it on myself. It was easy, almost too easy. Moments of my past, from the most mundane to the most monumental, scratched at the lower chambers of my memory, waiting for someone or something to open the door. While I was in the quiet solitude of my walk that morning, I did not gently open those doors, I kicked them open and the memories ran to me and jumped in my lap, kissing me and yelling loudly in gratitude for their liberation. I giggled and cried and giggled again. I returned to the palace several hours later, with an aura of desired solitude about me. I was granted that solitude for the rest of the day.

I could not savor another week of blissful pleasures, like the swan recommended, not as I had before. In my day of lone, concentrated, contemplative deliberation, the zeal of my commitment to God reawakened. The sensations of my years of study and fighting, of travel, discovery, and immense loss, returned to my heart with full vigor. I recalled every drop of my previous determination and aimed it at a new target, at mankind and the troubled world I left behind when I floated through the portal at Linderhof. I carried these concerns, along with a drastic alteration in my general air, to my husband.

As I sat with him on the edge of our bed that night, he whispered with foreboding sobriety, "Welcome back."

I had only sequestered myself for one day. My absence hardly warranted his comment. But the wise sincerity in his tone and expression suggested a deeper meaning.

"Welcome back to what?" I asked, half-expecting to know myself better with each word from his lips.

"Welcome back to your life."

"*Our* life," I quickly amended his statement.

"Yes, my Love, of course, *our* life. You know that everything you have suffered since I met you has pained me as well."

"I know," I assured him.

"Now that we are together and I am your husband, I will suffer every pain *with* you that I cannot take *from* you."

He stared into my eyes as he did when we met outside of Lina and Rüdiger's cave.

"What?" I asked him.

"You look familiar to me," he answered with more earnestness than jest.

I looked at him with a raised eyebrow and a facial expression that said, "I should hope so."

He maintained a sober air which sobered mine.

He ran his thumb along my jaw line and said, "Until a few weeks ago, I had never seen you blissful. Oh, I had seen you happy, even joyful, but always with a passionate engagement to duty, always with a constant underlying agitation."

"But I have not been myself these last weeks, have I?"

"I love to see you happy," he replied, "but I love much more to see you committed. For the first time, I see the fire of my Queen burning in the eyes of my wife… and I count myself the luckiest creature."

I had no words in response. I simply crawled onto his lap and nestled myself under his wrapping, feathered embrace.

With the first blink of dawn I beckoned the swan with my mind. He was not far from the palace and arrived in the main chamber within minutes. It was already filled with visitors, many who had entered with the light of the new

9

day, but many more who had remained there through the night. As The Ancient One sifted through the crowds, I experienced his thoughts. Felix's words had primed my mind for darker dreams of challenges and commitment. The swan was what he had always been, his mind and heart as committed and focused. I was again able to see that.

By the time I awoke that morning, the gifts, the gratitude, the praise, all became putrid to me. My mind reached with tender nostalgia toward the focused clarity of my more desperate days since coming through the portal. Even the most painful moments seemed alluring. The memory of them rooted me to an identity I knew much better than the decadent, spoiled Queen that had walked in my skin for several weeks. Commitment, turmoil, hardship, fear, and focus had come to define me. And I was ready for a return to self.

I sent the swan a simple request to clear the palace of visitors. Much more than the command came through with my thoughts. It was coated in the familiar determination of his student, and he was more than happy to oblige. My ears had worn the constant murmur of conversations since the day after my wedding. They enjoyed the palace's slow return to silence as the crowds cleared room by room. By the time the swan waddled into our bedchamber, he, Felix, and I were the only ones in the entire palace. I stared at the swan and grabbed Felix's hand as we all released simultaneous sighs, which pulled from their places of origin, deep within us, subtle smiles that they set gently on our faces.

With Felix and my teacher near me, the palace bedroom, that place that had only been mine during four surreal, spiritually foggy weeks, suddenly felt like home. A few more pieces needed to be set in place. I called for Lina and Cort, in a single inviting thought. Next, I sought Taufe. After the wedding, she had returned to St. Hildegard to

10

allow me my weeks of revelry before joining me to continue what she had begun on the day I met her. I found her maternal mind easily and instantly. I wrapped all appropriate honor and affection around a simple invitation to join us in the palace to resume her position as teacher to the Queen.

The simple life of an abbess was no longer hers to enjoy. Her position as my teacher was paramount — to me, to the sisters of St. Hildegard, to the creatures of the Sweeter Realm, and to her own precious heart. She had been awaiting my call. When it came, Taufe wasted no time. Each breed of the Land, and several of the Waters, had representatives in service to the Order of St. Hildegard. They lived in the city, prayed in the cathedral, and served the sisters. Upon my summons, several of the servants offered to take her with great haste. But she refused them. She needed a slow walk, to pray, think, and plan for something monumental. She knew what I had tried to forget — that the battle with Löwschock did not mark the end of my destiny. It only turned the first page of a much larger book.

CHAPTER 2
The Election

TAUFE WALKED TO THE PALACE ON HER OWN, enjoying the sweet smell of peace in the air along the way. The Land was still torn, ravaged, and healing. But every soul she encountered on her way to me was sweet and loving. There was nothing to fear from the pools and ponds along the way, and she savored the freedom of peaceful baths with the swimmers of the Shallow Waters. The Sweeter Realm owed her a great debt of gratitude, a debt that was joyfully paid by every pocket of creatures who had the pleasure of taking her in for a night, of sharing a bed and a meal with the spiritual leader of us all.

It took her almost three weeks to reach the palace. I used that time, with the advice and help of my husband and my dearest friends, to establish a realistic and healthier regimen of visits from my subjects. Hordes of creatures still gathered outside of the palace, waiting to resume their free wanderings of my home, and constant, unfettered access to me. Rules were put into place. Schedules were made and upheld. I was still touched like an ancient relic, but under controlled conditions and only during that designated hour of the day.

Cort became the Master of Ceremonies for all gatherings in the palace. All access to me was under his direction and by his standards. The creatures needed to connect with me. Being near me reminded them that the years of war were over and again a Queen sat in the throne of the lakeside palace. They had suffered and lost. They needed the comfort that I gave. And as awkward and unfitting as their praise and gratitude felt to me, they needed to praise me. So I connected with them. Outside of the designated hour for visitors, those gathered nearest the palace sent me their praise in instant waves of thought. At first, the few that were more emotionally powerful drowned out the others. But I quickly gained the ability to separate and decipher each individual thought. I sent my thoughts back to them — thoughts of love and devotion that relieved and softened them from the lingering scars of war, as they returned satisfied back to their homes.

I had wanted to reach for Acheriel. I thought of him daily. But the many Unicorns that seemed able to trot in and out of my mind at-will informed me that he was in mourning. Two months of isolation were required by Unicorn tradition. The time is used to communicate with the departed, to speak intimately to Prische and listen to what mystic signs she might offer from beyond. The Unicorns believe that without those months the dead will slip entirely away from the living and lose their connection to the collective of Unicorn ancestors. Acheriel's two-month isolation would provide their baby, and countless generations of future Unicorns, access to Prische's spirit. I kept my distance, but I missed him terribly. He and the goat were the first in my morning prayers, and my last thoughts to God as I went to sleep.

The morning that Taufe arrived, there were no crowds outside the palace for her to wade through on her way to me. As I wrestled with Lina in the main chamber, near the throne, Taufe's eager delight to see me unintentionally left her mind and flew to mine. I looked up to the palace entrance just in time to catch the morning rays ignite her radiant figure. For a moment, the reflection off of her water-like flesh stabbed at my eyes, eyes which despite the physical discomfort, tried to suck her beauty right through my eyelids and into my soul.

"I picked a good day to arrive," she announced from the entrance. "The crowds have all gone home to make their decision."

My heart and mind had been too filled with love that morning to notice the quiet. The area around the palace was as empty as it was the morning I first laid eyes on it. Even the young Vogelkrötes, who made a regular playground of the slope from the palace threshold toward the center of the lake, were gone. I froze as I sat, and I reached my mind to the areas around the palace. The beach was empty. The forest behind me and the Shallows in front were empty. I pieced together the emptiness with Taufe's words and I realized the event that drew them away. I knew what decision they had to make.

I had no reason to believe that they would elect anybody else. As The Ancient One had predicted, they venerated me well beyond my merits and heaped all credit for their liberation upon the easiest and most obvious target — me. Still, upon the realization that they were gathered at that moment in their respective capitals to elect their next Queen, I found myself shaking with nervousness. Taufe smiled at my obvious physical reaction. She saw it as evidence of her sound moral schooling. She knew that as long as I doubted my fitness for the honor I would strive to better deserve it. She also knew, as everyone else seemed to know, that I would be elected Queen without a single dissenting vote across the entire Sweeter Realm.

I was Queen before the election, not by merit but by the right of inheritance. That honor could not be denied. I was Ludwig's heir. He called me to Linderhof and led me to the journal and the portal. But now they could elect anyone. Why not the swan... or Acheriel? The truth is, I wanted to be Queen. I desired it so badly that I could not imagine my life without it. As foreign as the title seemed to me when Cort declared me to be the Queen of the Land and Shalow Waters, on the beach of the great lake, it seemed far stranger to consider myself in any other way. Who would I be as the only human in the Sweeter Realm if not the Queen? These questions rang too loudly in my thoughts and they projected themselves beyond the confines of my skull.

"You would be the greatest creature I know," Felix answered my thoughts from the entrance to the spiraling ramp. "And you would be my wife and the purpose for my existence."

Lina ran to Felix, climbed his bowed leg, and mounted triumphantly upon his shoulder, as if to shout her concurrence with her bold pose and lifted, pointy chin. I dropped my gaze from them to the floor in front of me, as I pondered my existence in the Sweeter Realm, as the fellow subject of some other Queen or King. I felt like there was a hole in my center, like somebody had ripped my queenship from my abdomen with jagged claws.

The nervousness quickly melted away and I began to drift into a shallow, comfortable trance. The cause of the transition became apparent when I noticed that I sat enveloped by Taufe's nurturing arms. She rubbed my temples with her delicate fingertips. Oh, how I missed the touch of the Brunnens, and the soothing, maternal company of Taufe. None of the attentions I received over the previous seven weeks, none of the gifts or foods, not even the magical effects of my Scherier armor could give the sense of well-being endowed by the loving caresses of Taufe.

The familiar pitter-patter of the swans webbed feet drew our attention as he appeared on the throne room's elevated platform, seemingly out of nowhere. His head shot back and forth from the statuesquely posed Federman and Scherier to the huddled human, curled in the protective embrace of a Brunnen.

"Good Heavens," he proclaimed, "what is going on here?"

He turned his eyes directly to Taufe's and shook his real wing in her direction as he said, "Good timing Taufe. You can begin her lessons on the very day she elected Queen. This is Providential!"

On those words, Felix softened his posture. Lina ran down his body and sprinted to us. She nestled herself tightly between Taufe's neck and mine. She released a sigh that expressed a special degree of comfort. Felix followed slowly behind her and knelt on the floor beside me. The Ancient One stood directly beside him. I asked them all, generally, with no expectation of an answer, how they can be sure that I would be their Queen after the election. There were three distinctly different responses, spoken concurrently, yet I was able to isolate the sentiments. The Ancient One said how absurd it was to suggest that anyone else deserved the honor. Taufe said that any title I might hold in the Sweeter Realm is irrelevant beside a much grander design that God has for me. Felix and Lina spoke the same sentiment — that my personal value to them transcended any title or honor.

There was wisdom and truth, beauty and love behind all three arguments. Together they relieved me of my worries. I would love and serve the Sweeter Realm, love and serve God, and love and serve my husband and friends, regardless of the decisions being made in the capital cities of the Sweeter Realm. Again, I raised the sails of my spirit and asked the Lord to push me where he willed.

Felix built a basin to collect the decisions of the different breeds. He placed it fittingly on the seat of the throne. The elections in the Sweeter Realm usually took

17

months. Creatures trickled in a breed or two at a time. But this election was different. Conferences in the capital were brief. Most breeds had their ballots ready for weeks, and only awaited the appropriate time for their representatives to carry the ballots into the palace.

The nomads were the first to return their decisions. The Friends of the Scheriers had little to discuss. Cort was first among them, and his particular relationship with me left little doubt about the will of his breed. He was the first to enter the palace. On the dried, shriveled casing of a local fruit, they had scratched a name. Cort stepped to the dead center of the palace opening, standing in water hip-deep to him. He paused there until he knew all of our eyes were on him. In a dramatically slow and deliberate march, he made his way to the steps that lead to the elevated platform. With regal, formal posture and a serious expression, he climbed the steps and approached the throne.

He reached for the basin with the ballot of his people, unable to come close to the rim. He stretched farther but was still half the length of his hand from being able to deposit the ballot. Lina made a quick gesture toward him, but Felix shushed her back. Cort rose onto his toes and grunted while he stretched, all the while maintaining his expression of formal pageantry. The scene was awkward but hilarious. I wanted it to end *and* to last forever. Finally, The Ancient One could hold back no longer. He dropped onto his tail feathers and let out a youthful laugh that reminded me of my little brother Karl. Taufe simply held her fingertips tightly against the bridge of her nose and pressed her palms against her mouth, vibrating ever so minutely, so as not to betray the laugh that must have been knocking desperately on the inside of her.

I could take no more. I stood and walked toward him, lifting my hands to gesture my assistance. Cort scowled at me, and his hand with the ballot flew behind his back to hide its secret. I raised my hands to the level of my head and slowly backed away. Felix, who had enjoyed the spectacle in silence from a distance, knew that Cort had to deposit the treasured ballot himself, while standing on his own two feet. He took the basin from the throne and set it on the floor. Cort resumed the regal form he had so clearly rehearsed, and he dropped the ballot into the basin with as much ceremonial grandeur as a Friend of the Scheriers can muster. He turned on his heals toward the palace entrance, glanced at me with a wink and a slight smile, and he marched out of the palace the same way he marched in.

The Federmensch came next, with a name scratched into a thin piece of slate. As the group of six Federmensch huddled before the throne with their slate secret, Felix left my side and joined them. They dared not deposit the ballot without him. So many feathered arms reached toward the basin, I could not tell whose were whose or which one held the ballot. The slate hit the bottom of the basin with a *clank*. All Federmensch but Felix walked from the throne and out of the palace, a few of them kissing and patting Felix tenderly as they parted. Felix stood as he had, directly against the throne, staring into the basin while he rubbed the rim. He was savoring the moment. He wanted to be able to tell the story of that moment vividly for many centuries to come. When his eyes left the basin and turned to me, they welled with tears that were held in place by eyes that were red and puffy, yet smiling immensely.

Ludwig was never elected King of the Land and Shallow Waters. He died before an election could take place. The Ancient One's election had been the last. Prior to that was Kandake's, thousands of years ago. There is no event in human society that can compare. As the other breeds marched, flew, and swam into the palace with their ballots, the weight of the rare occurrence was boldly stated on their faces and in their postures. The air in the main chamber seemed as ancient and solemn as the election itself. Streaks of nervousness flashed occasionally and suddenly through my body like lightening across the sky, declaring itself violently then disappearing entirely.

Electors trickled in over a few days. After the last breed dropped a ballot into the basin, Cort returned. As Master of Palace Ceremonies, he wanted to discuss my wishes for my coronation. I had given no thought to that. I had made no assumptions. A thick, black curtain was drawn in front of my imagination, preventing it from visualizing anything after the election, anything built on an assumed outcome. In response to his questions about *my* coronation, I studdered and twitched nervously.

Cort saw that the subject unsettled me. He changed the topic and asked me who *I* voted for.

"Individuals don't vote," I reminded him. "Each *breed* gets a vote."

"So…," he prodded, "how did the humans vote?"

"I am the only human here," I tentatively mumbled.

"So it looks like you must speak for your breed."

I looked to The Ancient One for guidance.

"He has a point," the swan answered after giving it some thought. "Every breed in the Sweeter Realm must submit a vote, and there is a human in the Sweeter Realm. What is your vote?"

"No no no," Cort interrupted, "the ballots are secret. The vote of the humans should be no exception."

"You are right, Friend," Lina shouted as she ran up the spiraling ramp.

She returned in seconds with a pen and a soft, tan, fleshy piece of paper. I wrote the vote of the humans and placed it gently in the basin. Within two seconds of my ballot touching the top of the pile, The Ancient One scooped the basin into his one wing and waddled up the ramp and disappeared into a side room. He returned within a few minutes.

"A unanimous decision I presume," Cort declared regally.

The swan waved his head in a small circle and answered, "No Cort, it was not."

Cort looked distressed. Taufe and Felix smiled. Lina held tightly to my ankle.

The swan continued, "Every vote was for Verena except one. There was one vote for you Cort, Friend of the

Scheriers, one vote written on a soft, tan, fleshy piece of paper."

At that announcement, Cort put off his own glow, a soft, light-green halo that touched every inch of the room. He turned to me with the widest smile I had ever seen on his face.

He bowed low to me, held it for several long seconds, returned upright and announced, "Long live the Queen. Long live Verena."

Taufe added much more subtly, "May God bless her and keep her on the path of her destiny."

All heads in the room dropped, mine lowest of all, as we responded in chorus, "Amen!"

The Sweeter Realm was rich with traditions tens of thousands of years in the making. Among them was the way news of the election was to pass to the various homelands. These traditions held firm before the arrival of a Swan Knight who could reach their minds from far away and project thoughts directly into their heads. I had to check my emotions after The Ancient One announced the results. My elation pulsed from me and wanted to touch every mind with the news, from the Nomadic Belt to beyond the Pfeifen Mountains. I also felt gratitude and love to every creature who honored me with a vote.

I had felt the burden of their cares, and I had felt their love before. But knowing they unanimously chose me to lead them and guide them, of every creature in the Sweeter Realm, they decided to put their faith in me, was an honor my self-control could barely check. I recalled the images of each breed processing to the throne and depositing their ballot in the basin. The memory of each face swelled me. To subdue my thoughts and keep them securely caged inside of my own head, so as not to jeopardize the ancient traditions, I focused on my dearest ones around me. I thought about my future with them and their futures with me as their Queen.

I deflated my honor *and* my pride by standing myself in comparison beside the Queens and Kings of the past. This worked. I still enjoyed a gloriously happy moment. But it was weighed down by a moderating sense of inadequacy and a squeezing desire to earn what had been given to me. I was not afraid of failure. I had something no other Queen had. I had The Ancient One, Taufe, Lina, and Acheriel. I had Felix and Cort. In my mind, *we* were elected that day, and every decision from the throne would bear their marks as well. I scanned the room, stopping to stare at each face, each feather. Combined, I did believe us worthy of the honor. Together, I thought us as formidable as Kandake.

My elation did not remain inside the confines of my own skull. But my focus kept it within the palace walls, to the precious few that were within reach of my physical senses. My thoughts flew freely to them and theirs to me. The rest of that evening and into the night, I kept our minds united. Conversation in the palace that night were a bizarre patchwork of spoken words and deluges of raw sentiment that erupted in silence directly from one heart to the others. After a late dinner, we all slept together in the dining room, after stories and speeches, jokes and effusions of gratitude slowly winded down. Mouths closed and hearts opened wider. We fell asleep in tight mental communion. We dreamed each other's dreams that night, while our arms, legs, and heads rested haphazardly on each other in a pile of celebratory affection.

CHAPTER 3
Requirements and Reunions

NEWS OF THE ELECTION RESULTS was sent to each capital. The coronation would occur as soon as the Master of Ceremonies had everything in order. Cort suggested that the ceremony take place on Der Mutterleib des Flusses (The River's Womb), the island at the mouth of the Achima River. That was where Kandake's coronation was held, and Cort thought that continuity with the Queens of old might make up for the fact that I am not from the Sweeter Realm. I could not go there. I certainly could not celebrate there. The last time I saw that island, Prische's body lay half-devoured on its shore. If there were still enemies in the Sweeter Realm, celebrating my coronation there might have held some powerful significance. But there was nobody to defy with such symbolism and I hoped that Acheriel might attend. I could not ask *him* to stand on that beach with thoughts of anyone but his wife.

Acheriel's period of mourning was to end one week after the election. I asked Cort to hold the coronation on that very day. Since passing through the portal, I had come to adore many beautiful natives of the Sweeter Realm. Acheriel was among the very dearest to me. Marriage and the swirling chaos of life since our victory had kept many of those friends from the front of my mind. With the election over and life settling substantially, my mind began to pull from its depths those tender sentiments that had napped quietly inside of me. I missed Acheriel. I mourned for him. And I could not wait to meet Prische's daughter. As the week between the election and the coronation passed, my anticipation for Acheriel's return to my life fevered my blood much more than any celebration of my queenship. It was only when Cort pressed me on matters of the coronation that any significant portion of my mind committed to it.

The Ancient One, Taufe, Lina, Cort, and I gathered in the palace throne room to discuss the coronation. The palace seemed the most ideal place to hold the ceremony. It was easily accessed by Land and Waters. And maintaining the unity achieved by Achima was widely considered the primary function of the Queen. The palace was new to me and foreign to most. It held none of the significance I wanted to associate with my queenship. The Ancient One and Taufe agreed. I wanted it to be in St. Hildegard. It is where my training began, and the last place I called home. It was relatively central and the approach into Brunnen land was light and level in all directions. Brunnen land, like the Brunnens themselves, is very gentle and welcoming. Even in the Brunnen wilderness, the ground is soft, the trees are tall and sparse, and the bark of the trees is tender and fleshy.

But it would be a rugged journey for the swimmers from the Queens Lake and the other distant bodies of water, and rallying the support of the swimmers was my first act after being declared the Queen by the Friends of the Scheriers. The swimmers rescued the swan, without whom I would have been lost. The war would have been lost, and there would be no Queen, no coronation. The safe and easy passage of the wet creatures to the coronation site was a paramount consideration in our discussions.

The Ancient One wanted to hold it near the Portal Point, under the tree that held his old nest. He believed that the location would remind everyone that I am also the Swan Knight. It was near the lake, on the southern end of the Nomadic Belt. It was far from Scherier land. But Scheriers had been making that trip for centuries, and the swan assured me that they would think nothing of the journey. I suggested that the ceremony take place in Gemeinsam, around the altar that hid the Holy Grail for so long. Connecting me symbolically with Kandake and the Queens of the past was simply not in my paradigm. The significance of the connection did not carry the weight in my mind that it did in the others. What was squarely within my cognitive framework was the Grail. To me, the obelisk and the Grail seemed like the most powerful symbols of my queenship.

Many suggestions were thrown forth, some with vehement insistence, with many good points of evidence in their favor. Others were whispered and forgotten. In my intimate circle, only one voice remained silent on the matter. Lina simply volleyed her eyes acroos the room as others spoke, as if she was watching a tennis match. Felix was the first to notice this. He asked her for her opinion.

She timidly and hesitantly responded, "Well Verena, my Queen, I'd like to hold the coronation in Gralkirsche. As the great swan reminded us, you are also the Swan Knight. The Boots of Lohengrin could perform the rites, linking reverence to the Queen with dedication to the Swan Knights. The order exists to secure Scherier dedication to the Swan Knights, the portal, and the Grail. It is the Boots of Lohengrin, more than any others, that are sworn to you. You *are* the Swan Knight they have been sworn to you long before the election. You are also the Queen of their homeland. It seems that if any group of any breed should host the ceremony, it should be them."

All eyes widened at the idea. Before Lina could continue her thoughts, others interjected.

The Ancient One said to me in a raspy whisper, "Yes, that would be ideal. The Boots could honor the line of Swan Knights and the line of Queens, ending both with the greatest of both, with you, my love."

My modesty had no time to rebut. Taufe added with her thoughtful practicality, "Oh yes, the swimmers could easily travel the river and the marsh, right to the doorstep of Gralkirsche."

Felix grabbed my hand as the others spoke. He rubbed the back of my hand with his thumb, quickly and excitedly, as if powered by an idea that churned inside of him. I looked to his eyes. They stared into the vacant air behind me as they widened.

"What is it?" I asked him.

"We will form another procession. Not to rescue the swan or gather an army. A peaceful parade will rally hearts for a peaceful purpose."

He looked to the floor, scratched his head as if in deep contemplation, lifted his head and continued, "The procession will begin at the Portal Point, where we will honor the Swan Knights. We will march you along the lakeshore, past the palace, where we will honor the Queens of old, parade you to the mouth of the river, where we will honor those who fell in battle. We will take you through the canyon, and honor your great victory there, to where the river runs nearest to Gemeinsam. There we will pause to honor Christ and the Grail. We will carry you through the Wendel Marsh and be received in Gralkirsche by the Stiefel von Lohengrin."

There was not a dissenting thought among us. It was done. It was decided to the delight of all. The procession would begin in one week, on the day of Acheriel's release from mourning. He could join us at any point along the way, whenever he is ready. Any particulars of the ceremony beyond that I was happy to leave entirely to

Cort's discretion. I asked Cort to go to Gralkirsche and work with Hüter and the other Boots. I called for a Unicorn to take him there. Not just any Unicorn would do, not to carry my Cort all the way to Gralkirsche. I called for Schwerthorn. She had served Veronika, and she was pleased to serve this mission.

Cort, who had spent more than a year of restless travel, preparing the Land and Shallow Waters to receive their Queen, was ready to perform a similar service.

"You will miss the procession," I reminded him.

"Miss it?" he giggled in response. "I will have the best view of all, watching your triumphant march into Gralkirsche from the top of the sacred spire. Besides, I am a Friend of the Scheriers. They will treat me well."

"They will certainly do that," Lina assured him. "The Scheriers have had no better creature-friend than you, Cort. You are truly a Friend of the Scheriers if ever we had one."

Cort bowed to Lina with an unnaturally wide smile. He turned toward the palace entrance and took a few steps.

"Where are you going?" I asked him.

"I am going to wait for my Unicorn, on the shore. There is no time to waste."

"We will wait with you. You kept me safe in the circle clearing, before I met any of the others. Now we will be *your* circle."

Few but I thought about those early days in the Sweeter Realm, when Cort was my only friend. Few realized how important that first contact was, how tragically differently it all might have happened, had Cort and his kind not kept me safe in their clearing, kept me from bathing in the lake and announcing myself to Löwschock while I was utterly unprepared to face him. My declaration reminded them all of what they owed to him.

We all walked with Cort to the shore outside of the palace, near where I awoke alone from my dream on that

29

strange morning with a mysterious bruise around my waist. We sat there and reminisced about joy, love, and loss for hours, until Schwerthorn trotted through the band of woods near that portion of the shore. I lifted Cort onto the Unicorn. But before I did, I held him at the height of my face and stared adoringly into his eyes. Without passing any thought straight from my mind to his, I relayed my affections for him as others must — though the softness of my embrace and the tenderness of the kiss I laid upon his forehead. As Schwerthorn sprinted away, Cort sat facing backwards on her shoulders, staring back at me with his signature smile.

With Cort off to plan the ceremony, and Felix organizing the procession, The Ancient One took me to himself and walked me along the beach. He began to explain some of the coronation traditions that must be upheld. He described how I should receive the visitors of each breed. He mentioned gifts.

"No more gifts!" I demanded. "No more banquets. No more. I can't receive another gift."

"You misunderstand, my dear one. After the coronation, it is you who must give the gifts... one gift to each breed."

"To thank them for electing me?"

"No, no. You think too minutely. The gifts are a symbol of a much bigger truth."

"That it is the Queen's duty to give to them, to serve them."

"Yes," he answered with a great deal of satisfaction.

"What sort of gifts should I give? I have nothing that they could use."

"You have everything that they will ever need from you. The treasures they seek from you do not sparkle, and they cannot be eaten or drunk. I can give you no more guidance on this matter. The sentiments must be entirely from your head. Just consider this. Not every gift need be carried away from Gralkirsche in the hands of the recipient."

I tried to manipulate around his reluctance to guide me on the matter, prying, "What gifts did you give at your coronation?"

"Oh my love," he replied with reminiscent sorrow, "there was no time for that, no time for rites, rituals, and celebrations. Our peril was immediate."

"So you gave no gifts?"

"I had no coronation. But I gave each breed the one thing that I believed they most needed."

Knowing him as I did, I quickly realized what that gift was, and I spoke it to him somberly, "It was your tour, wasn't it? Your gift was your presence. You risked your life to visit each breed, each homeland."

"That was what they needed, and I could think of no greater symbol of my love for them than to bury their dead and nurse their living. Yes, my dearest friend, my gift to them was my tour of the kingdom."

I smirked at him and turned the topic of conversation to the much brighter present, "Well, that doesn't help me at all. Times are very different now."

He maintained his serious tone, and added to my thought, "Yes, they are brighter for you than they were for me. They are brighter *because* of you. You have returned your queendom to the peace of old, and your gifts may resemble the coronation gifts of old. Now, love, stop trying to wiggle hints from me. I have told you all that I will on the subject. Truly, these gifts must come entirely from your heart. I am not King. My opinion is irrelevant."

He winked at me and I sat down directly where I stood. I wrapped my arms around themselves, dropped my head, and hummed one long, steady note.

The Ancient One kissed the top of my head, patted me a few times, and said, "These decisions are of great importance. I will leave you to consider them."

He jumped high into the air and flapped a few times, seeming to forget that he could not fly. When he came down hard on his feet, he simply waddled away, singing an old German song that I had never heard.

I had my work cut out for me. There was nothing in my mind, not one single idea for a gift to any of the many breeds of my queendom. The Ancient One declared that I could seek no advice. And I only had a few days to gather these gifts. I wanted so badly to be everything they expected me to be. The weight on my heart and head, as I strained to conjure ideas, was severe.

The procession was scheduled to begin at the Portal Point on the day after Acheriel's mourning ended. I begged Felix for one more day so that the greatest living Unicorn could join us at the beginning — perhaps carry me as his dear wife once had.

Felix, who was in charge of the procession, answered, "If you were only my wife, I could not deny you. If you were only my Queen, I could not. You are both, and your wishes hold absolute power over me. The procession will begin when you think it best. The queendom will gladly adjust."

My first thought in the decision was of Acheriel. But following shortly behind were thoughts of the gifts. I wanted so badly to ask Felix's advice. Few would know better of such things. But I knew I could not solicit his opinion, and I knew he would not give it if I did.

With all matters of the coronation securely in the hands of the fully capable, I set my mind on the gifts that would launch my lifelong queenship. The presentation of the gifts was to be the first interaction I would have with each breed after they elected and sanctified me, and a representation of my relationship with them until the day I die. There would be no second chances, no make-up gifts if I got the first one wrong. I was more nervous in the consideration of these gifts than I was in engaging the monsters in the Sicherheit Marsh.

I needed a place to sequester myself, to ponder under ideal conditions what must be ideal decisions. Only one place would do. I summoned a Wühlenvogel to fly me with haste to St. Hildegard. He was before me mere seconds after my mind disconnected from his, though he had been deep into Wöhlenvogel land. He landed only long enough to perform a slow, low bow, before wrapping his tail under my arms and swishing me through the thick air. He took my desire for haste to heart, and his heart relayed the order to his wings. The trees and streams, rocks and hills beneath us were a visual blur that provided few distinguishable features to identify one from another. By the time my eyes adjusted to the incredible rate of flashing shades, we were into the forest surrounding St. Hildegard and slowing for our descent.

I claimed a side chamber of the cathedral for my own use. The sisters were pleased to see me and more greatly pleased to offer me a room for such a sacred purpose. I entered the city with tremendous apprehension. But once on the ground, and strolling between the fleshy-barked trees of St. Hildegard, familiarity to the senses cradled and soothed me.

After the brief greetings, the sisters bathed me and caressed me. Once fully refreshed, I visited my old rooms underground. My Wühlenvogel joined me and spoke ceaselessly about the Schism and the preparations for the flight to the Black Forest. After touring the underground village, he flew home and I settled into the cathedral chamber that had been set-up by the sisters, ideally for my purpose. As they left me alone, they reminded me to be in the main chamber at sunset, to join them in the Vespers Hymn. My immediate reaction was of reluctance to sacrifice precious time to the sacred Benedictine tradition. But the atmosphere of the cathedral and the soothingly familiar voices of the sisters reminded me of the importance of prayer. If I were to make the right decisions, I must rely firmly on Divine guidance, as I had so steadily to that point.

So I sang the Psalter in the mornings, as I had during my training. I sang the Vespers Hymn in the evening. I was fed and bathed. In the hours between, I reflected on my monumental decisions to the dulcet accompaniment of the Brunnen choir. One at a time, with increasing delight, the answers came to me. As I pondered with the utmost focus each individual breed, what they mean to me and what I mean to them, our histories together, the laughs, the tears, the blood, and the deaths, the ideal gifts came to mind. So ideal was each gift, that I did not need to write them down. Each subsequent thought of a breed brought their ideal gift sharply to mind. Some gifts were ready to give. Many needed preparation. I worked feverishly until all gifts were decided upon. Most of the gifts could be prepared with the supplies at hand or quickly and easily fetched — all but one. I needed to go to the palace to prepare one gift.

As I was working on the design for my gift to the Zweigwesens, I received a special visitor. Three Brunnen sisters breached my chamber entrance with a young Zweigwesen — my godchild. I quickly pushed my secret plans aside and opened my arms to her. She sapped my forehead, lips, and chest, in a slow and emotional reenactment of her sapping ceremony. Then she embraced me as her parent, and kissed and stroked me passionately. She was the only creature in the Sweeter Realm who could claim the Queen as her godmother. But her pride in that honor was nothing beside her authentic affection for me, which was demonstrated dynamically with her kisses and caresses.

On the day we departed St. Hildegard in search of the Grail, just days after the sapping ceremony, my little Zweigwesen swore to protect me. She wanted to join our crusade. Of course, I denied her. But her stout spirit that day earned her a nickname. I have called her Eichengeist (Oaken Spirit) ever since.

Once she finally ceased her effusions of affection, Eichengeist stayed with me for the rest of that day. I knew that I was not supposed to seek advice in the choosing of gifts. But the gifts were already decided upon. It was only some particulars about the gifts that still needed work. I laid all my papers before my goddaughter and asked her if she wouldn't mind assisting me with finalizing the details. She sat on my lap and revealed her brilliance to me in the form of surprising and ingenious insights and contributions. With mock-formality, I swore her into an oath of silence until the gifts are revealed at the coronation. As if my hallowed position as her godmother had not sewn me firmly enough to her affections, this shared secret made her feel one with me. There was nothing "mock" about the formality in her heart. It was as if I had knighted her into a sacred quest. I had not seen such a happy creature since I saw my own reflection in Felix's eyes as he swore his wedding vow to me.

On the evening before the procession, with the blessing of her parents, I took Eichengeist with me to the palace. With her sharp wood-like fingers, she performed the final preparation for the presentation of gifts by completing my gift to the Pfutzeschilfs. Because of that gift, I had to close the palace to all. There could be no entering the main chamber without revealing the secret. So I spent the night before the procession with the Federmensch, and with the dearest Federman of all. Every moment outside of my husband's embrace is a lonely moment, regardless of the company I keep. Even the nurturing attentions of the Brunnen sisters of St. Hildegard could never replace him. My reunion with his feathered arms that night, though only a few days in the making, was as cozy a homecoming as could ever be.

The Federmensch celebrated boisterously that night. After all, one of their own was married to the Queen. But all of that was in the distant background of my senses. Foremost in my eyes, in my ears, and against my skin was my Felix. We spoke nothing of the coronation, nothing of the procession that he had so painstakingly coordinated. We spoke only of our love and devotion for each other. I awoke that next morning with greater energy and confidence than I had ever felt to that point in my life. The previous few days had given me much to galvanize my spirits. My return to St. Hildegard, the joining of my voice in prayer to those of the Brunnen choir, the completion of my gifts with my goddaughter, and my reunion with my husband, each offered my heart enough to fill it completely. Combined, I nearly burst with happiness.

Acheriel did not meet me at the Portal Point, as I had hoped. No, he met me in the Federmensch camp. He blocked his mind from me until he walked up behind me and touched his horn to the center of my spine. I began to sweat as such an immense rush of thought, affection, and memories poured through his horn and into my mind. With it all came the distinct presence of Prische, whose spirit had been permanently affixed to the front of his brain by his two months of devout mourning. I greeted them *both* lovingly, as I sent my response back through the horn connection.

Finishing my greeting was an earnest entreaty, my deep desire that he carry me during the procession from the Portal Point to Gralkirsche, covering ground that he and I traveled together under very different circumstances. He spoke his willingness to do so. But I heard nothing of his voice because it was drowned in a rush of thought directly from his head to mine, thoughts of undying devotion. Both his love for me and Prische's now lived inside of one head, one horn. And as he expressed his love, Prische's too flowed through his horn.

With only a kiss from my husband to delay me, I mounted Acheriel, gripped the base of his horn tightly while hugging him with a squeeze of my legs, and led the gathering crowd from the Federmensch camp to the Portal Point, where I had taken my first steps in the Sweeter Realm.

CHAPTER 4
The Procession

The Unicorns and Wühlenvogels were all working overtime. They were the only creatures in the Sweeter Realm capable of such speed as to arrive at the Portal Point in time. They served as taxis for the other breeds. Creatures of all shapes and sizes mounted Unicorn shoulders and clung to the grasping claws of the Wühlenvogels. Many breeds sent representatives to join in the procession. All sent emissaries to Gralkirsche for the coronation. Unicorns and Wühlenvogels crossed great swaths of ground and sky, shuttling creatures in the excited bustle of the ancient event. As they did, swimmers from across Rudolf's Map and beyond swam the final legs of their journey, begun the moment that Gralkirsche was announced as the site of the coronation.

The Portal Point brought a rush of memories for me to address, categorize, and decipher. I was not alone in this. Only the nomads and some Zweigwesens saw it regularly and had any associations with the area other than the portal. *My* memories were of one part of one day of my short life — though the extremity of sensations on that day made the recollection of them pungent. But The Ancient One was simultaneously pensive and stimulated by the familiar surroundings. His memories were of millions of moments over hundreds of years, as friend, teacher, custodian, and soldier for the Swan Knights.

His peculiar mood was so demonstratively displayed in his expression that it drew my thoughts away from my own memories and pulled my mind into his, accidentally at first, but followed by intentional probing. He let me in but did not guide me through his thoughts. I was free to wander his memories in a rich and lush mental safari. A great many extraordinary things occurred in and under the old nest. Kandake died there. The initial plans for Einigkeitstadt were drawn into the very dirt upon which I stood. These and many other profound realizations jolted me from my safari, just long enough to ponder them before diving back in.

As all of this occurred, groups from each breed in the procession joined what was becoming a massive company of creatures, many with their own centuries-old memories of the portal and the Swan Knights. One of the Scheriers bolted by me and caught my attention. I watched him as he ran several small circles.

"This is it," he proclaimed, more in a manner of internal thought than as a public address. "This is the Portal Point."

He rolled and bounced and tumbled on the ground, reenacting memories of his days at the old lodge and in the lush valley, keeping playful company with my storied ancestors. As he played, he spoke of Linderhof, of Earth and of humans.

I immediately suffered an acute sensation of home. Right there, where the Scherier stood, was the passage to Linderhof. My world felt very near, though I had no ability to access it. I stared into the air above the Scherier, half expecting the portal to be accidentally opened before my eyes by some distant cousin on the other side, or by my father, still roaming the Linderhof grounds in search of his daughter.

Although I had only heard the crackle of the opening portal once, and it terrified me at the time, I longed for it. I longed to step through it and smell the air of the Venus Grotto, to see humans walking in and out of the historical site. I wanted to walk through the portal into the past — to see Otto and Agnes, Elizabeth, and my dear Ludwig. I believe those thoughts came through my lingering connection to the swan's memories, as not doubt he wished the same.

In the company at-large, there was more reflection than conversation. But all was brought to a halt when the master of the procession demanded our attention. Felix sat high upon the shoulders of his oldest friend. It felt good to see them together. Mounted on Acheriel, he pointed his finger, flicked his hands, twirled his wrists, and waved his head like an orchestra conductor, guiding the creatures in concerted cadence into their place in the grand procession. A gap in the middle of a mix of Brunnens and Zweigwesens, about two thirds of the way from the front, sat empty until Acheriel filled it. Felix dismounted and gestured for me to take his place on Acheriel's shoulders. Before I could step, a familiar howl came from above. A small flock of Wühlenvogels descended upon us, some carrying Friends of the Scheriers, and others carrying the pieces of my armor, as I had instructed them to do.

They landed, and the Friends of the Scheriers strapped me in, like they had many times before. There were so many creatures around me. From high on Acheriel, I sought individuals, with my eyes and with my mind, wanting to pull them nearer to me. I sought Taufe, and she reminded me that those who had been dearest to me were placed at a distance for a reason, that those who had *not* marched beside me in the canyon of the Achima River, or through the bloody marshes, or across the Zweigwesen bridge, needed their moment at my side. The directive took

41

quickly to my heart and I turned my attention to those creatures before my eyes. There was one dear friend I demanded near me. My goddaughter rode on the shoulders of another Zweigwesen marching beside me. I insisted upon that and was not denied.

Although I showered attention on those surrounding me, I engaged in long conversations with Acheriel as we marched from the Portal Point to the shore of the lake. It was a good distraction from the confused memories of the last time I had traveled that stretch of land. Acheriel's goat had stayed with family in a Unicorn village not far from Gemeinsam during his period of mourning. She remained with them so Acheriel could attend the procession and coronation. He came directly from his isolation to join me. He had not seen his child since he and Prische left her to join the army in Gemeinsam. This was a bold testament to his devotion to me. I felt it keenly.

Acheriel assured me that we would meet the baby and the rest of his family when the procession passed Gemeinsam. As much as I had come to admire the oneness of the collective, and to understand it through my own ability to connect minds, the full depth of the Unicorn Collective's connection was still beyond me. Acheriel reared back his head and asked me to take his horn. I grabbed it and felt a bit of that connection, as my mind stood beside his family and baby, as near to them as I was to the Brunnens and Zweigwesens marching at my side. Acheriel sacrificed little to be with me. His mind touched his baby — so his baby touched her mother, and they all touched me as I rode on his shoulders and gripped his horn. Their physical distance from each other meant little.

The procession took us to the lake and around the eastern shore, to where I first met Cort. Cort was already in Gralkirsche, but I blasted his mind with the warmth of affection that the familiar surroundings enveloped me with.

His kindness to me during my first couple of days in the Sweeter Realm coated my spirits with a pleasant film that time and experience still had not washed off.

Evening came at about the same point that it did when I followed Cort and his friends into the circle clearing. There were no monsters to hide from anymore. The waters to our left were bright and clear, and swimmers splashed along beside the procession with happy, loyal, and grateful faces. It contrasted starkly with the dark waters and horrid sense of dread that haunted me from just beneath the surface on my first day through the portal. We camped on the lakeside, with nothing frightening but the memories of darker times.

Those memories pronounced themselves subtly, but just enough to add a rich austerity to our happiness and the appreciation of our blessings. Dangerous times, frightening times, mournful days of great loss were not so very far in our past, and certainly not faded from our memories. After so much war, fear was still our default emotion. But we awoke from our nightmares to a pure and beautiful Eden —and the rancid sting of our recent memories made our current surroundings all the more beautiful.

Over breakfast, I retold the story of my passage through the portal and my first several hours in the Sweeter Realm. I praised Cort for securing my safety and leading me to the Scheriers. Lina buried herself in my lap and wept as I recounted Rüdiger's brave excitement to rescue the swan. The stories had been told hundreds of times. But the members of my procession listened intently, and gasped and sighed, clapped and cried as if hearing them for the first time.

My voice faltered and my hands shook as I talked about meeting Felix and Acheriel. My love for them, fired and tempered in war, lost none of its potency under the calm and peaceful skies above us. I still shook when I thougth of them and choked when I spoke of them. I told the story up to the point when Prische joined us above the Scherier cave. I stopped there, unable to proceed. They all knew what brought the storytelling to such an abrupt end. We all sat and honored the most beautiful Unicorn of her generation. After an appropriate moment of silence, we reformed the procession and moved onward, along the lakeside, toward the Achima River.

All heaviness, all weighty thoughts and conversations as we walked along the beach were washed away by the playful splashing of the Queen's Lake Swimmers. They performed aquatic stunts that thrilled us. They made silly noises that made us laugh. We continued to march along at our previous pace while the Swimmer circus devoted their day to entertaining the procession. As much satisfaction as I took from the revival of the cities and shrines of the Land, I took much more from the health and liberty of the Swimmers, who suffered the greatest under the tyrannical rule of Löwschock. Their light-hearted antics along the shallow shore lifted us all and placed before our eyes and ears the most demonstrative evidence that the war was really over and nothing dark, nothing evil lurked beneath the surface of the Waters, waiting to abduct, imprison, torment, and devour.

In the late afternoon, a familiar sight found our eyes, ending the frolicking in the water beside us and slowing the pace of the procession, as if we waded through the mud of the marshes. The mud was not around our ankles, but around our hearts. Before I could see the mouth of the river, before seeing the beaches where we fought the knobby-headed serpents, I saw the island — the last place my eyes beheld Prische. The memory was putrid and renewed in me the sensation of experiencing her drowning. My chest ached. So did Acheriel's. Our minds connected intimately in the shared experience. The sensations were too

44

voluminous for the shallow rim of my spirits, and they poured over onto the minds of those around me, encumbering them and slowing them further.

But there *was* a lining of warmth behind the sorrow. Acheriel's period of mourning had adhered her spirit to his mind. In our connection, I was also with her. She spoke to me. The thoughts were unintelligible, as if whispered into a tunnel. Wispy, airy thoughts bounced around my skull. I could discern nothing specific. But the embrace of her love for me was unmistakable. My inability to channel her exact thought did not frustrate me. I thanked her and honored her, and I left Acheriel's mind to the two of them.

The procession grew as we worked our way up the river to the canyon. We were joined by dozens of Swimmers, four more Unicorns, and a flock of Wühlenvogels. Each new attendee greeted me before falling into their position as dictated by Felix. They came to me in rigidly formal pageantry. But my bumbling and failed attempts to respond properly quickly mortalized me, and an atmosphere of casual, familial comfort consumed all royal expectations. I was part of an ancient ceremony, to coronate the Queen of the Sweeter Realm. But I was also human. I was Verena Beth, the daughter of my silly father, and no amount of time in my queendom would lessen that.

We could have pressed on and made it to Gemeinsam by late evening. But there was no reason for expedience, nothing to rush torward, and nothing worrisome to rush away from. We camped outside of the canyon mouth, not far from where we camped after the Battle at the Achima River (as it came to be known). The day still had plenty of sunlight to offer and the grass of our campsite became the arena for hilarious games and wrestling. I left the crowd after sunset and found some solitude. Consciously, I wandered without aim. But my subconscious sought a direction, and took me to the remnants of the campfire, where The Ancient One and I had left the ground in the grasp of the Wühlenvogels, after our victory in the canyon.

With papers in hand, I put the finishing touches on some of the gifts I had so meticulously prepared to give the breeds of the queendom. I was nervous to present the gifts, suddenly doubtful that they were the sort of gifts expected from the Queen, or if there were any expectations at all. But as I put the final touches on each plan, they seemed right, and come-what-may, they would be gifted to the breeds soon.

Lina sought me out and broke my solitude. She convinced me to return to camp and get some sleep before another long day of travel. Whether exhausted or focused I could not tell. But the party settled quickly to sleep, most before the sun fully set. I was the last to settle in. I took a few minutes to enjoy the peaceful breaths of the dreaming creatures around me before joining them in slumber.

We wasted little time in the morning embarking on the day's travels. Few words passed among us as we worked our way into the canyon. There were reminders of the bloody battle at every turn of the head. Hoof and claw marks still told a tale of violence. Rocks remained rusty-crimson from blood stains that had not fully washed away. I looked around me to notice the huddling creatures, reshaping their procession to press more tightly together as they walked through the vivid flashbacks in their minds. Many in our procession fought in the battle, and lost loved ones between those canyon walls. A suitable amount of reverence was paid to the dead as we marched the battle-site. Scheriers and Wühlenvogels sang together songs of war and loss from their own ancient conflict.

One of those songs, sung in a patchwork-quilt of languages, I translate here, as well as I can into English verse.

Walls and stones, halls and homes

Bear no rank to hearts and bones
Secrets held inside the head
Turn to dirt inside the dead

Even the goodliest tooth or claw
When turned against a goodly
friend
Serves the demons that hunt us all
And releases poison to the wind

But the Queen, the Blessed Queen
will come
And wrap us all beneath her tail
And place the sparkle in our eyes
To reflect the sparkle of her scale
Now, one we are, one with her
And one with all who peace prefer
With claws and horns not to fight
But to work together in love and
right

The song spoke to the good that can come from
conflict. But it did not wash away the blood-stains from the
rocks. And it did not wash away the putrid memories of the
battle that raged in that very canyon. The tune was somber,
and it served only to further sink the morale of the
company.

Acheriel entered my head. He begged me to lift them
with a thought — any hopeful and loving thought to bring
the mood of the party back to a brighter place. I searched
Acheriel's deepest thoughts. His mind was on his daughter
and on the Unicorn capital that waited for us on the other
side of the canyon. Rather than sharing thoughts of my own
with the party, I shared Acheriel's. They were perfect.
They spoke of new life, of love, and of home, of the new,

47

young life that waited to grow and flourish in the wake of the losses of war.

My own memories began to wander, and they transmitted along with Acheriel's thoughts. They were memories of Gemeinsam, of finding the Holy Grail and of receiving Felix's letter, of confessing my admiration for him in a letter of my own. The memories lifted my heart. Every creature in our company sat upon my heart and was lifted with it. Felix's memories of writing his letter and receiving my response poured into the stream of grateful recollections and washed over the minds of the company.

A delightfully familiar sound greeted our senses, just as we left the battlefield section of the canyon. A flock of forty Eulesängers joined us from the east, specially selected emissaries sent from Eierheim to join our procession and attend the coronation. Their spirited whistles were our first intimation of their approach, as they descended upon us from the lip of the canyon walls above us. Such joy exuded from each note whistled that it elicited laughter from the company, beginning with the lightest of giggles as the sounds first met our ears, but growing to full-throated guffawing by the time the birds had settled among us.

The laughter morphed gradually and seamlessly into conversation. We pushed through the canyon with renewed vigor, not away from the horrors of the past, but toward the brightness of the future. By the time the canyon walls diminished to the soft plains between the Achima Mountains and Gemeinsam, the memories of war had settled deeply into the still and quiet corners of our minds. Our spirits and the open grasses of the Unicorn homeland cooperated to quicken the steps of the celebratory company. Led by the Unicorns, no doubt eager to take us into their capital, we increased our speed to a full trot, carrying our slower and smaller creatures on the backs and in the arms of the faster.

We came to Gemeinsam with plenty of afternoon sunlight ahead of us. Nearly every Unicorn in the Sweeter Realm had convened there. They swarmed us and enveloped us. Old friends greeted each other. Talk was loud and the scene became chaotic, almost unruly. One solitary somber thought pierced the ruckus. It was the swan. He had left the party and made his way to the fallen, broken obelisk, where the Grail had sat for over a century. I silenced the crowd with one forceful thought, shoved mercilessly into their heads. They obeyed immediately and turned their minds to the swan. The crowd parted, forming a corridor between me and the remains of the shrine. There, at the end of the corridor, sat The Ancient One, deep in his thoughts of Parsifal.

I joined him, surrounded by a halo of loving friends. The swan longed for the Grail — to touch it, to hold it and reconnect with his first human friend. I could not help him. But I could make one uplifting proclamation.

"You must rebuild the obelisk," I announced to the Unicorns.

A few gasps were all that was vocalized in response, but I heard their thoughts well enough. The altar of their ancestors was built long before any living Unicorn could remember. None felt qualified or authorized to reconstruct it. They had resigned themselves to its permanent loss the moment they decided to topple it in retrieving the Grail.

I challenged them, "There is no reason you cannot rebuild it. Your ancestors were no greater than you, no more deserving. Their generation built it and yours must rebuild it."

There was still doubt. Some had thoughts of agreement, but none dared express it.

I continued, "We rebuilt the cities and shrines of the Land and Shallow Waters without apprehension. Those too were built by your ancestors. How is this different?"

One Unicorn answered, "Those were destroyed by Löwschock. We rebuilt in defiance against him."

"Is this any different? Your altar was a casualty of the same war, was it not?"

I felt their concurrence, though they still dared not agree aloud. Doubt lingered until a voice broke the momentary silence.

The Ancient One declared, "The Swan Knight is right. Your obelisk fell in the war with the Deep, to retrieve the Grail hidden there by Kandake, hidden there from Löwschock. Do not let him keep you from your traditions. He is dead, killed by Verena. Do not give him this last victory over you. Rebuild your altar, noble Unicorns. Connect to your ancestors. Reclaim your ancient rites."

There were so many thoughts surrounding me. I could not feel the minds of the Unicorns who were not in Gemeinsam. But the ones around me were convinced. A strong sense of defiance against their vanquished enemy drove their determination to reconstruct the obelisk. Since childhood, each of them knew every contour of the replica of Senische's horn. Rebuilding it to identical specifications would not be difficult.

As it happened, I needed the altar rebuilt in order to present the Unicorns with their coronation gift. It was a crucial part of the symbolism behind the gift, and I had no idea what else to give them if the altar remained in pieces. But I needed it erected after the presentation of gifts. So I suggested that the efforts begin after the coronation. They dared not dispute the request, so everything was in perfect order for my gift to the Unicorns.

Those points being perfectly settled, our hearts were free to focus elsewhere. A long-overdue introduction awaited me. As the company blended into a diverse stew of breeds, Acheriel came to me, happier, lighter of spirit, and more deeply in love than I had ever seen him. At his side was a young goat, whose tiny nub of a horn was just beginning to lift the hairs atop her head. She was light-grey and white. The patches of grey blended smoothly into the white, so that no firm line of distinction could be drawn between the two. She had Prische's eyebrows and mouth, and Acheriel's posture and eyes. She was beautiful, stunningly so.

I called for my dearest few to gather around us to meet the daughter of our beloved Prische. Felix, Lina, Taufe, the swan, and I huddled tightly around the goat, squirming around each other to get the closest look at her face, all reaching to caress her and point out her similarities to her mother.

Acheriel whispered my name, dropping stillness and silence on the others, "Verena, my friend and Queen. Her horn will soon break through and I cannot name her. That is the honor of a Unicorn mother."

Lina innocently but bluntly reminded us all of the sad truth, "But her mother is dead."

"Yes she is," Acheriel acknowledged, "and a surrogate must be appointed. *That* honor is mine. The surrogate will serve as her mother from the moment the name is given until the end of time. I can think of none better than you, Verena."

No doubt I was honored, beyond any representation in language. I thought my gratitude directly into his head, followed by my spoken words for all of my dearest ones to hear, "I cannot be her mother. She should grow up here, with her own people, learning the traditions of the collective from other Unicorns. I cannot stay here with her. I am the Queen and must live at the palace, accessible by walkers, swimmers, and flyers alike. Likewise, she cannot grow up in the lakeside palace. Her hooves should be intimate with the grasses of her homeland."

Acheriel gave it a moment of thought. He knew I was right. The Queen would not make an ideal Unicorn surrogate. He scanned his eyes across our precious few, huffed through his beard, and focused his eyes on Lina.

"Will you be her mother, Lina? You are second only to the Queen in goodness and loyalty."

The rightness of the suggestion struck me immediately. Since Rüdiger's death, she had nobody to call her own. Because no Scherier children could be born outside of Eineklaue, and that city was abandoned during the war, Rüdiger and Lina had no children before his death. Lina stayed with me because I needed her. But the war was over and I was married, hoping to have children of my own soon. I could not hoard Lina for myself, leaving her to wait for those rare moments when a spare second fought its way to freedom from a Queen's schedule. I could not expect her to wait for me to need her. My life was busy and looked to get busier. It would be unfair to hold onto Lina for my own selfish comforts. Acheriel was right. There could be no better mother for the goat than Lina.

Lina looked at me awaiting my response. I placed my hand on her head, rubbed it along the side of her face, and cupped her pointed chin in my palm. I kissed her and told her that any creature in any world would be privileged to call her mother. Having been robbed of Prische, Acheriel's daughter could have no better to name her horn and raise her than the tenderest heart in the Sweeter Realm. Unicorn mothers had died. Surrogate mothers had been appointed. This was not uncommon, especially during the war. But the interaction of breeds in such delicate matters *was* rare. Every surrogate parent to a young Unicorn, in the known history of the breed, had been another Unicorn. Despite that well-known fact, nobody in attendance struggled with the idea of Lina naming the horn and raising Prische's daughter as her own.

Lina's reluctance to leave my side was quickly overcome. At the first suggestion of her surrogacy, the notion seemed providential, and we all felt the same. The matter was closed. Now a tremendous care burdened Lina's heart. She would have the Collective to help her mother the goat. But naming the horn was hers and hers alone. She spent the evening speaking to Unicorns, gathering in her open and loving mind all that she could learn of their history, traditions, rituals, and culture.

We decided that Lina would remain with the procession into Gralkirsche. The goat would stay in Gemeinsam and wait for Acheriel and Lina's return. The naming ceremony would take place when they came back from the coronation. In the meantime, the construction on the obelisk could begin, so long as it was not erected before the coronation, so my gift would maintain its potency. Lina stayed curled against the goat's belly through the night, in the center of our tightly cuddled group of friends. In the morning, she reluctantly left her new child and took her place in the procession as we left Gemeinsam, toward the Wendel Marsh that divided us from Scherier land and the holy site of Gralkirsche.

CHAPTER 5
The Coronation

I EXPERIENCED THE WENDEL MARSH very differently than I remembered it. All carcasses, friend and foe, had been removed from the site of the ambush. The rusty red of the blood-stained mud and reeds had faded back to their natural color. The desperation of my first trip through the marsh was a memory disconnected from my senses, senses that took the early sun off of the shallow water into my eyes, and the light-hearted conversations of the company into my ears. One thousand smells fought for supremacy over my nose, pleasant smells, smells of life and nature. My mind drifted back and forth from the perceptions of my senses in the marsh to my imagined portraits of the revitalized holy site of Gralkirsche ahead of us.

The marsh gave way to dry, hilly land, which gave way to the pyramids, mounds, and spires of the city. One Scherier monk met us outside of the city. She greeted us, welcomed us to Gralkirsche, and led us in a quick prayer before escorting us through the peripheral structures, directly to the ancient shrine with the high, spiraling spire. A flood of memories momentarily submerged all sensation of the moment. I thought of Hüter, of finding him emaciated at the top of the spire. I thought about his return to life and of the Christmas celebration. I thought of the fear and the hope that volleyed ceaselessly across my mind in those weeks before my battle with Löwschock.

I heard an excited giggle from the top of the spire. I looked up and saw the pointed chin of Hüter poking from a small, round window, only for a flash, before he disappeared. Within a few seconds, he stood at the threshold of the shrine. He had recovered his health almost beyond recognition. It was undoubtedly Hüter. But life sprang from him as abundantly as it has from any Scherier. He leaped and bounded off the shoulders and heads of the company in front of me, until he stood on Acheriel's head, holding the horn with two hands and staring adoringly into my eyes.

"It was here, you know my Swan Knight," he spoke in a soft and dreamy tone, "here that we gathered to decide on our vote, here that we chose you to remain our Queen."

"Hasn't that conference always taken place in Eineklaue?" I asked.

"You are right," he answered. "It has always been there. It has never before been here. But then, we have never chosen a Swan Knight to be Queen, so what better place than Gralkirsche to elect the Grail Blood to our throne?"

I don't know why I blushed so deeply. I had heard such talk for years. But never had it flattered me so.

I was about to thank him when he continued, "And that is why the shrine of the Boots of Lohengrin is the perfect place for your coronation. Every Scherier in the Sweeter Realm feels the honor."

His head drifted upward, and he whispered to the sky above us, "A Swan Knight Queen, thank you Lord. Soon the doors will be opened, your children will come home, and you will end your grievance with us."

Only the nearest circle around me could hear him. But he was loud enough for the ears of Taufe. I turned to her and caught her staring penetratingly at me. When our eyes met, she lowered her head with a slight grin, which contrasted with the worrisome expression on her brow. I gazed at her, trying to pull truth from her with my eyes, rather than peering into her mind.

The effort was interrupted by the voice of The Ancient One, laughing as he embraced Hüter and reciting in unison with him some ancient stanza of Scherier verse. The rest of the Boots appeared from the structures in all directions around us. They mingled with the company as our procession dispersed throughout the city. I followed Hüter and The Ancient One into the shrine, where I was met by a smile on Cort's bright face, so wide that I could not see the corners of his lips. They hid far on the sides of his head. He jumped into my arms, gave me one quick kiss, then immediately presented his report.

"Everything is ready for the ceremony, Verena. Everything except your gifts. Are they ready to present?"

"They are," I responded with false assuredness.

He smirked, with confident eyes that had more faith in me than I had in myself.

"They will be perfect, I know, my Queen. Everything you do is right."

I lifted him by the armpits and held his nose to mine, as I whispered to him with an air of dark austerity that swept his smile from his face, "If that is true, it is only because I have been guided by the wise. Without you all, I am just Verena."

He looked at me silently for a few seconds, then clinched one half of his face while lifting a smile with the other half, before saying, "Sometimes you say silly things. It is *you* who guide *us*, who fought for us and led us to victory and freedom."

After an awkward pause, he continued, "Now you will be our Queen forever. Let us sit and rest and discuss the ceremony."

Taufe, who was standing directly behind me, took Cort from my hands, kissed him, caressed him, and said, "Good idea, Master of Ceremonies, tell us what you have planned."

Cort jumped from Taufe's hands and gestured for us to follow him. He led us into a small room where papers were strewn from wall to wall, each documenting some facet of the elaborate ceremony. A thick curtain closing off the room at the entrance dropped behind us. Taufe and I cleared places to sit, while Cort embarrassingly organized his papers to present his plans to us. With his utmost pageantry and a tone even lofty for him, Cort laid forth all that he had organized for the ceremony. It was intricate, giving me much to memorize. Details as minute as they were implacable were embedded in each line of Cort's scribbling, on each paper in front of us. I grew increasingly nervous as Cort described each expectation. But I could not protest. This was their ceremony much more than it was mine. And pass or fail, I would do what I have always done — try desperately to meet the expectations of far superior creatures.

It all seemed too much, aggrandizing me well beyond my image of myself. I was terrified of failing, of drifting ever so slightly from expectations. I began to doubt the choices I had made for the gifts I had to present to the breeds. But Taufe was aware of every shiver, every goosebump that raised a hair on my arm. As only she can do, she soothed me with a caress of her soft Brunnen hand, or a grin and a wink, or an under-the-breath chuckle intended for my ears only. And she delivered them exactly when they were most needed.

There was no time to rehearse the ceremony, and hardly time for me to memorize my precisely choreographed part in the event. The coronation took place at sunrise the following morning and was slated to last the entire day — one entire, long day of meticulously scripted pageantry.

During the evening and night before, swarms of attendees arrived in Gralkirsche, in clusters of two and three and in waves of a hundred. I greeted them all as they entered the city. I blessed them as they settled to sleep. It was expected of me. In the last hour before dawn, Taufe pulled me into a small storage mound, where I snuggled between Felix and the already sleeping swan. Felix was perfectly still, but with eyes opened widely and welcomingly to mine. Taufe stripped me of my armor. She sat pressed firmly against my legs and began to sing. I remember little more than the first few notes. Those notes pulled me quickly and soundly to sleep.

The faintest hint of rose brushed the eastern horizon when I was aroused by a dozen Friends of the Scheriers. They escorted me from the mound to a pyramid behind the shrine. There, I was greeted by four Brunnens, each holding a piece of my coronation garments. The reddish-orange pants, bright-orange shirt with baggy sleeves and drooping cuffs, the grey cloak, and the scale-neckless were all placed ceremoniously on me by the Brunnens who made them, as they hummed their spirituals in rich and complex harmonies. They backed away from me and made room for the Friends of the Scheriers, entering the pyramid two-by-two with fruits and breads for my breakfast.

They gestured for me to begin.

"Not without Felix," I softly demanded.

With a panicked expression and frantic, spastic movements, one of them ran from the pyramid and returned within seconds with my husband. He wore a narrow cloak that hid the scars of missing feathers along his back. I sat in front of the food and he sat opposite of me. Everyone else left the pyramid.

"I dreamed of you," I told him, as we broke the bread together. "You flew high above me as I watched from the shore of the lake. You were just a speck in the sky, but I knew you were looking at me, looking and smiling."

"Of course I was."

I asked what he dreamed of.

"Of you," he said quickly and soberly. "You have been in every dream I have had since I met you outside of Rüdiger's cave. Some of my dreams are soft and loving, some terrifying, some thrilling, but all of them have been of you. From my first glance into your eyes, you have saturated me, bone to feathers."

The nervousness that was elevated as Cort explained the ceremony, and increased with the passing of each second that morning, was evicted from me by a sudden swell of love for my husband. Coronations, gifts, training and sacrifices, expectations and destiny — none of them could grip my nerves tightly. I realized that all of it came with one priceless gift, one sweet possession that made everything worth it. It came with Felix, with a husband whose love and admiration for me revealed new depths with each gesture, each word from his mouth, each kiss from the lips beneath that adorable, dangling nose.

We ate our breakfast in love. He took my hand and led me from the pyramid, handed me to Cort, and disappeared into the crowd of creatures that thickened around me by the second.

The gathering creatures left one clear bubble among them, where Cort and I stood. The bubble drifted around the shrine as if blown by the wind, as Cort and I walked inside of it to the entrance. The shrine was completely empty. A single high chair had been placed against the far wall. I received through thought an order to go to it. The thought came from many of the minds around me. I did not take the time to decipher the senders. I simply obeyed, walked alone to the chair, and took my seat.

Cort walked to the center of the chamber and cleared his throat. But before he spoke a word, Acheriel sent me a thought, a single request that I broadcast my experience of the ceremony to my many subjects spread throughout the Sweeter Realm. I reached for them all as Cort's first few words echoed hazily and eerily in my head. It was not a general broadcast. I sought them individually. Invigorating successes and frustrating failures dove in and out of my head, hundreds per second. I did not connect with them all. But those I did touch were united in thought more profoundly, more deeply and spiritually than any mass connection I had made before.

I could not maintain the connection while concentrating on the required details of the ceremony. So we all savored the connection for one more intense moment before separating into our own minds.

The coronation progressed. I sat, stood, and knelt exactly when I was supposed to. I recited my lines and said my prayers, made my oaths and promises. This went on for hours, grander and more intricate, I believe, than any coronation that had occurred before mine. Cort would have it no other way.

Then it was time for me to present the gifts. Each breed came forward, one at a time, with between two and five representatives. They bowed, or twisted, or dropped an ear to the floor in accordance with their own customs. Each representative spoke for their breed. They validated the vote of their kind and they swore their love and obedience. To each, I presented a gift. Some were tangible and handed directly to them. Others were promises or plans.

I gave the Scheriers my armor, all but the vambrace, the forearm plate that Löwschock bit through to draw my blood and open my portal. The material from which it was forged had belonged to the Scheriers since before the earliest Scherier memory, until they gifted it to the infant Elsa. Without its comforting effects, without the sense of well-being it gave me, I would have never embraced my destiny. Fear would have crippled me and my longing for home would have kept my eyes from the path laid before me by God. But I had no enemies left in the Sweeter Realm, and as Cort had put it, I became their Creature Queen, one of them, a product of the Sweeter Realm. It was time to bring the magical ore full-circle, and return it to the Scheriers. I presented it not as a gift from me, but from all Swan Knights from Elsa to the girl from Colorado.

The Ancient One once told me that the armor that Lohengrin made was not made for Elsa, but for me. He believed that everything, every story in the long line of Swan Knights happened to bring me to my destiny, including the Scheriers' gift to Elsa, Lohengrin's labors in forging the armor, Bechtold's decision to take it from his mother, and The Ancient One's agreement to hide it in the Sweeter Realm. I don't know why I kept the one vambrace for myself. I did not need its magical effects. Perhaps the fang holes reminded me of my vulnerability, or maybe it was because my blood flowed through those holes and created a portal, reminding me that I drank from the Grail.

At any rate, the rest of the armor was back in the claws of the Scheriers, where it belonged. All power and symbolism of the gift was felt in full weight, by the Scheriers, the crowd around them, and by The Ancient One, who glowed with pride in his student's wisdom.

I gave the Friends of the Scheriers the clothes I wore into the Sweeter Realm, the same jeans and t-shirt I wore as I stepped off of the bus at Linderhof Palace. I was in those clothes when I first met Cort and his kind. The Friends took great pride in being my first encounter on this side of Parsifal's Portal, of being the first to declare me the

Queen of the Land and Shallow Waters. Worn and tattered as they were, the clothes were accepted with boundless gratitude and with tender memories that were yanked about their hearts by what colors and scents still held to the old clothes.

Five Pfützeschilfs landed on the heads and shoulders of the Friends of the Scheriers. They greeted me with their singular, bulgy, smiling eyes. I connected the minds of those in and around the shrine. I vividly recalled my first encounter with their kind. With welling eyes, I thought of Rüdiger shouting into the puddle that held them. When the story ended with the sighs and nods of all around us, I announced to the Pfützeschilfs that my Zweigwesen goddaughter had already dug for them a puddle beside my throne in the palace. The puddle was for their use only, whenever they made the pilgrimage to the palace. From that post, they would serve as the liaisons between the Queen and the swimmers —if they accepted the position. Their slowly fluttering wings sped to create a faint but lovely hum that spoke clearly their approval and appreciation of the gift.

I gave the Unicorns a small vile of my blood, to be buried beneath the reconstructed altar. The ancient altar was destroyed to retrieve the Holy Grail from Kandake's hiding place.

I announced, "If the new altar cannot house the Holy Grail, as it did for so long, it can still house the Grail Blood."

The Unicorns in attendance stared wide-eyed at me. For a flash of a moment, I feared that the gift was inappropriate or not enough, until the grateful thoughts of the Unicorns were injected into my mind with excited force. The Boots of Lohengrin, whose notion of the Grail Blood was only surpassed by the swan's, erupted into cheers and applause. Schwerthorn took the vile reverently between her lips, nervous and shaking. The Unicorns thought much more of the gift than I thought they would. Many of them sent me their memories of fighting in the Portal Valley, with one Swan Knight or another riding high on their shoulders, defeating and evicting any and all manner of vile men.

In their hearts, I did not present them with Verena's blood, but with the Grail Blood. To some it was Otto's blood. To some it was Rudolf's. Each received the gift as the blood of those Swan Knights they loved and revered the most. No matter which of my ancestors they thought about as Schwerthorn took the vile, they were right. It was exactly that — a token artifact from each Swan Knight and a vivid reminder of the bond between the Unicorns and the children of Parsifal.

It seems that the Wittelsbach knack for architecture passed along with the many mysterious traits that bubbled unexpectantly in me since I first heard Ludwig's call. For the Zweigwesens I designed and commissioned a new hall for their sapping ceremonies, deep in the heart of Zweigwesen land. It featured a massive main hall and several smaller side chambers to serve as accommodations for the attendees. It would be the only building in a new town I named Erstersappe. Prior to the gift, there was no centralized location for the ceremonies. They happened in all corners of Zweigwesen land, depending upon the family of the celebrant. Family and friends often found it difficult to attend. Centrally located, Erstersappe is easily accessible from each extremity of the Zweigwesen homeland.

Not only was I the first human ever to take part in a sapping ceremony. I was the first Queen to serve as godparent to a young Zweigwesen. This was a source of tremendous pride for them. In their eyes, I became a Zweigwesen, a member of their breed and of their families, the moment I accepted the first sapping from Eichengeist's young fingertips on my forehead, lips, and chest. My goddaughter's ceremony was also the only first-sapping to occur outside of Zweigwesen land. They brought the ceremony to St. Hildegard because I was there.

Each future sapping ceremony performed in the new city would be a reminder of my familial connection to their breed. The plans needed some adjustments, but their acceptance of the blueprints put on bold display their approval of the plans and the gift. Along with the designs, I commissioned the best Sweeter Realm builders, an elite group of Zweigwesens, Scheriers, Wühlenvogels, and Brunnens, to perform the contruction.

My gift to the Brunnens was a song of my love for them. I wrote it for a full chorus of Brunnen voices. I reminded all in attendance of the time I spent in St. Hildegard Cathedral, learning how to be their Queen and Swan Knight. I declared 17 September, St. Hildegard's feast day, to be a holy holiday in the Sweeter Realm, requiring a pilgrimage to the cathedral at least once every five years for a day of honoring Hildegard and the Brunnen sisters who adore her. The song I gifted them is to be sung by the Brunnen choir and visiting pilgrims.

The gift honored the Brunnens deeply. It did exactly as I hoped it would. It expressed to them everything that they mean to me and elevated St. Hildegard Cathedral to the pinnacle of Sweeter Realm sacred sites. Taufe, who still served as abbess of St. Hildegard, albeit in more of an honorary capacity than a practical one (for she was more often away with me) received the gift and honored all in attendance with a solo rendition of the new composition. Hearing my words and sentiments of love for the Brunnens sung through the soft duel throats of Taufe sent shivers across my body and opened my pours, inviting each phrase, each harmonized note to be absorbed into my flesh as it entered my ears.

Each breed, wet and dry, came forward and received their gift. I saved one gift for last, to the giant swan who had been the rock of trust for every Swan Knight and every creature of Eden. To The Ancient One, I gave a small wooden helmet. I carved it to resemble Elsa's helmet, which was forged to imitate the little wooden trinket that sat upon Parsifal's shrine, the very trinket that Elsa played with as a child. The gift connected me intensely in his mind with his memories of his first human brother. As I passed the gift from my hand to his wing, I felt for a moment the full scope of his love for my bloodline, from Parsifal and Gütel to Otto and Agnes, from Adolf and Irmengard to Albert, from Ludwig to the silly little girl from Centennial, Colorado.

Comments and conversations crested and waned during the presentation of gifts. A constant low clamor serenaded the entire event — until The Ancient One stepped forward to receive his gift. Each flap of his webbed feet against the floor echoed in the otherwise silent city. After tucking the carving under his wing esuriently, as if the gazes from the crowd could do it some harm, he pressed himself against me, wrapped his neck around my face, and nestled his head against me cheek. The silent crowd erupted in chorus. The cheers were as much for him as for me. And he and I accepted the applause as two tightly-bound friends, singular of heart and grateful in the extreme for the presence of the other in our lives.

The gifts were successful, each considered by all to be ideal, wise, and poignant. My dearest ones glowed with pride. The gifts, which concluded the coronation ceremony, represented not only my relationship with the breeds, but defined their connection to their Queen for the life of my queenship. Everyone agreed that the gifts were inspired by God and were exactly as they ought to have been. I was relieved beyond measure.

By the time I was escorted out of the shrine and into the open air of Scherier land, the late afternoon sun had already lost the crisp brightness of its prime. A cool but sweet breeze blew through the city. Many groups departed immediately, with few goodbyes and in normal conversation, as if the day's events were quite ordinary. Many stayed behind to fill the mounds and huts of Gralkirsche for one more night. Once the coronation ended, very little was about me. I appreciated the rare moment of obscurity and I used it to gather with my dearest few. I survived a tremendous day on very little sleep. After receiving the congratulations, praise, and affection of The Ancient One, Taufe, Lina, Acheriel, and Cort, I took my husband to a Scherier mound relinquished to us by the Boots of Lohengrin, where I held the noblest creature I knew and slept soundly in his loving arms, knowing that I would be the subject of his dreams that night.

CHAPTER 6
New Life — Old Worries

THE MORNING AFTER THE CORONATION showed no signs of being extraordinary, except for the few gathered creatures who remained beyond the sunrise. Most had returned to their lives, leaving Gralkirsche and the Boots of Lohengrin to wait for the next wave of young Scheriers to be baptized and educated.

There was little reason for me to linger. Acheriel and Lina were eager to return to Gemeinsam and reunite with their young goat. I would not miss that reunion and I wanted to see how construction of the new Unicorn altar progressed. Lina had to present the young horn with a name. She was comfortably nervous about the decision. She showed no external signs of distress. But hints of anxiety coming from deep inside of her lapped against the outer shores of my mind like gentle waves on the sand. She had done her research. She studied the customs and traditions. She learned Acheriel's and Prische's family trees. She understood the importance of the task laid upon her.

All of those nearest and dearest to me during my years of training, those who knew Prische best, joined me in attending Acheriel and Lina to the Unicorn capital. Since no swimmers traveled with us, there was no reason to push through the sticky mud and sharp reeds of the marsh. So we rode along the Eulesänger border, between Eierheim and the eastern edge of the marsh. Three other Unicorns traveled with us, carrying Felix, Lina, Taufe, and The Ancient One. Acheriel carried his Queen and would have it no other way.

Cort left us. He went west with some Wühlenvogels, to consult on matters at the border between the Nomadic Belt and the Wühlenvogel forest.

Before we departed, I asked him, "Is this something that should concern me? Should I connect your thoughts?"

"Oh no, my Queen," he assured me with a few pats on my shin. "You be with Lina. I have this one. It is just a little misunderstanding, and I am just the one to fix it."

"Alright, if you think you have it. Reach for me if you need me. I will be listening for you."

Cort veered to the right, breaking from our path and heading southwest at a snail's pace, or at a Friend of the Scherier's waddle.

Our ride to Gemeinsam felt quite leisurely. But we made remarkable time. The Unicorns who carried us covered tremendous ground, but with little more effort than a trot. The Eulesängers offered us accommodations in their capital. I have no doubt that the boisterous little creatures would have given us quite the jubilee. But we were in need of intimate company, of telling and hearing stories we already knew, from voices as familiar to us as our own. So our little company camped quietly that night in an open field on the Eulesänger-Unicorn border, just southwest of Eierheim.

From departing Gralkische, to setting up camp in the field, to falling asleep and waking and resuming our course to Gemeinsam, no conversations began or ended. They had no such distinct borders. The journey was one long, casual and comfortable exchange of tales, ideas, and expressions of love. We were slow to break camp in the morning and much slower of pace on the second day.

We were in the capital by early evening. We ate and slept under the stars, with Lina's daughter center among us. The next morning's sunlight rose to illuminate a glorious new Unicorn altar. They had finished it in the few days we were away. The obelisk rested unused on its side, awaiting the vile of my blood. Once the vile was placed in the pit that had so long held the Holy Grail, the obelisk was raised, and the new altar was again the centerpiece of the illustrious capital. It looked just like the old one, minus the many centuries of weathering. It bore a polish that made it shine even brighter than the last. The rosy morning light joyfully slid down the spirals, seeming to laugh like children on a playground slide.

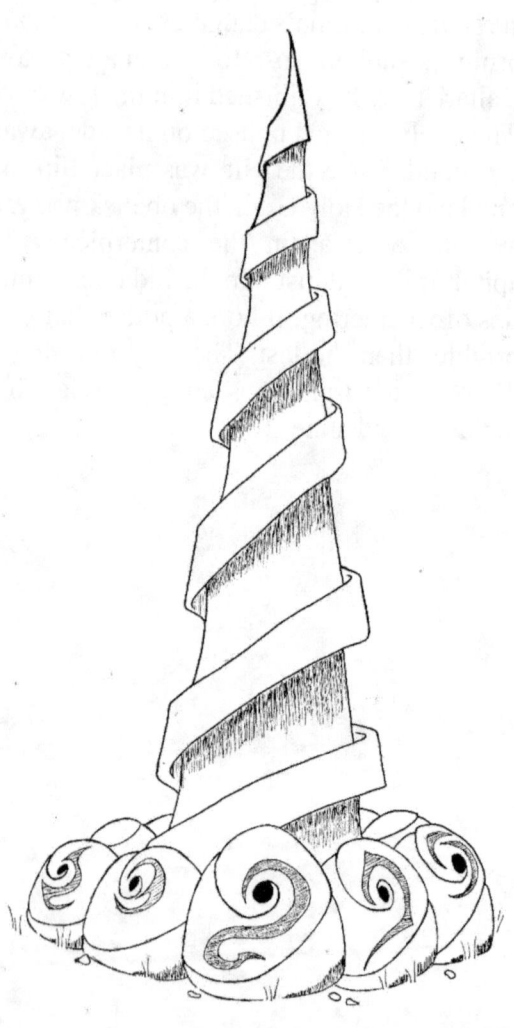

The new monument was the perfect backdrop for the naming ceremony. The goat's infant horn had grown in a few days. It protruded the length of my fingers from her sweet head. Her spirals were tight, wrapping three or four times around the three inches of horn. The horn was brilliantly white, with a deep burgundy trying to pronounce itself from within the tight ridges. The goat stood proud and excited near the foot of the obelisk. Taufe lifted Lina and placed her on one of the smaller stones encircling the monument. All eyes went to Lina. It was she who would name the horn. The next words from her mouth would dictate what name the goat would carry for the many long centuries of her life.

The intense anticipatory stares of the Unicorns unsettled Lina. Her awkwardness was as apparent as the city was silent.

Lina spoke a rough syllable, cleared her throat, and spoke clearly and loudly, "I name this horn, Senische."

Each Unicorn in attendance took one step away from the obelisk. The Ancient One twisted his neck, turning his head upside down. Taufe gasped. Poor Lina was mortified. She looked to me. I looked puzzled back at her. She looked to Acheriel.

Acheriel told her softly, but with a tone of intense gravity, "No horn has carried the name Senische since the founder of the collective. It has been forbidden."

Lina looked as if all air and blood left her body together. But it was done. The name was given, and nobody knew what to do next. They turned where they have always turned in such circumstances — to their Queen. One ancient Unicorn tradition had to fall that day. The answer came quickly to me.

"The new altar is complete," I reminded them, "so let her insert her young horn into a stone and communicate with her mother. Prische will know what is right."

The very moment my lips sealed behind my words, all eyes turned to the goat. She gingerly turned around to face Lina. She lowered her head and placed her tiny horn into the hole of the stone on which Lina stood. Acheriel and a few others lowered their heads and stepped toward the altar to share in the communion.

"No!" I shouted. "This is between the goat and her mother."

They all stopped where they stood. None would defy me.

When the horn was fully inserted, and her head pressed against the stone, every hair on the goat's body stood erect. She giggled, then cried, then giggled again.

She pulled away from the stone, winked at Lina, turned boldly to the company, and scanned her eyes silently, back and forth across the many Unicorns in attendance.

"What did your mother say to you, my daughter?" Acheriel pleaded.

The goat looked at me, and I whispered hoarsely, "What did Prische say?"

She lifted her thin, short beard and announced, "My mother said that the surrogate has named my horn. She said that she trusts my Scherier mother. She said that you should too."

The goat lowered her raised chin in deep contemplation for one so young, and announced in a much subtler tone, "She said that she loves me, and she called me Senische."

Well, that was all the convincing that Acheriel needed. He whispered the name Senische several times, getting slowly louder while he gazed at the daughter of his magnificent wife. The others joined, repeating the name with increasing volume and intensity.

"Senische, Senische, Senische..." rang out across the Unicorn capital.

It was done. She was no longer just "the goat". She was Senische, the one and only namesake of the founding matriarch of the Collective.

A few Unicorn warriors shouted in unison from the back of the herd, "Ohhl Ginshass Wahuff!"

The old phase struck me, and I connected my mind accidentally to hundreds of Unicorns throughout the Sweeter Realm.

The warriors repeated, "Ohhl Ginshass Wahuff!"

The phrase was repeated by me and every attendee of the ceremony — and by everyone in my mental connection. Young Senische's sweet little voice shouted the slogan. I believe she understood its meaning and felt its significance more than any living creature. Acheriel ran to her. She trotted a few laps around his front legs and under his belly. Acheriel reclined and Senische snuggled tightly to him. Lina leaped from the stone, over The Ancient One's head, and landed on Acheriel's back. She draped her upper half over Senische, so that she sloped sharply downward.

We all witnessed the beginning of a very intimate moment, the dawn of a new family. We had seen enough to delight us. But the rest of the day belonged to them. I thought a quick command to leave them in peace. The company scattered from the altar and went about the business of the day.

Felix took my hand and stared into my eyes.

"I adore you," he said in a long and melodic manner as we walked away from our friends. "You are as wise as you are brave, as brave as beautiful."

He knew I needed to hear that. He knew that Lina and I would seldom be together again. And he knew that among all the distractions of the Queen, his love was all that could comfort me in that loss.

We sought an old friend, one whose intense love for me had kept him at a distance during the chaotic weeks that followed the war. Georg met us at the entrance to the underground portion of the city. We walked several laps around Gemeinsam, the three of us, discussing topics from the most mundane to the most monumental. The entire Sweeter Realm had lightened in heart since the death of Löwschock — but not Georg. He was as austere as ever, agonizingly impassioned, and desperate to serve his Queen.

He had fought the attacks of the Deep on Gemeinsam. He trained me in St. Hildegard. Fighting and training to fight had become his identity, and he didn't know who he was without war. This truth showed itself first in his grinding teeth as Felix and I spoke of peaceful topics. It took only the briefest and shallowest peek into his thoughts to verify my suspicions. Georg needed a quest, a mission to give him purpose. My eyes and mind drifted together in search of an answer, until I caught a glimpse of the stain on Felix's arm. I bent down, dislodged a fistful of grass, grabbed the dirt beneath it, spat in it and kneaded it into a paste in my palm. I smeared it on Georg's right, front leg.

"Go find my special Guard," I commanded him, "those who still live."

I faked a seriousness in my voice to match his. He stood instantly erect, posing regally and attentively.

I continued, "Bring them to the palace and train them as you trained me. They are yours to captain. They will be called my Royal Guard and you are first among them."

Georg swirled his horn around in circles. As it cut the air above his head, it seemed to sing. Felix squeezed my hand twice, released it, and rubbed my back. He obviously approved of the measure. His face showed the delight he shared with Georg.

My new Captain kissed the top of my head, thought his love to me, then vocalized, "By the time you return to the palace, my Queen, you will have your Royal Guard, and training will be well underway."

He darted toward Zweigwesen land and was gone from our vision within seconds. His zealous elation projected far and wide, and remained in my head for the rest of the day. The gesture was out of kindness to Georg, not out of self-protection. I had no enemies and could imagine little usefulness of a Royal Guard for the Queen's protection. Thank God Georg's troubles touched my heart that day. I look back now and realize that my gesture of compassion toward my old combat teacher ultimately saved my life. But I will come to that later.

Felix and I retired alone into the underground village that evening, with warm thoughts of Acheriel, Lina, and Senische. We lit only two Wühlenvogel torches. The cavern was dim, and Felix's feathers were all that I saw clearly. In these conditions, he taught me an old Federman game. Each player has a stick and scratches symbols and marks in the dirt. It is something between Tic-Tac-Toe and Checkers. In the darkness, we knocked our sticks together accidentally, and even poked each other a few times. Each "Ouch!" was followed by a giggle, which ignited another giggle and spread to laughter. Impossible to see the symbols in the dirt, the game became all about poking and whacking each other with the sticks, until he caught ahold of my wrist and I of his opposite elbow. We wrestled. The wrestling slowed to a tender dance, which melted to a still embrace.

We draped in each other's arms and talked of our futures and the future of the Sweeter Realm, of our responsibilities as Queen and King.

"I am not the King of the Sweeter Realm," he said solemnly, but with tender and contented humility. "I am only the husband of its Queen."

"You may not be their King," I answered, followed by a kiss to his dangling nose, "but you are mine, and you have every bit of authority over me that I have over you. You have twice the claim at goodness and ten times the purity. Is not the King of their Queen also their King?"

He pulled his face from mine and looked at me with a puzzled expression, saying, "You do not know half of your own merit."

I pulled him tighter to me, touched his nose to mine, and responded without a breath of pause, "Nor you yours."

We stared at each other with deeply earnest expressions of admiration, which slowly and simultaneously morphed into matching smiles, until our adoring faces were much brighter than the two torches. Our mental embrace tightened as did our physical embrace. I felt painfully in love. We talked and prayed well into the night, until our conversations caught flame. And within a sphere of devout and the most faithful adoration, we conceived a child.

We began our *own* family. I knew the moment it happened. And my hysterical euphoria broadcasted unchecked across my queendom. The Sweeter Realm knew. Felix knew as I did, that we would have a family, that I held inside of me the first blood relative to touch me since I passed through Parsifal's Portal — that another human, or at least a half-human, was coming to Eden.

The morning had a particularly rosy glow about it. The Unicorns of Gemeinsam tried to give us our privacy. But the beards of the Unicorn capital were distorted that morning by the broadest smiles as they passed us. We had breakfast alone with Acheriel, Lina, and Senische. We spoke nothing of pregnancies or babies, nothing of the questions that tried to bury their heads into the sands of our brains. Ours would be the first child of a human and a creature of the Sweeter Realm since Brunhilde. We had no idea what to expect, no idea how long the pregnancy would last or what unique traits and abilities the child would have.

We concluded breakfast attempting to focus on the friends we would be leaving. But Felix and I both thought of little but the child inside of me, and shared a desperate desire to return to the palace and contemplate parenthood together. We walked home, slowly, stopping at every cave, pond, and tree where rest and refreshment were offered.

We thought of nothing but the pregnancy, but spoke nothing of it, until alone on a shaded path, near the border of the Nomadic Belt, when Felix stopped me, looked me in the eyes, and said, "This child is not only ours. This is of tremendous significance to your entire queendom and every creature within it. The child belongs to the Sweeter Realm."

I nodded and added, "And to God, and to mankind."

My comment came without thought, flying from my lips without consulting my consciousness. And it implied a truth of the most extreme gravity. It pulled the child within me from the peaceful, nurturing arms of Eden and placed it on a sacrificial altar, on a human altar. The daughter of Tannhäuser and his Brunnen lover involved herself intimately in the affairs of humans. The sweet, half-Brunnen little girl grew austere. She grew into a warrior. And there was no reason to imagine she did not still fly above the battlefields of Earth destroying the wicked-of-heart. Now, there in my belly, grew another half-human. The Sweeter Realm was settled. The toils of humanity were not. That thought brought immense darkness into our heads, accompanied by a premonition of terror.

Whatever vision we glimpsed, it was not a problem for current contemplation. We did not understand it and could see no further into it. We shook it off together and occupied our thoughts and conversations with the countless tasks at hand. I was Queen. He was my King. We had a realm to rule together, peace to maintain, a palace to prepare for a family, creatures to visit, appointments to make, and each other to adore. That was enough to consume our words as we met with the great lake and walked its shore to the palace.

Our leisure, and often mindlessly meandering stroll from Gemeinsam to the palace, took two weeks. Looking back, I can't say exactly which paths we took, which streams we crossed, and which hills we climbed over. During that time, my thoughts rarely drifted far from my womb. Between the many experiences of the journey, bubbled forth a constant awareness of the child, and many physical sensations, real and imagined, that I, in my silliness, attributed to some extraordinary trait of the next vessel of the Grail Blood.

Georg was as good as his word. Before the palace was in sight, he and the Royal Guard intercepted us on the beach. I did not think that the fire in Georg's eyes could burn any brighter than I had already known it. But the knowledge that protecting his Queen also meant protecting the next Swan Knight and his future student enflamed his passions further.

He saw every step I took as potentially disastrous. He directed the Guard to hoist me upon his back. Felix, with the slightest push on Georg's hip, vaulted himself to sit behind me. Georg huffed in surprise and swung his head quickly around to his left to glare at Felix. Felix wrapped his right arm around me and with his left hand, he grabbed the horn, transmitting in an instant his appreciation for the Unicorn's fervent loyalty, but passing with it a reminder of my ability to protect myself.

I snuck in through the back door of the exchange, viewing their minds in secrecy, until I reminded them both that Eden is pure, that every creature in the Sweeter Realm is peaceful and loyal to their Queen. Georg felt a little embarrassed by his intensely protective zeal until I reminded him that my ability to protect myself was a result of his diligent training, and that my life (and that of countless others) was saved by him during the battles against the sepents of the Deep.

Felix felt no embarrassment. He was happy to have the Guard surrounding us. The memory of our shared premonition remained sticky to the inside of his skull, unshared during the horn connection with Georg. We both saw a new darkness coming from God-knows-where, and knew it was connected to the precious life growing inside of me. I would have faced a dozen Löwschocks, a hundred knobby-headed serpents, rather than stare into the unknown darkness that seemed to have its eye on our child. No special Guard, no flock of Wühlenvogels or Unicorn-horned sword could fight back this sense of dread. I began to wish for the Scherier metal of my armor. I reached into our sack of trinkets and held the single piece of the armor I had kept for myself.

As we trotted along the beach to the palace, I left Felix's thoughts alone in his head. I did not need to look inside of him. His powerful feathered arms told me everything. He squeezed me in cycling pulses that subconsciously rode the rising and crashing waves of his thoughts. He buried his face into my neck and kissed me. He held my belly like a father holds his child. He twitched as his thoughts jolted in and out of his mind. His breath sped and slowed. There was quite a storm inside of him. But I took too much comfort in the subtle physical manifestations of his thoughts to enter his mind and soothe him. Within half an hour of mounting Georg, his splashing hooves reminded us that we were in the palace entrance. I kissed Georg's horn, thanked him, left him with the business of captaining the Guard, and I took my husband to bed, hoping that a new day would bring a new and promising perspective.

CHAPTER 7
The Conspicuous Scriptures

THE MORNING BROUGHT JUST ENOUGH COMMOTION to return a sense of normalcy to the palace. I had not taken three steps from my bedroom before being greeted by Taufe. Her voyage from Gemeinsam, though beginning one day after ours, was direct and with purpose. She arrived four days before we did.

"There is no time to waste, my love," she announced with greater than normal energy. "Things will be happening soon, and you must be prepared."

As menacing as those words should have felt, they emboldened me with the familiarity of urgency and turmoil. I slipped quickly into the state of mind that navigated my behavior for most of my years in the Sweeter Realm.

"I am ready," I responded with bold eagerness.

"The swan is in the throne room. He has your schedule fully mapped out."

"Of course he does," I answered with a wink and a smile.

Taufe and I met The Ancient One at the throne. But we did not linger there. They whisked me away quickly to one of the palace's quiet, lesser rooms. They sat me down on a chair made especially for my lessons in that room — made by Zweigwesens, under the direction and observation of the swan, made to replicate Ludmilla's desk chair in the old Linderhof lodge. My teachers stood side by side, squared to me, towering over me like they do when they scold me or pass grave news.

Taufe repeated the same prophesies she had so many times and so austerely delivered, each to the slow and menacing nod of the swan's head. She spoke of my duties to God, and my sacrifices and trials, but nothing of the child growing inside of me. With each of her quotations from scripture, each prognostication of St. Hildegard, I felt the words attach themselves to the baby — much more than they attached to me. But I don't believe they were meant that way. The sensations of dread that Felix and I shared on our walk seemed to adhere themselves only to us. Prophets and holy people long dead, visionaries like St. Hildegard, pointed their long, withered, skeletal fingers at my womb.

I was frustrated listening to Taufe, knowing how intimately the baby related to my fate and that of my species. The baby felt the same. So quickly after conception, impossibly so for a human, I felt the baby jump inside of me, in direct reaction to my feelings. What did it mean? How quickly would this child grow and fill my belly? How long would I carry the baby? Taufe's voice was momentarily muted in my ears by these sticky, clingy questions.

I thought I understood self-sacrifice. It had become a necessary part of my nature the moment Cort declared me to be the Queen, on the beach of the great lake, on that first day in the Sweeter Realm. But my sacrifices for the Sweeter Realm, though I accepted them, were never a pleasure. What a dramatic alteration the character of a woman undergoes when she feels that first throb of a new life within her. With those first movements of the baby, those first communications between child and mother, self-sacrifice ceases to be a mere necessity. There is a poignant joy in every pang suffered on behalf of her child, as if each is a down payment for the future fortunes of the baby. For this reason, and for others that I never really understood, I was frustrated with the placidity of peace, despite how hard I had worked to achieve it and how relieved I and my whole queendom were when it finally came.

I had an inexplicable desire to sweat, bleed, and suffer. I missed the extremities of emotion and the heights of intellect forced upon me by war. I won't say that I wanted an enemy. An enemy meant the suffering of others. I relished the blissful peace of the queendom, the relief and joy of my subjects. It was only my own turmoil that I yearned for, as some illogical accumulation of credit for the baby's future happiness. I was fidgety. I itched much more deeply than my fingernails could scratch. I knew I needed to study, to read, listen, and learn. But each second seated irritated me. I wanted to grab Albert's sword and fight. It was an illogical sensation — to inwardly rebel with such fury against the peace that so many dear friends suffered and died to bring about. Rüdiger and Prische, Kandake and Ludwig lost their lives to purchase the placid air around me, yet it was putrid to my nose. I did not know if my feelings were a weakness to be scorned and overcome, or an inner calling to be obeyed. I listened and learned. Perhaps it was the earliest communications of an unborn child whose wisdom would grow well beyond mine. So I sat and read. And I tried to ignore the burning of my blood.

The Ancient One and Taufe, along with the other creatures of my queendom, honored my unborn child as the next link in the chain of Swan Knights, a chain that was sacred to them all, to be sure. They viewed the baby as the descendant of Parsifal and Lohengrin, of Elsa, Otto, Rudolf, and Ludwig. That was no small thing, especially to The Ancient One. I felt that same connection, yet one more, not at all perceived by most and only thinly by a few. I saw the baby as the grandchild of my mother and father. I thought about my brother Karl and what a doting young uncle he would have been.

It was only in those thoughts that I realized that I would be a teenage mother. I had just turned eighteen years old during the pregnancy, very young indeed, among my own kind, to be having a baby and starting a family. It would have been quite scandalous, I'm sure, had I been in Centennial, Colorado. But I had lived several lifetimes of extreme experiences in my few years in the Sweeter Realm. I was a wife, a Queen, and a seasoned paladin of God. I had already buried more friends than my parents and grandparents combined. Both my fears and my love were not of an adolescent nature. In fact, the girl who rode with her family down her driveway, on her way to the airport for a trip to Germany, seemed like a distant relation to me, like an old friend I hadn't seen since my earliest memories. Yet, my memories of my parents and brother were fresh, unburied by the severe and uncalculatable experiences I had accumulated since I saw them last.

The Ancient One had studied my life and written it seamlessly into the Swan Knights history. He understood the pain of my disconnection from my family. Felix too understood. To him I was more than Queen and Swan Knight, much more than the vanquisher of Löwschock. I was Verena, the teenage girl that God had plucked from all that she had known and plunged into a role I was entirely unable to understand at the time. He saw my fresh and frightened face when I was just a couple of days in the Sweeter Realm. Felix had heard every story of my life that was still in my head and worth telling, and many that were not worth telling. He knew the girl I was, and he knew the woman I became.

While Taufe spoke of my sacrifices, and the baby leaped inside of me, I also thought about Felix. His

86

sacrifices would be great as well. The baby was not just a descendant of the Swan Knights, not just the child of my ancestors. This was also Felix's child, a Federkind, from an ancient and proud line of nomads. And life in God's creation never knew a prouder father, or one more in love with his child's mother. My love for him multiplied my anxieties with acute and agonizing sympathy for a Federman who married into a destiny I was not sure he would have chosen had he seen the whole picture. I know now that he would have suffered this and much, much more while still thanking God every night for allowing him to be my husband. There is no creature like him.

After the weighty introduction to my new phase of training, we slipped very much into the fashion of the old. Taufe took me alone for my spiritual schooling. The Ancient One, knowing no other way, continued my Swan Knight training, preparing me to protect the Sweeter Realm the way that Elsa protected the Portal Valley. And like the Swan Knights of old, I prepared for an unknown enemy, coming from an unknown origin, with unknown desires.

I resumed the courses of study I had abandoned when we departed St. Hildegard. Between all of this, I solved the petty disputes of my subjects, attended births and baptisms, blessed weddings and spoke at funerals. I connected the minds of loved ones set apart by various circumstances. In short, I lived the life of Kandake, performing every duty required of her, while living the life of Adolf, exiled in a new home that was far from my native land, preparing blindly for a destiny whose outline was vague to me at best. And above all of that, I had to project my thoughts into hundreds of heads per day, near and far. My efforts at the bottom of the lake may have purchased peace for my queendom, but it did not bring calmness and leisure into my life. For that I was thankful.

Except for my time with Taufe, all facets of my day provided distractions from my fiercest anxieties. My lessons with Taufe focused my attention squarely on God's ultimate plan for me. We reviewed what I had learned so far — that mankind left Eden, following the siren call of violence, that the divinity of human blood soiled and diluted on the other side of Abel's portal (as she called it), and that Eden itself ceased to be the dwelling garden of God. God nurtured a race of humans, his chosen people, to bear Christ and accept pure, divine blood back into humanity. When Christ saw his death at hand, he consecrated the first Holy Eucharist, so that human divinity remained on Earth after he did not, and to place within us a strain of divinity that would incline us toward God when we make our Final Judgment. Taufe believed that time to be near. The doors to Eden would again be opened and humans would choose — a return to oneness with God, as it was in the beginning, when we resided in Eden with God, or to remain shackled to violence and greed in a world of our own design.

What none of us could foresee was how and when the gates would be opened, and what event would initiate this miraculous event. The thought we shared, but rarely spoke of, was that the salvation of the lost would come at the cost of the righteous, as it always has. Since the moment humanity left Eden, the wise and faithful have bled, suffered, and died for the benefit of the blind and faithless. So consistent, so universal is this pattern, that its application in the events before us was a certainty to us all. It was for this unknown suffering that we tried to prepare.

I saw the scriptural evidence. Still, I protested, "I've studied the Bible. I've read the Gospels. Why don't they tell us plainly? Why didn't Jesus tell us plainly?"

"He did," she answered. "But *your* Gospels lay it shyly between the lines."

Taufe presented me with an old manuscript. It was untitled, but she introduced it as the "Conspicuous Scriptures", and a fanatical obsession of Archbishop Conrad.

"Read these words of Christ," she demanded, "from the Gospel of Phillip."

> I came to make the things
> below like the things above,
> and the things outside like
> those inside. I came to unite
> them in the place.

A few years earlier, those words would have been as enigmatic as every other cryptic clue tucked between the lines of scripture. But just then, they spoke clearly to me.

"Here," Taufe continued as she flipped the pages with speed and accuracy, "from the Gospel of Thomas."

> Where the beginning is,
> there will the end be.
> Blessed is he who will take
> his place in the beginning.

There it was, plain and clear, and in the words of the Messiah himself, Christ telling us why he came, and describing humanity's return to Eden. I was dumbfounded. These were not the coded mysteries of St. Hildegard's visions, to be interpreted by the wise and translated to me through the filter of their elite understanding. This was Jesus Christ telling Verena Elizabeth Kessler that her destiny was at hand. Taufe marked other portions of the Conspicuous Scriptures for me to read. I dove into them directly, as Taufe stood behind me and rubbed my temples with her nurturing Brunnen fingertips. I consumed the words gluttonously, returning to the beginning of the manuscript once I had read each of Taufe's marked passages. She knew I would not rest my eyes until I had read it all. She bent her long figure low to kiss the top of my head before she left the room without another word.

I read and reread for the rest of the day and evening. When I immerged, the fine details of my destiny were no clearer, except that I knew that I would be reunited with humanity. I knew that I, as Queen of the Sweeter Realm and reigning Swan Knight, would be instrumental in opening the gates of Eden and ushering in the faithful. My titles became far more of an honor than they had ever been a burden. The purification of Eden was only the beginning of my duties. The Conspicuous Scriptures told me that I would have the honor of bringing about the end of God's grievance against mankind.

But as Taufe and The Ancient One reminded me daily, the honor would come at a great cost. Much blood had already spilled on mankind's way to reunion with God, Parsifal's and the very blood of Christ included. And it was harrowingly clear to me that other blood, blood still being pumped by living hearts, would hit the ground in violence before God's will is fulfilled. I began to distinctly sense that the salvation of my species would cost me dearly. And my baby jostled and kicked in direct response to those ponderings.

The morning after I read the Conspicuous Scriptures, I developed a gradual desire to have the Grail in my hands. It began slowly, as flashes of memories of my time with the Grail. I could feel it in my hands as I envisioned holding it in front of me at the bottom of the lake. As the desire swelled into a panicked obsession, over the course of a few hours, the sensation spurred an experience that dwarfed my thoughts of the Grail. I saw the thoughts of the baby!

My Grail musings echoed in the mind of my unborn child, just weeks after conception. We felt each other's concerns, shared each thought. Every conversation I had, book I read, lecture I heard, was experienced by the baby. It was a boy. This I could see clearly. My mind and his were one — and *his* grew complex and deep, penetrating and expansive with each lesson and each drifting thought of his mother.

The sensation was too deep and real for me to even consider that it was my imagination. Another phenomenon confirmed the authenticity of the connection. After my first connection with the baby's mind, I could no longer see the thoughts of any other creature. What I had gained with the baby and what I had lost with my subjects, I kept to myself for several days. I hid away and fed my child's mind with everything I could read and reflect upon. My dearest ones thought nothing of it. Such self-sequestering was not out of my character. After a few days, I told Felix about the connection with the baby.

He wanted terribly to see the baby's thoughts, but I could not connect them. I could no longer reach into any other mind, including my husband's. I spoke directly to my baby's mind, felt the warmth of my own womb on his skin through his sensual perceptions, but could not share the experience with the only other creature with a right to it, nor could I put the sensations into words. It was frustrating to us both. The baby experienced his father, through my thoughts and senses, exactly as I did. But Felix remained outside of the connection. Still, he took comfort in rubbing my belly and speaking to the baby, knowing that his son perceived him clearly and knew his father well.

Felix insisted that this connection with the baby and the baby's phenomenally growing intelligence must be shared with my teachers. He was right, yet I refused to tell them at first, for Felix's sake. His wife was not his alone.

His child would be the same. He deserved this secret, at least for a few days, before sharing it with the Sweeter Realm. After a few days, with Felix by my side, I told Taufe and The Ancient One. Taufe nodded and smiled at the news, asking no question, seeking no elaboration, seeing the rightness of it as plainly as the color of the sky. The swan, on the other hand, was slow to grasp the truth. He pried and probed doubtfully, repeating the same questions despite my redundant answers.

It was only when seeing his reaction that the truth appeared as profound to me — until the baby seized control of my mouth and spoke directly to the swan. My voice, but not my words, not words that initiated in my own mind, but were born in the depth of my womb, broke through my lips, lips that glossed with the salty tears that poured profusely from my eyes. My son's thoughts struggled to push through my faltering voice as I convulsed in ecstatic emotion.

He told the swan, "My mother shares everything with me... her fears and hopes, her doubts and her love... her profound love for you. I feel it as she does."

As the baby spoke, and I shook violently, I dropped to my knees. When he released my face to my own control, I looked around me and saw that Felix had also dropped to his knees and The Ancient One plopped to one side. Taufe's long Brunnen body towered over us all, perfectly still, silvery, and almost transparent. She regained her color and full visual distinction as she rippled her way toward me and encompassed me in her embrace. Although I could not see into her mind, I knew that the embrace was one of greeting and congratulations to the baby. The baby felt every stroke of her fingers, every inch of Taufe's soft arms, and every sensation of affection perceived by my flesh. He did not speak to her as he spoke to the swan, but contented himself with the words I chose as I relayed his admiration for her.

The new revelation invigorated The Ancient One. He made many demands in its wake.

"A name!" he insisted, "Since we are already in conversation with the boy, he must have a name immediately."

The baby had no opinion on the matter and was ready to wear whatever we chose to call him. Felix, never fully mindful of his own greatness, felt so dwarfed by the events concerning his wife and son that he ventured no opinions. My connection to the baby was so intensely personal that a name felt unnecessary to me. But I understood the swan's desire for one and I agreed that we should name the child immediately.

We all stared at each other for what felt like several minutes, until Felix proclaimed, "The Federmensch godfathers name *our* children, but we don't even choose godparents until after the birth."

Before another second passed, the baby and I agreed that only one could fill that role.

"We want you," I said with a direct gaze into the swan's deep blue eyes. "You are his godfather. He is a Federkind, and you are his godfather. So what will you name him?"

The Ancient One had written my family tree into the Swan Knights history. He knew every name and many vivid stories connected to them.

"Joseph!" he declared with regal pageantry and his head held high atop his erect neck, as if he sat upon his throne in Neuschwanstein Castle. "Your grandfather was a great man and would have been a magnificent Swan Knight. The baby will carry his name."

The godfather had spoken. Joseph was content with the name. Nobody else felt qualified to dare venture an opinion, including me.

With that paramount mission accomplished, the swan moved on to his next demand. He insisted upon doubling my course of studies, knowing that as he taught me, he taught Joseph, that the baby recalled every word I read, every thought and sensation that brushed my mind.

"The Laws of Ermenrich have no place in these circumstances," the old teacher announced to the small room, as if he addressed a multitude, "Joseph's training begins in the womb. He will be born with more knowledge and wisdom than any Swan Knight in the long and storied line."

He meant it too. He was relentless in his regimen. He taught us more vigorously than he had taught any Swan Knight during his centuries of service to my ancestors. Latin, French and every language of the Sweeter Realm occupied the hours after my spiritual lessons with Taufe. Although all of my conversations in the Sweeter Realm were in German, I still thought often in English. For this reason, Joseph knew English before I knew of our connection. He knew and remembered every thought I had since his conception. Every word of every Sweeter Realm language, including German, that I spoke, read, or heard in that time was already set into his sublimely opulent mind.

With the loss of my ability to connect the minds of my subjects, I had much more time to feed Joseph's. Any dispute or incident that required my attention and intervention also required the related parties to travel to the palace. I did not know in advance who was coming to see me, who needed my guidance. I was, in short, like any Queen before me, on either side of the portal, needing to settle the affairs of the queendom face-to-face, with words delivered from my mouth.

The only exceptions came when I grasped Albert's Sword. But it only connected me to Unicorns, and not all Unicorns, only a few at a time, and not the Unicorns of my choosing. It carried my thoughts randomly and haphazardly to whichever horns it saw fit to visit, among those known to its original owner. Nevertheless, I used the sword often for this purpose, fruitless as those connections usually were. I began to miss cuddling up between the ears of those far away from me. Albert's Sword gave me that. And in those connections, Joseph joined me, giving him practice in interpreting the thoughts of others. He developed a particular affection for Unicorns, as they provided him his first experience inside of minds other than his mother's.

But I had little time to play with the sword, which had become little more than an exhibit in a throne room display of war-time relics. The settling of disputes and the giving of advice happened instantly before. With the loss of that ability, solutions had to plow through the clumsy jungle of language before emerging victorious. The Ancient One grew quickly impatient with the time required to fulfill my Queenly duties. He spoke to Cort. Cort still controlled the flow of visitors, and allowed much less of my day to be spent settling affairs. Each liberated second was redirected toward the swan and my lessons — *Joseph's* lessons.

Joseph was already steeped in scripture. All that I read, that was read or sung to me, and all that I prayed was stored securely in him. The Bible and the Conspicuous Scriptures, the writings of Taufe and of St. Hildegard, all bounced around in his head. He floated opinions to me, thoughts profoundly deep and beyond anything I would have considered. I was in constant conversation with him, but rarely in words. Our conversations reached into ideas that live far beyond the reach of language.

Joseph had a strong connection to the Grail. At the mention of Christ's Cup, he stirred inside of me and effused passionate thoughts on the subject. When my mind was elsewhere, on other studies, he often steered my thoughts to the Grail, keeping it almost as constant a companion as the thoughts of my son.

Joseph grew quickly, once The Ancient One implemented his regimen of study, as if the baby's body digested the information I read and used it as fuel to grow his bones. Within two weeks of his naming, he doubled in size. This was odd even for a Federkind. Although I often translated his thoughts to his father, Joseph relished kicking at Felix's touch, once he was large enough to be felt. It was direct and personal communication with his father, and both father and son savored it. Often, my belly would be noticeably larger in the evening than it was that very same morning.

Felix tried to keep one eye always on me, fearing that significant growth would occur, or any other notable event, and he would miss it while he glanced away. The baby was miraculous. That could not be denied. And Felix expected a new miracle to present itself during every passing second of the pregnancy. I often woke in the night to find Felix staring alertly at my belly, with one hand pressed on his son. I pretended to remain asleep, never wishing to interrupt those moments of intimacy, when he could communicate with Joseph alone. But as long as I was awake, there could be no privacy between Felix and Joseph. I could not block out the baby. I could not peel myself from his thoughts. We were of a single mind. Communication between us was instantaneous and entirely without effort. So even those tender-touching, midnight moments between Felix and Joseph were experienced and treasured by me.

Those were some of my happiest days. I was alert and enlivened by the anticipation of hardship and the return-to-self that came with my intense studies. I tingled with the newness of motherhood and the unprecedented oneness I felt with Joseph's mind, while still living in the bliss of a hard-earned peace. I had the peace I earned *and* the agitation I desired. And I fell more deeply in love with Felix every day. Joseph loved his father. And I felt Joseph's mind. My own love of my husband was magnified by Joseph's. My thoughts of Felix became multi-angular and profoundly, inexpressibly deep.

CHAPTER 8
Grail Blood at Linderhof

ONLY TWO AND A HALF MONTHS AFTER CONCEPTION, my belly was as large as I remembered any pregnant human being. I knew that the birth would be soon. I had swelled beyond the embrace of my clothes, and spent my days wearing no more than a narrow band of cloth, wrapped around my hips.

As I sat on my throne, awaiting the arrival of an envoy of Glühenchor, on some errand I have long forgotten, while my thoughts were intensely fixed on the impending birth, I was overcome by an exquisitely energetic sensation. The hairs on my arms and legs rose to attention. The feeling penetrated my skin, into my blood, through my bones, and to my marrow.

"This is it," I thought to myself.

I turned my attention to Joseph, and I asked him aloud, "Are you ready, son, to be held in my arms?"

Joseph was confused. He was not ready to be born. That was not the source of the sensation. The feeling was strange to Joseph and he could not account for it. He flipped through my memories like a scholar through a manuscript, trying to identify the strange phenomenon by some experience of my past. He found the memory that tied the sensation to my past, and pulled it to the forefront of my consciousness.

It was the portal — Parsifal's Portal at Linderhof. The last time I felt that tingle throughout my entire body, I was passing into the Sweeter Realm.

I began to ask myself and Joseph, "What does this mean?"

But before I could complete the thought, I knew the truth. The portal was open. Somebody was in the Venus Grotto, some relative, near or distant, had opened the portal from the other side.

My first thought was of my father. I was certain he was the one who opened the portal. A moment of brilliant delight at the idea of seeing him again was smashed by the suddenly descending understanding that it was not him, or anyone I knew. Delight turned to panic. I hollered for my Royal Guard. Georg, of course, led the surge of loyal warriors into the throne room. I could not think my thoughts to them. I was frustrated with the delay and clumsy slowness of vocal communication.

I pointed to a Wühlenvogel named Elisabeth who I affectionately called Lizzie, named after the daughter of Otto II, "Take me to the Portal Point!" I demanded. "As fast as you can fly."

"No, my Queen," Georg protested, "not in your condition. I will take you where you wish to go."

"No time!" I shouted.

Lizzie obeyed me, and in a flash, we were clear of the palace entrance and high into the air above the Nomadic Belt, flying south toward the Portal Point, at a dizzying speed.

Lizzie put me down and landed herself between me and a young man. He was in his mid-twenties, a handsome but terrified man caught between a fierce Wühlenvogel and the menacing crackle of the open portal behind him, and soaking wet from the water of the grotto's artificial lake. The portal snapped to a shut, which drew the man's attention and glance. When he saw that nothing was there, he turned frighteningly back to Lizzie's defensive scowl and growling fangs.

The poor man shook excessively and stumbled backward from his feet. He was armed only with a can of spray paint, shaking uncontrollably in his right hand.

I stepped between him and Lizzie, gestured her calm with a slow pat on her shoulders, and addressed the man in German, "You must be suffering quite a shock."

He answered crudely in broken German, in an accent that betrayed his American upbringing, "I am… It was… Who… What…"

I reached my hand for him, while addressing him in English, "I know this is unsettling. I will explain what you have gone through."

The sound of my English in his ears soothed him like a powerful drug, demonstrated clearly to my senses by his relaxed features and the sigh that released the air that his tense lungs had refused to relinquish. The man's tension seemed to transfer to Joseph. My unborn son, who was far wiser than knowledgeable, and could not easily explain the source of his opinions, sent his apprehensions forcefully into my mind.

"This is a human," I thought to him. "He is one of my kind, one of your kind. And he has Grail Blood."

The relief felt by my eyes at the sight of another human evicted the suspicious fears that would normally have accompanied the event. He was very handsome, muscular, with fiery eyes. He took my hand and allowed me to help him to his feet. He stood a full foot taller than me as he introduced himself as "Reid". To soothe his nerves, I introduced myself as "Verena, from Colorado."

Mere seconds after the introduction, all three of us were drawn to a bustle in the sky above us. Several Wühlenvogels descended upon us, each carrying passengers. Felix, The Ancient One, and several members of my Guard landed in a circle around us. Felix jumped to my side and wrapped an arm around me. This was immediately followed by the rapid thundering of Unicorn hooves, sprinting at us from the north. Taufe rode on the first of them.

There was a violent ferocity in the encircling party of creatures, all shifting from intimidating glares at Reid to assuring nods to me. Again, being without my ability to connect to their minds, I raised my hands high and calmed them all with a gentle introduction to the human in front of me. Reid inched closer to me, as if to seek my protection from the enclosing army of sharp horns, claws, and fangs.

The Ancient One trotted as quickly as his webbed feet could carry him, to stand directly in front of Reid. He raised his neck high, almost eye to eye with the intruder, looking for any trait that would remind him of his long line of students, and relieve him of his anxiety. The swan and Reid stared into each other's eyes, one in stringent, exacting evaluation, and the other in fearful surprise.

After a minute of his penetrating gaze, The Ancient One took a few steps back.

A Scherier voice shouted from behind me, "To the Queen's Jail, until we can make sense of this."

Reid's German was good enough to get the gist of the command. At those words, he began to shake. He knees grew weak and wobbled beneath him.

"No, no, no," I interjected, trying to speak in simple enough terms for Reid's poor German to keep up, "this is a friend, until he proves otherwise. He should be treated as such."

Taufe had dismounted her Unicorn and walked silently to my other side, opposite of Felix.

She placed her hand on my shoulder and spoke softly to me in Brunnen, "Good things will be happening soon.

Perhaps this is the beginning. But perhaps it is not. We should proceed carefully."

"Yes," The Ancient One continued, also in Brunnen, "listen to the abbess. Treachery, violence, and hate thrive in that world. We do not know what has crossed into the Sweeter Realm today."

"You are right," I answered in German.

I looked Reid in the eyes and continued in English, "We do not know what has come into my queendom today. Reid will teach us what makes up his character, and we will be patient students."

At the words "my queendom", Reid lowered himself shakily to one knee and dropped his wide eyes to the ground in front of my bare feet. My eyes joined his at my feet, which reminded me that I stood, bare-breasted, wrapped only by a cloth around my hips, in front of this stranger. It had been quite some time since I felt naked in front of the creatures of the Sweeter Realm. But my nudity leaped embarrassingly into my thoughts, as Reid continued his downward gaze. Before he could raise his eyes again, I grabbed Felix's other arm and covered my breasts with his feathers.

"Take him to the palace," I ordered a nearby Unicorn. "Do not let him touch your horn until we know the merits of his character."

Before Reid could lift his face, Felix grabbed me in his powerful arms and ran me northward. After several steps, Lizzie took him around the waist with her powerful tail and lifted us both high above the trees. Not a word was spoken between us while we flew to the palace. Joseph's only thoughts were unusually infantile. He sought only comfort from his mother, and allowed the warmth of my womb to encase and cradle all other thoughts, rocking them to sleep so that the only activity in his mind was that of an unborn child. I thought only comfort to him, as I sang in my mind a Scherier lullaby. For the sake of my frightened husband, my throat hummed along with the song in my head.

Never had I so terribly missed my ability to connect the minds of my queendom. We arrived to a palace entirely ignorant of the events of the morning. But the wings and hooves of the Sweeter Realm are swift, and they carried the news quickly to the startled ears of every homeland. Curious and defensive visitors began to arrive at the palace before The Ancient One and the others arrived with Reid. Georg was in no hurry to bring the stranger into my home.

In defiance of my orders, he carried Reid to the palace himself, flicking his sharp horn intimidatingly along the way, and speaking with his sternest, deepest growl. He wanted to give me a full report on the stranger before allowing him to step into the sanctity of the palace. Georg spoke no English. So he questioned Reid in German. It is unlikely Reid understood much. But the mood behind the questions must have been clear. The interview was harsh, thorough, and disquieting to the man's already shaken nerves.

Little intelligence was gathered by Georg, in the steady trot along the lakeside. Reid's German was weak at best, not much more than the few phrases a tourist would need to see the sights on his vacation. Georg was frustrated, and arrived at the palace with no more information than I had already discerned in the initial encounter. Georg left Reid on the beach near the palace entrance. He ordered the Guard to hold him there, speaking in the native languages of the Sweeter Realm. He marched into the palace with a stout determination that reminded me of his march into battle. Felix sat on the throne, and I on his lap.

Brunnens scurried to me with additions to my wardrobe that would fit my swollen state. Georg stepped to me as Felix slipped a shirt over my head.

"The man is outside on the beach," Georg proclaimed.

"Why doesn't he come in?" I asked.

"He is encaged by your Royal Guard until you give us orders."

"For Heaven's sake, my friend, bring him in."

Felix added forcefully, "Carefully! There should be a horn or a claw between him and the Queen at all times."

Georg nodded with a glare of agreement into Felix's eyes.

My nerves were still rattled, entirely unsoothed by my own lullaby. I ordered Georg to take Reid into one of the lesser rooms of the palace, which would be designated as his own until we could figure out what to do with him. I ordered the Guard to provide him food, company if he desired it, and any other comfort that could be thought of — but no information beyond what was immediately necessary. I placed two guards outside of his room, and I retired to bed with my husband. One of his arms wrapped underneath me, while the other hand pressed firmly against my belly. Joseph shoved both feet forcefully against his father's palm.

The physical comfort gave leave to my mind so it could wander to those notions I had been too disconcerted to consider. Reid's appearance in the forest blanketed many other thoughts that swam quickly into my head, in sharp and darting patterns, as I rested in Felix's embrace. I had stood before the open portal into Linderhof. Why did it not occur to me to go through before it closed? Aside from the fact that I was not properly clad for a stroll through Linderhof Park, it was my first chance to reconnect with my family. And the portal would always open for me from that side. I would not be leaving my queendom, my friends, and my husband forever. But the thought did not approach my most distant musings as I my ears were reintroduced to the signature crackle of Parsifal's Portal.

My thoughts were of curiosity at the man before me, and of defensive concerns for the Sweeter Realm and the Grail. I had given little thought to the can of paint that Reid brought with him through the portal, clasped covetously in his hand, as if it contained his immortal soul. It was a cheap can of spray paint, not the tool for revitalizing art. It was the tool of vandalism, of defilement. Only when in bed, in the arms of my husband, did I consider that Reid was there to vandalize the mural of Tannhäuser. Why else would he have been at the Portal Point, wet from the water of the grotto, with a can of cheap paint in his hand?

These thoughts would have set my teeth grinding in fury, had the image of his terrified face not elicited my deepest and familiar compassions. Joseph, who had retreated into his own thoughts and the comforts of his father's touch, offered his encouragement.

"The greatest figures in our history have had their moments of folly," he reminded me.

Being notoriously self-critical, my memory swept me cruelly across my own many moments of ill-judgment, irresponsibility, and immaturity, placing a soft filter over Reid's transgressions. With that softness, I released all concerns on the matter and let my husband's powerful arms and warm feathers incubate my lightest and freest reflections. It was upon the wings of those reflections that I sailed into sleep. My dreams were blithe and nurturing, but with Reid's face making an occasional and conspicuous cameo.

Joseph's thoughts spoke comfort to me, concerning Reid's appearance in the Sweeter Realm. But his heart moved very differently. He feared Reid, or feared some unknown evil associated with the human visitor. I believe it was those fears that kept Joseph in my womb. He grew larger than either a human baby or Federkind should be before birth. He spent the following day much more like a normal unborn baby, offering little communication, little movement. When I sought his thoughts, they were of the warmth and comfort of the womb and not the far-reaching and curious, probing thoughts he had displayed to that point.

The morning after Reid arrived demanded a complete disruption of the daily routines of the palace. Reid was in the Sweeter Realm with no ability to leave or be banished. The only known way out was my portal in the lake, and nobody knew where it led. Parsifal's Portal could not be opened from our side. These were the points and considerations made in an early morning meeting. Felix, Georg, the teachers, and I met in our sleeping chamber, at the highest point in the palace. We stared at each other, not even knowing how to initiate the discussion. Nobody knew what to do.

"There is no Swan Knight at Linderhof, to open the portal and receive him back, as Albert did with Gessner," the swan finally spoke up and reminded us.

"No," I shamefully answered, "I am not a traditional Swan Knight, living in Linderhof and protecting the portal from that side, keeping invaders out of Eden, as all Swan Knights have been sworn to do. The portal sits unguarded and there is nothing I can do about it."

Taufe scolded The Ancient One with a penetrating scowl. The room became awkward. Everyone wanted to defend me, to excuse my inability to serve as other Swan Knights had. But the truth could not be denied. I was unable to guard the portal and incidents like this were bound to occur.

Felix interrupted with some facts that balanced the mood of the room, "From what you tell us, there is no way a Swan Knight could live at Linderhof and protect the portal as they always had. Ludwig's palace and the Portal Valley are some sort of museum now."

The heads of the room nodded in agreement. And I knew he was right. Linderhof was under the control of the Bavarian Department of Palaces. Even if I was a sworn Swan Knight on the other side of the portal, I could not very well live at Linderhof and train with Unicorns in the valley. I could best guard the portal from my side in the Sweeter Realm.

"And," Felix continued, "Ludwig II secured the portal as well as could be with his grotto and lake."

Words of agreement joined the nodding heads.

I silenced the mouths and halted the nodding heads, adding, "In the old days, the Queen protected the Grail and the Swan Knight protected the portal. I can protect the Grail from here, as she did. But there is no Swan Knight on the other side, and as you say, there would be no way to perform that duty from Linderhof. So I must protect the portal from this side."

At those words, all eyes turned to The Ancient One, who lowered his head to the height of his shoulders, looked directly into my eyes, and asked, "How?"

Georg suggested, "Didn't your Parsifal build a house near the portal, so he could keep a close guard on it?"

"Out of the question," Felix rebutted. "That might allow her to more efficiently serve as the Swan Knight. But she is also the Queen, duly elected. The Swimmers could not come to her there, not easily. It is remote. This new house could not hold the gatherings required of a Queen's palace."

Georg nodded more vigorously with each of Felix's points, then added, "Yes, and her queenship needs the continuity of the ancient palaces. You are right. A house near the Portal Point will not do."

The Ancient One interrupted with a conspicuous clearing of his throat, then repeated his question, "So how do you protect the portal from this side?"

"Simple," I spoke in a matter-of-fact tone, "we build a cage around the Portal Point. Anyone who comes through will be instantly imprisoned, until we can determine the level of threat."

Taufe and Felix had apprehensions, both grabbing their chins and sighing in a perfect mirror of the other. Georg proclaimed the idea to be brilliant. The Ancient One began with the subtlest nod of his head, which grew larger as he slowly extended his neck upward.

Once his head sat as high as it could reach, and his nod was demonstrative, he spoke, "Yes, my dear. You will always know when the portal has opened. No accidental visitor will sit imprisoned for long. And if the intruder is good-hearted, he will surely forgive the precaution."

"If not," Georg added, "his forgiveness is something we neither seek nor desire."

Felix seemed to be warming to the idea. But Taufe's apprehensions showed even more clearly on her brow.

The Ancient One shook his head back and forth, looking at Taufe, anticipating her objection and speaking quickly and sharply to it, "Yes, yes, yes, the cage will be terrifying for anyone appearing in it, but no more terrifying than a heard of Wühlenvogels and Unicorns descending, as poor Reid experienced. Verena will notify us when the portal has opened and we will convene a welcome party, knowing that the visitor has not disappeared into the Zweigwesen forest before we arrive. And if he is injured, we know where we may find him to administer aide."

He allowed a few seconds of contemplation before continuing, "Yes, a cage around the Portal Point serves us perfectly. I fully endorse it."

Of course, the decision was mine to make. Since the portal is in the Nomadic Belt, no breed's authority on the matter rivaled mine. The endorsement of the only other living creature to have served as King cemented the plan.

Work on the design began immediately. As to the matter of Reid and what was to become of him, that decision could not be made by the heads in the room. Since I was unable to connect the minds of the leaders, a physical committee must meet, and that would take time. We sent messengers to the farthest reaches of the Sweeter Realm and planned a meeting at the palace in three weeks.

The Sweeter Realm was likely to be Reid's home for a very long time. I planned to use the three weeks to better learn of his character and to familiarize him with his new world. I had no intention of granting him permanent residence in the palace. But nobody was quite sure what else to do with him. So we decided to save those discussions for the committee as well.

When the meeting broke, I went directly to Reid's room. The guards at his door insisted upon accompanying me. But I denied them. I thought it best that I address him alone. Taufe agreed. From inside of Reid's room, I could hear Georg huffing and stomping his feet. I believe it was partly from his anxiety. But also so that both I and Reid would know he waited just outside.

Reid was slow to adjust to the new realities of his life. His fretful expressions from the day before had softened little. I explained to him that the passageway that brought him here was the same one that I had used years before, that I too was startled and scared. But I told him about my encounter with Cort and the other Friends. I spoke nothing of the Grail or the Swan Knights, nothing of Löwschock, or the war, or freeing the swan. I spoke only of the beauties of the Sweeter Realm. I also told him that there was no way for him to return to his home. This was an obvious blow to his spirits. His knees buckled beneath him and he fell to his hip.

He worked his way to his bed — a rather haphazard pile of my extra blankets and cloaks from my wardrobe, tossed upon a soft, gummy mound that extended a few feet from the floor. It was not unlike the beds in St. Hildegard. He held his face in his hand for a minute. I allowed him the moment of silent thought.

Finally, he pulled his palm from his face, turned his head slowly to me, and asked, "You say you are from Colorado? And you came through the same hole I came through?"

I nodded in silence.

"And now you are their Queen? You rule this entire world?"

"I don't rule them. God rules them and they rule themselves. I guide them when they need guidance."

"But they obey you. I can see that already. They do whatever you tell them."

Joseph heard the questions, through the muffling filter of my abdomen and through my own thoughts. He kicked and jolted in fear, sending shivers and goosebumps across my body. Joseph was right. Reid's words and his tone smacked of ambition. He had neither the benefit of Ludwig's journal, which did much to prepare me for the Sweeter Realm before *I* came through, nor had he the countless shared memories that gave me my understanding of my queendom. He did not have The Ancient One's training, or Taufe's spiritual guidance.

I had lived with the native creatures of Eden for years and still discovered delights daily. I could not expect Reid to understand after only one day, while still suffering the shock of his dramatic transplant.

I thought to Joseph, "Perhaps it is not ambition that we hear from his mouth, but confused thoughts, mutated as they are passed through his fears and ignorance. I am not ready to judge him yet. Let him adjust and learn, and we will see then if his words sound ambitious."

Reid disrupted my thoughts to Joseph, demanding, "They do, don't they? They obey your every wish. You control them, so you rule them."

I could not contain my frustration at this line of conversation, and I displayed it with a curt and forceful sigh, before answering, "They elected me. And in their elections, they do not consider who will give them what they want, or who will favor them over another breed. They do not look for a Queen to command them and control their lives. They look for a Queen who is willing to die for them, who loves them and respects them more than her own life."

"And did they find that Queen in you?"

I had no immediate words to answer him. I only stabbed his eyes with mine, powerfully enough to make him sheepishly turn away.

I walked to stand right against him, firmly placed my hand on his shoulder, and I spoke in a voice that sounded more like the swan's than my own, "It is their love and respect that gives me authority, not the title to which I was elected. Even as Queen, without the love, I have no influence over them. And even if I were not their Queen, my love for them would give me influence. The title is only a symbol of their trust in me… trust I earned with my own tears, with my own blood."

He was tall, and sat just a few inches lower than I stood. At the mention of blood, he turned quickly to face me, and my chin stood almost touching his nose as he looked upward at me. It was only in his reaction that I realized what I had done. In mentioning blood, I betrayed the conflicts of our recent past.

He asked, "You bled for them?"

I gave no explanation, but only responded, "I would do much more, if my duty as their servant-Queen demanded."

"Well," he huffed as he looked away again, "It seems to me that they serve you. They obviously think that they do."

A vocalized sigh that sounded more like a growl pushed through my clinched jaw. It seemed to come from my brow, as my disapproving eyes stabbed deeper into his. The directness of my eyes again pushed his gaze away from my face, this time downward, to my swollen belly.

Without raising his focus, he spoke of the belly he stared at, "You are pregnant. Is the baby... I mean, is the father from... who is the father?"

"*Felix* is my husband," my voice jabbed at him defensively.

"That little animal with the feathers? And you carry his baby?"

I walked away from him, to the threshold of the room, grinding my teeth and wanting to wad him into a little ball and shove him back into Linderhof —were that only an option.

I turned slowly to see him staring back at me, and said in a half-whisper, "You come from a very different world. Give it some time. You will come to understand."

With those words, I left him alone in his room. I wanted badly to know his inner thoughts, to be given some hint of his plans, his state of mind. His mind must have begun plotting his future, both immediate and distant. I wondered if I had misinterpreted his questions. He had a traumatic twenty-four hours, and could hardly be expected to display his real character under such strange conditions. These are the justifications that I presented to myself and Joseph in excuse of Reid's startling questions. From that encounter, I felt unable to resume the course of a normal day.

The throne room began to fill with curious and concerned creatures, waiting for their Queen to give them answers. In truth, I had no answers to give. I was not ready to reveal the unnerving particulars of my morning conversation with Reid, not to the creatures in the palace, or Taufe and The Ancient One, or even Felix, especially not Felix. I shared those confused contemplations with only Joseph, who seemed to retreat more deeply into his own mind with every thought of Reid.

Reid already unnerved Joseph. Our encounter with him that morning only frightened him further. Perhaps it was Joseph's uneasiness, more than any perceptions of my own, that instilled such apprehensions in my heart. Reid's curiosity was natural and the offensive things he said and asked were a mind trying to grasp realities far outside of his previous paradigm.

It was not until the next morning, when I was confronted by the swan, who insisted that my normal regimen of study resume, and by Cort, who demanded that I deal with the many pilgrims to the palace, that I told anyone the things that Reid had asked and said. I felt it best to leave Georg and the Guard out of that briefing. I spoke only to Felix, Taufe, Cort, and the swan. I wrapped my words in more excuses than worry, trying to soften their reactions. They interpreted Reid's words as confusion and curiosity, more than ambition. Their opinions comforted me, but did nothing to pull Joseph from his self-imposed isolation inside of my womb.

We decided to send Reid on a thoroughly guided and well-guarded tour of nearest cities and sights of the Land and Shallow Waters.

"Everything here is new to him," Taufe reminded us. "A little experience and understanding should set him right. He is, after all, from Parsifal. Just give him some Scherier hospitality and a Brunnen bath, let him sing with the Eulesängers and feel the penetrating harmonies of the Glühenchor."

Early the next morning, after forcing Reid to sit through our morning prayers, I sent him to tour the Land, with two young Unicorn warriors and two Wühlenvogels. I sent him with the prayer that nothing along his way would fuel his ambitions. I hoped that a little exposure to the creatures, as they live their daily lives, would clarify to some degree the nature of my relationship with my subjects. I prayed that the beauty of my queendom that filled my grateful eyes with every blink of my eyelids would saturate him as well, and a wiser, calmer, more settled and thoughtful man would return to the palace when the tour was complete.

CHAPTER 9
The Mark of Cain

THERE WAS SO MUCH FOR REID TO SEE, so much to feed his senses. I had no notion that he might return before the committee met. But I also stipulated no particular route or timetable. I should have. Gatherings of Sweeter Realm leaders, like the one we had planned, were not common. The fact that I asked for it stirred the tranquil air of my queendom. The oldest and wisest of each breed made the journey to the palace. Even Krummzahn, who rarely poked her head out of the Wühlenvogel capital, insisted on her voice being heard before the committee.

The keen interest in the matter of Reid's appearance was a testament to how rare and impactful human interaction with the Sweeter Realm had been. Parsifal was the first since mankind's banishment from Eden. He changed the Sweeter Realm immensely, bringing a unified language, and giving birth to their dedication to the Swan Knights and the portal. Tannhäuser was next. His breach of the portal brought into existence the first marriage of a human and a creature of Eden. It resulted in Brunhilde. Gessner's time in the Sweeter Realm awakened the evils of the Deep, resulting in war and death like the Sweeter Realm had never known. Then I came through, became their Queen, vanquished that evil and ended the war, spawning a new era of peace.

Each occurrence was monumental, to say the least. Now Reid was with us, and everyone wondered what the result would be. They only agreed on one thing — that his appearance would be tremendously impactful, as the others had been.

I wanted Joseph to be born in those weeks while Reid was away and the palace was calmly waiting for the arrival of the committee. My pregnancy had been brief, and I cherished his presence inside of me. But for some reason I could not explain, I did not want Reid near me for the birth. I had also hoped to present the baby to the honored friends converging upon the palace. But Joseph was increasingly withdrawn, despite my coaxing. His thoughts rarely left the bounds of his immediate senses. He did not engage in my lessons or philosophize with me during those quiet moments before sleep, as he had done before the portal reopened. I continued my daily routines, but with a nagging apprehension radiating outward from my womb, a sensation that was just about the only communication I had with my unborn son.

Two weeks after Reid left on his tour, well before the committee arrived, he returned to the palace with the chaperones I had sent with him. I was seated on the throne, discussing some construction projects with the Brunnens. Two weeks was not nearly enough, even on Unicorn-back, to see the places and meet the creatures I wanted him to meet. Unless he was very receptive, two weeks would not be enough for the goodness around him to saturate deeply.

He appeared under the arch of the palace entrance. I confess that a single glace into his face demonstrated an altered man. He seemed calmer, peaceful, and at-ease with his surroundings. He spoke casually and friendly with the creatures who accompanied him. It seemed that Taufe was right — that the pure, authentic, and holy love of the creatures he encountered had altered him for the better. His bond with the creatures around him seemed tight and authentic.

I was glad when he left, and loathed to see him return. But the alteration was a surprising delight, and my eyes relished the sight of him, particularly in light of the fact that my husband was away, and the palace had a stillness that begged for agitation. Felix was on the other side of the lake, presiding over ancient rituals, during a three-day Federmensch holiday. I had no way to reach for him. But I felt no need to. Reid's physical beauty was splendidly aggrandized by what appeared to be a prodigious and promising transformation in his character.

"You see, Joseph," I thought to my son, "With a little time, he is more of his true self. Now that the shock of the portal has faded, we can learn his character."

Joseph was not convinced. He buried his mind deep inside of his soft skull and projected nothing to me aside from his desire for the safety and comfort of his mother's womb.

Reid bid affectionate adieus to his Unicorn and Wühlenvogel guides. He bowed to me as he passed the throne. And he walked casually up the ramp to the upper rooms. Without dismissing the Brunnens, I gathered the chaperones and demanded a report of Reid's behavior during the tour.

"It took a few days, my Queen," one of the Unicorn warriors reported, "but he warmed up nicely."

"He's very charming," a Wühlenvogel added. "He told wonderful stories. Everyone we met with along the tour liked him."

This was wonderful news to my apprehensive ears. It shed a new light on the impending committee meeting. They could now convene under brighter circumstances. Deciding on Reid's place in the Sweeter Realm seemed a much pleasanter prospect. The Queen's Jail would have been a terribly unfitting home for the blood of Parsifal. And I admit having given the idea serious thought. It seemed that more peaceful options were in hand.

I did not see Reid for the rest of the day, which surprised me in light of his jovial entrance into the palace, and the glowing report of his behavior during the tour.

My shallow thoughts said, "He must be exhausted from his travels, and from all of the social interactions along the way."

But my deeper reflections were in line with Joseph, perhaps guided by his lingering misgivings, which seeped from my womb, into my blood and to my brain. But those thoughts were shoved downward by hope, and by what my own senses had perceived.

The next day, I only caught a few glimpses of Reid in passing, as the bustle of a busier-than-normal day in the palace kept me divided between many duties at once. Upon his return, I had rather hoped to develop the sort of bond he clearly shared with the Unicorns and Wühlenvogels who traveled with him. Our last interactions before his tour had been icy and suspicious. I longed for the warmth he had fostered with his chaperones and for the chance to begin again with the only other human in my life. The day offered no such opportunity. In our brief interactions, my looks of hopeful, familial good-will were not reflected back to me from his bright eyes. He was neither cold nor warm. Energy and activity swirled inside of his eyes and seemed to cloud me from their notice.

When evening descended and Cort had cleared the palace of visitors and settled into his own quarters, and Taufe and the swan had left for the day, I sat alone in the throne room, thinking of Reid, and longing for my first opportunity to authenticate the report of the chaperones with words and sentiments from Reid's own lips.

During my years as the only human in the Sweeter Realm, I missed the sight of my own kind, at least I thought I did. Seeing Reid at the portal that day did not bring relief or pleasure. He did not seem to be "of my kind", but rather some separate species entirely, some mysterious intruder from a foreign world. After his transformation, when he stood near the entrance to the palace and hugged the creatures who had accompanied him, he appeared truly human. And his beauty finally brought the relief that the sight of another human should have brought.

I wanted to speak to him — of his tour, of course, but also of his home town, his trip to Linderhof, of his friends, his family, his favorite television shows and sports, and all of the little things that our early years would have naturally had in common, those things over which I could relate to no other in my queendom. But I hesitated to seek him out. Joseph forbade it through his unspoken rejection. So I went alone to my sleeping chamber and resigned to waiting another day. I was not one minute in my room when Reid appeared.

"Can I talk to you?" he asked politely, but with stout confidence.

"Of course," I answered, with a rigid formality in my voice, intentionally designed to mask my eagerness. "I will be right with you."

Being alone with him in my bedroom held no scandalous implications in the Sweeter Realm. But enough of my human life remained stitched to my sensibilities to forbid it. I told him to meet me in the throne room, where palace business *should* be conducted. This was not the response he expected. But he obeyed, nodded his head slowly, and left my room.

I dressed fully, and added one more accoutrement. I strapped to my forearm my one remaining piece of Elsa'a armor, not for its magical properties. I was not in need of the Scherier sense of well-being. I wore it for its symbolism — of the ancient heritage to which we both belonged, and for its fang holes to remind me *and him* of the battles and the triumphs of my past. Those holes were an emblem of my sacrifices for the queendom. I wanted them boldly in his field of vision as he addressed me.

When I walked into the throne room, I saw Reid, oozing with self-assuredness, standing beside the Queen's throne, leaning with one hand against the throne and the other on his hip, as if he meticulously posed himself to display confidence. But it was no meticulously sculpted pose. No, a bone fide confidence placed him in that pose quite natuarally, and bordered on an unsettling degree of impudence.

I approached him casually, disguising my uneasiness, "Finally I can welcome you back from your tour. How did it go?"

"Well, that's what I wanted to talk to you about. It was wonderful. The animals —"

I interrupted him with a chastising grimace.

"Creatures!" he quickly amended. "They were amazing. The darling things were so accommodating."

He rolled his head and wore a broad smile as he spoke of them. His admiration seemed sincere. He spoke of a camp of Zweigwesens he encountered. Four Scheriers were in their party.

He recounted, "They listened very attentively to everything I told them. They sang for me and brought me food and drink the very moment I realized I wanted it."

Nothing in his words or tone inclined me to believe that his delight ran more deeply that pleasure. No sense of ardent admiration came across.

His tour guides were more than chaperones. They were guards and spies. I referenced them, "And the Unicorns and

Wühlenvogels who traveled with you, did you find them as accommodating?"

"They were a little stiff at first, but I won them over. By the end, they were as sweet as all the rest."

My heart volleyed back and forth between delight in his transformation and uneasiness at his childish understanding of his hosts.

Probing to end the volley, I asked, "Did you learn anything from your time away?"

His tone and expression grew austere, as he sat on the arm of the throne and answered, "I certainly did. Those... *creatures*... don't just adore you. They idolize you. You are a god to them."

I wanted to immediately refute his gross misunderstanding, but I waited for more.

He provided it, adding, "I know you say that *you* serve *them*, and that you guide, not rule. But you did not hear the way they speak of you. They would do anything you command, without question or hesitation. You own them. They are your obedient pets. This whole place belongs to you."

I could no longer bite my tongue, "Nothing you have just said approaches the truth. Loving them all and being their Queen is a painful pleasure. And it carries a burden you clearly do not understand."

"Oh, I understand. And that's exactly what I wanted to talk to you about."

He stood, backed toward the palace entrance, and gestured for me to sit on the throne. Hesitatingly, I sat as he had directed. My repugnance had a curiosity of its own. And it wanted to know what he would say next.

Once I sat down, he walked to touch his knees to mine, and he continued, "This is a big place, and you are a young woman, a *pregnant* woman. I am older. I am a man. I am stronger and it would be no burden to me."

I began to stand. He pushed gently on my shoulder with one hand. I sat down, but only to gather further justification for my souring opinion of him.

"Go on," I urged him.

"Let me take some of this off of your hands. Give me three or four homelands to rule at first. I will be a kind King. If you tell them that I am their King, then it will be so. They worship you. If motherhood becomes too much for you, I will take more off your hands. You and Felix could live with his people, where your child belongs. I could rule from here."

I felt Joseph turn inside of me, to put his back toward Reid. I glared at Reid through my lowered eyebrows, with a teeth-grinding scowl, shaking my head slowly back and forth.

He misinterpreted my disapproval and amended, "... or anywhere. You could remain in the palace. They can build me a new palace anywhere."

I stood slowly, pushing him backwards as I rose. I wanted inside his head. I had ordered his Unicorn guides not to make a horn connection with him. I wanted *our* secrets kept from him. But I would have gladly relinquished our secrets for his, and I intended to order a horn connection to his chest in the morning. Suddenly I remembered the Unicorn horn that was mine to use — Albert's Sword. It sat in its place of honor, mounted on an elevated platform against the wall of the throne room, for the doting visitors of the palace to gawk at and admire.

I stepped to the side and gestured to the throne, saying, "You would like to know how the throne feels beneath you. Have a seat."

With the smile of ambitious delight, he quickly took the seat. I walked to the sword display, took the relic in my hand and carried it toward Reid. I held it like a relic, not like a weapon I was wielding in conflict. Reid must have thought I was gifting it to him in some ritualistic transfer of power. When I stood directly before him, I gripped it by the handle and turned the sharp point toward him. His face grew fearful and he wiggled backward until he bumped the back of the throne. I inched the point toward his chest until it touched the fabric of his shirt. He thought I was going to kill him. That was clear in his wide-eyed, terrified expression.

Stone-faced, ready to welcome his thoughts into mine, I pushed the tip against his chest. His eyelids began blinking quickly, while his eyes rolled in every direction. He was receiving something from the horn. But I did not know what and I felt nothing in return. With my other hand I grabbed the base of the horn. I fell into the memories of the Unicorn who lost that horn centuries earlier. I felt it being sawed off by the prize hunter who defiled her. I saw Albert and the rich compassion in his dark eyes. When I broke from the vision, the sword was no longer touching Reid. He stood in front of the throne, towering over me and the tip of the sword rested on the floor between us.

Reid had a continually twisting and morphing grimace on his face, like he was trying to process what he just experienced. I hoped that he saw what I saw, that the experience would shed some light on the hidden contours of our miraculous presence in the Sweeter Realm, and of the many lives that have been committed to its protection. But I feared that the horn only revealed things that would fuel his ambitions. At any rate, I did not have the energy to deal with it then.

Looking harshly upward at the tall man, I sighed at him and spoke in a low and slow voice, "I am going to bed. A committee of leaders is coming here in a few days to discuss what to do with you. I do not recommend you pitch this plan of yours to them. In fact, it might be best if you do not speak at all."

125

I walked halfway from the throne to the entrance of the ramp, stopped sharply, turned slowly, and added, "You should trust me on this. I know them, *much* better than you."

I did not return the sword to its place of display. I carried it with me up the spiralling ramp to my bedroom. I went to bed, deeply agitated and stiff-bodied. When I finally slept, my dreams were violent. I dreamed of Löwschock — first of the unknown dread that dug into me as the sun set behind the lake on my first day in the Sweeter Realm, when I looked across the darkening water and imagined what hateful chaos stirred beneath the surface. Next, I dreamed of the swan's rescue, of mangled bodies being tossed at me from the lake. The lakeside turned into the canyon, and I saw every face that lost the twinkle of life in its eyes that day. I dreamed of my battle with Löwschock, and the darting eyes that stabbed at me from the blackness of the Deep.

I awoke entirely unrested, stiff-jointed, and low of spirit. My first thoughts of the day were of thanksgiving that Reid had no army of foul serpents at his command. He was all alone and his ambitions had no muscle. As I dressed, I tried to convince myself that ignorance, more than greed and ambition, propelled Reid's words from his mouth, and that the proper schooling by Taufe and The Ancient One might bring his thought more in line with the truth. I wanted badly to know what he saw in the horn connection. That knowledge may have given me some insight into his state of mind. It may have saved me a great deal of suffering and possibly saved Reid's life.

The Ancient One and Taufe greeted me as they always do, early for prayers and lessons. After morning prayers, which Reid unsurprisingly did not attend, I ate with my teachers and Cort. I told them nothing of the last evening's conversation. They would sit on the committee and hear the evidence with the rest of them. Together, as equal subjects of God, we would decide what to do with Reid.

I don't think Reid left his room all day. At least, I did not see him. I was glad not to see him. I preferred to imagine him burrowed away in prayer and contemplation, listening and learning from the wisdom of the winds, contemplating the lessons hidden in his experience of the horn connection. However, I did not expect that he did. I more easily saw him brooding, and composing his next speech, little good it would do him. I conducted my day as usual, divided between the mandates of my training and the whims of royal obligations.

The next couple of days were very similar. The Federmensch holiday ended, but Felix took the long way around the lake to meet up with some members of the committee and accompany them to the palace. On the day they were to arrive, Cort made all the preparations expected of a gathering of this magnitude. The food and decorations were a tribute to each breed represented in the committee. We were not sure how the meeting would go or how long it would last. Other than morning prayers and breakfast, no plans at all were made for the day.

I sat on the throne and waited. The travelers had convened on the beach, not far from the palace, to be escorted by Cort in a grand march. The Royal Guard arranged in a greeting formation outside of the palace entrance. When the chamber was entirely empty, and only Reid and I remained in the palace, I felt Joseph tossing and turning inside of me.

"Now?" I thought to him. "You choose *now* to be born?"

I stood from the throne and took one step toward the palace entrance, when I felt a sharp pain in my lower back. Before I could think about the first, another sharp pain hit my middle back, deeper and infinitely more excruciating.

This time, I felt the weapon being drawn from me. I heard Reid cursing behind me in a deep growl. By the time the third pain hit my side, I knew I was being attacked. I turned toward Reid and saw the greedy fury in his face, partially shielded by the flinging curtain of my blood as he withdrew the blade with a wide swing of his hand. I fell to my knees and watched a bloodied wooden knife, gripped tightly in Reid's red-stained fist, push through my attempt to block it, and plunge its full length into my belly.

I fell to my back as I yelled for my husband.

I stared up at Reid as he drew the knife above his head for a final and fatal strike. His image blurred behind the welling tears in my eyes. I wrapped my arms around my belly, around my son, doubtful that he or I would survive the day. Through the tears, I saw the distorted image of a Wühlenvogel wrap her tail around Reid, pinning his arms to his side. I saw the stain on the Wühlenvogel's wing, the "Mark of Sacrifice". It was Lizzie. She slammed the back of Reid's head with her hard horns, causing a cracking thud. Reid's head jerked forward. His chin bounced from his chest and his head flew back.

Reid went limp. His knees buckled and his legs turned soft. He remained upright only by the grip of a Wühlenvogel tail and the flap of her wings. Lizzie grabbed Reid's head with her claws and tilted his chin upward so that he looked at the ceiling of the throne room. He attempted to scream, but only an airy moan escaped his mouth. I felt Georg's beard brush against me as he thrusted his head upward and drove his horn through Reid's jaw and out the top of his skull. Lizzie released her grip on him. Georg held him off of his dangling, writhing legs. As my senses faltered and the room went dark, I saw hands, claws, and teeth, of all shapes, sizes, and colors, ripping and tearing at the helplessly suspended man. When I could see no more, I still felt Reid's blood, his Grail Blood, showering me from above. The sounds of tearing flesh and breaking bones — thuds, cracks, snaps, rips, and angry growls — sang in morbid concert with the strange, inhuman, gurgling sounds coming from Reid's mouth.

In the moments after my vision went black, images of all sorts, pleasant and vile, shot through my mind, too fast to interpret. I felt myself being jostled, but sound faded as sight had. The chaos of the throne room slowly muted into silence. The images flashing in my mind slowed until a single thought occupied my entire brain — Joseph. I called for his mind, but heard only sobbing, unsure if the sensation was received by my ears or my mind, if the crying I heard was Joseph or some poor, pathetic creature mourning the death of her Queen.

CHAPTER 10
Blades in the Darkness

THE SOUNDS, THE SOBBING, the sense of being jostled and moved around, all physical sensation winded down together into nothing, as if flushing down a drain. I was alone in the darkness. For the first time since my earliest communications with the Unicorns, there was nobody in my mind but me. There was nobody anywhere. My sense of loneliness was indescribable. I felt like I was floating in space, without a star in sight — nothing but silence and darkness in every direction, a vast, universal emptiness with me in its very center.

The return of sensation was gradual. The single whistle of a lone bird broke the nothingness. It beckoned a single speck of light, which appeared in the very center of my vision. Sound grew to include the wind through trees, and other birds. Sight grew to slowly reveal a blue sky with scattered clouds. Hills and trees appeared beneath the sky. My sense of touch perceived a crisp, cool, alpine breeze. The sensations swelled together, until I stood alone in a beautiful, blossoming, verdurous mountain valley.

I was wearing armor — not my armor, not Elsa'a armor. This armor was strange to me. I carried a sword at my hip and a bag over my shoulder. I spun slowly in place and scanned the area. The formation of the hills was familiar to me. I was in Linderhof valley. But there was no palace, no statues or fountains, no grotto. There was no hunting lodge. Nothing surrounded me but the natural wonders of God's hand.

I was alone in the valley, or so I thought, until a sweet, creamy, seductive voice rang a clear note through the alpine air. I turned to face the song. And there, floating down the side of the hill, as if riding on the wind, a beautiful woman walked toward me. Her long, flowing dress was pale green, with flower patterns. It blended into the hill beneath her, appearing as if the grass and flowers of the valley lifted from the earth and wrapped around her. She carried a basket overflowing with colorful blossoms.

She reached her arm toward me as she floated into the valley to stand directly in front of me. Her mouth went still, her voice silent. But her song continued from her eyes, eyes that seemed to sing directly into mine. I was utterly transfixed, intoxicated. I needed her more desperately than I needed the air in my lungs. She wrapped her arms around me and kissed me. I was locked to her mouth, rooted to her by lips that were so delicately soft, yet had a relentless hold on me. I felt like I was falling into her.

The pleasure of the kiss was immense. But it was sharply interrupted by a sensation familiar to me. The woman drove a blade into my side — not a wooden knife, like Reid's, but a long, cold, metal dagger. The pain of the piercing was nothing beside the sensation that followed. Iciness flowed from the tip of the blade, still buried deeply inside of me. A poison passed through blood, bone, and organs, and fill everything beneath my skin. My skin grew hard and grey, and felt like every inch was being pulled from me by flaming nails. Through this, my lips remained locked to hers. I could not pull away, and despite my fear and anguish, I did not want to release the kiss.

The woman released me and withdrew her blade from my side, precisely as I heard a scream. A shrill and terrified voice, high and powerful, yet immensely compassionate, rang across the valley. It frightened the woman away from me. She disappeared as I fell to the ground. The source of the scream soon revealed itself. It was a young local woman, wearing a plain beige dress. She knelt by my side. I knew her. Having never seen her face before, I knew her. She was Gütel, wife of Parsifal.

At that realization, the truth of the incident dawned on me. I was Parsifal, kissed and stabbed by an enchanted flowermaiden. Although I continued to experience everything from Parsifal's perspective, to feel and sense all that he did, I understood that I was not experiencing the events as Verena, but reliving the life of Parsifal, and through the pain, I cherished the memory. I remembered being stabbed by Reid and falling unconscious, and I imagined that my experience of Parsifal was his blood inside of me, declaring itself before spilling from the holes that Reid had put in my body.

I recited my lines as I knew them well, asking Gütel to pull the Grail from my bag, fill it with water, and return it to me. I felt myself slipping into death until being revived by the touch of the Grail rim to my lips. I drank, and I invigorated. The waves of poison drained from me as quickly as they were injected. I looked into the innocent, dulcet face of my rescuer and saw hints of myself, of Verena Elizabeth Kessler. My wound closed. My blood dropped to the ground. I heard the first opening of Parsifal's Portal. Then all went black and silent again.

Another pinhole of light expanded before my eyes. The birds of the valley returned to my ears. But I was not Parsifal. I was a young girl, eleven or twelve years old. By its description from The Ancient One, I recognized the Swan Knight lodge. I stood outside of its front door and heard a faint holler of angry men rise with my pulse. My hair was waist-long, black, and perfectly straight. I wore simple, baggy, grey pants and a white shirt. In my hand was a single dish — a small plate from the kitchen of the lodge. The yelling men grew loud as they immerged from the line of trees opposite of me. Nine men, screaming, wild men, with swords and filthy, smelly furs draping from them. I knew whose life I was experiencing. Only one Swan Knight had such hair. And I knew what moment of her life I would suffer, what wound would be inflicted upon me.

The scene unfolding before my eyes was one of my favorite, often-fantasized stories from the Swan Knights History. I was Veronika, and the wild men bounding toward the lodge came to avenge a clansman whom I had injured. I was alone in the valley, instructed by my absent parents to open the portal at dawn and summon the swan. But I anticipated the attack of the angry men, and I wanted to earn my teacher's respect by defeating them on my own. I recalled The Ancient One's lessons, of fighting with any tools or twigs at my disposal. My sword and armor were mere feet away, just inside of the lodge. But I thought I would challenge myself by fighting the band of armed men with only a single dish from the kitchen, wearing only the clothes I would wear to wrestle with the Scheriers or sing with the Eulesängers. This would surely impress The Ancient One.

I ran at the men, yelling as they yelled. Before they could form a circle around me, I leaped at one and threw my plate, striking him in the neck. The man fell to the ground grasping frantically at his throat and gasping for air. The plate fell to the ground and broke into two. The remaining eight stood with their hands at their sides in disbelief, the tips of their swords on the ground. I grabbed the shards, holding a half plate in each hand and I taunted them to come at me. They regathered their fury and encircled me, growling and cursing, beating their chests. Two came at me from opposite sides, one from my right and one from my left.

They swung their swords. I dodged the attack and spun to the side of the one at my left. I cut him across the face with the sharp, broken edge of the plate, and kicked him toward his brothers. I warned them to leave my valley and never return, promising to spare their lives. My words froze them in place. They stood silently for a few breaths, then broke into a roar of laughter. The one I had cut did not laugh with the others. He lunged at me and I thrusted the pointed tip of the plate shard into his left eye. He dropped his sword and screamed in pain, cursing me and ordering his brothers to kill me.

The others stood there until the wounded clansman dove at me and tackled me to the ground. Almost immediately as we hit the ground, the man went limp. As he fell on me, I used the force of the large man's own descent to drive a shard of the broken plate into his neck, between his jaws, and into the center of his head. I rolled him off of me and pulled on the buried shard. I could not dislodge it from the man's bloody, gurgling wound. I released it, withdrew my hand from his skull, and stood, drenched from neck to hips in the attacker's blood.

The other seven rushed at me together. I slashed one across the forehead with the other shard. But they quickly subdued me. Four of them held my small, young body to the ground, one on each limb, while a fifth placed the tip of his sword on the center of my chest. He raised the sword slightly. But as he thrusted it downward, I squirmed and wiggled, thrashed and flailed myself free. The descending blade drove through my right leg, entering high on the side of my thigh, running downward, and exiting cleanly between my knees.

He held his sword still, laughing while he said, "Now I've caught you, little insect."

I could not wiggle. I could not squirm. He began to twist and circle the sword, tearing at the muscle inside my gaping leg. I growled, but I did not cry. I grabbed a rock from the ground beside me and threw it into his eye. He withdrew his sword and I sprang to my one good leg. I limped and hobbled as quickly as I could, around the right side of the lodge and toward the Portal Point.

The men walked after me, matching my speed, spitting on my trail of blood, and mocking me with fake limps and fake whimpers. They followed me up the hill behind the lodge, to the Portal Point. They converged on me just before I reached my trigger point for opening the portal. They punched me in the face and head, while others kicked at my wounded leg. I reached my hand forward, and with the tiniest tip of my finger, I breached my trigger point. The Grail Blood that flowed through that extended fingertip opened the portal and the swan immerged.

Fortunately, he came with my riding teacher and friend, the Unicorn named Schwerthorn. For a flash of a moment, I thought as Verena, remembering my first encounter with Schwerthorn in the bloody marsh. But in an instant, I was Veronika again, bruised and bleeding, eyes swollen almost shut, and unable to stand. With the opening of the portal and the appearance of the swan and Unicorn, the men left me and took a few defensive steps backward, toward the lodge. My extended arm recoiled, and the portal snapped to a close, leaving a Unicorn, a swan, and a bloodied little girl to defeat the rest of the men.

Schwerthorn was more than a match for the barbarians. The Ancient One thought nothing of the angry men, certain of Schwerthorn's victory before the fight began, and consumed by his concerns for his young First-in-Training. I wanted to watch the battle unfolding just feet away from me. But The Ancient One held my face tightly to his. The clang of swords on horn, the tormented cries of men being lanced and lacerated by a long, sharp Unicorn horn, and the faint, final gasps for air as their bodies fell, one at a time, to die on the floor of the portal valley — these were my only experience of Schwerthorn's heroism.

The Ancient One dragged me a few steps toward the Portal Point, to Veronika's trigger point, which he knew well. Two Scheriers bounded through the portal, to enjoy the snacks in the lodge and a bit of wrestling with the young knight-in-training. Upon seeing the injuries and assessing the situation, they disappeared in a flash back through the portal. The Ancient One fetched bandages from the lodge and wrapped the wounds on my leg. The bleeding was profuse, and I began to feel faint. Within a few minutes, the Scheriers returned with a Zweigwesen, who carried in his clinched fists wads and bunches of leaves and stems. He removed the bandage and took quickly to sapping and packing the wounds with the flora in his hands and the secretions from his fingertips.

"Chew this," the Zweigwesen instructed, as he handed me a twig.

I bit the twig and grew suddenly weak. The valley around me spun in circles. My eyes grew heavy and the world went black for me again.

Sensation returned, as it had before, slowly. This time, it revealed the clopping sounds of distant horses on stone-paved streets, and a bridge upon which I stood. I was dressed again as a man, old and aching from years of toil. I was dressed regally, with the emblem of the Duke of Bavaria embroidered on my shirt. I knew who I was, and I knew that I would soon experience the thrust of another blade.

I stood in Kelheim, on the bridge where Duke Ludwig I, the Crusader, was assassinated. I abandoned the thoughts of Verena and wrapped myself in the reflections of the Duke and Swan Knight. Much weighed on my mind, but much more uplifted. I felt satisfaction in knowing that Brunhilde would have her own castle, where she could live in peace, away from the eyes of men. I felt gratitude to the Lord for the strength and wisdom of my son Otto, and for the family's great fortune in his choice of a wife.

Those thoughts left quickly, as they had when Ludwig the Crusader stood on the bridge that day and saw a man, a thug, on the bridge in front of him with a long blade drawn. I turned to run away. But two more men stood behind me. I feared nothing in Kelheim. Years of war and imprisonment were behind me. I enjoyed walks through Kelheim alone and unarmed. I ran toward the two men, begging them to defend me against the armed man. They had conspired with him. They held me by the arms while the armed man stabbed me over and over again, slashing and piercing every inch of my chest and abdomen. I fell to my back dying, but not before watching an angry mob of my loving and loyal subjects, the people of Kelheim, seize the three men, screaming for their deaths. With my eyes still open, my vision went black again, and it took all pain and all sounds and smells with it.

Sensation returned to me first in the weight of armor on my shoulders, and the squeeze of a tight helmet on my head. As sight returned to my eyes, revealing an elaborately decorated tournament combat arena, the noble confidence of a young First-in-Training entered my mind with it. The recent memory of an evening spent with a lovely young lady, telling stories and laughing by a fire, flew through my head. The love of a younger brother, the love of the valley, and the love of a white, winged sage, all converged in my head, bolstering my determination to make them all proud and win the tournament.

The sage, of course, was The Ancient One. The brother was Rudolf. I was Ludwig, first son of Duke Ludwig II.

The Ancient One! The thought of him stirred a memory, not in the head of the young knight whose life — and death — I was about to experience, but in the memory of Verena. The Ancient One watched the tournament in secret, from atop a nearby tree. Ludwig never knew this. My thoughts were his and Verena's, somehow melted together.

I scanned the nearby trees, but saw no swan. He was well hidden. I felt great sorrow for him, knowing what he would soon witness, and how atrociously disastrous the unfolding event would be to him. I returned my eyes to the arena before me, and saw my competitor, the saboteur who fixed my equipment with tree sap so I would not be able to draw my sword.

Simultaneously feeling Ludwig's confidence in his victory and Verena's terrified anticipation of the following moments, I reached for my sword. I pulled and yanked at the handle, but it would not let go of the sheath. Ludwig's panic met Verena's, as my sword-hand pulled desperately, and eyes focused sharply on the approaching knight. The sound of the man's drawing sword bit at my ears. Through the narrow slits and tiny holes of the helmet, I saw the flash of a well-polished sword, before hearing it tap against my breastplate and slide upward, followed by the pinch of the blade's tip pushing into my neck, and the frantic but fruitless need to draw breath.

With no sensation of falling, I felt my knees strike against the ground. I grasped my neck and strained my lungs to inhale. No air came. The bright air of Nürnberg went grey, then black. In the blackness, I heard the cry of the swan. I do not know if it was Ludwig's ears or Verena's imagination that perceived the mournful sound. With the fade of the departing swan's cries, all sensation left me, and again I floated in a senseless nothing.

When light returned again, it was not bright as before, not daylight at all, but the dim flicker of Wühlenvogel torches, held in the clay grasp of Wühlenvogel gargoyles, high above my head. I knew where I was, and by the fear in the face of the woman towering over me, I had a good idea who I was. I dreaded the blades coming for me, more than I dreaded any of the others. I was in Einigkeitstadt, and the woman squeezing me against her knees, huddling me tightly, along with another child my size, a toddler boy, an older girl, and a baby in her arms, was Irmengard, wife of Adolf, Rightful Swan Knight in the Black Forest. I knew them all. I knew them well. The toddler was Rupert. The older girl was my aunt, Mathilde, the daughter of Rudolf I, friend of the Eulesängers. I and the boy next to me were Adolf's twin sons.

Irmengard's dress was bloody. The hollers and screams of men and creatures seeped through the tiny holes in the forest floor above us. The muffled battle cries from above became clear, and echoed menacingly through the empty halls and buildings of the underground city. The soldiers of the greedy and ambitious Duke had entered our hidden city.

My twin brother cried.

"Shhhhhh. Quiet Friedrich!" Mathilde begged.

I began to cry with my brother.

"Adolf," she called me, "quiet, please."

I understood all that I had studied, all that I had learned as Verena, studying the Swan Knights History, while living every bit of a one-year old's terror and confusion. Irmengard kissed me and my twin brother. She ordered Mathilde to remain with us while she fled with the baby, Elizabeth.

The matriarch of the forest was gone in a flash, leaving Rupert, Friedrich, and me with Mathilde. The fighting above intensified. Wühlenvogels howled and Scheriers screamed. The creaking sound of dying Zweigwesens blended with the shrieking of terrified men to compose a wretched symphony of war. It was too much for the battle-

140

ready Mathilde to withstand. She had trained well for this moment, and her Grail Blood called her to battle.

She tucked Friedrich and me under a table, hid Rupert in a cabinet, "Stay here, little ones. Do not make a sound. Your mother will be back for you soon."

Knowing what was next, but fearing through the mind of a one-year old, I tried to ask her to stay. But my young mouth could not form the words in time. Mathilde kissed us each on the lips, drew a long knife from her belt, and darted out of sight. Friedrich sat down under the table. I plopped beside him. I looked Friedrich in the eyes. He did not have the knowledge, training, and experience of Verena Kessler, Queen of the Sweeter Realm. He whimpered in confused, scared, innocent ignorance.

This part of the Swan Knight History always churned my gut with each retelling. I knew The Ancient One was near. I wanted him so badly — for me, Verena, for the young boy beside me, and for the child whose final moments I was living. But I knew he would not find us until we were dead.

The Duke's vicious soldiers found us. Friedrich was startled by them, but relieved, not knowing that the swords they carried would be used to end our lives. Whether Adolf understood more, or the knowledge of Verena somehow stained his brain, he cried — *I* cried in terror, dreading the cold, bloody blades that waved before us.

The moment of the children's death was not described in the Swan Knights History. No creatures or other Grail Blood was there to witness it, other than poor Rupert. The swan found them after the slaughter, their pierced and broken bodies abandoned by their murderers.

The men argued, one of them reluctant to complete the order given, to destroy every living thing in the Black Forest. The other sternly recited the order, and a consensus was reached. I watched one of them yank Friedrich from

141

under the table by his right arm. With one hand, he suspended my twin brother at the level of his own eyes, and with the other hand, he hacked and stabbed at the baby. Friedrich did not cry. He died in pain but did not cry.

I screamed and tried to speak to the soldiers with the wisdom and understanding of a Queen. But nothing came from my mouth but the incoherent, terrified wailing of a one-year old. I felt a tight grip on my wrist. And in an instant, I was dangling above the ground by one arm, as Friedrich had. I waited for the sword. I wish it had come three seconds earlier. It was delayed long enough for me to hear the thud of Friedrich's little body hit the floor beneath me. I had one flash of nauseating compassion before my own body was sliced and pierced. It seemed to last for hours — countless, endless blows and slashes. I tried to cry, but the air inside of me was forced out too quickly by the violence, and never allowed to return.

The dim light of the torches grew dimmer, until completely black. I felt myself still being stabbed, but the pain faded with the light. My lungs were still. My heart was still. Yet I still experienced the moment. I heard the sound of my body, of Adolf's body, hit the floor with a dull thud. I felt only one thing — the cool floor of the city beneath my dead, bleeding body. I sensed poor Rupert standing beside me and my twin brother. His cries were the most soul-puncturing sound my heart had ever witnessed.

A familiar voice echoed above Rupert's voice, not off of the walls around me, but off of the walls of my mind. It was The Ancient One. The feel of the floor beneath me transitioned to a sensation intimately familiar and unequivocally comforting to me. The feathers of the swan's wing cradled me. He released an alarmingly mournful howl, cursed under his breath, and carried me and my brother, from the room, across the city, up the ramps that lead to the forest floor, through the frozen battle, to the threshold of the forest and the awaiting betrayer, Rudolf's brother Ludwig.

This I knew not from the perceptions of the moment, but from my knowledge of the event through the studies of Verena.

The young and powerful voice of the swan shouted, "Is this what you wanted? These children, the sons of your murdered nephew, the grandsons of your own brother, these children of Parsifal, Lohengrin, Elsa, and your own dear father, slaughtered by your hand. Is this what you wanted?"

I heard a subtle cry, a man's cry, followed by the diminishing clopping of a retreating horse. All sound faded to silence. All sensation of every kind went with it — all but one. The feel of the swan's feathers beneath me lingered. With no other sensations to divide my thoughts, I focused clearly and concentrated on the touch of the noble feathers. I expected them to fade also, and to awaken in the life of another doomed Swan Knight. But the feathers remained beneath me, and I was loathed to let them go.

I did not need to. With the touch of the swan's feathers still beneath me, another sensation joined it. I could see and hear the creatures from the battle, running and flying toward me. They were joined by countless others, of all kinds. Swimmers who did not join the Exodus to the Black Forest, Federmensch, Schildbüffels, Vogelkrötes, every breed of creature in the Sweeter Realm swarmed at me. They dove and leaped into me, into my mind, into my heart, depositing their most intense feelings of love, loyalty, and adoration into my soul.

Their thoughts brought a return of light with them. The light revealed my bedroom, my palace bedroom, and my own body, Verena Elizabeth Kessler's body, attached most intimately to the returning sensations. I was myself again. The touch of the swan's feathers remained, as I realized

143

that my neck and head were supported by The Ancient One's wing, while my forehead was caressed by the soft feathers beneath his beak. His thoughts and the thoughts of hundreds were in my head.

Two Brunnens and several Zweigwesens were in the room. I felt their thoughts. I felt them all, much more clearly than I had before Joseph's conception. Their thoughts were hopeful, confident, even a touch excited by what they knew would be my full recovery from Reid's attack.

With a sudden, distressed thought of Joseph, I reached for my belly. It was flat. My son was gone from me. Where I would have felt his kick, I felt only the sticky sap of a Zweigwesen bandage, glued to me over the stab wound. My sense of loss and fear for my son projected to the others in the room. They knew I was awake, and they knew I needed answers.

"Shhhhh, easy now, my love," the swan's soothingly familiar voice implored me.

"He is fine, my Queen," one of the Brunnens told me. "Your son was untouched by the blade."

The Ancient One ordered a Zweigwesen nurse to fetch my son and husband, while a Brunnen caressed my forehead and temples with her heavenly fingertips. Never had the touch of a Brunnen been so desperately needed or so gratefully accepted.

A caress that would otherwise have lulled me to sleep helped arouse me with excitement to see my husband, and to see the face of my son for the first time.

CHAPTER 11
Reid's Trial and the Presents

THE SIGHT OF FELIX, the shine of his face, and the swell of his devoted thoughts all entered my perception together. He carried an infant in his arms. He placed Joseph high upon my breast, carefully avoiding my wounds. I thought to Joseph, as I had since his mind first reached to mine. I felt him rebound, from the self-imprisoned, infantile thoughts of a normal newborn, to the deeply affectionate and intellectual cerebrations of my extraordinary son. His new arms were yet unable to embrace me. But his mind could. It could and it did, weakly and only for a brief moment. We did not share the depth of connection that we had before his birth. It felt more like the thought connections I had made with others. My lips kissed his head as my mind kissed his thoughts. Felix wrapped his powerful arms around us both, alternating kisses between my cheek and Joseph's shoulder. Felix deighted in the thoughts of love I was again able to place directly into his mind.

Aside from the expressions of immense thought and feeling on his face, Joseph looked much like we imagined a Federman-Human baby would look. His chest, tummy, shoulders and back were covered in the downy feathers of a Federkind, light-grey, as his father's were when he was an infant. On his head, seven white feathers stood among a thick head of white hair, matted against his scalp. His legs were bare, like a human baby, not like the downy feathered legs of an infant Federman.

His face, arms, and legs were plump like a human's. His nose was mine, not the dangling, bell-shaped flap that hangs from a Federman face. But he had the strength of a Federkind. Still, he was frustrated with his body's inability to catch up with his mind. On his first day, he wanted to walk, to wrap his arms around his father and the Zweigwesen nurses who withdrew him from my lacerated belly, but his infant body had all of the restriction of any newborn's body.

While he lay across my chest, he wanted to run his fingers through my hair and squeeze and kiss me, but he could hardly rock back and forth. His frustrations were soothed by the warmth of my chest, as he was swaddled against me by his father's warm feathered arms. Felix did as the Federmensch do. He heated his feathers for his son's tender skin. Joseph learned the skill immediately and heated his own feathers in response, though only slightly. The three of us held each other, in the radiance of heated feathers and immeasurable relief and adoration.

"How old is he?" I asked my husband.

"He is almost two weeks old. He was born just minutes after the attack."

"Two weeks. I have slept for two weeks?"

"No, my love. You died for one day, then revived, then slept before dying again. You died four times. Each time I mourned you, and each time you came back to me. Now you are alive and awake. You are strong and well. And the Zweigwesens say it is a miracle. I told them what I have always known… that you are a miracle, a miracle of a good and gracious God."

The memories of the last two weeks rushed rapidly through the minds of everyone in the room, and then through mine, displaying their doubts, hopes, sorrows and hopes again, as they witnessed the rallies and regressions of my body. Their most recent memory was of delight and thanksgiving to God, stitched tightly to their absolute confidence in my recovery.

Two Zweigwesen nurses remained in the room but withdrew to the edge of the rounded wall. All others left us in peace, including the swan, who said nothing, but felt a greater sense of satisfaction than my own mind had ever known, as he placed a few tender pats on Felix's shoulder before waddling from the room.

Few words were spoken between us. No words were needed. My penetration into the minds around me was deeper, more thorough, and more profound than before. I tried to block out the hordes that gathered in and around the palace and focus only on the minds of my husband and son.

Felix fed me attentively, thinking the simplest thoughts of devotion, before crawling beside me and holding me while I slept with the warmth of Joseph's soft infant skin and feathers against my breasts.

I awoke alone. But Felix was near, holding Joseph and speaking to him in language both paternal and intensely intellectual. Joseph's coo betrayed his young mouth's inability to form language. But Felix knew that his son understood him. With the help of the same two Zweigwesens, I sat up in bed and translated Joseph's responses to his father's welcoming ears and heart. It was the first conversation between father and son where Joseph's own voice played a part, and I was glad that Joseph could not speak to Felix. I was glad that the sentiments had to be relayed through me. It's funny, we so often see people in conversation and never ask what it is like to be the language that is spoken between them. What is it like to be the words that carry on their shoulders sentiments from the lips to a loved one's welcoming ear? I learned exactly what that was like. I was the language

147

spoken between them. I carried those sentiments, that precious cargo that bonded a father with his new-born son.

Cort entered the room and announced after a few adoring and relieved glances toward me, "The committee awaits."

"No, no," Felix quickly returned, "she is not leaving this room today. Bring the committee here, if this must happen now."

The long-awaited committee of creature-leaders filed into the room. They had remained in and around the palace since the day I was attacked. Each placed a tender kiss on my head and lips. Once they were gathered around me, Georg stepped forward and spoke.

"I hope you don't mind, but we held Reid's trial while you slept."

"His trial?" I responded with confusion. "But I watched him being torn to pieces. How is he not dead?"

"Oh, he is most certainly dead," Georg answered with a distinct tone of satisfaction. "The trial was an important point of justice for your subjects, who adore you and needed to perform retribution for the sin against you."

"And how did it go?" I asked with hesitant curiosity.

Krummzahn stepped forward and answered, "Reid was determined to be guilty of attacking you and your unborn child. He was first found guilty of trying to kill the Queen. The next day, we found him guilty of trying to kill the Swan Knight. On the third day of the trial, we convicted him of trying to murder Joseph."

"And his sentence… dare I ask?"

Acheriel stepped from the back of the crowd and answered, "When they rescued you, your Royal Guard, tore him into nine pieces. Those pieces were put on trial. Eight were distributed among eight homelands and homewaters of breeds willing to imprison him. His head sits in your jail, my Queen."

I vividly pictured what was described to me, driving from deep within me a long and violent shiver.

Taufe touched my shoulder, immediately calming my shiver, as she said, "Don't forget what King David said to Abishai, 'Who could raise his hand against God's anointed and go unpunished?'"

I thought for a brief second of Reid's Grail Blood, a thought that jetted unchecked into the surrounding minds.

The Ancient One responded, "He may have descended from my first human friend, but his blood bore the Mark of Cain, not the holiness of Parsifal. Nothing revered, and certainly nothing knightly spilled on the throne room floor from his body. The only thing precious and sacred to stain the palace that morning was your holy blood. You may rest your noble heart on that, my love."

Georg erupted unvoluntarily, "Oooh, it twists my horn to think of his rancid blood mixing with the sacred Grail Blood of our Queen. And to think of it pouring down on you and covering your Godly features."

He huffed through his beard and stompted all four hooves, not to intimidate, but in a raw release of emotion.

I began to recall the attack. But Joseph grabbed my mind with his and forcefully steered it exclusively toward the treasured hearts in the room. They were happy with my recovery, satisfyingly revenged from the trial and sentence, and honored to have played their part in both. Georg swelled with fulfilled purpose, and still relished the vivid and often visited memory of driving his horn through Reid's head. He and the Royal Guard saved my life. Without their intervention, Reid would surely have plunged his knife into me many more times, and into Joseph, until we were both beyond the help of Zweigwesen medicine.

As I felt him recalling the fury of that moment, I watched his beard shake from the tension in his jaw. Taufe calmed him with a long stroke of his horn, connecting his fiery thoughts with her much more harmonious mind. She released his horn and he grew fiery in reflection again. This cycle continued comically for several minutes. I took pleasure in watching it and it endeared them both to me.

I was not awake for long that day. I'm not sure what time it was when I awoke or what time I fell back to sleep. After the committee informed of their decisions and actions, they left the palace for their homes. They were given strict instructions from Cort that a single kiss and "Farewell" would suffice in my condition. Their other thoughts and concerns were not for me to consider then. So they left for their homes with their minds caged inside their heads. And I was forbidden by my dearest ones to encroach any mind but the tranquil ones within my physical reach.

Perhaps a few of their thoughts, projected randomly to me, would have done me good, and distracted my imagination from the wooden blade that must have passed perilously close to my baby. It was that image that spun in my brain as I drifted back into a dreamworld.

I dreamed of that prophetic dream I had during the war, while I slept with the Eulesängers, in which I stood in St. Hildegard Cathedral, looking up at Christ, with the nails of his crucifixion protruding from my abdomen. I did not have the same dream again, but rather dreamed of remembering it. The image of Reid's blade slicing so near the child in my belly, the terror of my old dream, now that the veiled message held a new tangible and immediate reality, penetrated my soul with violent, stabbing thrusts. Joseph lived the dream as I had. He did not fully understand it. But the image of his mother being pierced affected him, particularly in light of what we had just survived together. He was glad to be out of me. The wooden blade that nearly struck him and almost ended his mother, coupled with the dream of the nails in my abdomen, made the warmth of my womb foul and soured beside the heated feathers of his father's powerful and protective arms.

I awoke the next morning with much more energy than I had the day before. My ability to connect with my subjects strengthened ten-fold. The thoughts of the Sweeter Realm fell so quickly and desperately on me that morning, like a horse kicking at the gate before bolting at full speed onto the track. They were not reaching for me. Their thoughts sought me without their permission. Every thought, intense and mundane, of every creature in my queendom invaded a mind that had gotten used to the intimacy of sharing only a single other occupant. It was more than I could make sense of at once. I kept them just long enough to grab their attention and declare my return to service before shutting them out and focusing on the precious friend being carried into the room and handed to me by the tender palms of my Brunnen nurses.

I sat up, holding Joseph, and asked him about his birth and his first two weeks out of the womb. When his eyes met mine, he tried to speak to me, but only gurgled. He tried harder and failed equally. Our connection was not nearly as comprehensive as it was in the womb. Nor could he form language with his mouth. His desire to speak to me became desperate and frustrating. His body refused to comply with the wishes of his advanced mind. His body had been irrelivent to him before his birth. He relied on it for nothing. It sat suspended inside of me while his mind was free to wander and grow. He had developed quite a mastery of the mental and spiritual. After birth, he found himself bound in so many ways by the physical world. He began to weep in frustration. Though in my arms, he felt disconnected from me and he wanted to speak.

"Shhhhhh." I rubbed his chest and told him I love him.

He calmed, closed his eyes, and entered my mind, loosely and clumsily, not at all like the connection we felt before. It was no deeper, no more intimate than the connection I make with any creature. But this connection was not initiated by me. He pressed his mind into mine, an ability that few other than the Unicorns had.

Felix, who had been dealing with Queenly matters in my absence, joined us in the bedroom, with fruits for me and a bowl of thick Eulesänger nectar for Joseph. He dipped his finger in the bowl and coated it thickly in the nectar. He touched his fingertip against Joseph's lips. Joseph took his breakfast from his father's finger, grabbing him by the thumb and pinky finger with his tiny hands. That was the moment he realized that he could control things physically, by manipulating the physical world with his body. Most mothers cannot share in those moments of discovery in their newborns. They are present. But they have no idea what goes on in the child's mind. I did. Each breakthough was shared from his mind to mine, and we discussed and debated everything he encountered, everything he felt and learned as the physical world introduced itself to his tender new body.

When Felix withdrew his finger from Joseph's mouth, Joseph wanted to thank him —not for the breakfast, but for everything. Just as he sensed the evil in Reid, while still in the womb, he sensed the purity of his father's goodness. He tried to speak, but again managed only a few crude noises.

"No son," Felix begged him. "My mind is open to you. Speak to me as you speak to your mother."

Somehow he knew. He knew that his son would inherit my abilities.

I entered Felix's mind and witnessed Joseph's effusions of love to him. The connection was not made by me. Joseph entered Felix's mind on his own. He had the ability without me. The three of us remained there for a moment, in Felix's head, delighting in our first union of that sort. When I left Felix's mind, Joseph stayed. With only my physical senses, I watched the two of them giggle at each other's thoughts. As Felix laughed, tears streamed down his pale cheeks.

Later that day, I warned Joseph about entering the minds of others, about relaying his thoughts and seizing those of the dear creatures around him. It was an ability that came with tremendous moral obligations and practical considerations. Except for mine and Felix's, it was best that Joseph keep out of the heads of others until greater maturity accompanied the ability.

I was much recovered, able to move around on my own, albeit with much effort and pain. Our friends left us alone for the rest of that day, but were near if we should need them. The queendom kept their thoughts as quiet as possible, so as not to draw the attention of their Queen. The next day would be busy —many visitors with many gifts. But this day was ours. I gave only fleeting thoughts to Acheriel, Lina, and Senische, to Cort, Georg, and the many friends whose lives would be deeply affected by the birth, to humanity and the premonitions of the clerics. My thoughts dipped shallowly into those subjects and withdrew quickly, drawn back to the moment by the synchronized breath of my husband and son as their bodies seemed to sync with their minds.

Since word of the birth had spread quickly, as did the attack on the Queen, pilgrims from every homeland and homewater worked their way to the palace. Caravans from all directions traveled across land, water, and sky. Births are celebrated on a much grander scale in the Sweeter Realm. No matter how small, distant, or obscure the breed, how distant the relation, the birth of a Sweeter Realm creature is an event for all to celebrate. First, they are not nearly so frequent as they are among humans. Second, there is an assumption with each birth that the baby will be impactful in the lives of all of God's creatures. The child is not only seen as coming from the parents, but also as coming from God. Each child is honored as if God is the parent. Each other creature is seen as a beloved of God. If only humans thought that way. There would be no need for a Grail or a portal, no need for Swan Knights and magical armor or Unicorn-horn swords.

The creatures were on their way to the palace. As important as every birth is, Joseph's was more important. No assumptions needed to be made. Joseph would certainly impact the lives of all, if only as the child of their Queen. Mother, father, and child were allowed the one full day in peace, alone together, with only Zweigwesen tonics served to us by Zweigwesen hands, and meals presented by a host of Friends of the Scheriers.

A large band of Federmensch gathered outside of the palace, but none dared enter. None could enter if they tried. Georg sealed the entrance with a wall of my Royal Guard, representatives of several different breeds, many shapes and sizes, each marked with a dark stain upon the arm, fin, or wing.

Cort controlled the main chamber, permitting only those needed to prepare for the presentation of gifts to the baby. Even the Pfutzeschilfs, who had made a home of the puddle beside the throne, were evicted for the time being. The bustle of preparations was performed as stealthily as possible. Little hint of it reached our senses, tucked away in the highest room of the palace and smothered in our concentrated attention on each other.

At dawn the following day, Cort snuck his way into our chamber and asked if he could admit the guests. Felix looked to me. In the absence of an expressed opinion from my blank face, he answered Cort with a nod of his proud paternal head. I chose an outfit both colorful and comfortable. I buttoned my shirt as I stared at my feathered men. Felix held his son close to his face, looking downward at him so his nose hung loosely and brushed against the rounded button nose of Joseph. No intense thoughts were shared between them, just an adoring gaze.

We met Cort in the hallway. He led the way, followed by me, with Joseph in his father's arms behind me. Taufe and The Ancient One stood on either side of the entrance into the throne room. We marched past them and they fell into line behind Felix. I sat on my throne and Felix placed Joseph in my arms.

The wall of Guards opened and released a flow of visitors that crested and waned, trickled and poured throughout the day. The first to address us were the Federmensch. Joseph's birth would make them notorious — this small, relatively obscure breed from the Nomadic Belt. It was enough that one of their own married the Swan Knight-Queen. But now that only the second child to ever be born of a human and creature of Eden wore the signature white feathers of the Federmensch, every tongue in the queendom spoke of the nomads.

The Federmensch presented their gift. It was a scroll of Joseph's lineage, from his father, back, back hundreds of generations. As I wrote, the breed is small. The tree is not expansive. But the Federmensch had never kept such a written record before. As nomads, they keep few things to be lugged around. Their genealogy, as well as their histories, fables, and other traditions, are maintained orally and set to memory at an early age. They knew that such written records are consistent with human traditions, making the gift all the more thoughtful. After they opened the scroll and read to me for several minutes, Felix took the scroll covetously and ran it to a high chamber in the palace.

Most of the gifts were typical Sweeter Realm gifts for a child — toys and noise-makers, pens and books for his education, rare herbs and spices from the hidden corners of their homelands. Unlike similar ceremonies for other births, my baby was able to respond to the gifts, thinking his gratitude to me so I could relay them. In a few circumstances, with his father's people, the Scheriers, and the Unicorns, Joseph managed to press his gratitude and affection directly into the heads of the guests. Most believed the thought had come from me. Some knew otherwise. For those, the intimate connection with the extraordinary curiosity in my arms became a primary bragging point for years.

"Joseph spoke to me *before* he could speak," they would say in the gathering places of their homelands.

I warned him several times about the responsibilities that come with his abilities. He tried to keep his thoughts to only my mind and his father's. But self-control ranked high among the skills that proved to still be raw and underdeveloped in his infant mind.

The day exhausted me. Joseph was always in my mind. His thoughts were often confused, as his infant eyes took in new sights. I spoke with the visitors, sent them my thoughts, all while maintaining a constant internal communication with the baby. I shudder to imagine what nonsense came from my mouth as I juggled the many simultaneous conversations. It was a day of extreme over-stimulation and it nearly did me in. Cort was entirely too caught in the pomp and circumstance, the regal pageantry and formal royal atmosphere he tried to maintain amid the chaos, to recognize the toll it was all taking on me. Felix, generally highly attentive to such things, was too busy running gifts from the throne room to the upper chambers. It was a single Brunnen sister from St. Hildegard, one who had bathed me and soothed me through many trying periods of my Swan Knight training, who noticed my distress and brought it to The Ancient One's attention.

"Verena should rest now," the swan told Cort, with a few wing feathers poking the back of his little green head.

My dutiful Master of Ceremonies protested, "But the gifts… they have not all been presented."

Thoughtful and tactful as always, the swan answered, "You Cort, the only Friend of the Scheriers with a name, are the Queen's right hand. I am sure she will allow you to accept the gifts for the child."

Cort looked at me with eyes that nearly popped from his head.

I looked sharply down to Cort, who had inched his way to stand almost against my left leg as I sat on the throne, "Joseph would be honored, Cort, if you would accept the rest of the gifts in his name."

I spoke the words as if they had been thought to me by Joseph. They had not. But the infant quickly concurred with a struggled turn of his tiny head toward Cort. After crawling onto my lap and kissing Joseph's head, Cort leaped from the throne, hushed the room into silence, and announced that the Queen and her baby were retiring for the day, and that the ceremony would continue once we were clear from the bustle.

"But first," The Ancient One interrupted, "I will present my gift to the baby Swan Knight."

The anticipation of the gathered creatures was almost deafening, though no sound, not even breath, was heard.

The swan stepped around the throne to face Joseph and me, with his back to the entrance of the palace.

He spoke in a half-choked, deeply emotional voice, "My boy, the feathers of my left wing, these feathers you see here, came from your own dear father's back, Federman feathers like your own, a gift… a sacrifice of unspeakable value, from a friend of unspeakable worth. Your mother is dearer to me than any creature or human I have known in my many centuries. And now I must present a gift to you. I already love you more than any token could express. I have struggled for months to design the perfect

157

gift, but nothing reflects what is in my heart. So I gift to you my heart, my life. I live for nothing but to teach you, serve you, and love you."

Joseph wanted to respond on his own, with his mouth and voice. He opened his mouth and tried to speak. Rather than words, the air forcing up from his chest pushed a bubble of saliva to his mouth. It domed over his lips and grew, and grew, until it was half the size of Joseph's head. The enire room watched silently. The bubble popped and made a sound, which though quiet, echoed around the silent room. After a moment of collectively held breath, Cort let out a chuckle. It rolled into exuberant laughter and pulled from the necks of all an uproarious clamour of laughs at a variety of tones and tempos. The sweetest little baby giggle came from Joseph. His lungs convulsed. His extremities shook. His new body experienced its first full laugh. It delighted him and amused the others. They laughed at his laughter, which only pulled it more forcefully from Joseph. I did not look at his mind. I watched only his smiling face, and heard only the sweet, high giggle that gained momentum after being refueled by each inhale. The laughter of the room slowed and dwindled together, ending in a concerted sigh. Joseph found the laughter-ending sigh to be funny, and released one final giggle in the newly quieted room.

Joseph still had something to say to The Ancient One for the gift of his life. He opened his mouth wide, but made no sound. He knew the futility of attempting to speak with his infant mouth. He looked around the room, scanning his eyes wall to wall. He settled his focus on Cort, closed his eyes, slowed his breath to a near stop, and took control of Cort's face.

In the well-known voice of the Master of Palace Ceremonies, but in a very different tone, Joseph spoke through Cort's throat, "I have so many things to learn, so many things to see. Much of what I already know is vague. Most of what I experience is new to me. But one thing has been known to me since my conception. The swan is sacred, the noblest of creatures. It is he who held the hopes and aspirations of all high upon the tip of his wing. These thoughts have come into me from my mother before I was born, and from thousands since, from every creature who entered the palace today with a gift. I would say that your gift is too valuable for me to accept. But I accept it nevertheless… because I need it and I desire it. I receive the gift of your life with full understanding of its value."

Joseph released Cort's face to his own control. As he did, the expression Joseph had held on that pale-green face was replaced by a slowly widening smile that eventually wrapped halfway around Cort's head. The Master of Ceremonies bowed low to Joseph, replacing his head with the tail behind him. He turned to the swan, looking at him differently than he ever had before, and he bowed low again. The Ancient One returned the bow with a reverent nod of his head.

Felix took Joseph from my arms and helped me to my feet. The three of us walked slowly from the throne room to the applause and hurrahs of the gathered guests. Felix tucked us into bed and returned to the ceremony. Joseph and I were asleep within minutes, our minds diving together, hand-in-hand, into our shared dreams.

CHAPTER 12
Proliferation and Peril

THE MORNING PROVIDED NO RELIEF from the liveliness of the previous day. I was wakened by noises that were outside of my sensual range. Busy thoughts of deadlines and schedules barged into my head and aroused me from rest before a single sound broke the silent air of our sleeping chamber. They came from the swan, whose eagerness to resume lessons was doubled by the earnestness of his gift, and by his understanding that Joseph's training had begun in the womb. He knew that every point of learning passed to me since the day after Senische's naming ceremony had also been an investment in another student. The Ancient One knew that he had an opportunity that he had never had with any Swan Knight — to teach a beloved student from infancy, knowing that the lessons were seeping into an advanced mind that maintained lessons from the day of his conception.

He set himself up in the room we had designated for lessons. He brought with him Ludwig's journal, and every available relic and souvenir from the long history of the Swan Knights. Joseph did not have my memories. He only experienced my thoughts as they happened. Things that had remained out of my mind since his conception were entirely out of his, unless he went digging for them. And he had very few sensual memories. His lessons in the womb were theoretical, and he did well to understand them as he did. But lessons outside of the womb would be much more fruitful, with sensual connections and experiences to root them more deeply. After a rushed morning of preparations and a rapidly devoured breakfast, I brought Joseph to the classroom, where the swan refreshed my memory with a meticulous retelling of the Swan Knights History, this time with relics that Joseph could touch, see, and smell with his own senses. His new eyes traced the lines of Ludwig's penmanship. Wide-eyed, and with a raw, open tenderness of spirit, my infant son relished the expansion of his education into the physical world.

When the swan spoke of the foods gifted to the Swan Knights and their children, he had examples for Joseph to sample. Physical sensation multiplied the lessons by a thousand. It took three weeks, with few breaks. The swan hardly paused to draw breath as he anatomized the finest and obscurest details of his time in the Portal Valley and Black Forest, adding to those details much of what he experienced and thought when he was not in the valley, when he was home or with the Queen — details of the deepest inner-workings of his mind during the events covered by the history.

I came to know him much better. The history doubled in length with the inclusion of the minutest of details, left out of my earlier lessons and absent entirely from Ludwig's rushed manuscript. Joseph heard the stories with his own ears. But the freshness of the experience for me added to the pungency of the lessons on his tender young mind. Even the old teacher bore an aroma of freshness as he recalled the distant past with vibrancy and energy, as if it were yesterday.

With tender emotion, he recalled and described his long-lost thoughts and internal conversations he had with himself, sitting in the old nest near the Portal Point, waiting for some Swan Knight or another to open the portal and summon him. Tiny memories, too mundane to have ever been included in a young Swan Knight's lessons, were painstakingly detailed in those weeks. I delighted in these new insights into a subject that had gripped me since I discovered my heritage. The swan had delivered the history hundreds of times since he undertook the education of Lohengrin. But no student of his had ever received such a detailed account. He had never considered giving one. Many of the details had not been uncovered in his head since time and other events first buried them.

Joseph took the knowledge as routinely as learning that the sky is blue. Everything was equally zesty and dynamic to him. With few cemented opinions and no expectations, nothing shocked him as it did me. He also sensed my pride, as the swan reminded me of the exceptional abilities and accomplishments of my family. Joseph's baby eyes had seen so little. Discussions of crusades and invading knights, of castles and grottos, hand-cannons, angry mobs on a northern shore, violence and evil kings of the Deep Waters, made little sense to him. But each detail placed a piece in a puzzle that would fill in fully over time. The knowledge and understanding that swam chaotically around Joseph's newborn skull slowly took root and settled into wisdom.

After the history was taught, Taufe resumed her position, beginning each day with scriptural and spiritual training. It was in this arena that Joseph flourished, contributing as much as he received, with profound thoughts and connections that had even escaped the Sweeter Realm's wisest cleric. He may not have understood Klingsor and enchanted flowermaidens, hunting lodges or even the portal itself. But he understood God. He understood Christ. And his infant mind aroused and electrified at every mention of the Holy Grail. As disconnected as he was with the physical, as perplexing and slippery to his mental grasp, all things spiritual were concrete and were as surely inside of him as the palace air his young lungs drew in.

We began every morning as I had in St. Hildegard Cathedral, with recitations of the Psalms. The simple morality and devotion of King David's music struck a beautiful and reverberating chord in Joseph's heart. It echoed back to me with Joseph's signature moral tone. He set the Psalms to memory and conjured them aptly during his lessons, with as much sincere sentiments as King David himself.

In the few quiet moments, while I ate or prayed, or in the middle of the night, Joseph's mind spun in motion, and he entered my mind with burning questions and debates. His spirituality and grasp of all things divine and mystical was growing quickly beyond mine. Christ and God, love and rightiousness — he juggled these things masterfully and playfully, while I struggled to understand them. There was nothing I could teach him, nothing I could tell him in this area of his studies that he did not already comprehend much more thoroughly than I.

One morning, when Joseph was not yet seven months old, thinking of my parents and brother, I asked Taufe, "You say that my home will be coming to me, that my people will return to Eden. Who will come? Will all of them come?"

Taufe responded as a Benedictine Abbess should, with the recitation of a Psalm, "Lord, who may abide in your tent? Who may dwell on your holy mountain?"

Joseph answered with his first spoken words, with a clumsy but accurate recital of the following verse, "Whoever walks without blame, doing what is right, speaking truth from the heart... You know, Mother, the ones that are like you."

His sweet little voice, reciting the Psalms, sent Taufe into tears. Her silvery-blue skin rippled downward, from her scalp to her toes.

Joseph stared at her for several long seconds, then spoke his next words to her, "Holiest Brunnen…"

His next thoughts were not spoken, but sent directly into Taufe's tender and emotional mind. Joseph had an understanding of God's love that was beyond us all. He shared with Taufe God's love for her. She was a Brunnen cleric, the most revered holy-creature in the entire Sweeter Realm. She thought she understood God's love. Yet Joseph opened her to a new understanding, one infinitely wider, deeper, penetrating throughout, and permanently altering. It was as if he connected Taufe's mind to God's. Taufe fell to her knees.

Her rippling skin changed direction, upward, to God, and she whispered, repeating in the softest version of her dulcet Brunnen voice, "Thank you my Lord, I love you. Thank you my Lord, I love you."

Joseph and I stayed out of her mind. She shared a moment of intimate prayer with God, intimacy like she had never before felt. She fell silent, rolled onto her back, reached her hands to Joseph, and called him with a subtle curling of her long fingers.

I set Joseph on the floor and allowed him to crawl to her on his own. Taufe enveloped him in her loving arms. He seemed to sink into a pond of rippling Brunnen flesh. I envied him for a moment. I had spent much time in that embrace. There is nothing softer or more nurturing in all of God's creation than Taufe's embrace while she cries and ripples. She released one arm from Joseph, to gesture my invitation to join them. She held us until I slept — my face cradled in a Brunnen breast and my nose inhaling the scent of my son's hair and feathers. It was a level of bliss that few creatures of God ever knew, and I will not diminish it now by trying to encompass it with the rudimentary tools of language.

The next several months continued to provide staggering and altering advancements and insights from Joseph. As hard as I tried to help him, with vivid sensual recollections, he could not understand a middle school lunchroom or a shopping center and parking lot. While his grasp of all things spiritual was downright prophetic, material things, not yet witnessed by his own eyes, eluded his grasp. My earlier life — everything that I knew and was before crossing Parsifal's Portal — remained entirely foreign to him. Even much of my physical, sensually perceived experiences in the Sweeter Realm were beyond his ability to comprehend.

This was fine with Taufe, who belittled the physical in favor of the spiritual. But The Ancient One, still thoroughly steeped in Swan Knights tradition, was distressed by the deficiency. As Joseph's first birthday approached, though such events are barely recognized in the Sweeter Realm, The Ancient suggested a gift.

"Read to him from your journal… of all that you have done since coming to us. Visualize each moment with clarity. He lives in your mind, yet he does not know his mother, her heroism, her courage and sacrifice, her dutiful love of her subjects, and her devotion to the will of God. Recall the pain and recall the joy, the loss and the love, the scrapes, bruises, and punctures, the lacerations and loss of breath. Recall them as vividly as you can and allow him to experience them through your most expressive physical memories. Only then will he know you, and through that, know himself."

His head swirled with his words, as he stared at me in proud and vivacious adoration.

There were many horrors documented in that journal, many memories I shuddered to recall. I was not too keen to thrust those images into the young mind of my son. I expressed these concerns to the swan.

He answered, "If the clerics are right, he is likely to face much grander events than what *we* have been through together, my love. Walk him through your life. You are a Swan Knight, greater than any that was. He has heard the stories from my beak. But with your connection to him, he will understand them when they come from you, with your thoughts and memories accompanying the words. But it is not enough for you to recall them. You must relive them. In your mind, you must feel the physical pains and pleasures, so that in his mind he will understand them."

I saw his point but still hesitated. I asked Felix, who deferred to my judgment and the swan's. So, on Joseph's first birthday, he sat in his father's arms, with The Ancient One, Taufe, Cort, Lina, Acheriel, and many more of my dearest ones present, as I read to him from the journal that Taufe had given me years earlier, now filled with the stories I have written here and many, many more.

Joseph's mind filled me, as mine filled him. Neversince his birth had our connection been so comprehensive. He twitched as memories and visuals of the most dramatic and terrifying moments of my life sprang violently into my memory, dislodged from their hiding places by the words I had scratched in the journal. Felix caressed him. But he did not need calming. To his wise young heart, these stories were shards in a large mosaic, the extremities of which he saw much clearer than I. He could not see the trees for the forest, to reverse the old cliché. From a much broader perspective, the searing details of my life were only small contributors to a whole that he gripped more tightly than any of us. But in doing so, he did not experience the minute as the lesson was designed to do.

The stories succeeded in sparking Joseph's curiosity, particularly when my friends interjected with their perspectives of the same events. Joseph wanted to see these places with his own eyes — the Portal Point, Cort's circle clearing, where I spent my first nights in the Sweeter Realm, the Zweigwesen city where his father gifted the wing to the swan, the Glühenchor pond, where I was pulled into the Deep and rescued by Felix. He wanted to see the mountain pass where I fell, where his father's heroics saved me again. He wanted to hear the voices of the Brunnen choir echo off the walls of St. Hildegard Cathedral, to climb the sharp, craggy rocks of the Pfeifen Mountains and feel the bridge of Zweigwesens beneath his own feet. He wanted — he actually wanted to pierce his young feet with the sharp reeds of the marshes. His advanced mind was in deep conflict with the empty void of his physical experiences. And he felt a despotic hunger to reconcile his spiritual advancements with his physical deficiencies, and bring them into balance.

The Unicorn training ground, the Brunnen bathhouse we built in Eineklaue, the storage mound in Gemeinsam, where I hid from the Wühlenvogels and sampled the nectar, the Achima Canyon, my midnight flight with the swan, the floor of the great lake, and my portal that chewed through the King of the Deep and purified Eden, he wanted to see it all. And he wanted to see the Grail. He had an intense hunger to be at the bottom of the lake and hold the Grail in his own hands, to trigger my portal with the Grail Blood he inherited from me. The Grail was the bridge between the spiritual truths he already held tightly and the physical world he longed to understand. The truth of the Grail — its connection to Christ, its embodiment of divinity — had a tangible representative in the physical world, which was the Grail itself. He saw the Grail as his best opportunity to cross that bridge. He wanted to hold it in his hands, to feel its curves and textures, and press his lips against it, and to taste the Blood of Christ from within it.

The journey down the road of my memories, and of those friends around us who shared in the events, tired us all exceedingly. But it energized Joseph. His imagination went wild, and ravenous to see with his own eyes those thoughts I sent to him along with the words from my journal. Above all, he wanted to see the Grail. Early in the evening, on his birthday, after the telling of my story, all guests cleared out and Felix and I went to sleep. Joseph did not sleep, nor did I expect him to. But I did not expect his agitation and curiosity to endanger him.

Felix woke me at dawn, in a frantic panic. Joseph was not in the palace. I immediately sought his mind and found him. He was flying high above the Achima Mountains, in the grasp of a Wühlenvogel. He had taken control of the poor creature, while she remained entirely conscious of the events but did not have the strength to fight the boy's control over her. Joseph was too busy taking in all that was exposed to his virgin senses to see how terrified and mortified the Wühlenvogel was.

I dared not order my son to release the creature's body to her own mind. She might have dropped him. I ordered Joseph to come home. He flew from the mountains and out over the lake. He turned toward the palace in obedience of my order. But he could sense the Grail. He stopped and hovered over the place where I battled Löwschock. With all of his wisdom and knowledge, he still did not understand his own mortality and the perils of the physical world. As he flew above the lake, directly over the point where I killed Löwschock and lost the Grail, he released the Wühlenvogel to her own control. The Wühlenvogel went limp, releasing her grasp of Joseph and silencing her wings. They both dropped. The Wühlenvogel regained herself and steadied in the air. Joseph plunged into the lake.

169

He sank too deeply to resurface before drowning. I left Joseph's mind and sought those of my swimmers. Six Vogelkrötes were near him. I directed them to whisk him to the nearest breathable air, into the chambers of the Queen's Jail. They got him there, but not before he took in some water. He learned physical pain, and he learned fear. He coughed and seized, shivered and ached. The Vogelkrötes rolled him and slapped him until they evicted the water from his aching lungs.

I experienced it all with him, and it drew my memories to Prische's death. I could not have relived Prische's death, and I certainly could not have survived experiencing my son's death as I had Prische's. My heart would surely have stopped as his did. But the Vogelkrötes saved him. We all lived through it.

He was safe. He was in the jail where The Ancient One lived for more than a century. But the horrors of his captivity were not what my thoughts linked to Joseph's location. No, the jail had a current inmate that struck my memory much more ferociously. It held the skull of Reid. Reid was a full year dead, dismembered decayed, spread across the realm. But his skull was near my son, and flashbacks of those hungry, ambitious eyes, those eyes that screamed with such fury as he plunged his hand-crafted blade into me and at my child, shook and punched me with irrational anxiety. I wanted Joseph out of that jail and away from that evil artifact.

Bechtold and Hildemar, my faithful Schildbüffels, responded to my desperate call and moved at top speed from a small pond inside of Wühlenvogel land. They swam and ran (if it can be called running) and swam again, until they reached the jail. They returned Joseph to the surface under a Schildbüffel shell, some adolescent shell, discarded by some growing Schildbüffel long ago, filled with the jail's air that my son breathed all the way to the surface. Once they surfaced, the same Wühlenvogel, mortified by her role in Joseph's near demise, scooped him from the water and flew him directly to the palace.

I remember my mother telling a story of me, of not long after *my* first birthday, when I opened the front door of our house and toddled down the middle of our street. She always held her hand over her heart as she told the story. Her eyes widened and she spoke with such agitation, many years after it happened. I came to understand her that day — that brand of fear that only a mother can know, that sense of relief when an endangered child is again safe in a mother's arms. The Wühlenvogel apologized profusely for her part in the incident. But I thought nothing of that. There was no anger, no scolding, only the sweetest relief. I held Joseph, and Felix hoisted us both and ran us to the highest chamber of the palace, where we held each other in sequestered peace until midday.

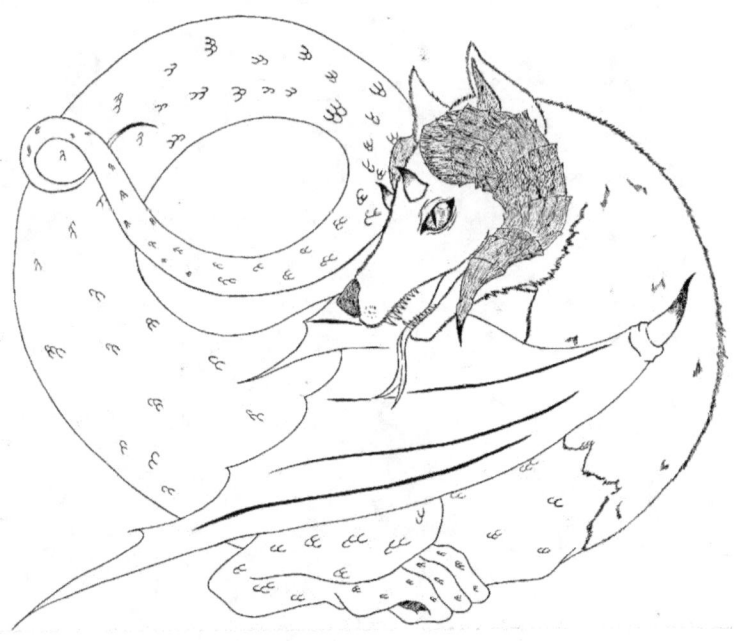

CHAPTER 13
Kingly Powers

THE ANCIENT ONE BLAMED HIMSELF for the incident with the Wühlenvogel. He had taught many Swan Knights, many of whom had extraordinary abilities. He taught them to control those abilities before harm was done by them. But he was so enthralled by Joseph's uniqueness, and so excited by his potential, that the precautions of the past eluded him in Joseph's earliest lessons. The incident with the lake was brutal evidence of that failing, and a reminder of similar failings from his past. He began his lessons in control and prudence first thing the following morning.

His first lesson was not of self-control, but of individual identity. The creatures of the Sweeter Realm have a right to their own bodies, their own functions. Joseph did not have the authority to take control of them without their permission.

"But my mother has done it," Joseph responded.

"She did it when it was necessary for her destiny and God's will. She did it to save lives."

"How will I know when it is God's will?"

Sternly, the swan answered, "Until you can answer that question on your own, it is best that you leave that ability alone."

The Ancient One reduced Joseph's vision, diminishing it from its lofty spiritual perch, that elevated perspective he gained in the lessons with Taufe, to a smaller, more

173

individualistic view of life and time. He taught Joseph to be introspective, to see his own identity separate from his mother and the creatures around him. As a result, Joseph spent less time in the thoughts of others. When he was in the company of others, he learned how to delight in the words that they expressed vocally, to enjoy the surprise of their slowly revealed thoughts. He was a quick-minded child, much quicker than anyone he encountered. And he found it difficult to wait for thoughts, feelings, and stories to be expressed through the slow and comparatively clumsy modes of common expression. He battled his impatient desires to extract the thoughts quickly and forcefully. He battled, and he won.

During his lessons with Taufe, he applied the scriptures to his own morality, his immediate feelings and behavior, and he began to craft his own personality, individual from his destiny and the will of God. Aside from his entirely singular knowledge and wisdom, he began to resemble a child. Prior to this evolution, any one food was just like another — not relevant to the grand scheme of his universal and timeless perspective. But after the change, he had foods that he preferred and some he did not like at all. He developed preferences of all kinds, and he expressed them readily. He became aware of his individual tastes in all things. With this came an awareness of his senses, the pleasures and pains that his own brain perceived.

The incident in the lake, and the lessons that sprang from it, put fear into a young mind that had not previously known fear. He abhorred the lake, and any water pooled in large amounts. He shuddered to enter the throne room and look out across the shallow pool entrance to the lake beyond. His first baths after the incident were battles. He did not want to touch the water, and his reaction was infantile, in other words, they were not extraordinary. For several months, only the Brunnens could bathe him. He avoided all things that pained him and obsessed over the things that pleased him. He did not become narcissistic. He was still intensely compassionate. He delighted more in the pleasures of others than in his own, anguished in the pain of others more than his own.

From his conception, I had no expectation that our child would be like any human child. But the develop of some human normalcy was surely welcomed. For such parenthood, I at least had some blueprint of experience to follow. Joseph still displayed insights beyond the capacity of any creature in existence. But in the mundane moments of family life, he was a child, even capable, from time to time, of selfishness, in which I delighted. Isolated inside of his own thoughts, he often lost the wider perspective that came with connected minds. He put his desires above the needs of others. He grew irritated when others did not immediately understand him. But he fought his yearning to project his thoughts directly into their minds, having been forbidden by the swan to do so. So he shouted his aggravation in the form of very childlike tantrums. In other words, he resembled a normal child.

Through this transition, he developed a much closer relationship with Felix, who could relate much better with Joseph's normacies than his more extraordinary traits. The childish outbursts that irritated The Ancient One, and at times even Taufe, endeared Felix's son to him. It was in those moments when Joseph was not a First-in-Training, not a symbol of an impending reunion of God and humans, rather only a child, and a Federkind. Felix was no longer a nomad, like his people. He lived in the palace with me. Joseph was not a nomad either. Felix thought nothing of the sacrifices-of-self he had to make to be my husband and lover. But he thought often of Joseph's, and of the Federman half of a boy whose life was so unlike that of his people.

It was important to Felix that his son recognize and relish his Sweeter Realm heritage. Yes, Joseph was the son of a Swan Knight and the only child of the Queen. But he was also a Federkind, and nothing of his childhood resembled his father's upbringing. To remedy this, when Joseph was about a year and half old, Felix took his son for a week to live and interact with his nomadic relatives, along the western shore of the great lake. The timing was propitious. The old Eulesänger leader had died, and my attendance in Eierheim was required.

Felix and Joseph left one day before I did. For only the second time since his conception, Joseph was away from me, and the first did not go well. He was far away in both body and mind. I fought my maternal instincts to connect with him. He needed time to be a Federkind, Felix's son, and part of a proud clan of nomads. To console me in my loss, Acheriel agreed to escort me to Eierheim, with Lina and Senische in company. Of course, Georg and a parade of my Royal Guard made the journey as well. Georg would not have taken no for an answer. Acheriel and his family met me at the palace and we all embarked for Eierheim.

It was only a year and a half since Reid's attack. In seeing and speaking to Georg, you would think it was just hours into our past. His protectiveness encrusted his character and hid from me, and from the others, those subtle traits that made the noble Unicorn dear to us. He was the Captain of the Guard and nothing else. I missed him. I missed the friend who spoke frankly to me during our studies, travels, and battles together. The trip to Eierheim softened his austere encasement. We were not out of the Nomadic belt before Georg and the Guard relaxed the rigid formality of their formations. They mingled with us and we traveled like a leisure band of old friends.

It took weeks of travel for us to reach Eierheim. Our pace was unsteady, constantly interrupted by passing creatures who demanded the attention of their Queen and the other heroes of the war who traveled with me. Lina and Senische were as much of a draw as I was. It was not the way of the Sweeter Realm for breeds to become intimate in the lives of other breeds. Lina serving as surrogate mother to Senische was remarkable in every corner of the Sweeter Realm. The bonds formed between the members of my traveling company, forged in battle and turmoil, but polished to a gloss during blissful peace, were uncommon and a point of curiosity for all we encountered. Unicorns and Scheriers, Wühlenvogels and Zweigwesens, and several other breeds all marching together in friendly, leisure company, was a sight that both confounded and delighted spectators. Pilgrims to our path demanded stories of the war, and anecdotes of daily life in the palace. They wanted to know about Joseph — how he grew in both size and mind, and what delightful new abilities were being discovered in him.

There was hope and excitement, and a great portion of laughter during the rambling, traipsing trip to Eierheim. Spirits were high when we encountered them, and made higher by the company of traveling heroes. But the moment we mounted the rim of the giant nest of Eierheim, all frivolity, all lightheartedness was silenced under the pall of the city's mourning. Their beloved leader was dead, just a couple of years after regaining their capital. I had never before imagined that the spirited whistles of the Eulesängers could sound so doleful and forlorn. Had their songs not cheered me in my darkest moments, the contrast would not have struck me so. But their sadness had sharpened their passionate song enough for it to cut easily and deeply into my spirits. I found it intensely painful to hear. I wanted to block it out, to think of brighter, pleasanter things. But I dared not. I made the voyage to suffer with them, and suffer I would.

In the quiet times of the late evenings, when I was alone with my Guard, there was enough distraction in conversation for my thought to comfortably depart from the pain of the Eulesängers. I even found my mind distant from my husband and child — that is, until something as unexpected as it was miraculous occurred.

Felix and Joseph were walking with a caravan of Federmensch, gathering fruits and seeking a campsite for the night. Joseph's fear of the lake to his right proved fortuitous. He was skirting the edge of the woods, as far as possible from the water. Most of the band traveled along the water's edge. Joseph walked with one of Felix's cousins, a young Federman named Flaumig. Flaumig climbed a high tree to retrieve some fruit. The tree branch broke and the Federman fell. Two nearby trees bent low to catch Flaumig in their branches. They did this at Joseph's command. The sand between the trees rose to receive the trembling Federman from the bent trees, after which the trees returned to their normal positions and the sand slowly lowered to its previous state, gently laying its passenger on the ground.

Flaumig hollered when he fell, catching the attention of the rest of the band. In the high emotions of the fall, my mind connected to Joseph and Felix, and to several of the witnesses. The cousin had broken an arm on one of the branches that caught him. I watched through Felix's thoughts as our son commanded the bone to heal. The bone obeyed. The pain of the injury lingered until Joseph soothed it away by nurturing Flaumig's senses from within. He held Flaumig's mind in his and caressed it with compassion until the pain of the injury was gone.

Without invading his mind, Joseph sent a quick and simple message to the swan, "I understand now."

Flaumig's accident and Joseph's immediate, instinctual reaction to it evicted the immaturities that had just begun to normalize inside of him. The child that I desired was obliterated by the Swan Knight-King that The Ancient One worked hard to develop inside of my son. The incident with Flaumig placed squarely on Joseph's shoulders the immense responsibility that comes with his abilities. He felt himself not only responsible for his cousin, father, and other Federmensch relatives, not only for me, the swan, and Taufe, but for every creature he could reach with either hand or mind. At a year and a half old, while his bones were still soft and his infantile muscles barely able to follow the commands of his extravagant mind, he strapped the concerns of his world onto his back and bore them with the determination of a true hero and prophet. There was no war raging in my queendom. But my subjects suffered all of the accidents, losses, and heartaches typical of any society during peacetime. Joseph's profound abilities came with a profound mandate. I did not see it that way. Neither did Felix. But the teachers did, and Joseph did.

Word of the incident spread quickly across the queendom. There was much debate over what it meant for Joseph, his destiny, and the connection between the world of humans and the Sweeter Realm. Joseph's new-found powers would have much greater potential in the world of humans, with their violent and destructive natures, than in the Sweeter Realm, where accidents like Flaumig's and the heartaches of normal life would be the only employment those powers could find.

Taufe reminded me, "The reunion of worlds in inevitable, a dramatic chapter in a book written before time. It is the destiny of humanity to return to Eden and regain oneness with God. Just like with Brunhilde, when humanity mixes with Eden, it regains a bit of its divinity. It is no wonder that your son has such abilities. He is a step toward reunification. He is the result of reunification. Only

God knows what he is capable of. But I tell you this, he gives us a glimpse of what is in store for us all. And it is exciting."

Defensively I asked, "But must he use these abilities there? The humans are not his people. We are."

She gave me the look she always gave when she expected me to answer my own question. It was only under that look that I realized how I spoke, referring to humans as if I was not one, and Joseph was not half-human. I thought of my father and mother, my grandparents and aunts and uncles who had given me so much. I felt the shame of forsaking them and displayed that shame boldly enough for Taufe to read it clearly.

She softened her face and answered my question, "Not necessarily. His abilities may not be intended for a particular use. They may have nothing to do with mankind's return to Eden. I view them simply as evidence of divinity. His beauty is reflective of God's and he is a window into the future of your species."

She was not wrong when she called it exciting. The incident with the Federmensch caused quite a buzz of excitement within every city, circle, and gathering place of the Sweeter Realm. The very air seemed sweeter and Godlier after that day. Something big was coming. We all sensed it, and it excited the hearts of all my subjects — except The Ancient One, Taufe, Felix, and me. For us, a darkness, a distinct melancholy accompanied the excitement. We could not help but acknowledge what the others could not see — that such a miracle does not happen without cost, and the cost would be *ours* to pay. For the salvation of both worlds, *we* must sacrifice. At times, in shared contemplation on the subject, the realization of this unknown and unforeseeable pain crippled us with its squeezing, clenching, digging and biting grip.

The sensation was deliciously rancid. We giggled and cried at the same time, as we thanked God for our part in his plan, while we tried to reconcile ourselves to whatever pain and destruction that plan would bring into our lives. Joseph felt the darkness as well. And his new-found individuality gave that darkness a hideous hue. But he also maintained a perspective that none of us had. The hideous was beautiful to him. It was a peppery seasoning in a succulent dish, served up by Christ himself. It was not until I tasted that dish, many years later, that I understood what Joseph knew then, at only a year and a half old.

CHAPTER 14
Commitment to the Unknown

JOSEPH CONTINUED TO STUDY EVERY DAY with the teachers. He rode and trained with Georg as soon as his body grew large and strong enough. His Federman strength came as it would in any normal Federkind. But it came with a mind infinitely more aware of how to use it. While Joseph was still not much taller than my mid-thigh, Georg initiated his riding and combat training, reuniting with Joseph the trinity of teachers who had taught me in St. Hildegard.

His unusual life in the Sweeter Realm offered him plenty to occupy his time and his thoughts. At least it would have been plenty for anyone else. But his mind moved faster, which allowed his thoughts, despite his schedule, the ability to drift beyond the lessons at hand. And the nearer his destiny came, the more impatient he became to embrace it. Between the lessons he absorbed from me while he was still in the womb, and those lessons given directly to him after his birth, he clung to one central theme — the Holy Grail, the central motif of the long and storied Swan Knights History. It and the swan had been the centerpiece of his own mother's story. Joseph remained keenly aware of the Grail's intimacy with our fate, and he saw his own future as a seemless continuation from Parsifal and Lohengrin, through the Ottos and Ludwigs, through me and to him.

Joseph wanted the Holy Grail. It seemed to speak to him the way the portal spoke to Rudolf. Despite Joseph's uncommonly broad perspective and the daily temperance of his impulses by his steady and devout teachers, he showed occasional recklessness. Every now and then, his youth would reveal itself in the form of impatience. His desire for the Grail displayed itself with bursts of irritation, in which language that bordered on cruelness shot from his lips.

The Grail was safe at the bottom of the lake, where no swimmers dared to go. The death of the Deep creatures and the opening of my portal by my spilled blood gave the area a morbid reverence that no creature dared to defile. The Grail was not lost. It was not in danger. It did not need rescuing or retrieval. It was at the bottom of the lake, and neither I nor my teachers saw any reason to recall it from that safe hiding place, not until by some sign or mystical directive, God demanded its retrieval. But Joseph's obsession only grew as he did.

Joseph did not see the Grail as we did. To him, it was not some dusty old relic, to be revered from afar. To him it was a tool that had not been put away properly. He looked at the queendom around him and saw daily opportunities to put that tool to use. Ever since I read to him from my journal, he viewed the Grail as mine, as a gift to me from God, like my eyes, my hands, my friends, and my destiny. He wanted it in my hands, near him, where it could do the most good. Not only did I have a humbler devotion to the Grail than Joseph understood. I was afraid of it. I was not so much afraid of the Grail itself as I was of the role I imagined it would play in a destiny I was content to keep out of immediate reach. A distant Grail meant a distant destiny and a postponement of any terrible sacrifices required of me. I was in no hurry to bring about the miracles foreseen by Taufe and Hüter. I was committed, ready to train, to work *slowly* toward whatever the will of God had in store for me. But each sign of its approach, including the blossoming of Joseph's abilities, startled me, frightened me, and inclined me to push destiny into the unforeseeable future.

Joseph raised the subject of the Grail daily, both inside and outside of related conversations. With an appropriate amount of remorse, I think about how impatient I grew with him. His aversion to the lake was the only thing that kept his desire for the Grail behind a healthy curtain of apprehension. To dampen his desires, I played upon that weakness. I shared with him my memories of fading from consciousness at the bottom of the lake. During his peaceful moments I allowed other memories to casually leave the vaults of my mind and wander into his — being pulled into the icy blackness of the Glühenchor pond, Prische's death, and even my motherly experience of Joseph's own near-drowning.

These things did much to "sour the milk". He could not help but associate the Grail with the water that enshrouds it. And the water bore a repugnance that he could not shake. Perhaps it was the cruelest way to separate my son from the immediate fate of the Grail. And I felt remorse for the fear I stoked inside of him. But this lasted only as long as he feared the water.

The playfulness and innocence of the Shallow Waters creatures, particularly the Vogelkrötes, coaxed him into reconciliation with the water, beginning with the swimmers who came to play in the entrance to the palace. With little to fear from the ankle-high water, Joseph began to release his fears. With every giggling splash in the shallow pool in front of the throne, the Waters came to represent friendship instead of pain and mortality. Within a few years of his plunge into the lake, his desire to connect his senses with the stories of the Grail grew to outweigh his waning fear of water.

Before long, the shallow pool was an insufficient playground for his friends. They wanted to swim freely and they wanted Joseph to play with them. He began to venture into deeper water — knee-deep, waste-deep, neck-deep, until the fears of his infancy ceased to inhibit him at all. A small, lonely apprehension to the water always resided in the dusty, rarely visited corners of his mind. But shout as it may, it could not be heard over the laughing and splashing of his swimming friends. The more time he spent in the lake, and the farther out he went, the weaker seemed the daunting vault that encased the Grail. In direct proportion to that evolution grew in volume and influence the siren call of the Grail.

Joseph's outbursts of impatience grew beyond what I and his teachers viewed as tolerable. When he was five years old, during a lesson with Taufe, he pushed it too far. The wise abbess was speaking of the goodness of Christ, speaking of the Grail as a metaphor for God's love. Joseph could no longer abide such distant, hazy, theoretical speech about an object very real and very near to him. He shoved a thought of disgust loudly into Taufe's mind, so violent, so powerfully angry that it buckled her knees beneath her and caused her nose to bleed. The transfer of thought was one-sided. Joseph received nothing in return. He did not see the pain, the insult, the vast disrespect of his outburst against the most revered cleric in the Sweeter Realm. He stomped out of the room not knowing the physical and spiritual damage he had caused.

Joseph's Grail-fever reached an uncontrollable pitch. It was early the next morning, during our recitation of the Psalms, that he demanded the Grail.

On Chapter 116 of the Psalms, as we recited in unison,
How can I repay the Lord

For all the great good done
for me?

Joseph stood abruptly and continued the next verse in a determined and demanding voice that startled us,

I will lift the *Cup of Salvation*
And call on the name of the Lord

The great Benedictine Abbess glared at him, castigating him for his interruption, with deep and powerful eyes. It was enough to shake the obsession from his head for a moment. It startled *me*, though I had been on the receiving end of that scornful gaze many times. It was much more than a remonstrance for disturbing the prayers. Taufe sensed a degree of impatience in him that could endanger Joseph's life and the Grail. She had felt first-hand the power of his mind to cause pain. After morning scriptures, she spoke with The Ancient One. The two teachers decided on a course of action to subdue Joseph's passions until they could be useful.

Joseph had displayed abilities, with the trees and the sand, and with his influence over the minds and bodies of others, that rose high above the capabilities of any creature in the queendom. For this reason, and to distract him from his own impatience, the teachers decided to compliment his training with service, to pull him from his sense of destiny and place him into a sense of duty. They decided to commission him into the Queen's Royal Guard. After all, alloyed with his own particular abilities was the strength of the Federmensch. It was not only to placate our concerns. He could be useful to the Royal Guard, small as he was. Our recommendation to Georg was sincere. But my primary motivation was not the strengthening of the Guard. As a member of the Guard, he would be under Georg's diligent and discerning watch, and I had not forgotten the strong doses of humility that Georg's training had forced me to drink.

It was only after the teachers suggested the measure to me that Taufe told me of Joseph's attack on her mind. The details both fightened and enfuriated me. Taufe would have never presumed to lecture me on parenting my own child. But she asked that I not address the incident with Joseph. I was severely angry with him, and I wanted to punish him harshly. Taufe told me that Joseph did not receive her thoughts in return and was unaware of the pain he caused. She thought that such a response would trigger in him a crippling level of guilt that would block the path down which they wanted to steer his ambitions, and it could jeopardize their plans for his immediate improvement.

Joseph's Grail obsession was not selfish. He did not wish to have the Grail for his own betterment. He was no Klingsor, and nothing like the many ambitious hands that grasped at the Grail since it left that holy chamber where the Last Supper took place. The Grail, like the Holy Eucharist, was given by Christ to mankind, for mankind. Through this understanding, Joseph could not help but tie intimately his desire for the Grail with an insatiable drive to benefit humanity. He knew the Conspicuous Scriptures as well as I. They drew a clear line connecting God's love of his children and the line of heroic Swan Knights of which he was a part. His internal eye was perpetually on the world of humans and what he believed to be his destiny to bring them to Eden. As he grew in height and depth, his ability to remain in the present, with mind and senses on his surroundings, decreased exponentially. He knew his abilities were remarkable, entirely singular among God's creation. And any slight moment not putting those abilities to full employment itched him like a rash inside of his bones.

If Joseph had weaknesses in his education, it was in Georg's arena of study. Georg was precisely the sort of influence he needed to humble him and make him view his destiny with realistic apprehension. My riding and combat teacher terrified me into greatness during my lessons in St. Hildegard. Georg trained the members of the Guard very similarly to the ways he trained me. Joseph's induction into the Royal Guard would not only give his mind an occupation that was sure to grasp his sense of duty. It would force upon him the intense and humbly fearful training regulated by Georg.

Taufe appealed to Joseph's love of the Sweeter Realm and its creatures, and convinced him to commit to the Guard, with all of its immediate and practical responsibilities, with a quotation from the visions of St. Hildegard, "If we give up this world, we shall be destroyed by demons and deprived of the Angels' protection."

She appealed to him, "Protect your mother. Protect the palace and your friends. Protect your home as a member of the Royal Guard. That is where your mind should be. Whatever awaits you, these duties will prepare you. Give them your attention. This is your world right now, the Sweeter Realm. Serve it, your mother, and your Captain."

The quotation, with its intended sentiment, hit its mark. Joseph's fiercely protective love of his mother's queendom swelled inside of him. With the Captain's approval, Felix stained his son's upper arm, with a smudge to match his own. Joseph, being thoroughly versed in the history of his parents, wore the emblem with pride. His sense of service to others, and of connection to the stories of his parents' past, loosened the grip of impatience on his heart. His zeal found another avenue by which to release its immense pressure on his mind. He fully embraced his new role. To stoke his excitement, Georg planned a royal tour of the capital cities to begin immediately upon the completion of Joseph's Royal Guard training.

The completion of training was not determined by any set period of time, but by the completion of skills to Georg's satisfaction. While not in the rigors of his excersizes, Joseph served as an active member of the Guard. He watched. He learned from the advice and examples of the other members. And he clung to every word of his Captain. Surprising me, but not at all Georg, Joseph completed his training in two weeks. He was a fully initiated member of the Queen's Royal Guard, wearing a stain that matched his father's. As promised, Georg's planned tour of the capital cities could commence. I looked forward to putting my feet on the paths, hills, forests, and shrines of my beloved queendom. My heart sought that. But my curiosity saw the tour as an opportunity to see my son in this new light, with a new identity.

My Guard must accompany me, which allowed Joseph to serve his new title while retracing many of his mother's earliest steps in the Land and Shallow Waters. He remained my son as we embarked. But beyond that, he was a member of the Royal Guard. At only five years old, and standing only waist-high to me, he had the physical strength of a powerful human man, complimented of course by his more extraordinary abilities.

The realization of his new identity puffed his chest. He was already so wise at five years old, displaying spiritual understanding that befuddled our wisest. But the way he walked around the traveling party, canting his stained arm toward every eye that passed him, strutting with raised chin, was distinctly juvenile. He wanted to be like his fellow Guards, to walk like them, and especially to talk like them. The slow and grossly inadequate verbal communication between his colleagues brought him delight rather than frustration. He admired them all, and in doing so admired everything about them. Despite that admiration, there was an obvious fact, obvious to us all, staring him in the face. He was my son and he was entirely unique.

He walked among his comrades, rarely addressing me directly and hardly ever at my side. He knew that his capabilities rose above the most equipped members of the Guard. He saw all of our lives as squarely in his hands, though little between the capitals could do any of us harm. It was a strange mix of feelings for him. While admiring the veteran members of his team, he knew that only he could command the trees and sand, command bones to heal, and seize the functions of any body in our traveling party. *He* knew it and *we* knew it. But despite his superiority, he mingled with the Guard while very subserviently requesting and absorbing any piece of advice they might have to give him. He did not do this to patronize them. He truly valued their words and holstered each point of guidance to be drawn and utilized when needed.

There was an air of austerity around him that was entirely absent from his comrades. Joseph was a serious bubble in a jovial ocean of creatures. The rest of them understood that we had nothing to fear from the woods or waters around us. Even Georg saw little reason to protect the Queen. For this reason, he served more as teacher than as Captain, as we worked our way down the paths of travel. Joseph's new position, and newly stained arm, focused his mind on his combat teacher, priming him for the crucial influence that would follow. His duty was to unquestioningly obey his Captain.

Georg kept tight reins on Joseph's attention while he slyly slipped his lessons under the disguise of duty. My son's pride and sense of purpose filled me with love for him, and love for the wise teachers who again served me, the Sweeter Realm, humanity, and God to delightful results. In the cities and among the creatures we encountered on the road, Joseph was nothing more than a protective soldier, not elevating himself above the lowest of them. He obeyed his Captain with humility and complete deference.

Felix traveled with us into Zweigwesen land, past the Portal Point, where he and The Ancient One broke from the caravan and returned to the palace together. Taufe remained with us. We picked up friends along the way. Creatures from each breed joined and broke off, as our path winded in directions they needed to go. We were gone from the palace for seven months, spending hours with some, days with others, sleeping in Brunnen buildings and Eulesänger nests, Zweigwesen huts and Unicorn fields. We waded into the Shallows of every pool and pond in our path. We were welcomed by every swimmer, crawler, runner, and flyer. It was a grand tour of the queendom indeed, and one long-overdue.

In each homeland and at every stop, I served my hosts. I worked their fields and cleaned their homes. I bathed them and nurtured them. I prepared their foods and fed them from my own hands. I put my laborious efforts on bold display — not for my sake, not in the service of my own vanity, but to show Joseph that leadership was not always glorious, and that there is nothing nobler than improving, however minutely, the lives of those we encounter. The improvement is not always healing bones and saving lives. It can be the gentlest of gestures. A leader can show more greatness holding a broom than holding the Holy Grail. I ended every day tired, sweaty, and thoroughly fulfilled. The lesson was received. Joseph, whose powers greatly exceeded my own, felt inadequate beside his mother's ability to serve. But he tried. He toiled beside the creatures of the queendom, while obeying the mandates of his new office and sparing a rare moment to kiss his mother, like a five-year old should.

I encountered many old friends on the tour, creatures who were dear, treasured parts of daily life, at a time when sensations were heightened and affections magnified. They never left my mind, but sat much lower in my consciousness since the war ended. During the tour, they occupied my most immediate attention. I hardly saw Joseph. He mingled with the Guard, assuming his assigned posts on his assigned shifts. The position on the Guard gave him an independence he had never felt, and an identity beyond being my son and the student of the great teachers. Georg knew when to scold him, when to teach him, and when to let him be a free and equal member of an elite fellowship. The heroics of the Royal Guard on the beach of the Queen's Lake, when they battled the vile serpents of the Deep while protecting me from harm, had already become the stuff of legends. Those stories were as deeply rooted to the creature-psyche of the queendom as the oldest and most cherished chapters in Sweeter Realm lore. The Mark of Sacrifice drew gazes of admiration from every pocket of creatures we encountered, as much or more than the human features of their Queen. Although the heroics of the war happened well before Joseph's conception, his arm was stained, and he shared in all of the glory that came with the designation.

In addition to his duties and socializing with his comrades, he had to entertain the attentions of the Guard's adoring fans, allowing them to run their fingers across his stained feathers. Still, several times a day, Joseph and I connected our minds and shared our thoughts and experiences of the tour. He kept one thought hidden deeply from me, where his most private ambitions brewed. His obsession with the Grail may have been covered from view by his new title. But burying it beneath his duties only let it cook under greater heat. It was only a matter of time before it boiled over. I did not pry into his mind to learn this. I saw it in his eyes. That same fiery gleam that possessed him when he spoke of the Grail still showed its spark, in the subtlest of twinkles that only his mother recognized.

I had not forgotten my husband since he broke from our caravan and returned to the palace. There were matters he needed to attend to. He was as busy — and walked as many steps — as those of us who remained on the tour. I missed him terribly while I traveled, but I sought his mind daily and walked through his dreams at night. The Ancient One's departure from the tour was more enigmatic. I assumed he would travel with me, using the opportunity to teach and train me under a variety of conditions. I supposed that he had some service or another to perform for some breed or another. Such was not the case. I snuck into his mind when I could, when it would go unnoticed and unprotested.

With Joseph tucked-in tightly to his new position and training, now more under Georg's eye than his, The Ancient One returned his focus to me. He remained my teacher after gifting himself to my infant son. But he had been true to his word. His life and his focus belonged to Joseph. His student's position in the Royal Guard liberated the old bird's mind to canvas the past and to dwell on the worries he had for me. He thought me to be grossly unequipped to defeat the faceless, epic demon he believed I must soon encounter. The purification of Eden required the defeat of Löwschock and the dangerous monsters we fought. Many of our lives were lost. The Ancient One assumed that a much larger prize would require the defeat of a much deadlier enemy. He returned to the palace to rework my training — more intense, more elaborate, more comprehensive. An engrossing and frenzied anticipation

194

consumed him. He twitched at every sound he took in, expecting me to be whisked away to fight some evil and sacrifice myself for God.

There was something I did not understand about him until I stood silently at the window ledge of his mind and observed him in secret. He was still haunted by the part he played in pulling me out onto the lake to face Löwschock. Despite the fact that it had to be done and it was all for the best, those moments tormented his memory. His willingness to escort me to my assumed death scratched, irritated, and enflamed his guilt more wretchedly as his love for me grew.

He thought daily of that moment, recalling it more vividly with each recollection. On that day, with every stroke of his webbed feet that pulled me toward the center of the lake, he felt more like my executioner, and he cursed himself the whole way. He saw himself, like Simon of Cyrene, helping me by quickening my march to death. This put a wound on his heart that was reopened every time he looked at me and every time he thought of me, made more painful as that heart became more dependent on my love. He feared what enemies awaited us in the completion of God's will. But far more than that, he feared being instrumental in my demise. He could not bear the thought of ushering me into another battle, into another dark place to face a dark demon. He feared it, and he assumed it to be his unavoidable destiny — and it ripped him apart. He was desperate to prepare me to survive, knowing that causing my death would suck him dry of everything that lives inside of him.

I had seen so many minds, so many thoughts and experiences of loss, pain, and despair. But none of them stood tall beside those memories of the swan that he had hidden from me. They did not just haunt him, they navigated his every decision and propelled his every movement since I plunged into the lake with the Grail that day. Everything he did since was in an attempt to cut that wound from his heart, a wound whose rancid poison filled him thoroughly. As devoted as he was to the will of God, he could not be instrumental in my potential demise, not again. He swore it to himself. And in the silence of his fortified thoughts, he swore it to me. While I was far away on the tour of the queendom, busy traveling, cooking, cleaning, and toiling with my subjects, he relaxed the security of his most cloaked and guarded thoughts, exposing them to my probing mind. His love for me was immense, his fears for me debilitating, and his prayers for me ever-fervent.

The swan assumed that victory for God would require me to be Otto's axe, Brunhilde's knife, and Ludwig the Crusader's cunning diplomacy, all rolled into one. He knew enough of human nature, of the human propensity for cruelty and betrayal, and he knew that my destiny was to face the evils of my own breed. 1,300 years among humans, countless violent battles, greed and ambition, had shown him destruction and loss to a scale that I was unable to comprehend. He knew humans better than I did. He had known more of them, good and evil. He had to prepare me for my own species through an accumulation of experiences that no human could boast.

When he broke from the traveling party, he returned to the palace to prepare his lessons for my return from the tour. He did exactly that. Had I been given the chance, I believe I could have slept for five days straight, after pushing my reluctant bones through the shallow pool at the entrance to the palace, after several months of toil and travel. The Ancient One allowed me not a single hour of recovery before implementing his new syllabus. Georg posted Joseph nearest his mother, at the times when our proximity would yield us the most calm and familial conversations. I thanked my old friend and teacher profusely for his thoughtfulness, for allowing us *some* time to be a family. But those times grew rarer by the day.

CHAPTER 15
Bruised and Ablaze

JUST LIKE AFTER THE SERPENT ATTACK on St. Hildegard Cathedral, The Ancient One was focused, at the cost of his tenderness. He drove me hard, with incessant talk of violence and evil. We pored over the most distressing portions of the Swan Knights History, obsessing over human weakness and propensity for self-destruction. Daily he prayed that I might find Brunhilde at my side in my battles to come. Balance came to me in two forms — in the warm, feathered arms of my husband, who spoke only of his love for me, and in the spiritual, calm, and confident lessons with Taufe. Her lips brought me comfort during the day with their words, and comfort in the evening with their kisses.

She spoke of destiny very differently than the swan. There was a grateful air around her, a contentedness with God's plan, that took a little of the biting edge off of The Ancient One's panicked warnings. I came to Taufe each morning with the lingering distress of the previous day's training with the swan.

I asked her one morning, how will I know what to do, when to do it, where to go. How can God put the fate of mankind into my hands with no directions?

"I am surprised at you," she softly replied. "Have you forgotten already? As a young child, you felt the reach of

God's hand. You felt it, acknowledged it, and reached for God in return."

Defensively, but in search for her calm assurance, I refuted, "I didn't know what I was doing. I was a kid, following a childish obsession."

"You obeyed a subtle and cryptic summons that most would have ignored in favor of the distractions around them. You crossed from your world, where you left all that you knew to blindly follow your faith. And look at the results. You answered God's call to the portal at Linderhof. God brought you to Cort, who took you to Rüdiger, who brought you to the great swan, who took you to me. You risked your life and abandoned your identity to serve Eden as its paladin and Queen. You dove to a death you were certain of, to sacrifice yourself for God's will. But you did not die. The Cup of Christ saved you and vanquished your enemies. And now, after all of that has transpired before your eyes, do you choose now to doubt God's methods, and doubt your own fitness as his weapon of choice? Look at your heart for a moment, my love, and tell me, where is your faith right now? Do you doubt God?"

Her words lifted me over the fears of the swan, as they walked me through the wondrous truths of my Providential experiences, only to drop me to the ground with a large and heavy ball of guilt on my lap. I was mortified for having doubted. Taufe's tongue could be as soft as the skin of her belly, and as sharp as the tip of a young Unicorn warrior's horn.

The swan spoke so grimly of my destiny, and he trained me more to avoid it than to embrace it. Perhaps he loved me too much. He was training me to survive. Taufe spoke of my trials ahead, even of the painful sacrifices she knew I must endure, as pleasures in themselves, as gifts from God for which I should be grateful. I could not yet see the trials of my future as pleasures deserving my gratitude, and I feared my failure even more than my suffering, with so much at stake.

I asked Taufe, "Is the will of God so fragile, that my weakness could crumble it, that my flaws could jeopardize the salvation of so many?"

She stared at me for half a minute, with eyes that churned with depth, as if entire oceans had been shrunk and placed above her cheeks.

"I cannot speak to the fragility of God's will," she finally answered. "But I have clarity on two points where you do not."

I waited for her to continue, but she only stared as before, until I prompted her, "The first?"

She stepped closer to me and slouched slightly so that her eyes were all that I could see, and she answered me with both throats, in a voice that seemed to echo off of my skin, "The first is *your* greatness. The second is that good creatures will make great sacrifices for you, and brave creatures will be willing to suffer... no, not *willing*. They will be pleased to suffer. The will of God requires Verena. But with Verena comes others. Your strength is broader and more complex than you see."

I struggled to reconcile the view points of my two teachers. The truth is, they were both right. There was much to fear and prepare for, many treacherous truths to be acknowledged. But those preparations needed to be coated with a layer of Taufe's faith. After speaking to Taufe that morning, while still adhering to the demands of The Ancient One, with all of his wretched experiences, I approached my training with balance, still with trepidation, but cooled and soothed with an ointment of faith and an honest acknowledgement of the miracles that had already transpired before me.

In the previous several years of my life, I had lived ten lifetimes of danger, love, loss, and gain. Yet there I stood, whole and wholly-blessed. I took my love and faith into my training, so that I could embrace every terrifying, winless scenario placed before me by the swan with confidence that, whether I live or die, no matter what I lose, I will ultimately succeed. I reminded myself often of Taufe's words on the shore of the lake, as I prepared to face the King of the Deep, "Do you believe that the Lord has brought her here to fail?" She was right then. Eden was purified and I survived. In my most desperate hours of doubt, I thought of that.

The training was fierce. I often crawled to bed more bruised and bloody than at any point during the war with the Deep. I climbed and fell, took blows to every part of my body, rode and ran, swam and fought. Each day pitted me against another set of volunteers gathered by The Ancient One, friends who left the day's challenges as cut up as I was, but did so willingly and gladly in service to God and their Queen. I was in the best physical shape of my life. I sprinted up steep hills while Unicorns poked at me with their sharp horns. I swam across the lake while Vogelkrötes tugged me downward. I sparred with Wühlenvogels, who were instructed by the swan to fight against me as if they were fighting for me. I dodged the blows of their hard horns and parried the thrusts of their chomping snouts. I flipped and spun and swung from trees until my arms could barely lift the weight of my hands. Had I been so well-trained, so fit for battle during the war, I could have vanquished many serpents single-handedly, and saved many sweet, innocent lives.

I saw so little of Joseph during those long months of intense training. As much as I missed him, I was relieved to have him so removed from the preparations for war, removed from the aches and pains that attacked me every night, skin to bone, and removed from the fate that the training prepared me to face. I'm not really sure who conducted the day-to-day business of the queendom. I was walled entirely from it in favor of my training. Either no thoughts came for me from the needy minds of my subjects, or my own mind simply could not juggle one more ball than the ones thrown at me by the swan's protective precautions.

Felix's love and attention each night revived me with a vengeance. I was reborn each morning, as new and fresh and ready for the day as any schoolgirl's first morning of summer break. I could never have done it without the greatest husband any human woman ever had. The healing power of his heated feathers and the miraculous tonic of his unfaltering love were the very ground upon which my body and spirit took their last steps every night and their first steps every morning. If I was to be the hand of God in the events to come, then Felix was the arm that held that hand in the air — and I have never known a stronger arm.

Nobody knew what battlefield would be chosen for the trials ahead of us. There were many debates and disagreements among those who had an opinion. There was just one notion we all shared, that whatever would happen was on its way, and would soon be upon us. And there was one more thing that only a few of us knew — that it would come at a great expense of blood. The cost of salvation has always been blood. It was true in the Gospels, true in the Swan Knights History, and so wretchedly true in my own experiences.

Joseph was left out of my training. He worked with Georg, who did plenty to keep the Guard ready for any eventuality. But his training was not associated with the Grail or the fate of mankind. It had to do with serving the Queen and protecting the palace. Joseph grew, in height and abilities. So did Senische, a fact that afforded both Lina and Acheriel greater liberty with each passing month. As the fever of destiny gripped the Sweeter Realm, as Eden felt its reunion with God's chosen creatures approach, Acheriel and his family made longer and more regular visits to the palace. Joseph and Senische grew close. They spent most of Joseph's free time gallivanting into the woods surrounding the lake, reaching farther out, for longer stretches, as their friendship grew.

The two of them spoke little to each other. Except when they wanted their conversation to be heard by others, they communicated directly into the other's mind. Under the stout and thoughtful guidance from her father, and the sentimental common-sense of Lina, Senische grew wise. Her influence over Joseph was as advantageous as it was profound. In keeping their most sacred correspondence private, however, they kept from me the burning ambitions that they stoked in each other's minds. They too trained as I did, secretly, in the hills and forests outside of the palace, unguided, and in preparation for a world entirely foreign to them both.

Despite Joseph's wisdom, his clandestined training with Senische bore all of the light heroics of children at play. They laughed as they slashed though imaginary enemies. And their mock-battles often transitioned in an instant to peaceful jaunts through a peaceful forest. I caught them in the palace one day, when Joseph was almost seven years old. They were in the throes of an imagined battle. Somehow, in their connected minds, the enemies they envisioned transitioned into a crowd of visitors, in the palace to view their collaborated works of art. The mob of imagined art-enthusiasts evolved into an audience gathered to watch them dance. In a matter of minutes, the war-cries of enemy soldiers became the applause of an audience witnessing their clumsy duet. I stood alone at the entrance to their room, watching in maternal delight as my son had fun with his friend, young, innocent, juvenile fun. I watched and delighted because I knew that such moments were few and in dire danger of extinction.

Since Joseph took his post in the Guard, and removed himself from his constant connection to me, his mind was absent from my lessons with Taufe and the swan, absent from the terrors that were piled upon my exhausted heart. This did not bother The Ancient One. He firmly believed that God's will was mine alone to bring about, and that Joseph's attention served only as another distraction from my preparations. I felt otherwise. That hint of darkness that infected Felix and me while Joseph was still in the womb lingered in our heads. Every second of my training carried a touch of dread with my son's name on it. Although he was kept from me by so many demands on us both. We still sought each other for a few moments each day, where we would share our thoughts, often over great distances, and I would hold his mind like an infant and sing to him the songs that soothed him to sleep when he was a baby. And I fell asleep with memories of his high-pitched laugh blending with Senische's as they fell upon each other in their playful dance.

The sight of my son at play, and even thoughts of my dearest ones, became increasingly rare. Demands from my subjects began to find me, despite The Ancient One's attempts to segregate and insulate me. Beside all that was thrust upon me, I slowly resumed many of the often-tedious tasks of queenship. Each day they crept into my schedule in greater number, until I was training just as vigorously with The Ancient One *and* settling the needs of the queendom, from mundane disputes to rare and monumental occurneces.

Months of busily balancing the duties of my elected position with the swan's relentless training and the spiritual guidance of Taufe seemed to speed time. Weeks rolled by like days and months like weeks. Joseph's seventh birthday came and went without my notice. Although the event carried little weight in the Sweeter Realm, it was unusual for me to allow a birthday to pass without recognition of some kind.

My duties caused me to travel, usually without my husband or son. In one instance, I was beckoned to Zweigwesen land, to a village called Wurzelstadt, to consult with their leadership over changes in their laws. Joseph came with me as a member of the small band of my Royal Guard. Georg and most of the Guard remained near the palace. My trip to Wurzelstadt was not part of any grand tour. It was less than half a day of travel, two days and two nights in consultation, then an immediate return to the palace. Georg entrusted my protection to Joseph and four other members of my Guard — a Wühlenvogel and three Scheriers. The event was to be quite ordinary, not promising anything to break the calendar's relentless spinning. But something did happen in Wurzelstadt, something significant.

Other than being a bit rushed, the trip to Wurzelstadt was unremarkable. The Scheriers of my Guard encountered an old friend from their days in the Portal Valley. She was a Zweigwesen who lived in the woods surrounding the lodge during the reign of King Ludwig I. She repaired and maintained the lodge while the Swan Knight Family was away. My Scheriers had not seen her since before I came through Parsifal's Portal. When they saw each other, the Scheriers sprinted at the Zweigwesen, appearing as one large, rolling ball of white fur. They dove on their old friend and wrestled with her on the floor of the forest. The spectacle ended as quickly as it began, delaying our voyage for only a few minutes. They all kissed each other, bid their adieus, and we were on our way again.

The details that impelled the visit were settled within our first few hours in Wurzelstadt, leaving that evening and the whole next day for leisure and celebrating the town's rare royal visit. The entire town gathered in the main hall, a large, cone-shaped building, made of at least two hundred logs on end, leaning against each other like the supports of a teepee. The space between the logs was filled with a sort of muddy thatch. In some sections, the thatch was hard and thick. In other areas, it was loose and thin enough to push a hand through. The entrance doorway was low, so that even I had to duck not to bump my head. Once inside, looking up, the room seemed to go on indefinitely.

A table was set on an elevated stage, about two feet higher than the floor. Seats at the table were reserved for the town leaders, my Royal Guard, Joseph, and me, with my seat and Joseph's centered. The rest of the congregation sat on the floor. Dinner was served. The food was blessed by Wurzelstadt's oldest resident — a Zweigwesen named Heilungslied. She had been in Albert's Battle as part of the Zweigwesen tree that descended upon the hunters and prize-seekers who attacked the valley that day. She had also worked beside the Swan Knight Milli as she constructed her medical manuscript. She was very dear to Milli, who affectionately nick-named her Helsie. The name stuck among her own kind. The whole town called her Helsie and revered her for her accomplishments in the

Portal Valley. She was among the leaders seated at our table.

The Zweigwesens are healers, and every breed in the Sweeter Realm had benefitted from their particular skills. For this reason, they, above all other breeds, were fascinated with Joseph's ability to mend bones and heal wounds. They hounded him on the subject, hardly allowing him to swallow a bite of food between questions. Finally, he collected their minds into a single pool of thought and answered all of their questions while his silent mouth went about the business of eating. The entire town delighted in the connection. They were very taken with him, and the evening, the entire visit to Wurzelstadt, became about Joseph, much more than it was about the laws we amended.

After dinner, they were reluctant to release Joseph's attention and return to their own huts. They begged for his answers to this and that, and for stories from the first seven years of his life. He regaled them graciously, but had already put in a strenuous day. He calmed them, gathered their attention, and led us all in the Vespers Hymn. For the first few verses, the crowd sang along — those few who knew it. But all voices quickly fell off, leaving only Joseph's. His sweet, young voice filled the entire hall, saturating the hearts of all in attendance. They were so touched by the holy purity and dynamic passion with which he sang, that they demanded more from him.

Joseph stood on his chair, at the middle of the table, and recited scripture. He included fiery personal commentary, delivered with impassioned eloquence, yielding insights that blew their minds and reshaped their faith. His high, young voice, his gestures, every wave of his little feathered arms was vivacious to an extraordinary degree. He spoke and he sang and he spoke some more. They were all mesmerized. I found *myself* captivated by his charisma. I was more intruiged by the reaction of the

Zweigwesens. I passed my eyes across them all and saw a crowd of creatures drinking his presentation as if their lives depended on it.

One Zweigwesen caught my particular attention. Helsie's eyes seemed to glow brighter than the others as she stared at my son. They seemed to reflect some invisible light radiating from Joseph whenever he sang. It is easy to understand. He was all ablaze from the sparks of inner-vision that shot from his eyes as he spoke and sang, and seemed to catch his bright, searing-hot feathers on fire. He shone with passion and he lit the room.

Something passed intimately between Joseph and Helsie, some thought shared by only the two of them, something entirely outside of the perceptions of us all. He turned quickly to face her, holding steady the one pure note he struck with his voice just before he turned. His note appeared to coax a dramatic change in her. The shy hints of orange that had been so reluctant to peek around her coarse brown hairs raised on the peaks of her heightened skin, transforming her color before our eyes and giving an outward reflection to the inner frenzy of spiritual hysteria brought forth by Joseph's song, like a cobra from a basket by a snake-charmer's flute. Within a second, a wave of bright-orange that began in the center of her chest washed outward to her extremities until her dearest relations would have no longer recognized the radiantly glowing figure who cast her orange glow onto the walls, furniture, and creatures around her. Her orange hair seemed to be reflecting the bright passions bellowing from Joseph's throat. He was the sun and she was the moon.

Nobody could help but witness Helsie's transformation and the effect that Joseph had on her. Few of us thought much of it. We understood. Joseph's address moved us all. Joseph thought more of it. Within seconds of witnessing Helsie's color change, his voice faltered before going silent. He stared at her, as mesmerized by her bright orange hair as she had been by his song. But when his steady note broke and died away, her orange inner hairs returned to the hermits they had always been. Her color transformed just as quickly back to the deep brown she was known for.

Her focus dropped downward, to her hands and long, splintery fingers that were stacked upon themselves on the table in front of her. His gaze to her remained fixed. His mouth hung open exactly as it had while he still sang his note, as if his jaw did not realize that his throat had gone silent and had no more to say. She looked up slowly at him, her eyes just barely beginning to swell. The mental chord of communion between them was obviously thick. I wondered what passed along it. I tried to look into his mind, but the thoughts were beyond me, too fast to make sense of and too bright to stare at for long. I abandoned the effort and turned my attention to her.

I saw easily into her mind. Her admiration for him was extreme. Her thoughts to him were prayerful — thoughts of great hope. There was an ardent love that could not be denied. But it was not at all a romantic love. It was connected tightly to her faith. It was not fondness. It was more than esteem. There was a glorification going on in her head. She gilded Joseph into some divine ornament on the face of God. I sensed a very different sort of emotion in Joseph, the particulars of which I could not discern. I was not uneasy with the strange connection. But it was something extraordinary and I intended to observe it closely.

I broke the awkward silence and the staring Zweigwesen eyes by rising from my seat and seizing the stage. I sang a recessional song from my old church in Colorado. I sang it in English and few understood. But the mood of the melody must have spoken to them. The hall began to empty as small clusters broke a few at a time and returned to their homes. I took Joseph by the hand and severed his chord of connection to Helsie by pulling him from the hall, into the paths of the town.

Outside of the hall, he began to shake, as if cold. I lifted him into my arms and carried him to the hut that was designated for me. He did not sleep with the Guard that night. He slept in his mother's arms, twitching thoughout the night from dreams that I could not see or soothe. Something had begun that night. Of that, I was certain. But the scope, depth, and nature of it was mysterious. I had never seen him so affected by another creature, never heard his voice falter or felt him shake under the influence of another — not since Reid. This was an event to be observed, an affair to be monitored.

CHAPTER 16
A Boy in Love

WITH THE BUSINESS OF THE TRIP so quickly settled, the following day was to have been calm and leisurely. Food, conversation, and casual strolls around the town should have been the only orders of the day. I was mere seconds out of sleep when I realized that the following hours had very different experiences to offer. I did not awaken with Joseph in my arms. I was alone. The only intimation of Joseph's proximity was the bursting sighs that bookended my son's agitated wimper. He was in extreme distress. This translated clearly to me through my ears. No other perceptions were necessary.

Joseph paced circles outside of our small hut. I thought a quick greeting to him, alerting him that I was awake. He ran inside, toe-to-toe with me, as if to consult with me on the direst, most urgent of matters.

"Is it too early?" he asked, "Is it too soon to reach for her mind? Do you think she is still asleep?"

The panting between his syllables, his inability to catch his breath, might lead one to believe he had been running for hours, rather than walking steady paces in a circle. Everything about him in that moment, the frantic speed of his thoughts, his crippling self-doubt, the rising of his feathers, and the heat coming off of his body, all struck me as intimately familiar. I had stood where he stood. Joseph was in love. He was only seven years old, and

Helsie was nearly a thousand. But that did not seem strange to me. What was strange was how very ordinary his feelings were, coming from a child who bore little of what is called common.

But still he was extraordinary. The pure and authentic depth of his affections are seldom met by the wisest adults. His young body forbade the interference of physical attraction with the admiration in his heart and head, making the spiritual attraction richer in its purity. Also very strange to me, as I peeked into his mind, was the disparity between the adolescence on display before my eyes and ears and the unalloyed concentration of mature affection that I struggled to grasp with my inferior mind. This was no childish crush. There was a refinement to his adoration that bordered on the divine.

He stood, panting, and desperately awaiting my answers to his questions. I did not know how to react. I could neither encourage nor discourage his love. I studdered in response, unable to shove a coherent thought to my lips. He dipped into my mind and found no more clarity there. Frustrated, he slammed his arms to his side and dove onto the bed where we had slept. He buried his face into the bed, with a rigid little body belly-down. He squeezed every muscle but did not move. I could scarcely even see the subtle rise and drop of his breathing.

I wanted to hold him, but he did not. I wanted to speak to him, but every word on the matter ran for cover deep inside of me and hid effectively from my probing throat. With a new sort of twist in my gut, I stared at him for several minutes before walking from the hut and seeking any company that might distract me out of the awkward and uncomfortable feeling I was under.

It is the way of the Zweigwesens to be up, amid the trees and grasses in time to greet the rising sun. By the time I left our hut, the sun had cleared the horizon by twice its width. Yet only a few of the Wurzelstadt natives broke the still air of the town. Helsie was among them. This was ideal. While the others recovered from a much later, much fuller night than their normal circumstances provided, I could speak with the subject of my son's affections and try to place the matter into some form that could be carried into our indefinite futures.

As I approached her, I notced immediately the vast and conspicuous difference between her disposition and Joseph's. Helsie was calm, blissful, and prayerful. She stood on the outskirts of the town, facing the rising sun, where a single beam of morning light wiggled its way between the trees to paint her face yellow. The rest of her body was not the brilliant orange that rose to attention at the call of Joseph's passionate voice the night before. It was her ordinary deep-brown. But there was a softness about her that I had never seen.

I whispered her name as I approached her from the side. She turned slowly to face me, as if the passage of time around her was distorted. Her face boasted no joyful smile, rather a contented grin. I begged her pardon. In a melodic half-whisper, she proudly told me that she had been in prayer, prayers of thanksgiving for the gift of Joseph to the creatures of the Sweeter Realm — not to her, but to every creature under that rising sun. I confess that I was greatly relieved to see that her esteem for Joseph was not of the same nature as his admiration of her. She thanked me for everything that I had done and been for them since coming to the Sweeter Realm.

I humbly accepted her gratitude and had just formed my mouth to mention Joseph's name when she raised the topic herself.

"Your son is the Godliest creature I have ever met."

The compliment from one who had known so many rinsed my anxiety away like mud under a heavy rain. In how many cases had my closeness to him and my maternal insticts blinded me to the miracle of his existence and the divine gift of his uniqueness? From their distance, my subjects seemed to have a clearer view of my son.

Helsie continued, "He is evidence that God has embraced us again. I awoke early this morning, after little sleep. But I awoke refreshed, by Divine love."

Her face went austere as she reached her long fingers to wrap around my forearm and added, "… still enshrouded by Joseph's words and the succulent complexity of his sweet little voice."

Her words were complimentary in the extreme, and they were words of love, but not love for Joseph. They spoke to her love of God, and Joseph was no more than a shining, brilliant representative of God's devotion to his creation. I am not going to say that it would have been imposible for a nine-hundred year old creature, with all of her vast experience, to fall in love with Joseph. But it was not the case here, not with Helsie.

Although I had spoken quite casually with her before, she looked at me, now sharing her beam of morning light, with new reverence. She ran her oaken fingertip along my jaw, from my right earlobe to my chin, leaving a trail of her sap. She stared into my eyes with a smile that widened as her eyes swelled shut. She whispered a thank-you, dropped slowly to her knees, and rubbed her face against the top of my feet, dropping a kiss as the tip her lips made contact with my skin. I gave her a blessing, lifted her to her feet, and left her to her drifting beam of sunlight, saying nothing to her of Joseph's feelings.

My encounter with Helsie left a euphoric sensation through me. But it deflated with my next thought of Joseph. He suffered an ache that was new to him and unlikely to fade quickly. There was nothing I could do and little I could say to him that would bear useful fruit. He was authentically devoted to her. He had the richness of mind and depth of spirit to fall into a real and ardent love. But he was seven. He had never felt anything like that before and he was entirely unequipped to decifer, categorize, and compartmentalize his feelings.

I returned to the hut where we had slept. Joseph stood in the center of the room, his arms flatly at his side and even his feathers seeming to droop in the wretched squalor of unobtainable desire. He wanted nearness to her in both body and mind. He would not enter her mind to gauge her affections. But he rode stealthily on the back of mine while I spoke to Helsie that morning. He saw what I saw, heard what I hear, and he knew the nature of her regard for him. His eyes were wide and his cheeks were dry, until he called to me, "Mother", in the sadest little voice. The word unplugged the cork of his emotions, freeing the torrent of tears that stood awaiting their release. I knelt on the floor and he stumbled into my arms.

He wept loudly. He didn't care who heard. Deep inside of the parts of him that only I could see, he wanted Helsie to hear him weep. It was the only way he permitted himself to express to her the depth of his affection. Of course we were in our hut and she was on the other side of the town. Most of the inhabitants still slept. Nobody heard him. It was a moment between a parent and her child, and as painful as it was to see him suffer, I took some pleasure in the rare opportunity to serve him as a mother should serve her son, comforting the pains of life.

The rest of the trip to Wurzelstadt would not go as planned. The festivities of the royal visit were an inappropriate backdrop to Joseph's fresh and stinging sorrows. I bid quiet, unstately farewells to our hosts and I took my son alone on the paths that lead back to the Nomadic Belt and the shore of the Queen's Lake, leaving my Wühlenvogel and four Scheriers as representatives on my behalf for the celebrations in Wurzelstadt.

Neither of us being large creatures, and both encumbered by the weight in our chests, we walked slowly. Joseph's spirit was as dark as the deepest part of the Deep Waters while they were still ruled by Löwschock. Back in Wurzelstadt, many thoughts were of us, many toasts raised in our honor, particularly Joseph's. These sentiments flew free and wild from their places of origin and found my mind. They found Joseph as well. But under the extreme gravity of his sorrow, they were sucked into oblivion. The Zweigwesens celebrated Joseph's rich mind and deep spirit — those precise attributes that allowed him to fall into such a real and captivating love, causing him such anguish. As I walked with him, seeing him, feeling them, the irony in the air was thick and pungent.

Evening came as we approached the Nomadic Belt. Some bands of Nomads were near, a cluster of Friends of the Scheriers, and some of Joseph's own Federmensch cousins. I beckoned them to join us and camp for the night on the southeast shore of the lake. Felix heard the call and rode Georg from the palace to our campsite. Felix sensed the heaviness in the air but could not imagine its source. The others remained entirely ignorant of the chaos that churned in Joseph's spirit. They spoke and joked with Joseph, whose lethargic responses did not seem to arouse suspicion. Even the Friends of the Scheriers, whose unintentional silliness always guaranteed a giggle from Joseph, could not contaminate him with their jovial antics.

Felix, being a Federman of heightened perception, asked me what was wrong. I prodded Joseph to confide in his father the way he had in me. He obeyed and entered his father's mind, sharing with him all that the previous day had brought into his life. The two of them went for a walk along the tree-line. When they returned, Joseph was determined to recover. Determination does not eliminate the trials required of success. All three of us understood that. And we braced ourselves for an indefinite period of mutual mourning.

We slept on the beach that night, the three of us in a tightly huddled bunch. It took me well into the night to close my eyes. They were held open by the silvery shimmer of the moonlight off the feathers of my family. Joseph blended into his father under the dim light. In trying to determine whose feathers were whose, I was struck by how similar they were, Felix and Joseph. I looked at Felix and saw, as I have always seen, all the goodness that adhered him to my affections in the first place. My eyes drifted to Joseph and I realized that he held all of those same traits, all of that goodness that I, in my weakness, struggle to understand.

That realization came with another. Felix fell in love with me the moment he saw me outside of Lina and Rüdiger's cave. Had he lost me, or had I for some reason been beyond his reach, he would have never loved another. That is the nature of his character, a nature, a purity and goodness inherited by his son. I knew that Joseph would never have Helsie, not as he desired her. He wanted her constantly with him, body and mind. He was ready to commit his life to her in a union modeled after his parents' marriage. He would have married her that night in Wurzelstadt, if he could have. His current pain brought a pinch to my heart. But an understanding of his character brought a much deeper sort of pain, one that reverberated off the walls of my inner-self like the dong of a heavy bell off the high walls and arches of an empty cathedral.

I knew that Joseph would never love like that again. A creature of his character does not recover from such a passion. He cannot simply gather the broken parts, reassemble them, and gift them to another later in life. Rare men of his sort are like that. They love that deeply only once in their lives. Unfortunately for him, it came when he was seven years old, and many circumstances converged to forbid the fruition of his desires. Joseph would never have the benefit of marrying the source of his passions, like his mother did and like his father did. Oh he could find romance. He could love. But what he felt for Helsie would never pass to another and it would haunt him for the rest of his life. I knew this as surely as I knew, from the moment I realized the depth and nature of Felix's love for me, that he would be mine forever.

Joseph had been stained by a curse only suffered by the noblest of creatures. I did not know what that meant for him, his happiness, or his fate. But I knew that he would never know the sort of bliss I experience every time I find myself in my husband's company. And the realization stabbed me more viciously than any serpent's fang or any hand-crafted wooden blade ever had.

Well before sunrise, while the nomads lay stone-still around us, Joseph aroused Felix and me when he wiggled free of our embrace. We watched him stand and start walking slowly toward the lake. We followed, hand-in-hand a few paces behind him. He waded knee-deep into the water, stopped, and stood still. He began to shake, convulsing from a cry he held back. Ripples from his shaking legs haloed out over the lake. A sound came up from the water in front of him, followed by an arc of tiny ripples returning to him, crashing against those that radiated from his knees. The source of both the sound and the ripples revealed themselves with the emergence of tiny, capped Vogelkröte heads. Several of them, a dozen perhaps, encircled him. They cried. Somehow they knew. I sensed no broadcast of his feelings across the water. Maybe the ripples themselves spoke to the compassionate little creatures. One thing is for certain. They mourned for him.

They sang their cries to him in doleful harmonies. Felix and I stood silently behind him, rubbing our thumbs against the other's hand.

After a few minutes, the Vogelkrötes disappeared into the lake and Joseph turned to face us. He looked better — relieved, however minutely, of the burden on his heart. The Nomads still slept. Joseph walked between us and wrapped his arms around our waists. With a slight push, he directed us along the shore, toward home.

"The Nomads," Felix reminded us, "if they awaken and we are gone..."

I stopped sharp, halting my feathered men, closed my eyes and crept into the shallow dreams of the nomads. I wove a simple message into the narratives of their dreams.

"Let's go," I told my family. "When the Nomads awaken, they will know where we are."

There was some lightness in the halo of love around us as we walked. We tried to keep conversation flowing. Every time there was a lull, Joseph reached his mind for Helsie, but was snapped back to his immediate company by the spark of a new topic. We arrived at the palace in late morning, just as the bustle of daily activities hit its zenith.

The palace was full, as I expected it to be. But it was not busy. That is to say, all business ceased before we broke the threshold of the entrance arch. Cort stood on an arm of the throne, surrounded by a group of Glühenchor. A Schildbüffel stood on his rear flippers, leaning against the other arm, like he was whispering something in Cort's ear. Georg and a few members of the Royal Guard stood behind the throne, frozen in a snapshot of some imagined battle. Every head in the main chamber was turned toward us before we came into their vision. They felt us. They felt Joseph. His sorrow proclaimed itself and froze the creatures as they stood. Felix begged them to return to their business as if we were not there. They slowly regained their

221

previous animation and the scene returned to normal as the three of us winded up the ramp to our rooms.

Joseph went immediately to bed and fell quickly to sleep. Throughout the afternnon and evening, I wandered into his room, sat beside him, and rubbed his head. I peaked into his dreams. The poor thing, too much like his father, dreamed of nothing but Helsie. They were ordinary dreams in ordinary circumstances. He sat beside her in conversation. They read to each other. They walked and sang. Dream after dream was of her, but calm, normal, everyday dreams. He rested soundly and I went to bed that night without alarm.

While I slept, my mind sought his and I fell into his dream. It was *not* an ordinary situation. It began similarly to the others. Joseph and Helsie sat atop a tall tree, facing each other and holding hands. She tenderly sapped his forehead. As she withdrew her fingertip, Joseph's fingers began to sap, followed by his toes, his elbows and knees, his nose, his eyelids, until sap seeped from every part of him. He was covered entirely in thick Zweigwesen secretions from his own body. Helsie called for him but her voice was muffled, and he could only see shadows through his amber encasing. She began wiping the sap from him, carving out thicker clumps as she tried to unbury him. Joseph was not beneath it. He had *become* the sap, and he stuck to her hands and arms as she frantically searched for him. Although still muffled, he could hear her calling to him.

Helsie sat at the top of the tree alone. Joseph coated her, more part of her than an individual. He seeped into her hair and skin. He was entirely inside of her, part of her. Yet she continued to call for him. He gathered himself into the sap glands of her forearms. She tried to secrete him through her fingertips, but he did not flow — until she began to sing. She sang to him. And as she did, he flowed through her hands and out of her fingertips, onto a young Zweigwesen, whose broken body healed instantly. With the opening of the young Zweigwesen's eyes, our eyes too opened, and we awoke from the dream together. Neither of us slept for the rest of that night. I lay still beside my sleeping husband while Joseph stared wide-eyed at the ceiling of his room. I did not communicate with him, but my mind simply held his mind. We remained like that until the sun rose and we could hear the first whispers of the day's palace activity.

We were not up for long when the realities behind our shared dream revealed themselves. Helsie's great-great nephew, a young Zweigwesen named Weichkern, built himself a playhouse. Late on the evening of our dream, his family could not find him. They searched the Zweigwesen wilderness and found the collapsed playhouse with Weichkern inside. He had been crushed beneath the collapsed structure for hours. His breath was shallow and what was left of his heartbeat was weak and irregular. His cousins extracted him from the structure and rushed him to Wurzelstadt. He had two feet in the grave. Life had little more than a few of his course hairs pinched between its fingers. Perhaps if he had been near Heiligborke they may have been able to save him. But their greatest healers and the great stores of Zweigwesen medicines were nowhere near Wurzelstadt. Weichkern would have died that night if not for Helsie's peculiar connection to Joseph.

Joseph slept when the Zweigwesens discovered the injured boy. But his mind was on Helsie and her mind was on her nephew. She reached for Joseph's mind, begging for his notorious healing power. She felt nothing in return. She sang to the dying boy. The power of her despair rode on the notes of her song, easily finding a sleeping mind that sought her subconsciously. The song connected her mind to his. She used him. While she sang, she healed the boy using Joseph's abilities. The dream was Joseph's thoughts trying to make sense of what happened while he slept.

According to those who witnessed it. Weichkern healed within a few seconds — entirely, from the edge of death to flawless health. It was only through Helsie's singing that she could channel Joseph's powers while he slept. Her song found a mind that wanted to be found by her. I summoned Helsie to the palace to discuss the incident with her and with the teachers. It was not uncommon for me to be dumbfounded by the events surrounding my son. But hesitation and anxiety always trailed closely behind. I trusted Helsie, and I never imagined she would abuse Joseph's affections for her. But her access to his mind and her ability to steer his powers to her own will made me very uneasy.

In a private room, with only the teachers and me, Helsie explained her degree of desperation to save her young clansman. She wanted us to be certain of that before she explained the event from her perspective. In her mind, she was not calling on Joseph, not exploiting a seven year old's abilities. She was calling on God and asking that the tools of God come to her call. Joseph's subconscious healing of the young Zweigwesen was God's favorite tool being wielded by the hand of God. That is how she saw it and Taufe agreed. A sticky film of apprehention remained affixed to the swan and me, unable to be washed away by Taufe's unfaultering faith.

I asked Helsie to speak nothing of what had happened and sent a rather stern decree to all who knew of the incident. The last thing I wanted was to open Joseph's mind to any and all who could gain by entering it and commandeering his unique gifts. Helsie was old and wise enough to understand my concerns, and she was too loyal to rebut, though she did not entirely agree. She returned to her home under a sworn oath of silence and a promise never again to sing her way into Joseph's dreams.

As it happened, she did not need to aim for Joseph's mind with her songs. His bond with her had already been profound, before Weichkern's healing. Any hope that Felix and I had of Joseph's speedy recovery from his obsession was dashed. When she ceased her song that night and recoiled into her own mind, she left a part of herself behind. Her voice, her melody, a portion of her very soul stained his brain. His desire to be with her increased and he was in severe, acute agony every moment he did not embrace her body and mind. He joined none of his normal activities. He did not study with the teachers. He did not ride with Senische. He hardly ate, and what little sleep he got was short and restless.

All of this was worsened daily by a phenomenon that took ahold of my son. Whenever Helsie sang, no matter how far away she was, whether alone or with others, the songs resonated loudly in Joseph's skull. More often than not, she remained unaware of the intrusion of her voice into his mind. But it gripped him ruthlessly. He sang along with her through his broken voice and violent sobs. This went on for weeks, and every possible distraction was thrown in front of him by his parents, teachers, and friends. None could gain traction. Things he had previously adored, things that had always seized his fancy, slid quickly from his attention no matter how aggressively we threw them at him. Helsie was all that existed, and her singing voice found him and haunted him each time she so much as hummed beneath her breath.

As desperate as I was to free my son from this relentless tether, it is not within the authority of the Queen of the Sweeter Realm to restrict the liberties of her subjects. I could not stop Helsie from singing. Even if the authority had been mine, I would never have wielded it. Nor could I go about my daily routines as if my son did not suffer. He was under a torment I could not fathom. The Ancient One compared it to his captivity in the Queen's Jail and the torturous things done to him there. I could give no orders to relieve my son, but I could make requests, appealing to the goodness of a creature whose nature ensured her cooperation.

I traveled alone to Wurzelstadt, unannounced, with no expectation or desire for the fanfare of a royal visit. My presence was noticed. But the inhabitants of the town knew that my visit was personal, and aside from the pleasantries that my celebrity natuarally attracted, they allowed me to go about my business in peace. I found Helsie and walked alone with her, deep into the neighboring woods. I explained the depths of Joseph's obsession for her. She was flattered beyond measure that she, among all of the fine creatures he has encountered, would be the one to strike him so deeply.

I told her about the songs that found him and gripped him so tightly that he could neither eat nor sleep. It distressed her profoundly that he was in such a state. And although she was deeply sorry for having used her song to find his mind and heal her nephew, she did not regret it. She felt in great debt to us and to Joseph, in light of what had ensued in its wake. For the life of her nephew, it was a debt she was willing to pay at any price. I asked her not to sing — not to hum or whistle or create music in any way. I was deeply hesitant to make such a request. But I was desperate. Her compassionate heart would have relieved my desperation at any cost. Between that and the debt she believed herself to owe, she happily submitted. She apologized in advance for any slip of the throat, any accidental tune that might escape her lips in a moment of mental wandering. I assured her that I was grateful for a whole-hearted attempt and I left the town as quietly as I had entered.

When I arrived back at the palace, Joseph was just as taciturn. But he seemed significantly less haunted. His obsession was much like any, not fueled by the pipeline of seductive melodies that had flowed almost constantly onto him before I spoke with Helsie. I was confident that time would eventually numb his pain, though I knew it would never remove it or fully bury it.

CHAPTER 17
A Friend's Healing Horn

HELSIE WAS TRUE TO HER PROMISE. She refrained from creating music with hands, throat, or lips. Unfortunately, the connection between them was much deeper than we knew. The melodies that she thought of found him and echoed in his skull as if nothing else was there. Memories of her own mother's voice and the songs she used to sing when Helsie was young flowed to Joseph the moment they immerged from the frozen depths of her deepest memories to flash for an instant in her conscious thoughts. He sang in time with the speed of her memories and she knew that he did. She tried to subdue every thought of music. It was quite consuming and torturous to a Zweigwesen whose long history was sewn together by songs.

Nevertheless she tried. The effort came with great sacrifices for her. In her goodness, she thought nothing of that, only of her loyalty and the debt she believed herself to owe to Joseph, to me as the Queen and vanquisher of Löwschock, and to her Swan Knight friends whose blood swam through my veins. Try as she might, it was no use. She could not help the memories that bubbled unannounced and uninvited to the surface of her thoughts. She did all that she could, but the obsession continued to grow and the melodies from Helsie's memories were often the only sounds to resonate in Joseph's throat during the course of an entire week.

Acheriel's position of prominence amoung his breed kept him always on his cloven hooves and saw him trotting the paths and streets on all corners of Rudolf's map, leaving Lina and Senische more regularly at the palace. Senische was increasingly frustrated with her inability to catch the eye of her best friend. One morning, seven or eight weeks after Joseph met Helsie and raised her orange hairs, I sat after breakfast with Lina and Senische.

Senische complained of her loneliness in Joseph's absence from her life, to which Lina responded, "You are the daughter of Prische, the greatest Unicorn of her age. Go to him and cure him as only a Unicorn can."

Senische bent her knees, slouched, and lowered her horn to the floor in front of Lina and said, "I am the daughter of Lina, the greatest Scherier of her age. I will cure him as only a Scherier can."

She slid her horn underneath Lina and flung her surrogate mother onto her shoulders. Lina pretended to be annoyed as Senische galloped around the room yelling, "Look at me. What a tall Scherier I am. I am the fastest Scherier in the Sweeter Realm."

She stopped beside me, bucked Lina from her shoulders into my arms, winked at us both and trotted up the spiraling ramp to Joseph's room.

I connected Lina's mind to mine and Senische's. We witnessed her enter Joseph's room. He was flat on his back in the center of the floor, humming a song from deep in Helsie's past, some tune I doubt Helsie knew she was recalling. Senische pushed the tip of her horn against Joseph neck. His singing stopped as if her horn dammed the flow between his heart and his mouth. His eyes flew open as hers struggled to push upward enough to see him through her shaggy eyebrows.

"Take my horn," she growled at him.

He tentatively pressed the fingertips of his right hand on her horn, lightly, as if holding something fragile.

"Grab my horn!" she yelled.

In an almost fearful reaction, he grabbed the horn with both hands and squeezed tightly. She lifted her head and raised him to his feet. She struggled to force her thoughts into his head, an action usually performed quite easily by Unicorns in a horn-connection. But his head was reluctant to push thoughts of Helsie aside to clear room for another.

Under the mental connection that I maintained, Lina whispered to her daughter, "Music, my daughter, wiggle your way in with music."

Senische thought of her favorite songs, Scherier songs, Unicorn songs, human and Federman songs that Joseph used to sing to her. The music found their way in and seeped through the tiny cracks in his obsession. Senische continued pushing them through her horn-connection to Joseph until the music they had shared reached the deepest parts of his mind. The moment his features softened in response, my excitement would no longer allow me to stay away. Lina and I ran up the ramp to Joseph's room, to witness the powerful miracle of a friend's love. I called to Felix's mind and he responded in seconds. He stood pressed against me. Lina climbed my back and stood on my shoulder while draping her chin across the top of Felix's head.

The tension that had rooted itself to Joseph's every muscle rolled off of him like water off The Ancient One's back. His mind was not free of his passion for Helsie, but his body was no longer clamped to the same fate. Senische's songs washed through him as his tears washed his cheeks.

With the gentlest, softest expression on his little face, he let go of the horn and looked up to Senische, who stood well taller than him. He placed his hands on the sides of her head and ran his palms along her long jaw, until his fingers met at her thin beard.

He dropped his gaze to the floor between her front hooves, as he rolled her beard hairs between his thumbs and fingers, repeating remorsefully, "I'm sorry. I'm sorry."

Thoughts passed between them that I cannot articulate. They were beyond language, thoughts and feelings that no word has ever been able to put its hands on. Sensiche giggled. Joseph did not. There was no happiness or bliss in his heart. But there was relief — tremendous relief from a torment that had nearly done him in. His love for Helsie was by no means weaker or less omnipresent inside of him. But it had to share him with his other loves that had been reawakened by Senische and her songs. Songs, music — that was the key. It was the key Helsie used to open his mind, though she was unable to pull it from the lock when she was done. It was the key Senische used to let herself into him. And it would be the key I must use to reclaim my son and restore some sense of balance to his life.

Joseph resumed his rides with Senische, allowing me to resume the often bruising training regimen prepared for me by The Ancient One. In the evenings, however, and first thing in the morning, my concerns were not over my own healing and recovery. I did not seek the comforts of my husband's arms. I sang. I sang to Joseph, filling his ears to the brim with melodies. In every spare moment of my day, in those sparse seconds when my thoughts could stray from my immediate surroundings and tasks, I connected with Joseph, trying to push music into him the way that Senische did. I strove to imitate the accomplishments of an eight-year-old Unicorn, and seep the notes from my childhood songs deeply enough into him to repel his obsession with Helsie to a safer distance.

Felix, having witnessed Joseph's horn-connection to Senische and the power of music over his son, sang to

Joseph throughout the day while I was away placing myself into violent scenarios and straining my body to its limits. He was joined in the effort by Cort, who had put into song almost everything I had done since coming into the Sweeter Realm and was so much more than pleased to recite his compositions to Joseph. Cort assembled a choir of Shallow swimmers to enrich his compositions through full orchestration. Buisiness in the palace remained as usual, but the motions of the throne room moved to the accompaniment of Cort's music. It was impossible to be in the palace without ears filled with melodies and the stories that rode upon the backs of the notes. With Helsie subduing her thoughts, and the constant songs flying from wall to wall in the palace, Joseph found himself more attached to his immediate surroundings than to the fossilized musical memories pressed into the deepest sediments of Helsie's past.

Joseph was in recovery mode. Everyone saw it that way, even the teachers, who placed no expectations on him beyond the gentle search for peace. Recovery was gradual. Acitivities in and around the palace regained a slight tint of normalcy. Joseph even began to mingle with the Royal Guard and on occasion stand a post. He played with Senische for hours at a time, still in love, still obsessed, but not crippled. As the following months went by, he cried less at night and slept more. Poor Helsie's life was on high alert, always terrified of mindlessly whistling a tune or thinking a powerful thought of Joseph that would yank him back into the gravity of his attraction to her. Only a creature of remarkable self-control could have done as she did. Only a friend of the deepest loyalty would have tried.

It took a year of ginger coaxing to bring Joseph back to the life and routines he had before that night in Wurzelstadt. He was again capable of lightheartedness, but always with a dark underlining of hopeless longing. There was a Helsie-colored stain on his heart that was as permanent as the dark smudge on Felix's arm. He had always been a thoughtful child. But in his case, thoughtfulness was perilous. Georg increased his shifts and patrols, never alone, always with a company of fellow Guards to keep conversation and distractions abundant. My and Felix's attentions to Joseph's tender heart slowly gave way to the demands of normal life. We did not forget about his broken heart, but we went days and weeks at a time without thinking of it. Life seemed to be back on track.

Ever-conscious of his oath, The Ancient One took responsibility for Joseph's recovery and growth. *All* efforts to that end were under his direction. He often took Joseph for long walks and conversed with him over topics collosal and mundane. The old swan had guided and motivated many of Parsifal's descendants, often saving them from themselves and their worse inclinations. He had gotten very good at it. His lessons with Joseph were not the sort of training inflicted upon me. They were purely philosophical and designed to keep him from any distraction, any fork in the road that might lead him away from his destiny.

This is how things went, month by month, for more than a year, until a rather unremarkable event broke that spinning cycle. Joseph turned nine, and The Ancient One's lingering and habitual loyalty to the Laws of Ermenrich enflamed. He was known for that, for occasional eruptions of sentiment and phases of obsession with some thing or another from the Swan Knights History. The centuries of strict adherence to the Laws of Ermenrich rooted the traditions deeply to his sensibilities. As Joseph's ninth birthday approached, the swan was dreamy and easily flustered. When the birthday came, the routines that had governed us for the previous years had to yield to the arcane rules of bygone days.

Joseph took a greater share of the teachers' attention, preparing him to "assist" his mother in her trials ahead. His long walks with The Ancient One turned to much more rigorous training. There was no Swan Knight in Linderhof to slowly walk Joseph toward his portal trigger-point, to delight in his surprise as the hole of nothingness crackled open in front of him for the first time. The swan could not appear through the portal and introduce himself to the new First-in-Training. The Ancient One felt this deficiently keenly in his nostalgic old head. To compensate, he reembraced — perhaps over-embraced — what Swan Knight traditions *were* at his disposal.

Joseph's ninth birthday brought the boy a dramatic change in lifestyle. His position with the Guard became more honorary than practical, as his schedule forbade the regimen of shifts and training required of the Guards. Senische joined him in the classroom. Georg, while still serving as Captain, took control of Joseph's practical training. Joseph trained like so many First-in-Training did before him, preparing him for battles like those fought in the earliest days of the Portal Valley.

There was no question that he was First-in-Training and I was the Swan Knight. Despite the gravity of the unknown tasks ahead, foreshadowed by scripture and the visions of the clerics, his training was designed to be light and often frivolous, not at all like the dire and dangerous preparations that carved out the majority of my days. But Joseph attacked his lessons very differently than they were intended. There were things he knew that none of us knew, things he saw that were beyond the most penetrating visions of the clerics.

He laughed, but not the laugh of ignorant bliss. His was the laugh of infinite perspective. He cherished moments like his playful times with Senische because he knew how precious they were. He was aware of the brevity of life, but rather than terrorizing him, as that realization does in most, it only served to gild the pleasures of life more resplendently in his eyes. His Helsie-stained heart no longer looked dirty and pathetic. Still in love, the stain was a badge of nobility he wore with more pride than pain.

In his mind, he did not ride and train to assist his mother. He had a much greater awareness of his destiny than Georg or Senische. He grew up before his time. The theological symposiums that he attended in the womb launched a life that was destined to be extraordinary — or doomed to be. He fell deeply into an authentic, mature love at the age of seven. He had his heart broken and he recovered. There was nothing shallow and frivolous about him. And his long philosophical walks with The Ancient One ignited his fervent sense of duty.

At nine years old, there was little that was child-like left inside of him. He trained with a vicious seriousness and the fire of holy righteousness. He was ready to sacrifice his life for God. And in our daily connections, he proclaimed as much to me, which frightened me exceedingly. But he did all of this with a lighter heart than his own understandings should have permitted. I suffered and bled in my training. So did Joseph. But while I did so through a deeply rooted sense of obligation, Joseph suffered with pleasure. His pain brought a smile to his face, as did all premonitions of future struggles and sacrifice. He was so much better than me, so far above and beyond me, even at nine years old.

Senische had too much Scherier influence to be so austere. It was only in her company that Joseph showed signs of being a child. Scherier playfulness shone off her coat with a gleam that spoke of Lina's parenting. But as powerful as Scherier playfulness, is Scherier heroism. This too displayed itself demonstratively in Senische's signature spirit. It was in this area that Joseph and Senische bonded most tightly. Senische reached her full height by the age of three. But she was gangly, awkward and underweight until she was seven. By the time she trained with Joseph, she had grown tall and stout, strong, fast, and remarkably insightful. The daughter of Acheriel and Prische, raised with the Scherier traditions and sensibilities of her surrogate mother, constructed a child unlike anything the Sweeter Realm had seen. She carried the best of both breeds, the best of each of her many eclectic influences, and she was the perfect friend for my son. She kept him playful like the Scheriers, loyal and self-sacrificing like Lina, but with all of the staunch merits of the Unicorn Collective.

Joseph was small, even for a Federman. Senische was almost too much Unicorn for him to ride. But he continued to grow long after she had stopped. By the time he was ten, he had reached his father's height. A year later, he was as tall as me. The hair on his head grew coarse, something between hair and feathers, but soft to the stroke. The feathers of his head and back were fully grown, strong, thick, and course, and able to warm to a searing heat at his command. His training had brought his strength to rival Felix's. He and Senische made a powerful team, with speed and agility matched only by the other. No Swan Knight, not even Elsa or Otto could match his skills on Unicorn-back. He and Senische rode as one. They rode through the lands of the Sweeter Realm. They saw every lake, every forest and hill, every city. Yet with all of that, they still portioned the necessary time to Georg, the Ancient One, and Taufe — and occasionally to their parents.

Lina missed her daughter terribly, as I did my son. But we found shared comfort in our shared distress, and in the renewed intimacy of that friendship that saw me through my first few years in the Sweeter Realm. When we needed to be alone and have only each other and our shared memories as company, Lina and I went to her old cave where she lived with Rüdiger. In that cave, where I first met her, those sentiments that bound us most tightly were further thickened and strengthened. Lina was again mine, and I hers. Belonging to each other had much more depth than it did when she guided me through Eineklaue all those years earlier. She had mothered a Unicorn and lived in the Unicorn culture, while ever mourning her husband. Our paths had diverged when she accepted Senische as her own. Our reconnection easily bridged that divide. My love for her had forgotten nothing, and it wore the newness of our reconnection as a beautiful accessory above all that we shared.

Those were strenuous years for me. Training bloodied me. Queenship spread me thin. My marriage wiped up the last few drops of my time and energy. I hardly saw my son, hardly had time to connect with his mind. But when it all became too much for me, there, waiting to wisk me away and soothe me with familiar conversation and some bark tea, was Lina. She was the strongest line of continuity in a life that had given and taken so much from me. Much of what I have documented in this account was dislodged from the hardened depths of my memory by my nostalgic reminiscing with Lina. I often thought about Senische's service to Joseph, cramming music into his head and healing him with the love of a friend. Lina provided a similar service to me, but instead of song, she used stories, like only she can tell them.

CHAPTER 18
Expansion and Beckoning

THE MANY PULLS ON JOSEPH'S TIME and attention permitted few hobbies. What leisure time he had, he committed to singing. Usually this was only in passing between his various obligations. He was always a singing child, since his earliest days. It was often his emotional outlet, for his love of God, friends, and parents. I sang to him (as well as I could) since the morning after his conception. His exposure to the Benedictine Psalter and the Vespers Hymn gave him an extensive education in music before he took a single formal lesson. But his deepest draw to music was attached to him through his lingering love for Helsie. That night when she commandeered his abilities with song, she paved a highway to his heart, a passage exclusively for music's use.

The hand that had squeezed his heart with that relentlessly clutching grip had musical fingers. As the emotions of the matter gradually yielded to his reasoning, he began to appreciate the power that music had over his heart. He gained the ability to view the whole thing academically. As he did, he began to see the power of music over all creatures. It intrigued him. He saw the potential for good that music could provide to his already phenomenal abilities.

He made an independent study of music theory, and as he grew older, and he and Senische ventured deeper into the wider realm, he took a strong interest in the musical traditions of the various breeds. His compassion for the creatures attracted him to their most passionate outlet. Much of the Sweeter Realm's oral histories and folklore have been passed in song. Their stories transfixed Joseph, a power that was tightened by the allure that music still held for him and had quick and easy access to his innermost being along that direct highway that music had already paved into his heart.

The folksongs of the various breeds became Joseph's deepest connection to the creatures. While he sang their songs, particularly when singing with them, he connected deeply to their thoughts — not only their thoughts, but much more. He saw memories that were not at the tops of their minds, even memories long forgotten. He felt feelings from their childhoods, hundreds, and in some cases, more than a thousand years old. He began to connect with songs being sung far away. Thoughts that would have sought him anyway, rode to him more quickly and freely on the wings of music.

Eventually, he was able to reconnect intimately with Helsie, without placing his heart on a slippery slope to obsession. She sang again, and he allowed his heart's weakness for her to expand the experience. She was old and kept many of her breed's stories in songs that sat tucked away in her head, waiting for a good reason to be rejuvenated by fresh and eager ears. Joseph allowed his love for her to take him more deeply and vividly through her mind than he could through others. In doing so, he doubled his abilities and broadened his access to all minds.

Late one night, when he was eleven years old, I heard Joseph's singing voice echoing through the palace halls. It rang with rich compassion and deep spirituality. I followed his voice into the throne room, where I saw him standing at the edge of the entrance pool, singing to the lake in front of him. He sang in Vogelkröte.

"What are you doing?" I interrupted from behind.

He took a few seconds to complete the phrase and bring the song to a gentle conclusion.

He turned slowly to me, to reveal the full journey of a few tears, from eyes to chin, where they seemed to reluctantly release his face and fall to the floor.

"Oh sweetheart," I inquired in a panic, "what is wrong?"

Joseph began to speak, but his first syllable was interrupted by a burst of an impromptu giggle through his nose.

He calmed himself and answered, "He is all better now. I fixed him."

I gave him an inquisitive look that beckoned an explanation. He closed his eyes and connected my mind to a young Vogelkröte named Gaier. He pulled me through Gaier's memories. It was so much clearer, so vivid and abundant, much, much more than anything I could have accomplished with my own abilities. I saw a brave young Vogelkröte alone, exploring the abandoned passageways of the Deep. A tunnel collapsed on him, injuring his back. He spent the day alone, unable to move, helplessly squeezed, crushed by the fallen structure. He was not in the Queen's lake, but beneath the bed of a deep lake on the far northern edge of Wühlenvogel land.

Gaier lay immobile into the night. As he felt himself slipping from life, he sang. He sang the prayers of his breed, in an ancient melody passed through the centuries. The song easisly found its way into Joseph's mind while he slept, waking him and connecting him immediately and intimately to the poor creature. Joseph ran to the edge of the water, at the entrance pool of the palace. He sang the Vogelkröte song, rippling the water in front of him and sending the vibrations across the Queen's Lake. Joseph's voice followed every hidden tunnel and wet passage between the palace and the distant lake. Every Vogelkröte between my son and Gaier heard the call.

In Gaier's memory, I felt Joseph's voice reach the collapsed tunnel, travel through Gaier's broken body, and begin the healing. The fallen rock and sand lifted and packed, regaining its previous form and opening the passage for a school of rescuers. By the time Gaier's kin reached him, his body tingled with Joseph's voice, reverberating off of water, stone, and bone, until Gaier was healed of all injuries. The rescuers were not needed. The adventurous young Vogelkröte swam from the tunnel under the strength of his own back. The entire school of creatures sang their prayers of thanksgiving to God for Joseph's compassion and powers. Joseph stood in the throne room of the palace, far away from the Vogelkrötes, and sang with them. It was that song that I interrupted.

When Joseph pulled me from Gaier's memories and returned my consciousness to my own skull, I was sweating. I stood within inches of my son and felt the heat radiating from his feathers. When I pulled him into me for the proudest embrace I had ever given him, his feathers were almost too hot to touch. But I bore the discomfort with joy in my heart, and I refused to release him, even when he asked to go back to bed. I sat him on my lap, seated on the throne, held him, and sang his favorite Federman lullabies until he fell asleep. While I held him and sang, I pondered strenuously on what I had just experienced.

Joseph had not sought Gaier. The prayerful song of the Vogelkröte found him, woke him, and drew him into service. He was only eleven, still my baby. But every painful or sorrowful song, sung anywhere in the entire Sweeter Realm, seemed to knock at his door with great liberty. I felt myself losing him to the needs of the queendom. My motherhood repelled the idea, while my queenship embraced it. Such duality of spirit put a tremendous strain on me. But I continued to sing, and my child rested in my arms with the peaceful face of a sleeping newborn. Another apposing duality struck my maternal heart. The boy I held was a soft and innocent child, while being a creature of immense power. My heart tried to reconcile the contrast while I sang. In the ultimate failure of that attempt, I carried my son to his bed and returned to the comfort of my husband's feathers.

After the incident with the Vogelkröte, Joseph's compassion was heightened. His tender heart was an antenna, receiving the most extreme emotions felt in the world around him. Many of those feelings came with the conscious thoughts of forlorn creatures who sought Joseph's abilities. Most did not. Most of the thoughts sought Joseph's receptive and tender benevolence without the will of their owners. Those were the most penetrating — those peppery, stinging sentiments and sensations felt most agonizingly severe by the suffering.

All extremities of emotion traveled the Sweeter Realm to find Joseph. But the brighter feelings took their time, wandering freely and enjoying the journey. Those emotions most excruciating, most putrid, rushed to Joseph quickly and directly, and did not slow upon approach. They crashed into him violently. Taufe tried to encourage the ability, seeing only the beauty of God in the rich compassionate fits that seized my son in the blink of an Eulesänger. The Ancient One, more cerebral than spiritual, felt differently. He saw the pain that glossed Joseph's benevolent and commiserative eyes as unnecessary and even disruptive to his development.

Both teachers intensified their lessons, both in opposition to the will of the other. With a heart full of love for them both, my maternal instincts inclined me in favor of the swan. I, who had suffered the experience of death inside of the mind of a beloved friend, whose mind had been seized by the tormented thoughts of another, was the only one who approached an understanding of Joseph's long, sleepless nights. There was always someone to help or to heal, always someone in pain or distress, someone lonely or sad. And Joseph would not allow a moment of pain, in the entire queendom, that he could prevent.

The Ancient One tried to occupy Joseph's mind with academic study and physical exertion, which would have worked on me. But Joseph's mind was so much more complex than mine. He could recite the legends of Sweeter Realm lore to the swan while caressing the saddened hearts and mending the broken bodies of many creatures at a time, spread across the homelands, though the toll on him was severe.

The more creatures he connected to, and the more he shared in their joys and pains, the more Joseph came to love the Sweeter Realm and its inhabitants. He knew them far better than I, in many cases, better than their own families. Each day more minds found him, adding to a pool of thought in his head that seemed to have no limits. His mental activities began to seep into his physical functions, as he struggled to isolate and individualize the many voices inside of him.

One evening, while enjoying a rare dinner alone as a family, Felix, Joseph, and I were soothing ourselves and each other with an ordinary, mundane conversation about petty matters. In the middle of a sentence about walking in thick mud, Joseph transitioned instantly into one of the multitude of mental conversations he was having with some creature far away. Joseph did not realize that his mouth spoke to his parents what his mind was saying to the distant creature, that his voice released our conversation and gripped another. The experience was deeply unsettling for Felix and me.

We stared at him, trying to make sense of the abrupt change in subject matter and tone. I figured out the phenomenon behind the behavior before Felix did. Another mental connection hijacked Joseph's mouth in mid-sentence, displaying another dramatic and abrupt alteration in subject and tone. When it happened a third time, the language of the conversation changed from German to Schildbüffel. That is when Felix realized that Joseph's voice bounced from one simultaneous conversation to another.

Felix gasped with the realization, jolting Joseph's consciousness back to his physical surroundings. At that moment, he finished his thought about running in thick mud, as if it had not been interrupted. The whole bizarre scene made it clear that, as vast as Joseph's mind was, his abilities were beginning to interfere with the functions of daily life. But there seemed to be no barrier we could construct around him that would keep the creatures from seeking him and his constant mental companionship. So we tried to expand his mind so that he could hold all of those conversations while conducting his routines with some semblance of normalcy.

By the time he was thirteen, he must have had thousands, tens of thousands of individuals in his head at any given moment, night or day. And he loved them all dearly. He could not simply heal, detach, and move on to the next. Once he connected closely with a creature, he was in love, and had to remain an intimate part of that creature's life. The days simply did not provide enough hours. The wear on Joseph was obvious. His bloom faded. He was often sick and always under-slept.

I began to long for the days when his richly empassioned love had only one target, Helsie. I even asked

Helsie to draw him in, if only deeply enough to drown out a few hundred of the other connections in his head. She tried. Had she been in love with him, and the prospect of a life with her been possible, it probably would have worked. But it was his love for Helsie that heightened his ability, and each time she reconnected with him, the effort seemed only to broaden and strengthen his connection to the wider realm.

His deteriorating state worried me excessively. I tried to leap into his thoughts. But they swirled chaotically with so much more than my mind could grasp — too many voices, too many experiences, pains and pleasures. I had connected with each creature in my queendom. I had even projected thoughts to them all at once. But Joseph lived their lives with them, moment by moment, through the profound and mundane moments of their days and nights. They took great comfort and pleasure in his constant company and refused to relinquish his connection. They felt invincible and deeply loved when he shared their minds, as if they walked, flew, and swam with God's angels.

He was as loathed to leave them as they were to let him go. But Felix and I, Joseph's Federmensch family, the teachers, and our dearest ones were greatly concerned by the rapid decline in his health. I was intensely jealous of Joseph's time and focus that was once mine alone. I did not envy him for having abilities so far beyond mine. I envied the creatures of my queendom for sharing and intimacy with Joseph that once belonged only to his mother. I felt him slipping from me, both mind and body. I often held him at night. He was half-asleep, half-awake. His exhausted body twitched as it tried to sleep but was kept in agitation by the thousands of lives in his mind. I wanted to shove him back into my womb and enjoy the intimate mental connection that was ours alone before he was born.

I tried to relieve his burden by seeking the pains of my subjects and soothing them myself. My own ability to connect the minds of my queendom, which seemed so magnificent when it first blossomed inside of me, paled in comparison to Joseph's. I could take sereral burdens at a time, from small groups of creatures, but only when they were together and shared the same distress. Other than that, I could only take one at a time, like taking one pebble at a time when trying to level a mountain.

Still, I tried. And the obvious futility of my efforts only motivated me to try harder — and fail harder. No amount of busy assignments, intense study or distractions could shield him from the incessant bombardment of thoughts. He still rode with Senische, and conversed with her, laughed with her, but he did so in the mental company of a multitude. And just like that evening at the dinner table, the words and movements of his body would often suddenly and inadvertently react to what his mind was experiencing with some other creature near or far.

I tried to forbid the connections. I appealed to the queendom with all of my authority and influence. But it did little. Most of the connections to Joseph were made subconsciously or in the spur of a desperate moment. Many were sought by Joseph simply because he had grown to love them. All my intervention managed to do was create guilt in the minds of those who, whether consciously or not, found themselves in communion with Joseph.

Taufe, ever alert to my slightest signs of distress, left me abruptly. She went to St. Hildegard, claiming that a matter of paramount importance must be decided among the sisters there. When she returned, Joseph had just turned fourteen. She abandoned all of her lessons with me and most of her lessons with Joseph. In their place was an all-consuming curriculum of music. Joseph spent all of his time with Taufe. It was the one subject capable of consuming and distracting him, at least momentarily, from the thousands of minds tugging on his attention.

The songs focused him on the subject at hand and incoming thoughts that sought his mind seemed to bounce off of the melodies reverberating inside of his chest and throat. The subject was music, an activity that had magnified, not diminished, the width and intensity of his connections. But the subject of the songs chosen by Taufe was the Grail. She gathered every Grail song in the Sweeter Realm. The Boots of Lohengrin had hundreds of such songs. Taufe decided to rekindle his fixation. She knew that Joseph's obsession with the Grail and his love of music would combine to focus him. She was right. It worked.

Joseph's days were filled with melodies, both new and ancient, each dedicated to his favorite topic. His concentration on the Grail, the portal, and the Swan Knights pulled another divine ability from him. He found himself in hazy, weak, but undoubted communication with the Swan Knights. Their spirits swam in his Grail Blood and his receptive mind gave them a window into the world of the living. This new ability fascinated the swan, who was desperate to reconnect with so many lost loved ones. Joseph's skull became like the Unicorn altar in Gemeinsam, only no horn and no stone was needed. He connected with his ancestors over their shared dedication to the Holy Grail.

No Swan Knight ever really understood what life in the valley was like for The Ancient One. He helped kindle the romances that resulted in the births of the children he taught and raised. He buried the Swan Knights, only to swear the next one into duty. He fought beside them, held them when they cried, sang with them when they were joyful, and shook with them when they faced their shared dangers. He was teacher, father, brother, and counselor to them all. But they died and he lived on. He ran his wing across the infant hairs of their heads when they were born, only to kiss their grey, wrinkled heads when they died. Joseph gave him the opportunity to be with them again.

I had performed that service. I connected him with Parsifal, quite accidentally, when I uncovered the Grail in Gemeinsam. But Joseph could do it on command, with whichever Swan Knight had something to say to him. It became the swan's only reason to wake in the morning. He followed Joseph everywhere. He sat in on Taufe's music lessons, just waiting for Joseph to toss him a morsel of thought from his abundant table of Swan Knights. I was afraid that his connections with the Swan Knights of old would simply replace the minds of the Sweeter Realm with a different kind of strain. But I was wrong. The spirits of the Swan Knights did not tax Joseph's mind like the desperation of the living. During his waking hours, despite the swan hanging perpetually on his heels, Joseph was calm, and his mind seemed to carry no more than it was comfortable carrying.

But his nights were still haunted by the lonely and suffering, whose conscious and unconscious minds still sought him jealously. Things were better, but Joseph's health required isolating a mind that no walls could contain.

When Lent came that year, Taufe suggested that he spend it in St. Hildegard, cloistered like a monk with the Brunnen sisters of the city.

"It will slow him down," she promised me. "Prayer and music all day and night... by Easter, he should be calmer, tranquil and reflective, a different creature entirely from the burdened boy we see now."

Reflective, she said, with his thoughts inward and his magnificent abilities set on healing himself, rather than others. I desired that greatly. Plus, I knew how distracting and indulgent the tender and benevolent hands of the

Brunnens can be. I thought it a perfect scheme. Taufe arranged it all. Joseph joined the choir of St. Hildegard Cathedral and entered a Benedictine life on Ash Wednesday of his fifteenth year.

Every Brunnen of St. Hildegard came to the palace to escort him. I rode with them to the edge of the Nomadic Belt. Under the strenuously suggested advice of the Brunnens, I left the party there and returned alone to the palace. Leaving him was not difficult. I never felt so good about departing from my son. There was a bright, warm sense of hope in the scheme that I allowed to shine on me while I slowly walked back to the shore. Perhaps I would have been apprehensive had those same Brunnens, that same city and cathedral, those same soft beds and baths not already performed for me exactly that which I hoped they would perform for Joseph. I could not have been more shattered of spirit than I was after the fall from the cliff, when I thought I had killed Felix. My spiritual recovery in the hands of Taufe and the Brunnens of St. Hildegard was miraculous. I could imagine Joseph in no better situation.

The sisters calmed him as promised. He kept his thoughts in his own head and left the thoughts of others alone. He studied, prayed, and sang, rarely leaving the cathedral and its many side chambers — never leaving the city. The songs he sang were not the songs of Sweeter Realm lore, or the wailing warbling of sad creatures. They were Lenten songs of Christ's love. They were reminders of the Passion of Christ and all that the Lord suffered on our behalf. They were Benedictine songs of contrition. They were spirituals that served to connect his mind to God. During song, his voice and his thoughts were locked into the sounds of the Brunnen choir of St. Hildegard, implacably fixed between the harmonies, like a layer of sediment deep beneath the surface. Nothing else touched him and he touched nothing else.

He received the nurturing caresses of Brunnen fingers, and he relished his own healing, his own pleasures. He rediscovered the momentary sensations of his body. The hunger of fasting, the relief of eating again, the taste of foods, the sweet breeze of Brunnen land through his feathers, Brunnen fingertips across his forehead and temples were all given his full attention in their turn. He listened to the intelligence of nature, allowing himself to be spoken to by the growth patterns of the grass, the whisper of the wind, the giggle of flowing water. The Brunnens managed to clear his mind enough for these things to speak to him.

I learned of Joseph's progress through Taufe. I sought her mind nightly for updates. The news was so encouraging, and lifted my concerns so effectively, it liberated me again to miss my son, to wish him again in my arms. I felt quite lonely without our regular connections of the mind. The absence of his thoughts gave me a cold and hollow feeling. But I dared no breach the dam around his mind constructed by the sisters. My senses missed him equally. They were suddenly and comprehensively bereft of the sight, sound, touch, and smell of him. But I knew what good could come of it, and I left him in the peaceful, placid company of the Brunnens. Two weeks before Easter, Taufe returned to me, to help prepare me for our holiest holiday.

Joseph was to remain in St. Hildegard until after Good Friday, and join his mother and father for the Easter Celebrations in the palace, escorted on the swift shoulders of Senische. He surprised me, when without the slightest intimation, he appeared at the palace on Palm Sunday, one week before Easter. I was startled to see him, and I ran my thoughts through the many possible misfortunes that could have conspired to bring him home early.

"No, no, no Mother, it is nothing like that," he comforted me after peeking into my thoughts, while he splashed his way across the submerged court in front of the throne.

"It is about the Grail," he continued in a ghostly whisper.

Both curious and disturbed, I began to ask him to explain. He quieted me with a thought, then summoned his father.

Felix was in a hilly portion of forest, just outside of the beach, not far from where I first met Cort. A clan of Friends of the Scheriers hosted him. At his son's call, and without a word to his hosts, Felix ran at full speed along the beach and to the palace, never resting or even slowing his pace, and leaving the frantically following Friends completely behind him.

Joseph would not elaborate on his hint until Felix arrived. We met him in the throne room. Joseph led us to his classroom and called his teachers to join. The Ancient One and Taufe entered together, as intrigued as I.

Once we all settled in, Joseph explained, "Three nights ago, I had a dream. I stood on the rim of the Holy Grail. I was no larger than a Scherier's finger. Christ held the Cup and lifted it to his lips. I called to my Lord, but he did not hear me. He did not acknowledge me. When he tilted the Grail toward him, I fell in. Jesus drank from the Grail and swallowed me. Everything went black and silent. The blackness turned to bright and the silence turned to the noises of battle. Swords clanged. Men and women screamed. Guns fired. It was all so loud."

Joseph was clearly disturbed by the recollection. He held his hands over his ears and hunched as if in pain. I rubbed his head and kissed his cheek. Taufe caressed his arm, while Felix and the swan followed in kind.

"Go on," The Ancient One prompted him with both compassion and impatience.

Joseph recovered his stance and resumed, "I fell from the wound in Jesus' side, onto a field where men and women fought. They hit and kicked each other. They bit and scratched and struck each other with objects of all kinds, things from their lives, trinkets and jewelry, books and purses and figurines, pens and eye glasses, chairs and picture frames. There were no armies, no sides pitted against each other. It was each against all, in chaotic and mindless violence. They screamed words that I have never heard, in languages I did not know."

Joseph began to cry as he spoke. Tears streamed down his cloud-white cheeks and rolled off of his chest feathers and onto his feet. I cried with him. The sensual complexities of his memories did not pass directly into my mind, only the distress that he felt as he spoke. His agitation was severe.

Taufe gave him a long and steady "Shhhhhh", accompanied by gentle strokes on his temples with her fingertips. Felix held his hands and kissed his knuckles.

After about a minute, the swan interrupted, "Go on, boy. What happened next?"

"I could not see their thoughts. They could not hear mine. I could not command their bodies or heal their wounds. I dropped to my knees and screamed. The scream softened as my breath weakened. When my breath ran dry, the scream continued. But it was not mine. It turned to a sweet tone, a Brunnen voice, harmonizing with itself. My mouth was closed, but the pure note came from me, radiating outward from my feathers. I looked at myself but could not tell where the music came from. When I looked up again, the fighting had stopped. An endless field, filled with an endless lake of people, stood motionless, staring at me, still bruised and bleeding from their deep lacerations.

Their blood poured from them, pooling at their feet, rising, covering the field, rising up to our knees, higher and higher, until we swam in it. From standing, to wading, to swimming in their blood, they just stared at me as if to beg for my help."

One forceful thought interrupted his narrative. It was his memory of almost drowning in the Queen's Lake, when he was one year old. He held his breath and began to shake. I begged him to breathe. When he did again, he did so with desperate gasps, like the air in the palace did not satisfy his lungs.

He slowed his gasps and continued, short of breath, unprompted by the swan, whose compassion overpowered his curiosity, "We sank. We sank into the blood of the people. I fought for the surface. When I found it, I was again in the Holy Grail, with all of God's people, all around me, all fighting to stay afloat. Again, Christ took the Cup and swallowed us all. I felt as if I was falling. When the sensation subsided, I opened my eyes. I was in the Unicorn fields, and God's people walked in all directions around me, casually, happily, peacefully, with loving, contented smiles. They talked to one another in the languages of the Sweeter Realm. They did not see me. They did not know me. I began to melt into the high grass. I called for you, Mother. But I could not find you before I melted away."

He gave a long sigh, followed by a much longer held breath before drawing in the air of the palace.

"What happened next?" I asked him.

"I woke up... with a forceful sense of finality, both peaceful and remorseful, content and regretful. I told nobody of the dream. The next night, I had the dream again, exactly as before. I left for home that morning on the shoulders of Senische. I stayed that night in Gemeinsam, where I had the dream a third time. My mind spun as I traveled. I prayed. I listened for God's command. By the time I saw the palace, I knew what the dream was meant to tell me. God wants me to retrieve the Holy Grail, to have it in my hands on Thursday, when we commemorate his Last Supper and the first consecration of the Holy Eucharist."

"For what purpose?" Taufe asked, ready to commit her faithful heart to whatever came from his prophetic lips.

I was unfairly skeptical. I look back at that moment with shame and gnawing regret. Seeing my son in such a state of distress engaged my fiercest and most defensive maternal instincts. Deep in my subconscious, I wanted to detach Joseph from the fate of the Grail, and from the sacrifices that were destined to accompany it. I was ready to make whatever sacrifices were required of *me*, so long as it did not mean pain for my son — anything and anyone but him. My maternal protectiveness took full control of my reaction to that moment. I said things that I did not mean, things I knew to be untrue.

Of course, Joseph understood my fears. He read them like a neon street sign. I began by defending the Grail's right to remain unmolested where it sat, safely at the bottom of the lake. When that argument failed, I attacked my own son's right to possess the Grail.

"You are not the Swan Knight!" I sharply snapped. "I am the Queen, not you. You are the son of a nomad. You should be content with that!"

With that childish outburst, I managed to insult some of my dearest loved ones, family, friends, and the noblest hearts in God's creation.

The Grail Blood was not needed to understand the source of my drastic change of character. With only the thoughts in their *own* heads, Felix, Taufe, and The Ancient One understood me. They did not judge me by my behavior.

The swan knew that little could be settled, or even properly considered, while the emotions of the moment remained so high.

With shades of his younger, whole self, he gently interjected, "Welcome home, my boy. You have been missed in the palace. Come. Eat and recover, and tell us how the Brunnen sisters are doing."

With all of my powers, and those of my son, The Ancient One's wise words again proved to be the most potent asset of the Swan Knights. The tension in the air diffused instantly. With curious thoughts of St. Hildegard Cathedral and Joseph's time there, we scuttled off to the dining room, our minds on the comforts of the immediate past, not on the perils of the future.

CHAPTER 19
Into the Service of the Righteous

A LEISURE MEAL AND A NIGHT OF SLEEP placed a façade of normalcy over tumultuous thoughts and frantic concerns. I was not the only one who felt the story of the Holy Grail approaching its climax. Nor was I the only one who clearly foresaw Joseph's intimate involvement. There was no denying it. Everything about the child was extraordinary and Providential, from the moment of his conception. He was as good a creature as God had ever created. He was dear in the extreme to all who called him their own. And with each year of his life, his abilities grew Godlier. We were all disturbed to the marrow by our collective premonitions of his fate.

I did not fear for his life, but for his pain. From the first moment he demanded the Grail, years earlier, my thoughts never drifted far from the subject. I determined to train harder, to prepare myself for any trial God may have intended for Joseph. I concentrated, trying to expand my abilities to match his, so that I could replace him in any trial God had in store. I encompassed the thoughts of many within my mental grasp, but failed tremendously in my effort to do what Joseph did effortlessly. At only fourteen, he was already so far beyond me. I should have trusted my wise son and trusted God, as my husband and teachers reminded me.

I awoke the next morning exhausted from a long night of trying to expand my powers. Half of my heart saw my son as a beautiful, shining tool of God, just slightly less precious than the Grail itself. The other half saw the child I had held, the very mortal cheeks where I had placed a million motherly kisses. Never had I been tormented by such polar and opposing duplexity of spirit.

Taufe met me early to continue our daily practices, as if the previous day's revelations changed nothing. But things were different, and she acknowledged as much by greeting me differently.

"He *is* young," she admitted. "But how fortunate it is," she continued, "that *you* were so young when you came through the portal at Linderhof."

While her voice was still speaking, sensing my gentle intrusion into her mind, she thought to me, "You were less than one year older, and had none of his training."

She continued speaking, "You had more faith than sense. You carried the courage of ignorance. With a couple more years of life experiences, you may not have followed the call of your Grail Blood. The difficult decisions you needed to make would have been weighted and bound by opinions and expectations. You would not have been light enough of spirit to be 'a feather on the breath of God.'"

The legitimacy of her argument settled heavily on my shoulders. I sent my acknowledgement of her wisdom and the truths of her recollections to her in thoughts.

I confessed as much vocally, "He is infinitely more prepared than I was. But I lost so much and suffered greatly."

She added to my one-sided recital of events, taking it down a brighter path, "And gained so much and grew so much."

After a few seconds of silent and personal pondering, she added, "Have more faith in your son, and have much more in the hand of God."

The irrefutable truths lying before me did little to relieve me of my anxiety. I projected a thought to those around me, "Enough of this talk for now. Let us pick this up after Easter."

Joseph was not pleased by my attempt to delay his desires. Throughout that day, he sent short, simple thoughts into my head. They came uninvited, forced into the middle of my own musings, interrupting the conversations I had with others, and conspicuously slamming my mental doors on their way in. He did not want those thoughts to bubble gently to the surface of my consciousness. He wanted me to know that he put them there. And he wanted my mind on nothing else.

On Wednesday evening after dinner, he sent everyone from the table with a mental command that he kept from my head. Between my last swallow of food and the following breath, everyone else was gone and I sat alone with my son.

"Tomorrow is Holy Thursday," he reminded me as if the fact was not keenly on my mind. "Our services should feature the Cup of Christ."

"All right!" I snapped, "I will go into the lake tomorrow morning, to the place where *I* defeated Löwschock and his serpents, to where *I* last held the Grail. I will bring it from its hiding place... because I am the Swan Knight and the Grail has been placed in *my* keeping."

"Mother," he whispered, "You were younger than I am now when you first felt the pull of your Grail Blood. You followed it and it eventually led you here. You were not much older than I when Cort declared you Queen. Father, the swan, Acheriel, Rüdiger and Lina, the entire Land and

Shallow Waters put their faith in the voices from your veins. They staked their lives upon it."

I had no rebuttal. And hearing the points made from his wise lips hit me more profoundly than hearing them from Taufe.

He continued, "And I am not only a decedent of Parsifal, carrying his Grail Blood as you do. I am the son of the greatest Swan Knight ever. *You* drank from the Grail. I have second generation Grail Blood, like Lohengrin himself. Would you have trusted Lohengrin to fetch the Grail?"

"Not at fourteen years old," I responded calmly. "At your age, Lohengrin was as foolish as any child... as foolish as I was."

"And yet, he played the part given to him by God, exactly as it was meant to be, as did you, Mother. Young and foolish as you may have been, God led you to the Grail in Gemeinsam, led you to the lake and to Löwschock. Surely you understand, *you* did not do all of those things. God did them, and you were his tool. I feel myself firmly in God's hand, a tool, ready for his use."

"You will be. I have known that since the moment you came into being. But this is not the time, not yet, not now."

With a churning discomposure in his eyes, he reached to his face and pinched his lips tightly between his thumb and index finger. It looked like it must have hurt him. But he showed no signs of physical pain. It was clearly overpowered by the turmoil within.

He let out a few rapid bursts of exhales, followed by a long, slow inhale, before asking, "If not now, when I feel it the strongest, then when, Mother?"

Unable to legitimize my feelings with my own words, I turned to scripture, flinging at my son the words of Christ, "It is not for you to know the times or seasons that God has established by his own authority."

The quotation hit him with its intended force. The swirling passions in his eyes calmed as he pondered the words and applied them to the situation at hand. His resolve to gather the Grail was not subdued. But the fury with which that resolve raged inside of him slowed to a mild storm. I watched the change take him halfway to where I wanted him — but not all the way. He was still determined, and I had no more arguments to throw.

I was done with words. I gathered every maternal terror, all of my heaviest dread, from my very depths to my flesh. I held it in one tight ball, then sent it to Joseph. It settled deeply inside of him. He sank in his seat, pondering the sensation of his mother's greatest fears. He cried, but not for himself. He cried in sympathy for me, for the pain I had been holding and for all that I had not yet experienced.

After a few minutes of silence, with him staring at his knees and my eyes fixed implacably on his face, he lifted his face to me and yielded, "You are right. You are the Swan Knight and retrieving the Grail from the lake is your responsibility. I will accompany you first thing in the morning. Our swimmers will take you down, and I will wait for you on the shore."

"We will see," I responded lethargically.

To those words, he writhed his face into a distorted grimace, stood slowly from his seat, placed his hand on my shoulder with a long and heavy sigh, patted me twice, and walked from the room. I had no intention of retrieving the Grail first thing the next morning. It was my intention to delay the Grail's fate as long as I could. I would make an indisputable decree — that the Grail would be brought to the palace *after* Easter, after enough time to construct an appropriate altar for its display.

Those were my plans. I knew that we would never see eye-to-eye on the subject, and I had no more energy for argument. I was still a student of the teachers. But I was also Queen, and no longer a young woman. My decree would be obeyed, if I presented it forcefully. I buried all thoughts of the Grail deeply into the hidden chambers of my heart and head. I found my son and kissed him goodnight, with only the adoration of a doting mother. He did not take my placidity as acquiescence. He went to bed agitated but determined.

Felix woke me the following morning. He was up and alert, and had obviously been so for some time.

"Joseph is not in the palace," he told me with a slight hint of alarm in his voice.

I responded calmly, "He thinks that I am going to get the Grail this morning. He is gathering swimmers by the shore."

"I don't think so. I was up before dawn and he was already gone. I think you should go to him now."

I sought Joseph with my mind, unraveling the mental scroll that held my decree, ready to deliver it to him and to all, with the authority of their Queen. I could not find him. More frustration than fear followed my failure. He had long been able to keep his thought from projecting to me. But he had not been able to avoid me when I sought his mind. I assumed this to be yet another new skill he had developed.

"I cannot find him," I told Felix. "He is blocking my mind."

After a pause, and with a touch of panic in his voice, Felix added, "Or he is beyond your reach, injured, unconscious, or worse. Call the Wühlenvogels and Unicorns, gather some Zweigwesens. Send the swimmers to every inch of every pool and pond. Let's find our son."

I did as my husband commanded. His apprehensions were contagious. I soaked in them, and they slowly seeped beyond my skin, into my blood and down to my bones, which began to shiver and rattle, though I was quite warm. I continued to seek his mind, to call for him. Every creature in the Sweeter Realm heard my cries for Joseph. And every creature able to respond did so with feverish frenzy.

The queendom was all abuzz. Nobody rested. Nobody ate. All of Eden swam in a collective pool of worry. Senische, quickly becoming wise among her kind, sprinted at full gallop all the way to Gemeinsam. She planted her horn into the Unicorn altar and consulted with her mother.

I was in the grasp of a Wühlenvogel, on the western shore of the great lake, scouring the hidden homesteads of the Federmensch. Senische, in intimate contact with Prische's spirit, connected me to her mother.

"He is gone" is all that came to me, in the simultaneous thoughts of mother and daughter.

The Wühlenvogel flew me to Gemeinsam as quickly as she could flap. The landscape between the western shore of the lake and the altar at the heart of the Unicorn capital blurred past my eyes in an indistinguishable flash of natural tones. I had never moved so quickly. In no more breaths than feathers on the swan, I was on the ground, before the altar and the best friend of my missing son.

She was wet, entirely soaked, horn to hoof.

I reached pensively to her, fearing her explanation as I asked, "You are wet… why?"

"Those are the tears of Prische," she answered in a broken voice. "Joseph is gone. My mother has told me."

My knees buckled. The weight of a thousand worlds crashed onto my head, and I collapsed to the ground.

"My son is dead," I repeated a few times. "I have lost my Joseph."

Senische shook her head in contradiction, but no other thought could penetrate my despair, as I repeated, "My son is dead."

Senische continued to shake her head. I looked to her and asked, "Did he drown? Is he in the lake? Was he going after the Grail? I should have listened to him. I have killed my son."

"No, my Queen!" Senische shouted impatiently at me. "He is not dead! He is gone!"

I looked sharply at her, and with a stern scowl I invaded her mind and demanded an explanation.

"He is gone from the Sweeter Realm."

I left her mind and spoke aloud, "The portal cannot open from this side. Where could he have gone."

Senische interrupted me, snapping, "Not through Parsifal's Portal, through yours!"

The lake! Joseph went after the Grail and went through my portal, the one that opened with my blood, spilled by Löwschock's fangs. I thought intensely of the Holy Grail, suddenly more fearful for it than for my son. It was gone. I sensed nothing of it, nothing from it. Even when it hid from me under the obelisk, in the years after following its call through the portal at Linderhof, as it waited patiently for me in its seaweed wrapping, I felt it. I grew accustomed to its proximity. After the war, while it sat in the lake, I felt it. It was near me. Now it was gone, and a dark, haunted, aching, Grail-shaped hole sat hollow deep inside of me. It was worse than anything I had imagined.

Nobody knew where my portal landed. The serpents of the Deep were sent there. Did it lead to my home world, somewhere in Germany or beyond, or did it lead to some other world entirely? Are the Grail and my son in the hands of the slimy serpents I sent through my portal? These thoughts rang around my head and called directly to The Ancient One. He met me on the shore of the lake, exactly where we embarked from the beach, in the little boat, on the day my portal first opened.

The swan's feathers were ruffled and loose. A few had fallen from his breast to the sand between his feet. The familiar sound of a Federman's running footsteps on the sand drew our attention. Felix joined us, fearing, as we did, for the Grail and for his son.

The Ancient One, with a sickly and raspy voice, reminded us, "Even Parsifal could not protect the Grail from the evils of your world. That is why he gave to me, and I gave it to Kandake. Now it has been taken back, away from the protection of Eden and its Queen. Mankind has not been in such peril since Klingsor sought the Grail."

Felix, more in love with his son than steeped in the Swan Knights History, suggested, "Joseph has powers and abilities that Parsifal did not. Surely it is safer in his hands."

The swan shook his head, hanging low at the end of his long neck, "Parsifal was a seasoned knight, and Joseph's abilities might not carry into that world. It is an ungodly world, a forsaken world. Joseph has never met evil, has never seen a road, a gun, an army. He is entirely unprepared to deal with the world he faces. With any luck, he and the Grail are embedded in the heart of some mountain, along with the bones of the serpents Verena sent through."

The comment should have seemed heartless to the parents of a child he wished dead. But Felix and I both understood the gravity of the situation, and the greater good, the grander plan of human salvation weighed more heavily, even in *our* hearts, than the welfare of our beloved son.

Resolve entered my mind as forcefully as the idea it brought with it.

"I cannot leave this to luck, nor can I abandon Joseph to an unknown fate."

By this point, several Vogelkrötes had met us at the shore, poking their heads from the water while their bellies rested on the shallowly submerged sand. Without a word, or even so much as a projected thought, I ran into the water.

265

Eight Vogelkrötes grabbed me and swam me quickly to the bottom of the lake.

My heart pounded, exhausting the oxygen in my blood. My lungs demanded breath. But I would not give in. Too much was at stake. I ached and my vision grew dim. I went limp while I prayed to the Lord. In an instant, I lost the need to draw breath. My vision, along with all of my senses, returned to their full height. I surveyed the surroundings and quickly gained my bearings. I knew where I was, and I knew where to go. I directed the Vogelkrötes to the place where I fought Löwschock.

The muted crackle of my opening portal as we approached did not startle me. I was expecting it, desiring it. It terrified the Vogelkrötes. They released me and retreated from its sound, which was accompanied by a wide circle of nothing, screaming its crackle through the water.

I thought nothing of the Vogelkrötes. I thought only on Joseph, the Grail, and the portal, my portal, that would take me to them. I peered deeply, decidedly, and entirely resolved into the portal, until I saw nothing but its indescribable center. Whether I pulled it or it pulled me I cannot say. But I was upon it instantly.

To my senses, traveling through my portal was identical to traveling through Parsifal's. But this time I was no ignorant, confused girl. I was a woman, a wife and mother, a Queen and Swan Knight. The sensations were filtered through a heart that had lived several lifetimes of love and loss. I relished the brief experience of passing through my own portal, mindless for a moment to what might await me on the other side.

Deep inside, I did not believe I would be joining Joseph's lifeless body and the bones of the serpents in the heart of some mountain. Parsifal's Portal opened precisely where it needed to, to find The Ancient One, deliver the Grail, and introduce to the line of Parsifal that one figure of continuity, the true protagonist of our story, our teacher and friend. It opened where it needed to open in the fulfillment of God's will. As I savored the experience of passing through, my heart believed that my portal would serve the same purpose.

The brief sensation of passing ended in a flash, and my skin and lungs encountered the distant familiarity of the dry, cooler air of my home world.

CHAPTER 20
A Drastically Altered World

WHEN MY VISION REGAINED CLARITY, I found myself lying flatly on my left side in a dark room, with a cool, hard floor. When I propped myself with my left hand, the motion triggered the room's lights. It was a large room with oak trim and marbled flooring. The walls were covered in elegantly patterned wallpaper. The room was obviously meant to be seen. But it was empty except for several large crates, still stacked and resting on palates. The room bore the smell of newness. It seemed eager for a life it had not yet grown into, designed for grand public display, but not yet put to that employment.

I frantically scanned the room for Joseph. I was alone. I closed my eyes and sought his mind — but could not find him. A shiny brass plaque was on the wall, half hidden by a stack of crates. I wedged myself between the crates and the wall, hoping that the plaque might give some indication of my location. It gave one big clue at first glance. The inscription on the plaque was in German.

It read, "Here, on 10 August 2021, the mysterious Niemitz Skeletons were discovered by construction crews, attracting the attention of the scientific world, challenging assumptions of this region's geological past, and adding fascinating new species to the pages of our planet's zoological history."

I'm not sure why, but I felt a swell of embarrassment, having opened the portal in the lake and sent those "fascinating new species" to their new hosts. There was a resurgence of a forgotten concern. As I cleared Eden of Löwschock's serpents, I wondered whose problem they had become. The thought woke me from many a restless sleep in the first few years after the war. It appeared that their skeletons were found underground during construction, embedded in the earth. No harm was done.

The terror of narrowly averted disaster struck me instantly, as I thought to myself, "If not for the construction, and the discovery of the monsters, Joseph would have been embedded in rock beside them... and so would I."

The faith of my Benedictine teacher swelled in me as I realized that the monsters passed through the portal into rock, where they could do no harm, and their discovery cleared the way for Joseph and me to pass safely. The whole thing smacked heavily of Divine guidance.

Joseph was not in the room, but he had been several hours earlier. He could have been near. My focus left the past and regained the immediate moment. As it did, I became aware of the noises beyond the walls surrounding me. The murmur of calm, hushed voices barely scraped the lowest levels of my audible range, accented by the drops of lake water still dripping from my clothes and landing on the marble floor.

The sound of the water drops gave me my first thoughts of self-awareness. I wore a flamboyantly bright, yellowish shirt, loose and flowing, with over-sized sleeves and ruffled cuffs. Tails extended in the back, like a tuxedo, fanning out and ribbed to resemble Kandake's tail. The tail of Kandake had come to be the emblem of the Queen of the Land and Shallow Waters during her reign, a tradition kept in full vigor when I assumed the post.

Upon each collar of my shirt, a thumb-sized image of a Brunnen tree was embroidered by the Brunnen sisters who made the clothes. My pants were equally conspicuous — reddish-brown, tight around the waist, but flailing out to look more like a long skirt than a pair of pants. Between the shirt and the pants, with all of the redundant fabric, they retained a heavy, burdensome amount of lake water. My shoes were crafted by the Zweigwesens. The soles were of fruit casings, threaded by crossed straps, like sandals. These were the clothes I had, and I wore nothing beneath them. In them I must venture from the room, into the wider world, in search of my son.

The room had two doors, on opposite ends. The muffled voices led me to one. I opened the door to a long, straight staircase. The reverent mumbling gently rolled down the stairs. I allowed myself to hope, to almost expect to see Joseph in the room above, chairing some theological symposium with the best religious minds in Germany. My eyes took in a very different picture as they breached the horizon of the highest step.

The stairs opened into a tremendous gallery, as large as the main hall of St. Hildegard Cathedral. A few scatterings of two to six people congregated around display cases along the walls. The largest group, fifteen to twenty people surrounded an exhibit in the middle of the room. The quickest of glances would have been enough for me to identify the central attraction. It was the skeletal remains of Löwschock's lower half. I did not give it the quickest of glances. My eyes were fixed upon it, as my imagination filled in what time and decay had stripped. The room, if not the entire building, seemed to be a museum, dedicated, or at least motivated by the discovery of the serpents of the Deep.

Beside the bones was a plaster cast of Löwschock's tail, painted inaccurately in a shiny green, closer to that of

Bechtold's shell than Löwschock's tail. The display's subconscious grip on me was unyielding. I walked toward it, brushing against the museum patrons, drenching their arms and shoulders with water from another world. They too were interested in the display. But it did not grip them tyrannically, as it did me. Their attention easily shifted to the wet, brightly dressed woman shuffling in a trance across the floor like a sleep-walking slug.

I stood in wonder of the display. When I finally managed to unshackle my attention, I noticed that I drew more attention than the scientific curiosity in front of us, more looks, more whispers, more pointed fingers. Finally, one nice young man asked me if I was well. I wanted to ask him if he had seen a feathered boy pass through. My mind shoved the question into my mouth, but my reluctant lips would not let it pass. I collected myself, nodded to the man, and walked away from the Löwschock display. I walked the perimeter of the room, looking at the people, but enthralled by the forty or so cased displays with the remains of Löwschock's minions.

When I battled those very serpents, the darkness of the Deep Waters obscured most of their features. Only their eyes remained adhered to my memories, making the figures before me as new and fascinating to me as they were to the museum patrons. Three college-aged women and an elderly couple stared fascinated at the strangest skeleton any of us had ever seen. It had two heads and two tails, but shared a single body and a single set of four clawed flippers. I did not linger to study it. I sought my son and the Holy Grail. The curiosities of the museum were not a luxury for my amusement. They were a reminder of my obligations to God and my queendom.

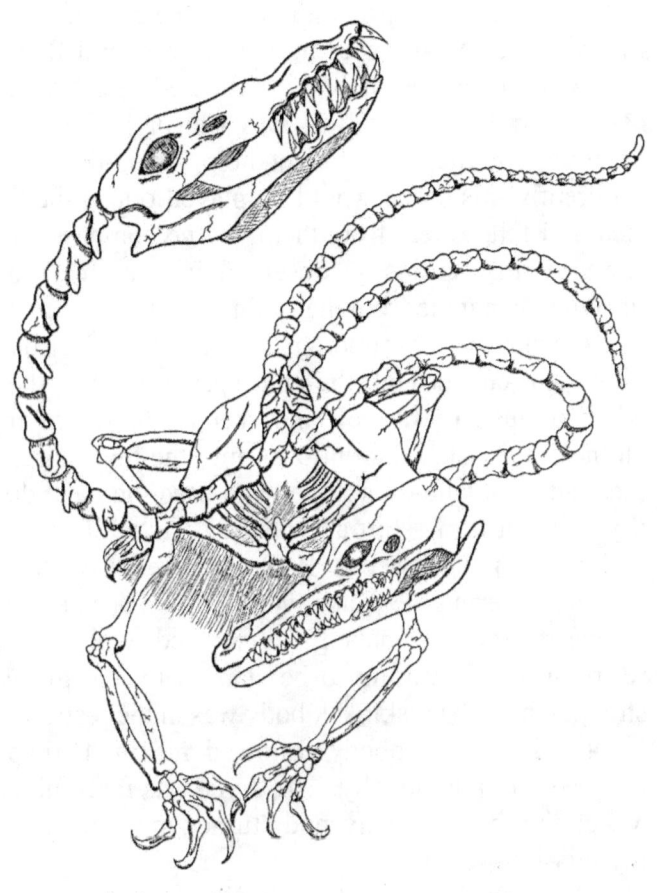

I scanned my eyes over the displays, as I followed the splash of sun that poured through the double-doored entrance to the building. I shuffled toward the entrance, as if sliding down the sunlight. The bones still kept enough of my attention to draw my eyes back. Quick, head-snapping glances behind me were directed by and in imitation of my quick, jerky, staccato thoughts of the decayed serpents behind me. But my backward glances revealed more than the featured displays. I continued to catch the timid stares of those I passed. Patrons slipped on the trail of water I left in my wake. A janitor came with a mop and floor-signs. Yet with all of this, nobody addressed me. Nobody else asked how I was or why I was wet or if they could do anything for me. I could not help but notice how very differently this scene would be played out in the Sweeter Realm. I felt no fear from them, yet no compassion either. I was a mild curiosity, observed in a moment of mild intrigue, then gone from their minds as if erased from time.

Outside of the building, it was a beautiful day. The direct sun cut through the cold spring air. But the wind, when it gusted, was icy and seemed to freeze my wet clothes to my skin. I went back into the museum and into the restroom, where I stripped and used the hand dryers to dry and warm my shirt and pants. I had walked the paths and halls of the Sweeter Realm for years, with little or nothing covering me. But never did I feel as naked as I did in that restroom — naked and exposed, with eyes on the restroom door, waiting to be startled by the glance of a stranger at my bare skin. Nobody was in the restroom when I entered it, and nobody followed me in. Perhaps they avoided me intentionally. The dryer was forceful and hot. My clothes dried quickly, and I turned my thoughts back to my mission.

With brighter, lighter, flowing, but dry and warm clothes, I walked back into the German air, focused and determined to find Joseph and the Grail. There were not many people in and around the museum. But I walked among those I saw. None spoke of a wet and feathered boy leaving the building. Joseph's immergence from the marble-floored room would have drawn attention, had anybody perceived him. But they paid such little mind to me, with my dripping, flamboyantly bright and flowing clothes. Perhaps they had experienced Joseph similarly and jettisoned him as readily.

I meandered through the small huddles of people, eavesdropping on every conversation, anatomizing every facial expression and hand gesture, trying to piece the clues together into some discernable language. It was a skill I had not needed until then. I could not simply flip through the files of their minds for my answers, as I had grown accustomed. I was at a loss. I could not simply step between a couple, interrupting their tiny sphere of conversation, and ask, "Have you seen a young Federman carrying the Holy Cup of Christ?"

I decided to look at my surroundings as Joseph might have, to be drawn by what might have drawn him. A large sign stood outside of the museum entrance. On it was a map of the region. Surely Joseph would have consulted the map to get his bearings. The museum was clearly marked on a map of the larger region. I was in northwestern Bavaria, near the Hessen border. I was a stone's throw from my ancestral town, where I would have traveled with my family had I not passed through Parsifal's Portal.

The museum sat just southeast of a town called Grossostheim, nestled snugly near the western bank of the Main River. Shuttle buses sat near the entrance to the museum, waiting to take patrons back to the town center. I boarded the bus very apprehensive of my next steps. I had no money, nothing to trade or sell except a set of Brunnen-made clothes made in a mash-up of styles that would not have fit into any era of human fashions. Still stronger on my mind was the fact that Joseph had no money. He had no clothes, and was covered only by his feathers. His feathers would have made obscurity impossible for him. But where did he go? How did he get there? And what were his intentions? Nothing in what I had seen so far could answer any of these questions.

The town center of Grossostheim yielded no more guidance for me. But it did delight me. I'm not sure what I expected. But the town was quaint, almost medieval. Grossostheim boomed in the wake of the discovery of the bones. Charter colleges opened in the area. Many were still under construction. Every sort of business needed to sustain the growth was sprouting in place of the fields that had long cradled the town. But the town center remained unspoiled by modernity. Half-timbered buildings, cobblestone roads, and worn old fountains made the imagination expect the clopping of horse hooves more than the hum of car motors.

I walked the town for about an hour, looking in every place I could imagine Joseph hiding. But then, it was not in his nature to hide, and possession of the Grail would have dissolved what thin threads of trepidation he had. I found the town's Catholic church. My spirit had me seated inside, in deep prayer, before my conscious mind realized I had taken a step.

I begged God for help, help in finding Joseph, and help in securing the Holy Grail. The only answers that came back to me were thoughts of Taufe. I could almost hear her voice and feel her caress, as lectures both stern and nurturing clutched and squeezed my memory. The chaos of my thoughts settled to a single lesson from long ago. I remembered Taufe telling me that nature had an intelligence that I, in my youthful ignorance, had refused to listen to. The sound of running water, or of the breeze through trees, the direction of the wind and the manner in which a leaf falls to the ground, all are conversations. Nature speaks to us whether or not we are smart enough to listen and wise enough to interpret the message.

Nature had nothing to say to me in the church. I walked briskly outside and stood in the open air. A faint whistle, followed by a low howl, drew my attention to the wind. My skin became hyper-aware of the subtle stroke of the moving air. The breeze seemed to swirl around me, graze and tickle my cheek attentively, then embrace me before breaking to the south. I did not follow it like a bumbling fool, going wherever a finger points. I listened with my heart for a much more complicated message.

The sound of the wind took my attention upward, to the sparse scattering of high, light, and independent clouds. Each curve in the cottony wisps spoke to me. The flap of the wings of a small bird that crossed the path of my focus, along with the color of its feathers, its direction of travel, and the inconsistent pattern of its flight conveyed part of a message to my open heart.

Everything communicated in concert, many aspects of a single voice directing me — leading me to Linderhof, to Ludwig's palace, to Parsifal's Portal, where the life that had come to define me began. I went directly for the train station that I had passed several times while I was searching the town. There was no ticket booth, no turnstiles, no kiosks to accept payment, just a platform with a small but pleasantly boisterous herd of people waiting to board, most of whom spoke entirely of the museum and its marvels. The sign on the train told me that it headed for Vienna, with many stops between. As I boarded the train, the ride appeared to be free. Nobody stood, asking for my ticket or pass. The passengers freely entered the train and took random seats of their choosing. I had little to lose and everything to gain. I boarded the train with the others and took a seat.

One minute out of the city center, the medieval atmosphere dissolved completely. There was technology all around me, much that I had once known and much that was entirely foreign to me. The cars on the road were sleek and rounded, like a bullet. The passengers on the train ended their conversations within seconds of departing the station. They fixed their eyes and their complete attention to the gadgets and gizmos in their hands. Several placed their focus on the screens on the backs of the seats in front of them. At first, I found it all intriguing, even delightful. But intrigue turned to disgust, as my fellow riders plugged their ears and eyes into their electronics, to the absolute dismissal of everything and everyone around them. Every flashing light and beeping, buzzing trinket made me more homesick.

I grew ill longing for the touch of the fleshy bark on the Brunnen trees, and for the infinite number of other soul-soothing sensations abundant in the Sweeter Realm. Some murmuring remained, but one conversation took my attention. An older couple sitting in front of me spoke lightly and gaily in English. In my many years in the Sweeter Realm, I spoke many languages, heard many languages, but rarely my own native tongue. I had not spoken in English since my awkward and frustrating conversations with Reid. I had forgotten what English felt like in my ears and in my mouth.

The couple's words were meant only for each other. But I seized each syllable. It filled and enveloped me with warm, welcoming, and nurturing recollections. The sound of every classmate, friend, relative, and neighbor from my childhood erupted together from the dusty, neglected vaults of my deepest memories. When I blurted out a half-giggle, half-cry it caught the attention of the couple. They turned to me and asked if I was okay. The English that came from my mouth in response came quickly and naturally, without needing to be translated from some other language. But it sounded like a memory of myself, like looking at a photograph from my early childhood. I recognized it as a past version of me that no longer exists.

I spoke with the couple for several minutes. They sensed how giddy I was to talk to them, but could not have guessed why. They also sensed the underlying darkness of my mission. The desperate sadness of a mother who lost her child, and of a Swan Knight who lost the Grail, stabbed upward against the thin film of delight that coated the conversation. They prodded and probed delicately for answers to explain that mysterious darkness eyeing them from beneath my exterior features. Strong was my yearning for companionship. And warm and welcoming were the nurturing voices and compassionate words of the couple. But my lips were stoutly devoted to the Swan Knight's oath, and I gave no satisfaction to the benevolent curiosity of the couple.

They returned to their private conversation and I was left with nothing but the screen that stared at me from the back of the seat in front of me. I looked up and down the train and saw many passengers scrolling through words and videos with a flick of the finger across the screen. I touched mine and was presented with a menu of options. Music, movies, news, books, encyclopedias were all at my disposal. I chose to view the news, believing that a little research might help me. It quickly revealed the state of affairs in a drastically altered world.

The Americas and Western Europe had formed into a loosely united confederation. The East and Eastern Europe had done the same. Northern Africa had joined the East and Southern Africa joined the West. A few countries in the center had maintained their neutrality. In Europe, only the German speaking countries remained neutral and independent of the larger confederations. Even Vatican City took a side, affiliating itself and the church it represented with the West. Germany, Austria, and Switzerland tightened on their shared island of neutrality, but maintained complete autonomy.

The East and the West stood strongly in opposition, in a new Cold War. The German speaking countries traded with both sides, bringing them unprecedented wealth. It was illegal in the East and the West to trade with the other. Every commodity that made the trip from East to West or vice versa, passed through Germany, Austria, or Switzerland. The East and the West spoke in such hateful, derogatory words of the other. From the neutral perspective of the German news, I saw how wrong both sides were. It saddened me greatly to think of Centennial Colorado, and of my family living under those conditions. I imagined for a moment that they never returned from Germany — that they remained in southern Bavaria, waiting for me to return from my mysterious disappearance.

I decided to employ the search function on the screen. I entered my family name and address. It revealed a single written article from my old local newspaper, announcing my father's death. The article was five years old and told of a loving husband, father, and grandfather who died of a heart attack. I held back a cry that beat at the inside of my face, trying to escape loudly into the train. I read the article through the blur of my watering eyes. It mentioned my mother and brother, my brother's wife and child — and it mentioned me, the daughter my parents had lost, whose body was never recovered. My poor mother. I ached desperately for her. I instinctively tried to connect my mind to hers. After so many years with that ability, it was my default reaction to a compassionate moment. All I felt was pain, and I was not sure if it was hers or mine that I felt.

I dwelled on my father, trying to revive in my memory the sound of his laugh, his scent, and the feel of his hand stroking my head as he used to do. But every tender thought of him brought sorrowful sympathy for my mother. I spent much of the rest of the train ride trying to use my queenly abilities and connect to my mother. When that failed, I tried to connect my mind to anybody's. I reached outward in frenzied, furious, grasping attempts. I felt nothing from the people around me, frustrating me as much as it exhausted me, and making me feel very much alone — until I found something so beautifully familiar in the widely casted net of my mind. It was the thoughts of a Unicorn. That signature boldness of a Unicorn's thoughts could be mistaken for nothing else.

At first, I only listened, and did not announce myself. The Unicorn's thoughts grew clearer as I traveled, as I approached Linderhof. His mind was worried, but so used to worry that the emotion had lost most of its potency. At the moment I connected with him, he was restful and at-ease. He was with trusted friends who had spent so many years with him that he considered them his only family. Memories of his Unicorn clan were still vibrant, but lived beneath the love he had for the creatures that surrounded him. He lived underground, in a cavern that he and his friends labored together to create.

With each field, each patch of forest, each city and village that the train passed, the thoughts of the Unicorn came clearer. He thought of the other lives around him, of those he loved most dearly. It was an unusual assortment of creatures — three Scheriers, a Wühlenvogel, and a Brunnen. He also thought quite passionately about two Eulesängers. But those thoughts were mournful. Clearly they had died. The rich, deep, dark thoughts of loss were well known to me and I recognized them at a glance. The Unicorn loved the birds, and his sense of loss was blended with strains of guilt. His name is Lenelil.

Thoughts of Linderhof, of recent Linderhof, with its hordes of tourists, skipped across the upper regions of his mind. That is where they were, this Unicorn and his friends. These isolated creatures of the Land and Shallow Waters, my subjects, would soon meet their Queen. The last they knew, The Ancient One was dead, the line of Swan Knights

281

broken, and Löwschock with his minions terrorized the kind creatures of their homelands.

"The Brunnen!" I interrupted my own thoughts. "Is this the Brunnen who received the journal from Ludwig? Did she place it on the boat for me to find? Was it her voice I heard echoing my words back to me in the Venus Grotto?"

It was time to introduce myself. The Unicorn's thoughts were clear to me. I could very weakly see the minds of the others, but they were scattered and blended together. I could make little sense of them. Lenelil's thoughts became as clear to me as my own. I placed my greeting into the mind of the Unicorn.

"Lenelil," I thought to him, "don't be alarmed. I am a friend."

He interrupted me with a forceful mental proclamation, "Verena! Swan Knight! I hear your thoughts."

"How do you know me?"

"I heard your thoughts many years ago, as you wandered into the Grotto looking for your family. That is how we knew."

"Knew what? What did you know?'

"We knew that you came from Parsifal, from Elsa. You came to guide us, to resume the line of Swan Knights. Tinyn placed the book for you to find."

When he thought of Tinyn, his heart leaped with love for the Brunnen of their party. She was dear to them all.

"We did not" he continued, "expect you to open the portal from that distance, nor did we expect the portal to pull you through. How is it that you communicate with me? Where are you? Is there peace in the Sweeter Realm?"

These questions and many more flew at me faster than I could decipher them all.

"I am here," I informed him, "in Germany. I am coming to you. I have answers, so many answers for you that we will discuss in person. I also have questions, which I pray you can answer. For now, I have just one thought to share with you. Lower your head and instruct the others to touch your horn. This is for all of them."

Lenelil obeyed, as did the others. When they were all linked by the horn connection, I sent one grand thought. The Ancient One is alive and living in a cleansed Sweeter Realm. The jubilant reaction returned so boisterously to my head that I looked around the train, fearing it was heard by all. Of course it was not. It rang only in my head. There was more to tell them, tragic news of great loss to pepper the sweetness of their celebration. But those words would be shared mouth-to-ears, and after they savored the only reason to celebrate in their recent memories.

When their excitement settled, Friedrich, the Wühlenvogel, took command of the conversation, "You will have to break free of the crowds, Swan Knight. Go up the hill to the far side of the Grotto. I will wait for you there."

I had as many questions for them as they had for me. How had they lived at Linderhof for so long? What did they do during the long daylight hours, while people roamed the park and palace? Most importantly, have they seen Joseph, heard of him, or felt his thoughts? My mind was worn from the connection and the emotions of the day. My questions would keep until I arrived. My mind released the connection and drifted unguided through a hundred waking dreams, until I left the train in Oberammergau and boarded a bus to Linderhof.

CHAPTER 21
Where It All Began

THE BUSES TAKING TOURISTS TO LINDERHOF had finished for the day. Fortunately, I caught a shuttle leaving from Oberammergau to pick up a tour group that was already at the palace grounds. I told the driver that my family was among the tour. He allowed me aboard and the brief trip was filled with light talk between the driver and me, the only passenger.

When the bus arrived at Linderhof, visitors were still walking the grounds. The palace was already closed. There were not many visitors that day, nothing like the crowds that filled Parsifal's Valley the last time I was there. I was certain to be conspicuous. The beauty of the park's glorious features proved distracting enough to keep most eyes off of me and my flamboyant clothes. I received a few nods, stares, and under-breath comments as I worked my way through the park, to the Venus Grotto. The last few visitors were exiting the grotto as I approached it. The park employee shuffled off with them, toward the palace parking lot and the awaiting buses. They walked right by me, without a second glance in my direction.

It was a strange sensation, being there again, again in search of family. But familiarity was just a thin strain of the experience. I was a very different woman that day, from the little girl who ran from the screaming and scowling portrait of Ludwig. My childhood before the Sweeter

Realm was like a few flakes of skin from the back of my elbow — just some tiny, insignificant part of me compared to the whole.

There I stood, alone, at the entrance to the grotto, for the second time in my life. But this time, my home was in front of me, across the artificial lake and through the crackling circle of nothing, not across the ocean and up a suburban driveway in Centennial, Colorado. The park was clearing for the day. It was almost too easy. The grounds crew was nowhere near me. I felt a strong draw to enter the grotto. The portal was right there. My husband, my teachers, my friends and queendom were just through the stone entrance. But I felt the eager anticipation of the abandoned creatures of Linderhof. So I followed Friedrich's instructions and climbed the hill beyond the grotto.

I looked to the trees and brush, to any nook and cranny in the hill that could hide a creature of the Sweeter Realm.

"Pssst", I hesitantly whispered, "I'm here. It's me, Verena."

I sought Lenelil's mind and found it immediately. Before I could decipher the rush of complex thoughts, I felt a Wühlenvogel tail wrap around my waist and pull me downward. The light of the afternoon disappeared in a blink and was replaced by the torchlight of a Wühlenvogel village.

Friedrich squeezed me a bit too tightly. It hurt. But the tightness of his tail spoke no ill-will to me. It spoke what his mind (now clearly projected into my head) spoke to me — the love and loyalty of a servant of the Swan Knights, of a faithful Portal Steward, finally relieved of a long and heavy burden. Under the shower of his thoughts, I felt like a daughter of Rudolf, a Swan Knight, a Wittelsbach. He was proud to show me his constructs. They lived beneath Linderhof in a cave no larger than the palace above. It was plenty for the five creatures who hid there with no expectation of reinforcements or replacements.

The creatures spent the long years since Ludwig's death protecting the valley as well as they could. They witnessed two World Wars and stared into the face of a third. They saw Löwschock drag a poor man across the grotto lake and through the portal. And they waited. They waited for someone to arrive in the valley and present herself, in one way or another, as the new Swan Knight. They waited for me, and they found me as a young teenager, only to lose me when I went through the portal on the day that Cort proclaimed me the Queen.

Friedrich placed me gently on the floor of their underground palace. The most ecstatically delighted faces greeted me. Three Scheriers, Rupert, Syllia, and Agnes, gripped each other tightly, squeezing the fur of the others with clinched fists. Their faces were lit by the reflection of Wühlenvogel torches shining off of their tear-drenched cheeks, but lit much more brightly by their eyes, eyes that scoped me up and down with equal portions of love and homage.

Lenelil, a short, stout Unicorn, light grey of coat, mane, and beard, with an almost awkwardly long and thin horn stood beside a tall, rippling Brunnen whose beauty rivaled Taufe's. Tinyn stood taller than Lenelil, narrower than any Brunnen I had ever met, but as fair as any. I spoke my greeting to her in Brunnen, as well as my single, human throat could manage. She broke from the Unicorn and wrapped both of her long arms around me. She answered my greeting in the duel tones of a rich Brunnen voice. Her voices were both uncommonly high and low, reaching an octave in both directions beyond the common greetings. She smothered me in her embrace as she cried and sang. Her skin rippled downward, caressing me as she held me against her. Her Brunnen charms worked their magic on me. Her voice and skin joined in perfect teamwork to seduce my mind from any thought but the pleasure of her embrace.

Lenelil broke the moment with a strong thought of the high grass of the Unicorn homeland, sent to me accidentally. My appearance that day meant many things to them, not the least of which was access to the portal and a chance to finally go home. But what sort of home awaited them? I was pleased to fill their ears and thoughts with much brighter images than they dared to hope for. I gave them a brief chronicle of events in their homelands since Ludwig's death. Of course, they were ecstatic to hear that Löwschock was dead and the Waters were clear, but infinitely more pleased the hear that The Ancient One lives.

"The portal!" I proclaimed, interrupting my story. "You would like to go home and I would love to see my husband."

With the potent thought of Felix, I projected my love for him into the minds of my new friends.

"A Federman? You married a Federman?" Agnes the Scherier asked in disbelief.

"I did. And he is as much my King as I am his Queen."

Every eye in the underground palace grew wide.

"Of course," Lenelil whispered. "You are the heir to Ludwig. You are the Queen of the Land and Shallow Waters."

I nodded and he continued in confusion, "But the King, the Swan lives."

"Yes, but as you know, he was presumed dead, and Ludwig became King. When I arrived in the Nomadic Belt, I was pronounced Queen, then the swan was rescued from the lake."

"Was there an election?" he followed.

"Yes. And I am still their Queen, but with the wise guidance of the swan and many others."

"You married Felix. I know your husband. And how are his friends, Acheriel and Prische?"

I could not bring myself to list the dead, and answered him only with, "There is so much to tell you, but I will leave that to better story-tellers than I. Let's go to the grotto and see you home."

They declined the offer, insisting that we remain below ground until sundown, at which point they would delight in the crackling sound of their passage home. In the hours between, they spoke of me, of how much I had grown since they saw me last. They wondered how I came back to Germany. I described finding the Grail in Gemeinsam and fighting Löwschock, of being bitten, and of the opening of my portal. I told them that I came to find my son, who came with the Grail through my portal. I left all other stories for another day and another story-teller.

While we waited for darkness, the Portal Stewards led me through a tour of their underground palace. There were many unused rooms, as if their dirt palace was built for a party ten times their numbers. We passed most rooms without a glance and focused on the areas that they used. In a carved out cubby, in the hallway near the entrance of Tinyn's room, sat some folded fabric. Tinyn took it unceremoniously and placed it over her head. It unfolded and cascaded down her delicate form to reveal its nature — a long, sleeveless, woolen, white tunic. It hung down to her knees. A large, black cross spanned the width of her chest. Its identity was undeniable. It was the tunic of a Teutonic Knight.

"What is that?" I asked.

"Can't you guess, Swan Knight? It belonged to your cousin."

She distorted her lovely face to be disturbingly unpleasant, as she added, "… and a man I misjudged."

289

In a vocalized whisper, both firm and reverent, I said, "Tannhäuser."

She nodded.

I ran my hand across her chest, along the cross, and down the side of the tunic to her hip. The fabric was soft and strong, the stitches still firm and tight. It did not look or feel like a relic of its age.

"It's so unweathered." I remarked.

The other creatures had gathered in a semi-circle around us, delighting in the exchange.

Rupert interjected with a playful slap at Tinyn's leg, "It has been well cared for."

I stared at the artifact from the Swan Knights history, then lifted my eyes to Tinyn's and commented, "I think Brunhilde would be interested in such a well-preserved token of her father."

She answered, "I imagine she would."

She looked downward to Agnes, who was wringing her hands in front of her thoughtful, teary little Scherier face, and spoke compassionately to her little friend, "Don't you think so, Agnes?"

Agnes nodded, shaking loose the tears that held to her eyes and sending them to the point of her chin and to the floor.

Rupert explained the exchange, "Agnes is the oldest of us. She was friends with Elizabeth and Brunhilde. In fact, she is Brunhilde's special friend, isn't that true, Agnes?"

Agnes answered, "Well, we were very close when she was young and living in the valley. I taught her how to wrestle and fight."

All of the other creatures cleared their throats in unison.

"Well, I suppose that The Ancient One and Otto helped to teach her. But she *was* my special friend until she left us to live in the castle."

Intrigued as I was by this revelation of a quaint personal account of Swan Knights history, I brought the conversation back to its roots, "I think Brunhilde would want her father's tunic."

"And that is why I keep it here," Tinyn said calmly but with a hint of melancholy, "waiting for her return. But honestly speaking, I have grown accustomed to it and will be loathed to part with it, should the day ever come. It serves me as it would serve Brunhilde, as a token of remembrance of one very dear to me."

"Where did *you* get it?" I asked.

She dropped her gaze to the floor between us, as if frozen in a trance. And in her stillness, she turned almost invisible. The tunic seemed to float around vapors that bore a slight resemblance to a woman's figure. Her skin began to ripple downward in slow, swaying pulses, bringing her pensive form into plain view for us all. More out of compassion than curiosity, I subconsciously peered into her thoughts.

"Please don't," she thought to me. "In searching for those memories, you will pull me through recollections I do not have the strength to relive."

I left her mind immediately, snapping back to myself, jolting my body backward and forcing a sharp gasp.

"Please forgive me, Swan Knight," she said in a sincere apologetic tone, with her head lowered and one hand upon her chest.

I responded with words from my mouth, and my mind entirely inside of my own head, "Oh no, no. *I* am sorry."

Raising her head and recovering from her submissive posture, she suggested casually, "So there is nothing for either of us to forgive. Let us please leave it there."

She reached her palm under my chin, ran it up the side of my cheek, drew her fingertips across shut eyes, and back again across my lips. A great deal of respect, admiration, and dutiful loyalty was expressed in that exquisitely soft gesture.

She pulled the tunic from her, folded it as it was before, and handed it to me with a sigh, saying, "This is an artifact of the Swan Knights, a relic from a war where *your* family fought and bled. Perhaps it is better in your hands than mine."

I took it from her, looking at her with eyes of uncertainty. She released it easily and gracefully. She turned from me and the tunic without hesitation. I placed it back in the cubby that had been created for its display. We continued the tour with neither thought nor glance at the cherished relic.

When the sun set, we all went above ground and entered the grotto giddily. The voices in my Grail Blood shouted a thousand memories of the portal and the valley as I waded across the lake to the Tannhäuser mural. Every Swan Knight knew their own trigger point. They knew it well. I was excited to get to know mine. I did not have a father-Swan Knight to walk me slowly toward the Portal Point and begin my days of training according to the Laws of Ermenrich. But I could recreate the tradition in my own way. This one facet of being a Swan Knight, like many others, was not mine to have. I was different. I stared at the Portal Point as I splashed toward it. It opened quickly. A sharp, crisp crackle snapped, and the portal was open in an instant. Then it closed.

When the portal closed, I stopped in confusion, gazing confounded at the mural. The portal opened again, just as quickly. Then it closed and reopened slowly in the shape of a giant feather. Only when it took the feather form did I realize that the portal did not open at my trigger point, but at my subconscious command. It beckoned the feathered creatures I desired to see, my husband and my teacher. I closed it again, intentionally, then opened it normally. I still stood in the middle of the lake when The Ancient One walked through. Lenelil and the others laughed at the sight of the old swan. The Scheriers, ever good swimmers, dove into the shallow lake, swam along the bottom, and sprang from the water onto the small stage.

They dove on the swan and began wrestling with him. The Ancient One pushed back at them with his one wing, while the prosthetic stuck awkwardly to the side. The Scheriers stopped and examined the swan. They saw the harness that held the prosthetic, and followed the straps closely to where they connected to the artificial wing.

"Teacher!" Syllia said with great sadness in her voice, "Your wing."

"It is a tragic story," I announced.

The Ancient One quickly added, "One with a happy and heroic ending."

He turned to me with brightness in his eyes and continued, "Oh Verena, we were lost, with no idea where you went. 'The portal' I told them, 'Parsifal's Portal.' I knew you would find your way to the valley. We rushed to the Portal Point and waited. When it opened, we knew you had come for us. When it formed to a feather, we knew you called for us."

As he spoke those words, Felix walked through. He stumbled to avoid stepping on the swan. In doing so, he fell face first into the lake. By the time his face immerged from the water, both of my arms were around him. The water was cold, but Felix's feathers reacted to the touch of his lover and heated me throughout. I squeezed him with eyes closed. When I opened my eyes and looked around, I saw the Portal Stewards, bowing low to Felix. In my strong thoughts of my husband, I passed to them my admiration for him. The saw all of his heroics. And they venerated him as I did. They bowed to their King, though he would denounce the honor as above him.

Nobody else came through the portal. I stared at it in anticipation until Felix thought, "It is only us. We thought it best until we knew what we were facing."

His thoughts came clearly to me, just as did those of the other creatures gathered around the Portal Point in the Sweeter Realm. I closed the portal with a gentle blink of my eyes. The Ancient One swelled with pride. He had not seen that sort of control over the portal since Elsa, and he reminded us all of that fact.

Turning quickly from the swan to me, Felix interrupted him, "Joseph! Where is our son?"

"I don't know. I can't feel him. I can't hear him."

"Yours is a big world." The swan gingerly added.

Felix thought in a defensive rebuke, "*This* is not *her* world. She is the Queen of the Sweeter Realm."

The thought was meant for his own head. But I heard him, and I squeezed him more tightly.

I answered the swan, "This *is* a big world. But there are very few places he would have reason to go, and I don't believe he would wander aimlessly."

After a short pause, filled with many thoughts of our company, all projected loudly into my head, I added, "Nature led me to Linderhof. I will count on her again. We will find Joseph and the Grail."

As I said that, I thought of Taufe, who taught me to listen to nature. I wondered what she would say. I thought I heard her thoughts, "… if God wishes them found."

I focused hard on her and saw her praying in the Cathedral of St. Hildegard, preparing her heart and soul for what she believed to be the imminent completion of God's will.

I put my suspicions to the test, asking The Ancient One, "Where is Taufe? Is she not coming too?"

"When you disappeared, she rushed to the cathedral in the grasp of a Wühlenvogel. She has been leading the sisters in constant prayer."

My mind *had* connected to her, through the portal, all the way to the heart of Brunnen land.

I asked Felix, "Who knows that I am here, that I have left?"

"What are you talking about?" the swan answered for him. "They *all* know. We felt your absence the moment you went through. Whether you are conscious of it or not, you coat the hearts of your queendom with your love. There is a sense of Godliness that exudes from you and comforts us all. Of course we knew when that sensation was pulled from us. The air and water across your entire queendom changed and announced your departure to all who breathe."

I detected a hint of disapproval from him, at least for the manner *in which* I left the queendom. A clear paternal protectiveness came through with his words, not in his tone, but in his deep thoughts — deeper, I believe, than even he knew.

He shook off his consternation and continued more calmly, "A plan, my dear. We must make a plan. You have three Scheriers, a Unicorn, a Brunnen, a Wühlenvogel, a Federman, and one crippled old swan."

"No," I stopped him short, "these friends need to go home. They have been in Linderhof, hiding and afraid, for too long already, protecting the valley in the absence of a Swan Knight."

"You are right, Swan Knight," Lenelil said in a somber tone. "We should go home, see our families, pay respects to our lost loved ones. Then we will return to continue what we have sworn to do. We are stewards of the Portal Valley and servants of the Swan Knights. We will not discard that oath, now that there is finally a Swan Knight to serve."

I looked to the others. Not a hint of dissention was in their brave, noble faces.

"How long do you need?"

"I will take Tinyn home. Friedrich can take the Scheriers. We will all sleep with our own tonight. One full day to say the things that must be said, for me to connect to my ancestors at the shrine of Gemeinsam, for the Scheriers to wrestle and play with their clan, for Tinyn to pray with her sisters, and for Friedrich to… do whatever Wühlenvogels do in their underground villages. We will leave for the portal early the next morning and wait for you to let us through."

I stared very gratefully into his eyes. He tilted his head as he stared back and said, "You have King Ludwig's eyes, Verena."

"But my eyes are blueish-green, and his were…"

He interrupted me, "I am not looking at the color, but far beyond that, to the fire within."

I kissed Lenelil on the nose, dropped my head, and opened the portal. My eager new friends were gone in a flash and I closed the portal behind them, leaving me alone with Felix and the swan, in the constructs of The Ancient One's last Wittelsbach student.

We left the grotto together and I took them to the small, hidden entrance to the underground palace.

Felix's eyes darted around the cave in amazement. "Incredible," he said in awe of his surroundings. "They have been hiding here this whole time, living beneath the bustling site above."

"Yes," the swan included, "it is a bustling site. We must proceed cautiously."

"Well, there we are in luck," I informed them. "It is Easter weekend, and the park and palace will be closed. We just need to stay put for one day. After that, *we* are not doing anything. I must be here, to find Joseph and the Grail.

Not because I am the Swan Knight and it is my duty, but because I am human and can travel among the crowds. The realm is without me. It cannot be without you too. You must go back and lead in my place."

The Ancient One shook his head and Felix giggled. I saw Felix's thoughts, and they accompanied the swan's words, "The realm is in good hands. They are being led, as they should, by the one with the second most votes."

It was perfect. Cort already lived in the palace, and the palace could not have been left in better hands.

I announced my approval in a rather formal tone, considering the intimacy of the audience, "The Friend of the Scheriers is a friend to all. He is adored and honored. He is wise and just."

The matter did not need authenticating by me. But Felix and the swan bowed low in deferent response to my proclamation. And that settled the matter. The queendom was in Cort's hands.

CHAPTER 22
A Sentimental Reunion

EACH OF THE PORTAL STEWARDS had a private chamber. We found the only one that promised comfort to us all. In the corner of Tinyn's room, beside a desk that had only the Bible and a Rosary upon it, was a soft Brunnen bed. I slept with loving feathers on both sides, pressed firmly between the teacher of the Swan Knights and the Swan Knight's only lover. My mind was on Joseph, torn into equal portions between great faith in his abilities and the soul-wrenching terror of a mother in fear for her child. As I began to drift, I feared what wretched dreams might saturate my soul that night. With my body nestled against my beloved feathered ones, my mind went to my other source of comfort, and it took my dreams with it.

The moment my consciousness lost grip of my thoughts, my mind sought Taufe. It found her as she was — in twenty-four hour vigil, singing her prayers to God with the sisters of her order. She knew I was with her, and my voice came from one of her Brunnen throats, harmonizing in prayer with the choir of St. Hildegard. From there my dreams took control. I felt myself propelled from Taufe's throat, as a single harmony that floated to the high arches of the cathedral and blended with the voices of the other sisters. I was a note of music, holding hands and dancing with dozens of other soft, prayerful Brunnen notes.

We were not mournful notes, nor did we dance in selfish demands. We were grateful notes, sung in thanksgiving of God's goodness. We bounced off of the ceiling and walls, floating through the sweet, humid air of Brunnen land, entering the ears of the sisters, swirling around their hearts and heads, and exiting through their eyes, only to float into the air and repeat the dance again and again, until I awoke under one feathered arm and one feathered wing.

It was Friday, and the park and palace above came to life with waves of tourists. We had no choice but to remain underground and wait out the day. The bustle of the crowds echoed in the Stewards' home. I was drawn to the murmurs, as if I could walk into the park and see my parents and brother looking for me and calling my name. The day seemed to last for months. With the only light coming from torches, held in the hands of Wühlenvogel gargoyles, time was undeterminable. Each second was stretched to many times its natural length. The three of us had the entire underground palace to ourselves. We roamed and explored, sometimes together, sometimes alone.

We passed some light conversations, but in general we spoke little. The weight on our heads was severe. It held down all of the frivolous words that might usually help pass a long day in such intimate company. But our mouths were reluctant to send into the air those more meaningful words that encumbered our hearts. So we remained mostly silent. I tried to stay out of their heads. It was a needed day of prayer and reflection for each of us, and I was afraid that bearing the weight of their thoughts and mine might prove too much from my fragile spirit.

Eventually the day ended. The crowds left. And Felix, The Ancient One, and I all went above ground and walked brisk laps around Linderhof Park. The nighttime Spring air was biting on skin that was used to the Sweeter Realm and not well-warmed by light hearts within. With many more steps than words shared between us, we wore ourselves out and went back to bed. We knew the park would be closed for the Easter weekend, and we would have the valley to ourselves.

My eyes opened on Saturday morning to a smooth, alabaster pair of legs, attached to the delicate bare feet of a figure who needed no introduction. I sat up slowly, scanning the woman from feet to face, slowly, as if afraid to overdose on her magnificent beauty. She swayed slightly back and forth, her skin rippling with the movements. Around her waist was wrapped a braided band of her own light-brown hair, attached to which was a small knife. There before my eyes was the bare figure of Brunhilde. As my eyes scanned upward, they were reluctant to release what they left behind. But each inch of her was more beautiful and alluring than the last. When I got to her face, I was utterly transfixed.

She looked to be ageless, timeless. Her complexion was as fair as an infant child. But just beneath it was clear evidence of an ancient wisdom, and countless generations of experience.

I parted my lips to speak her name. But instead of my voice, I heard the voice of the swan.

His head rose to the height of mine, as he spoke in a raspy tone of disbelief, "Brunhilde? Is it really my beloved?"

In exquisite antiquated German, but in a mix of a hundred accents, she answered him, "I have come back to you, faithful friend and teacher. I have come back to the valley where I was raised. I have come for her."

She pointed to me, then drifted her pointed finger to the desk and continued, "And I have come with this."

Between her body and her voice, I was as captivated as the thousands of evil men she had vanquished over the centuries. The trance was broken by the gasp of The Ancient One. It shook me free from the spell of her beauty and allowed me to follow her pointed finger. There, on Tinyn's desk, between the Rosary and the Bible, sat the Holy Grail.

Any grip that Brunhilde's figure had of my attention was shattered by the sight of the Grail. My Swan Knights Blood took complete control of me. I lunged at the Grail, as if to protect it from some immediate and unknown danger. I grabbed it and held its rim against my chest. In doing so, I aroused Felix from sleep. The air of the room was charged with excitement. Felix felt it and his feathers stood rigid. His attention went to the one stranger in the room — to Brunhilde. He stared at her, but not captivated by her beauty. After a couple of seconds scanning her up and down, he turned his eyes easily to me, along with an expression of intrigue and bewilderment.

"Is this Brunhilde?" he asked me.

Before I could answer, he noticed what I pressed against my chest. His thoughts went to his son.

He turned his attention back to the daughter of Tannhäuser, sprang to his feet and demanded, "Joseph! You have seen Joseph! Where is he?"

Brunhilde was infinitely more concerned for the Grail than for the feathered boy she received it from. Her response was calm and entirely too slow for Felix.

Brunhilde barely had time to part her lips in response before Felix followed, "He had the Holy Grail. Now it is here. Where is our son? Is he here with you?"

Felix did not wait for Brunhilde. He frantically looked around. He ran to the doorway of Tinyn's bedchamber, turned back to Brunhilde and demanded again, "Where is he?"

Brunhilde placed her palm on Felix's cheek. The skin of her arm began to ripple downward, from the shoulder to the palm that held Felix's face.

Her voice rang out in Brunnen harmony, but speaking softly in German, "Yours is the purest and noblest heart I have met in centuries. And I feel your pain."

Felix's breath slowed with Brunhilde's hypnotic voice and touch.

He was calmer, but insisted again, "Where is Joseph?"

"He is not with me. I am here on his errand, at his command. He is like *me*. And unlike me. Eat your breakfast. Refresh yourselves. I have much to tell you."

Her vague report gave us enough relief to obey her. Her calm manner, her beauty, and her rich authoritative voice left us little choice. Added to that was The Ancient One's validation. His faith in Brunhilde was comprehensive. He trusted her unreservedly. And we trusted him. So we gathered in the main hall and ate from the Steward's pantry small, green cakes made of God-knows-what. They were earthy-tasting, mildly unpleasant, but perfectly filling.

The swan was glued to Brunhilde's side, imploring her for any morsel of information about her life since she left him in the Black Forest centuries earlier. She answered rather coldly, with little more than yes or no. But when she looked at him, her iciness melted, and her eyes glowed with love and warmth. Several times he wrapped his wing around her. Each time, her skin turned from that of a naturally pale woman to bluish-green, and it waved upward. Once or twice, it raised her off of her seat.

Under different circumstances, I would have delighted in the reunion. I knew what they meant to each other. But the joy that would otherwise have lit that morning ablaze was smothered by the direness of the situation. My thoughts skipped like a stone on a pond, across topics mundane and monumental. I thought about the Grail and was glad to have it. I thought about the scriptures and the will of God. I thought about my queendom and the creatures I love so much. But towering from the center of all of it, was the thought of my son. The Grail had shared an equal allocation of my concerns. With it safe in my possession, it dumped its portion of my burden onto my thoughts of Joseph.

My breath sped and slowed. I clinched and relaxed, as my mind drifted from subject to subject. But every thought brought me back to Joseph, and I subconsciously whispered his name several times. Each time brought a squeeze of my husband's hand in response, and a look of compassion from the swan. Brunhilde showed little reaction to me and my swinging disposition. Her eyes were deep as they looked at me, as if they saw me comprehensively in a glance, every inch of my body, mind, and spirit. She had an indescribable, unspeakable power that had aggrandized and enriched with each century since she had last seen the swan. I dared not defy her. I asked nothing of her as we ate. After breakfast, she told us of her encounter with Joseph.

Brunhilde's ability to sense the hearts of people continued to sharpen during her 800 years of life. Joseph's pious, noble passion drew her attention the moment he went through my portal.

She stood, positioned herself in front of me and described the sensation, "The children of Parsifal are on every continent. Most are good. Many are not. Your son shined beyond them all. After he appeared, I sensed none of them but him, like I stared into a bright light that blinded me to all else. I felt his Grail Blood, but differently than the rest. It was magnified. I know now that you drank from the Grail… that he has Parsifal's Grail Blood and yours."

As she spoke of *my* Grail Blood, she bowed slightly, and she reverently softened her voice. When she raised her eyes back to mine, I could see in them that she revered me above Felix and the swan, above all others. There was an adoration in her gaze that I had not seen until that moment. But once revealed to me, it never left. Every word and every glance to me afterward was laced with veneration and awe. She had given no thought to keeping the Grail, to keeping it safe under her far more capable watch. In her eyes, I was the only creature in God's creation entitled to hold it. I was the Queen and Swan Knight. Her years of upbringing with the swan and the children of Parsifal deeply implanted her respect for both of my titles.

I urged her to proceed and she obeyed, "I followed his bright beacon, from where I was, in the far northeast, through Germany and across the border to the West, into France. That is where I found your son. He was in search of his grandparents and uncle. His destination was Colorado. But he is like me. He feels the goodness or evil of human hearts. Unlike me, the evil does not illicit fury. It spawns in him love, and overwhelming compassion… so overwhelming that it kept him from his destination."

She spoke those last words with such dire gravity that I burst into tears. She hummed and rubbed her thumb back and forth across my lips until I regained myself. Felix hoisted me and placed me on his lap, wrapping both arms around me tightly.

Confident in my recovery, Brunhilde continued, "Your son crossed the border into the West and encountered evil-hearted men and women. They were soldiers. He could have easily slipped past them. But he was drawn to their evil hearts, and he felt an unconquerable desire to redeem them. He pitied them, walked to them and reached to stroke their faces. They were beyond the redeeming qualities of his compassion. Goodness to your

305

son's degree was not in their ability to understand. They saw your feathered boy. And in a mix of fear, confusion, and bigotry, they surrounded him and taunted him. They shot their guns at his feet, telling him to flap his arms and fly away. They asked him what sort of creature he is and threatened to roast him and serve him with potatoes."

Felix's rage grew with the revelation of each terrible detail. His feathers turned searing hot, like I had never felt them before, and he squeezed me painfully tight.

"Felix!" The Ancient One yelled at him, "The Queen!"

Felix relaxed his grip and cooled his feathers while kissing the back of my head repeatedly. I reached back to stroke his cheek, then begged Brunhilde to continue.

"They would have killed him had I not arrived. I was drawn at first to Joseph's goodness. But in the midst of the soldiers, all I could sense was their hate. I killed them all before they could harm a feather on Joseph's back."

As she said that, she recalled the event with vivid detail. I looked into her eyes and fell through them, landing with a thud on the floor of her memories. I saw what she envisioned. About twenty soldiers, mostly men, but a few women, surrounded Joseph in a forest. Most kept their weapons down or holstered. A few shot their guns at his feet and taunted him, like Brunhilde described. This I saw from her perspective, descending from the tops of the trees. She landed beside Joseph. I saw him. I saw him through the eyes of her memory. He looked alert but not frightened. He stood nobly and regally, but with softness and tenderness. His face showed no concern for the soldiers' guns, only for their souls.

Brunhilde held her little knife in her right hand. She flew at the closest soldier, the one shooting nearest to Joseph's feet. She slid effortlessly across the forest floor, with little movement of her legs, like the earth tilted toward the soldier and she rode the slope like a skier on a hill. The soldier, like most violent men she encountered, was thoroughly encased in her beauty, unable and unwilling to raise his gun against her. In the blink of a Wühlenvogel's eye, she made three deep holes in the man's skull with her blade.

I doubt he felt pain. He fell to the forest floor with the same expression of bewildered delight that seized his face the moment she landed beside Joseph. The intense violence of the scene shook a few of the soldiers from their shared trance. Blood flung from Brunhilde's retreating blade, hitting those nearest and decorating their frozen, mesmerized faces with deep red splashed and spattered patterns. They stood like painted statues in a museum, as Brunhilde identified those who had broken from her spell and ended their threat before they could raise their guns and fire. She swirled around and between them, slashing and puncturing them on all sides. Her blade found the backs of their necks, the sides of their heads, their hearts, their arms, and their legs before they realized she was upon them.

A few triggers were pulled. A few bullets left their guns. But nothing came close to endangering Brunhilde or Joseph. Many of them never broke from the spell of her beauty. Those soldiers died peacefully. Falling lifeless to the ground after a single, precise strike. Like the first, they still wore expressions of exquisite bliss. They died with their eyes experiencing sensual pleasure like they had never known and their imaginations wrapping around every inch of Brunhilde's bright, bare, dulcet figure. Others discovered terror for the first time, just as Brunhilde's blade punctured them. They fell to the ground with the most horrid expressions fixed to their lifeless faces.

After the last soldier fell to the ground, her attention was drawn to the sobs of Joseph. He did not cry in relief of his danger, nor in gratitude for his rescuer. He cried for the men and women whose bodies still oozed blood from their wounds. He cried for the families who would mourn them. And he cried for the lost opportunity of their redemption.

I was not sure how much of the imagery in my head came directly from Brunhilde's memories of the event and how much sprang from my imagination as my ears continued to hear her tell the story. I pulled myself from her head in time to hear her tell of Joseph's tears.

The Ancient One was torn between reveling in a story of Brunhilde's heroics and wishing to know the welfare and whereabouts of his young student. Felix and I were not torn.

"Where is Joseph?" Felix demanded.

Brunhilde answered, more perplexed than judgmental, "Your son wept for the destroyed evil. He held his hands against their wounds, prayed for them, and begged them to return to life. He ordered their wounds to close, expecting the bodies of the dead to obey him. He pulled the Grail from a pouch that strapped over his shoulder. I had never seen the Grail. But I knew in a glance what it was. It seemed at home in his hand. It appeared to grow from him like a fingernail."

I dropped my head and interrupted with words meant for my own heart, more than for the audience before me, "I was so wrong. He was right and I was so very blind."

The Ancient One reached forward and rubbed my upper arm, and tried to comfort me, saying, "Many things have brought us here, perhaps the hand of God. You have reacted as a loving mother, a Queen, and a Swan Knight."

"No," I rebutted, "my jealousy and short-sightedness brought us to this… brought *him* to this."

"Enough!" Felix scolded. "These points are moot." He looked quickly, but less sternly than before to Brunhilde and added, "For heaven's sake, where is he?"

"He filled the Grail with water from the soldiers' bottles and poured it on their wounds and into their mouths.

They were dead, beyond the power of the Grail... or undeserving of it. I stayed with him while he tried to save them, gathering what information I could from him between his prayers and his sobs."

Brunhilde sat, as if suddenly exhausted. Ripples ran across her bare skin, violently in different directions, crashing against each other. She turned a deep purple, which faded to blue as she continued to stare at the floor in front of her. She returned to her normal, pale flesh-color as she raised her eyes to me. For the first time, she looked like a woman to me, a normal, though strikingly beautiful woman.

She reached one hand to rest on my knee and spoke hoarsely through one throat, "I have seen enough of soldiers to know that they would be quickly missed and harshly avenged, especially during these times. I begged him to retreat with me. I could have protected him. I could have taken him here and sent him through the portal to his own home. But he refused."

She stood sharply and puffed her chest in imitation of Joseph's posture, and in a disturbingly precise impression of his voice, she quoted him, "These are men and women, like my mother's people. They deserve to be respected. I will not leave their bodies here, not like this, with the writhing expressions of terror still on the lifeless faces of the ones who died in fear."

Brunhilde resumed her natural posture and continued in her natural voice, "He wiped the blood from their faces, hoisted two of them over his shoulders, and started walking west, along the road, deeper into France. I leaped into the air and landed in front of him. I implored him to abandon his mission and come with me. I warned him of the soulless fury of the world he faced. He stopped, looked at me with the same expression of compassion he first showed the soldiers. He placed the bodies gently on the road, as if they

309

still felt pain. He pulled the Grail from the pouch and ordered me sternly to take it to Linderhof, through the portal, and to his noble mother, the Queen and Swan Knight. When I arrived in the grotto and opened the portal, it spoke to me. It told me that you are here, in this world. My heart led me to this Wühlenvogel construct. And I found the three of you asleep."

Never had my maternal heart known greater fear. My own anguish was compounded by Felix's, whose thoughts charged wildly into my head.

Through my breaking voice, I scolded Brunhilde, "Why did you not take him, force him to come with you?"

Brunhilde looked to Felix, then back to me and responded, "How could I? I am not worthy to defy him. He is your son. There is no sound tree that produces rotten fruit."

She went pale-white, stone-still, then disappeared almost entirely from sight. She began to sway gently, returning to our vision before continuing, "The kiln tests the work of the potter, the test of a person is in conversation. Your son spoke honestly, words of love, divine words of Godly meaning. I knew him immediately to be my better. And he held the Cup of Christ. Its deep brown protruded from his palm like words from the poet's lips. All of this told me that he is sent by God and far above my judgment, far beyond my control."

"We will take that as an endorsement." The swan replied with a proud chuckle.

I turned to him, and looked at him like he had just stabbed me with Reid's wooden knife.

"Do not look at me like that," he sang softly with a tilt of his head. "Such favorable praise from Brunhilde should not go uncelebrated. She sees into the heart like you see into the mind. If the merits of his heart are as she describes, then he is beyond the tutelage and direction of *any* of us.

He is on a mission that we cannot touch, and dare not alter. Only God can guide him now."

The swan's words brought me pride, but not comfort. The Grail was back in my possession. Its fate was in my hands. But Joseph's was not. As badly as I wanted the Grail under my control, I wished it still safely tucked away in Joseph's shoulder pouch, where it could save him in battle as it did me.

Felix stood determined. He looked at me, pointed to the Grail, and ordered me, "Take the Grail. Let's go find our son."

Brunhilde stood in front of him and turned smooth and silvery. The white of his skin and feathers reflected from her belly and breasts. His face reflected from hers, distorted by her delicate contours. Her entire front side looked like a surreal painting of a Federman, twisted and altered into the voluptuous figure of a magnificent human beauty.

She placed her palms on the sides of his face, lowered her forehead to rest against his, and spoke low and harmonized, in the purest of notes from her two throats, "You are brave and strong. But in much greater abundance than your courage and strength is your faith. I left your son because his words were from God, his actions divine. And for these reasons, you too must leave him to his fate."

Tears flowed down Felix's cheeks and neck, as rapid and abundant as a steady brook on a steep slope. Ripples on Brunhilde's skin mimicked my husband's tears, running from beneath her eyes to the tips of her toes.

Felix tried to pull his face from her grasp, but she squeezed him more tightly and added, "Are you to rush across the Western border, another strange-looking feathered man with no knowledge of the local languages or customs?"

He answered feebly, "I… I have Verena. She is of their kind, an American. They will let her home."

The Ancient One stuck his long neck between Brunhilde's elbows and spoke with his beak nearly touching Felix's mouth, "With no identification, no documents?"

I tugged on the swan's neck and pulled him from between Felix and Brunhilde. I stood at Felix's side and ran my hand along Brunhilde's cheek and through the hair on the side of her head. I struggle to describe the sensations of my fingers. They swam through her hair like Glöhenchor through a clear pond, frolicking and reluctant to leave the pleasure of their environment. But my love of my husband was infinitely stronger than the sensual allurements of Brunhilde. I withdrew my hand as she backed away and allowed me to replace her in front of Felix.

"They are right," I said between kisses on his dangling nose. "It pains me to say, but they are right. I am a Swan Knight, sworn to protect the portal. I cannot traipse across the countryside, Grail in hand, looking for our son and endangering everything the Swan Knights have fought for. I am also the Queen and cannot afford to be as Albert V was, endangering our home for the will of my own desires. We will keep camp here. I can wander Germany without identification, without arousing suspicion. If anything happens to Joseph, it will make news, and the public computers will tell us everything."

The Ancient One and Brunhilde readily agreed. Felix acquiesced reluctantly. And our immediate plan was set.

"You cannot wander Germany like that," Brunhilde told me, gesturing to my clothes. "Leave that to me."

She and The Ancient One went above ground. They walked several laps around the valley together, while Felix and I sat under a tree. The Ancient One returned to us alone. He told me that his dear Brunhilde left to fetch me a gift. As the sun lowered in the sky, she returned to us, holding in her soft but deadly hands a pair of pants, a shirt, socks, and a pair of shoes. I did not know where she got them, how she got them. I did not care. I took them from her with gratitude.

That night, I sent the swan back through Parsifal's Portal with the Grail, instructing him to take it to Gralkirsche and place it under the care of the Boots of Lohengrin, then return to me with the Portal Stewards and any other volunteers he can find.

As we all stood at the threshold of the grotto, under the dim light of a partial moon, Brunhilde kissed her old friend goodbye.

The swan rambled in protest, "No, no, where are you going? You have come back to me after so long. I need you now, more than ever. Verena needs you."

"And I will serve her, as I have served God and every Swan Knight, with the abilities that God has given me. My rage is a gift from God, like my beauty and my flight. The skills *you* taught me are a gift from God, like the blade given to me by the Duke. I must use these gifts as I always have, following my heart and extinguishing evil, tilting the scales toward goodness in the time given to me."

I seized her attention, in sudden remembrance of her father's tunic, "Wait! I have something for you."

I ran into the underground palace, to the cubby where the tunic was on display, removed it with both hands, as if it were fragile, and ran it back to Brunhilde. It glowed magically under the moonlight.

"This was your father's…"

I was not allowed to finish. Brunhilde swiped in from my hand like a starving man taking a loaf of bread. She held it in front of her face, too closely to focus upon in. She dropped to her knees, pressed the fabric against her face, and inhaled slowly and deeply. She exhaled as quickly as she could so she could draw another slow inhale, searching for some scent of her father, fossilized within the weaves of the garment.

She began to weep out loud, mournful cries that were muted by the thick wool pressed against her face. She cried into the tunic, kneeling as she had dropped, for several minutes. We stood around her, all of us, not knowing how to comfort her and unwilling to disturb whatever precious memories were drawn to the forefront of her thoughts by the smells she fished from deep in the fabric with her keen senses.

Finally, she dropped her hands to her knees, stopped her sobs as quickly as she began them, rose to her feet, and handed me the tunic in a haphazard bundle, saying, "This is not a useful tool to me. It is not a luxury my duties will indulge. Do as you wish with it."

She took the swan's head with both hands, kissed his beak, and told him that she loves him. She turned from him to Felix, gently lifted his dangling nose from his face and giggled. She turned to me, knelt at my feet with a bow of her head, whispered a prayer, rose, submerged my lips within hers with a silent and sustained kiss, then pulled away from me, looked to the sky and disappeared into the dark above. The swan wept loudly and unashamed. His heart was broken by her departure, as it had been before.

I stood to face him, stroked his neck with one hand and tapped the Grail under his wing with the other, saying, "She has her mission and we have ours. Get it safely to Hüter and come back to me. I need you much more than I need Brunhilde. My father is dead. You are my father now and you are more important to me than ever."

He recovered immediately after my words, stiffening his neck and raising his head high, as he said to me in his calm, blissful voice, "I amend my words, my love. I do not need Brunhilde. I desire her. I need *you*. All of God's creation needs you."

I pulled the swan and Felix into a tight embrace, and said, "It is a good thing I cannot float away into the sky. I am your same old Verena, and you know where *I* will be… here, awaiting the return of the Swan Knights' most trusted friend and father."

On those words, we waddled our tight embrace into the grotto. Felix and I stopped short of the artificial lake. The swan swam gracefully across it, toward the mural of Tannhäuser, with the Grail tucked under his wing. He hopped onto the small stage, kissed the ground beneath him, and whispered a few words to Kandake, whose remains were beneath him. He turned to me and nodded. With a thought from my stone-still body, I opened the portal and watched The Ancient One disappear. The snap of the closing portal accompanied a tremendous surge of love for my husband, who stood alone with me as the only creature I knew in the Portal Valley. Even the grass stood still and silent as we made our way back to the underground accommodations. The embrace of the other was our only tonic for the ailments of our souls. We took that medicine voraciously and remained in the tightest embrace through the night.

CHAPTER 23
From the Lips of a Child

I AWOKE IN A STATE OF SEVERE AGITATION, from dreams I do not remember. My poor mind was being pulled in too many directions to commit much of myself to any one thing. At that point, I understood King Ludwig's decision to abdicate his throne and the Swan Knighthood to become the King of the Land and Shallow Waters. The duties of the Swan Knight and the concerns of the Queen, though always in service to the same master, were often in contradiction and never meant to be held by the same creature. I was more confused than in fear for my son. I was numbed to my faith in my destiny, my passion for God, even to the caress of my husband. I stood abruptly, dressed in the clothes that Brunhilde brought me, and made my way to the Venus Grotto, not knowing what I intended to do, but desiring to open the portal, hoping its crackle would speak to me, the way it spoke to Rudolf.

I stood inside of the grotto, exactly where I was when I opened the portal the night before. I looked into the mural of Tannhäuser. I felt nothing from it or from the constructions of my dear King Ludwig II. I thought about the sound of the opening portal, and it opened. Several Scheriers came bounding through, followed by some Zweigwesens and Friends of the Scheriers, all knocking the ones before into the artificial lake. The last one through was

317

a Federman. I closed the portal behind him. None of them were the Portal Stewards I hoped to see.

One of the Scheriers swam back to the stage in front of the mural, climbed onto the shoulder of the Federman, and announced. "We have been waiting at the Portal Point, waiting to serve you. Hundreds more wait..."

He paused, looked behind him to the mural, and asked, "Why did you close the portal, my Queen? An army is coming to serve you, to retrieve your son from this unholy place."

The whole grotto went silent, except for the subtle splashing from the Scheriers and Friends of the Scheriers who paddled to keep their heads above the water.

"Go home," I told them just above a whisper. "The Portal Stewards will return, and I will let them know what I need. Please go. You will know when I need you."

They all looked so devastated by my command, so I softened it, adding, "This is a delicate situation. An army of Eden's creatures erupting from Ludwig's cave and flowing across the world could ruin everything. I will need you. I assure you of that. I just don't yet know how. Please go home and wait. I will let you know. I promise."

I reopened the portal. A few more Federmensch came into the grotto. The others pushed them back through. The first Federman through stood at the portal, ushering the creatures back. When he was the only one left, I noticed that he looked beyond me with a smile. His eyes were on Felix, who stood beside me. Only then did I realize that he was there, and that his hand rested on my shoulder.

I turned to Felix and begged, "Go with them."

"No!" he insisted. "My place is always with you, to comfort you."

"That is just it. I don't need comfort right now. I need agitation. I need the battles in my mind to run their course and declare a winner, so that I might have some idea of what I am supposed to do. Those battles cannot rage under the warmth of your feathers. I assure you, I will be in desperate need of what you offer me, before this is done, but not now. Stay at the Portal Point if you must. I will open it soon."

His face fell. He felt useless to me, a sensation that cut him from the inside out.

"How long?" he asked.

"You know I can't be without you long. Just... give me some time."

He obeyed me. He followed his clansman through the portal and I closed it behind him. I was alone in the Swan Knights' valley.

As I had hoped, the battle raged in my head, resuming its violence the moment the portal closed. I left the grotto and wandered into the park. It did not feel like home to me, neither did my lakeside palace, St. Hildegard, or Centennial Colorado. Everything was prickly to me, every thought a torture. I strolled aimlessly from the valley until I came across a road. I was picked up by a family who offered me a ride. I accepted the ride with no idea or care for direction or destination. I sat in the back with three children. Although they were very different from each other, and even more different from my own son, they reminded me of Joseph.

Each seat in the car had a computer screen in front of it. The children scrolled through endless information, allowing their eyes to surf what seemed to be an ocean of news and knowledge. The family drove by Oberammergau. I asked them to drop me off there. They had not intended to stop there. But they did, and they bought me a delicious breakfast of meats and cheeses. They ate with me, wished me well, and were on their way.

The computers in the family's car reminded me of the ones on the train. I boarded the train in Oberammergau, in who-knows-which direction. I didn't care. I cared only for the computers on board, those wells of news and knowledge that might have some information on a lost feathered boy.

I found his trail quickly. The news spoke of a troop of Western soldiers, slaughtered near the French-German border. I scrolled frantically for a continuation of the story, for word of a boy carrying the bodies back to their people, but I found nothing.

A girl sat alone across the aisle from me. She looked to be eleven or twelve years old. She had pulled her feet up onto the seat so that her knees were as high as her cheeks. She had both arms wrapped around her legs, and her nose buried between her knees — and she was whimpering. Her long, course, wavy hair shook behind her as her entire body vibrated in distress. She took my attention entirely away from the all-knowing screen in front of me. My mind swept through several thoughts in a few seconds. My first thoughts were of compassion. But my eyes quickly left her and darted up and down the train in search of her people. She seemed to be alone.

My eyes went back to her, but not compassionately. When that same image of that same little girl, still whimpering into her knees, returned to my senses, it brought with it a heavy and dark sense of dread, well, more of a burning beneath my skin. I was repelled by her. I wanted to move farther from her. But my maternal instincts overcame that. I abandoned my computer terminal and my quest for information. I moved across the aisle and sat beside the girl.

She lifted her face to look at me, revealing puffy eyes and cheeks saturated with tears. After one quick glance at me, she returned her face downward, crying more loudly and shaking more disturbingly. I looked around the train again. Not only was nobody looking for her. Nobody seemed to notice her cry. I leaned in to her and put my arm around her. She shoved my arm aside and scrambled away from me, until her back was pressed against the side of the train and the back of her head shoved against the window.

In a shaking voice, much more disgusted and angry than frightened, she yelled at me, "Keep your hugs! Your arms cannot save me from a nuclear blast."

Her raised voice caught the attention of a few of the nearer passengers. But after a some judgmental whispers, more annoyed by her noise than moved by her words, they reattached their attention to the screens in front of them or the gadgets on their laps. When I returned my eyes to the girl, she was on her knees, leaning toward me, with eyes furiously focused on mine.

With reddened cheeks, shaking with anger, she scolded me, "This is your world now. It does not belong to your parents anymore. You cannot blame them for anything that happens now. It is yours to fix or ruin."

She sat back against the side of the train, folded her arms, and took a deep breath, looking to the floor of the train, but with a gaze that looked far beyond what her eyes could see, and speaking more to herself than to me, she continued, "At this rate, it will never be my world. It will never be mine. I will be *dead*. There will be no new generation to inherit the world from the last, and no world to inherit."

She regathered herself, shook off her daze, sat primly on her seat, looking forward, before turning her head to face me again, as she said calmly, "So, what are you going to do with *your* world while it *is* yours?"

I did not know if she wanted me to answer. I had the feeling that nothing I could think to say would satisfy her. Her vision was beyond mine and I didn't really know what she was talking about. It seemed that her question was rhetorical. She did not give me time to consider an answer.

She followed quickly with, "Do you want to be the ones who lost it all? Get out there and fix this. For Christ's sake, save your children."

She was not speaking to me, but to all adults, through me. I turned to face the front of the train, in the seat beside her. I lifted my face upward and covered my eyes with the palms of my hands. I filled my lungs to capacity and held that deep breath until my chest begged me to exhale. I let the breath out slowly through a slightly opened mouth and rounded lips, creating a whistling wind sound. The sound spoke to my young friend that her words took root.

When I opened my eyes, lowered my head and turned to face her again, she simply nodded, said, "Hmmm", and poked at the screen in front of her. She brought up a cartoon and watched it like any other child. I felt a strong inexplicable need to get off the train and away from the girl. I took the next stop. I watched from the platform as she sped away from me, before crossing the track and taking the very next train back to Oberammergau, this time with a widened sense of purpose, with my same sense of duty, but immensely expanded by the words of the little stranger I met on the train.

I searched the news again but found no further mention of my son. I thought about moving my camp to the abandoned city beneath the Black Forest, assuming it to remain undiscovered, and desiring to be closer to France and to Joseph. The thought was interrupted by the train's arrival in Oberammergau. Having drained what little could be taken from the computers, I had no reason to remain on the train. And I wanted to get back to Linderhof. I had no desire to travel aimlessly, nor did I want to welcome a crowd of my subjects through the portal.

In the quaint and relatively quiet town, I went to church. It was Easter Sunday. I celebrated the resurrection of the Lord with strangers. I received the Holy Eucharist, taking the body and blood of Christ with hands that recently held the Holy Grail. As the priest handed the cup to me, I thirsted terribly for its holy contents. At that moment, the wooden cup used by the priest in Oberammergau was as holy and divine to me as the very cup that Christ held at the Last Supper. The Eucharist filled me, and I felt connected to God, to Taufe and the Brunnen sisters, to my father and family.

These feelings blended with the words of the girl on the train, still rolling in constant motion around my head. By the time I walked out of the church in Oberammergau I had an impatient, jigging, bit-chomping drive toward a target I could not identify. I wanted to run at full speed but did not know where. I did the only thing I could think to do. I ran. I ran through the rest of the day and into the night, until I reached the Portal Valley. I walked slowly through the valley, with aching legs and lungs, past the Venus Grotto, to the underground home of the Portal Stewards. I lay alone in the Brunnen bed, thinking of the child on the train.

"The world is mine to fix."

This was the mantra I chanted to myself for hours, wanting to act upon it but having no idea how, until I fell asleep. I slept alone there, hoping to awaken with some focus for my relentlessly pulsing determination. I begged God for direction. I even took the immature step of listing all that I had done in service to God, hoping I could barter it for a single, clear sign of what to do. No sign came clearly to me before I fell asleep.

CHAPTER 24
News of Joseph

I AWOKE EARLY ON MONDAY, before the sunrise, tense-muscled and wholly unrested. I had spent the night alone because I wanted to think. But by morning I could not bear another moment in isolation with my own thoughts. I marched with aching joints directly to the grotto, opening the portal before I left the Brunnen bedroom. The Portal Stewards were waiting for me as they had promised. I felt their anxious thoughts as they paced around the Portal Point in the Nomadic Belt. The Ancient One was not with them and I could not sense his mind. Calmer, less anxious, but equally excited to step into Linderhof, was Felix and Acheriel, accompanied by a small cluster of creature-volunteers who pushed their way through the portal.

They all came into the grotto before I passed the stone door. The Linderhof grounds crew was already at work. The palace was lit, and employees of the Bavarian Department of Palaces were preparing for a busy day of tourism. Under the dim light of the early dawn, I crept with my loyal subjects back to the stealth and cover of the Stewards' underground home. Before the crowds arrived, we debated and determined that I would cross the Western border and search for signs of Joseph.

The only matter still undecided was my mode of transportation. Acheriel wanted to take me. But at ground level, he would be conspicuous in the extreme. Agnes, the

Scherier, suggested that Friedrich take me west. He had been trapped in Linderhof for a century and a half. He knew the area well. He knew the dangers. And he could fly me well above the human eyes on the ground. It was a dangerous mission. The West had grown suspicious. The liberties that had defined them for so long were dissolved by their desire for security. Yes, I was American. But I had disappeared and was presumed dead. I had no identification. If I were captured, along with a Wühlenvogel, we would both be in danger.

Despite these concerns, we could think of nothing else to do. I would not risk many lives. The Grail was secure in Gralkirsche. This mission was for the rescue of my son, not for the salvation of God's people. The portal was as safe and hidden as it had been. The Sweeter Realm was not at risk. My obligation to the mission was as a mother, not as a Queen or Swan Knight. So we all agreed. Friedrich would fly me west and I would walk the roads of France until I found my son or died trying.

We were to embark that night, while a minimal crew of my Royal Guard remained beneath Linderhof. I called for the Guard and sent all but Felix and Acheriel back to their homes and families. The Portal Stewards remained. We were in their home, hiding in a cave of their construction, in rooms and halls that they saw daily since Ludwig's death. I did not have the authority to evict them. Although I was the Swan Knight, the heir of Ludwig and the Wittelsbach Swan Knights, a child of Parsifal, who first claimed that valley as his home, the valley belonged to the Portal Stewards much more than it did to me or the Bavarian Department of Palaces, or anyone else who might make a claim. They remained. The Stewards and the Guard knew what they risked. If I were lost and Joseph never found, Brunhilde would be the only being who both knew of their existence and could open the portal. And her involvement in anything was less than predictable.

While the morning passed on, and the Guard trickled through the portal, the crowds of tourists to the palace thickened and thinned in waves. I closed the portal for the day and took the opportunity to pass into the park and mix among the crowds. With the very first conversation I overheard, I learned news of Joseph.

A group of young friends, students from Berlin, spoke of the newest tensions between the West and the East. They spoke of a spy, a genetically altered, feathered boy who killed an entire patrol of Western soldiers, not far from the German border. My breath stopped and my heart seemed to join it. I panicked and shook and caught the attention of the students.

They rushed to my assistance, holding me on my feet, above my weakened knees. I assured them that I was all right, brushed them from my arms, and sat shakily on the ground. They backed away hesitantly, asking repeatedly if I needed help. I did not convince them, but after my repeated demands, they let me be and continued to stroll the grounds.

When I recovered my strength, I joined a crowd as they walked from the grotto to the palace entrance, listening to their conversations for any news. They spoke of the beauty of the grounds. They bragged of their wealth. And they regaled each other with inaccurate anecdotes of King Ludwig's life. The world remained ignorant to the truths about the last Wittelsbach Swan Knight. In my impatience to hear about Joseph, I almost corrected them. I bit my tongue and my patience paid off.

At the entrance to the palace was a kiosk. It was a computer with information about the palace, the Wittelsbach, King Ludwig II, the architects of the palace and designers of the gardens. But it was also connected to the media world around it. Like the terminals on the trains, it was another all-knowing, all-telling resource of world news and entertainment. I did not have to search long. The West was furious about the feathered boy who killed their soldiers. Joseph's youth rallied their sensibilities. They declared it a human rights travesty, to have altered the child for military purposes. And they used the incident as a propaganda dagger against the East, blasting the story and their disapproval across every news organization that wanted a scoop.

I pieced together Brunhilde's story with the information in the news and determined that Joseph carried the two dead soldiers back to their base and was arrested there for the deaths of everyone slaughtered by Brunhilde that day. The mysterious, genetically altered, feathered boy spoke in broken English, exquisite German, and a host of unknown languages. There was nothing in the report about a portal to another world, nothing of the Federmensch and Unicorns, nothing of the Grail. I knew that Joseph would not betray us, not that any such reports would be believed from the mouth of a suspected spy.

They tested Joseph's DNA and found that he was more than a quarter German, with traces of Italian and Scottish from my mother's side. Felix's genetic contribution was an enigma to them. They determined that a German child was kidnapped by the East and experimented upon for the creation of a better soldier. At least that was the story they sent across Germany, trying to incense the Germans and break the bonds of trade between them and the East. They depicted Joseph as some innocent German child, stolen from his family and brutally mutated with ungodly experiments, turned into a killer and unleashed on the innocent soldiers of the West. The world news was plastered with images of a purely human Joseph, a computer-generated depiction of what he might look like with no Federman features. The Western governments asked for the parents of the stolen German boy to come claim their child. I knew it would not be so easy.

Nevertheless, the propaganda angle taken by the West relieved me tremendously. As long as they used him as a victim, as a tool to stir the disgust of the world, they would not harm him. Of this I was certain. But they also saw him as a weapon of the East and would not release him without tests and interrogation, the thought of which clawed ferociously at my heart. Above all, I wanted to know that he was not afraid, that he knew I was coming for him, and that he was not in pain. I reached so hard for his mind but could not connect with him. I stood at the kiosk, at the entrance to the palace, straining to touch his thoughts, however slightly. But all I managed was to cause myself an excruciating headache and a bloody nose that spilled onto the screen of the kiosk.

Palace staff cleaned my mess and medics tended to me. When I shook free of them all, I returned to the underground rooms and reported what I had learned. New plans had to be hatched. I would not find Joseph on the streets of France. He would be held in a military facility, probably in America. No army of Eden's creatures could free him, and my responsibilities to the Swecter Realm as its Queen, and to the portal as its Swan Knight, weighed as heavily on me as the mountain of maternal concerns over the welfare of my son.

Acheriel, whose counsel was almost as valuable to me as The Ancient One's and Taufe's, and whose own child was dear to Joseph, saw no choice but for me to turn myself in to Western authorities, claim my motherhood of Joseph, play along with their propaganda narrative, and throw myself on their compassion. Lenelil agreed with his distant cousin and suggested that I tell them that my son was stolen from me by the evil military scientists of the East and that

329

his return to his German mother would sway German relations in favor of the West. I did not trust my ability to lie so well and pull it off with Joseph's life and mine on the line.

Never had I so desperately needed the advice of my teachers, and neither were with me. I reached for the swan's mind, asking him, "Where are you? Why haven't you come back?"

I felt no connection to him. In something of a jealous stupor, I added, "Now that you have seen your Brunhilde, there is no room in your heart for me."

The penetrating pungency of the jealousy and distress that accompanied that thought found the old bird. He was in Gemeinsam, gathering with their leaders and the leaders of the Boots of Lohengrin to determine where the Grail should be hidden until my return — and where it should remain in the increasingly probable case that I never returned.

The Ancient One heeded my mental call, answering, "My Queen, my most precious student, and my most cherished friend, I serve you at this very moment. But in your distress, I will leave these matters to the wisdom of others and join you immediately."

He mounted Senische, who had become the fastest of all Unicorns, and rushed from Gemeinsam to the Portal Point. In his youth, he would have flown himself almost as swiftly. But his difficult ride on the shoulders of a young Unicorn endeared him tenderly to me and made the gift of his presence all the more precious. He was with me in a few hours and allowed no signs of his trying travels to be noticed by me. I snuck into the grotto during a rare lull in visitors, snuck him through the portal, out of the grotto and in a flash through a tiny Wühlenvogel hole in the ground, in the grasp of Friedrich's tail.

While I walked around to the other entrance, I sought Taufe and invited her to remain in my mind while we pondered our options. In the cave, looking at my new friends and old friends gathered together for my cause, a wave of confidence rushed over me. And riding on the elevation of that wave, I found Taufe's mind. She had received almost every distressed thought that I had projected wildly since I swam through my portal. But I had been too wild, too distracted, too lost in the swirling and chaotic clouds of worry and confusion to perceive her responses. On my wave of confidence, both soothing and energizing, I heard her.

We wasted no time attending the matters at hand. Acheriel's plan seemed the most sound. But it made me terribly uncomfortable. I would be alone. I could not take Felix or any of the creatures. And I did not trust my ability to deceive, to pretend to be a German mother whose child was stolen.

"What else can we do?" The Ancient One asked, "You can't very well tell them that you were pulled through a portal at Linderhof Palace, became the Queen, killed the King of the Deep, and married a Federman. Any attempt at honesty would be devastating on many levels."

"But we don't know what Joseph has told them," I reminded them.

Acheriel answered without a breath in between, "Nor *can* we know, until after you have already committed to a plan of action. This plan is all we have. We must pray that it works."

Syllia, in the signature enthusiasm of her kind, added, "They might just give him to you, and we can all go home."

Every other creature in attendance looked at her with a mix of delight and disappointment. They too knew that it would not be so easy.

None of us saw good reason to delay the plan. We decided it was best to fly through the night. After a couple hours of sleep, Friedrich would fly me by cover of dark to the Western border, leave me to my own faculties in the hands of the Western government, make his way to the Black Forest before sunrise, and spend the day in the abandoned city of Einigkeitstadt before returning to Linderhof the next night.

Felix and I were left alone in Tinyn's room. Tinyn contented herself with the floor of the main hall. The Ancient One wanted to sleep with us, but he dared not ask. Acheriel invited him to nestle against him for the almost two hours of rest allotted by our plan. But the swan did not let me part from him easily. Knowing the departure would be difficult enough, he said his good-byes to me then, kissing me dozens of times and begging me to keep a thought-connection with Acheriel or Lenelil, so that he could grasp their horns and connect with me through them.

I had no expectation of sleep, but Felix's warm feathers and my memories of Brunnen lullabies lulled me into a shallow rest. Felix and I were awakened as planned by Tinyn's soft Brunnen fingertips on our cheeks. We rose and we ate. We spoke little. Only Felix accompanied Friedrich and me to the surface. His powerful Federman arms, those arms that hoisted me effortlessly onto Acheriel on the day that we met, that carried me through the woods as we ran from the Glühenchor pond after I was attacked by the serpents of the Deep, those arms that spun me as I fell from the cliff, so that he would break my fall, that stained arm that wiped the smudge from my armor and carried that heroic emblem forever, hugged me good-bye.

"Please come back to me," he whispered in the midst of an almost unbearably tight embrace, "and bring our son home."

All of the concerns in my head — Joseph, the portal, the Grail, my queendom, the creatures — all disappeared behind a single thought. I once thought I had killed him. I broke every bone in his body. But he recovered from that, strengthened by his love for me. If I die, and fail to free our son, Felix would be irrevocably broken. My pity for him as we said good-bye was the single most strangling thought I had ever had. It forbade the Bavarian air to enter my lungs and it seemed to coat every cell in my body with lead. I kissed my husband, told him I would see him soon, then nodded to Friedrich. The Wühlenvogel took me with his tail and flew me west, toward France.

CHAPTER 25
Into the West

FRIEDRICH FLEW ME TO A PATCH of dense forest just north of a small German town called Auenheim, on the east bank of the Rhine River, bordering France. His Wühlenvogel wings moved like lightning and we landed well before the sunrise. I allowed him half an hour to recover and catch his breath. He did not need so much, and he probed me for details about my plans. I had little in mind beyond what he already knew. I had a decision to make. During the flight, I had begun to doubt the plan. I thought about flying deep into France, or maybe into England, as resuming my former identity, as Verena Kessler, the American. But I would have to explain my nearly two-decade disappearance without revealing my precious secrets. And I could not see how that would get me my son. No — they had written my new identity for me, as a German mother who lost a child to the godless heathens of the East. They handed me that identity like Brunhilde handed me my clothes, and I had to put it on and wear it just the same.

I sat in the forest with Friedrich for hours and whispered my thought process to him as it occurred in my head. He agreed with my final decision. After discarding my doubts, but certainly not my fears, Friedrich took me into the rose sky of the infant dawn. He left me at the edge of a golf course, east of the town of Kehl. I told him to rush to the Black Forest without rest, to avoid the towns and roads as much as possible, and to hide under the Black Forest until nighttime. He swore his obedience and admiration, whispered a choppy form of the Lord's Prayer, then he flew toward the rising sun.

I walked into Kehl, which took me at least an hour. I strolled through the town, past stores and cafes, a movie theater and a lovely public rose garden, just beginning to bud. The morning sun shone off of the tower of St. Johannes Church. The moment I looked up at the tower, the church bell chimed. I took it as a sign and attended the morning mass. There was nothing special about the mass. I sank into intensely personal prayer, while my mouth and body mindlessly performed the rituals of the Catholic mass. The church interior reminded me of St. Hildegard, but brighter. The inner walls were lined with statues. I felt like they were praying with me. Behind the altar was a crucifix.

My heart jumped as a vivid flashback of that horrible dream leaped from the back of my mind and punched me in the chest. I thought about the nail pounding into my abdomen — into my womb. The hammering sound reverberated in my memory, as my inner-eye watched the nail sink into me. I had relived that dream countless times. But only then, in St. Johannes Church, did I seriously consider it an attack on my womb, a foreboding warning of the fate of my child. With this new realization, I began rolling through every prediction of Taufe, every prophetic scripture I had studied, fearing that I might recall one that would, like my dream, target my son.

My mind was only drawn back to the moment at hand when we rose to receive the Eucharist. I followed the line toward the altar. The Crucifix loomed menacingly over me as I received the sacrament. I took the cup and pressed my lips to it as reverently as I had matched the lip-marks of Parsifal on the Holy Grail. The Eucharist did not purge me of fear or erase the morbid memories of that awful dream. But it made me okay with whatever fate awaited me. It allowed me to again be a feather on the breath of God. I floated like a feather from the church, passing only simple pleasantries to the people around me.

I walked along the front of the church, down one block to a road that led to a pedestrian bridge across the Rhine, into France, into the West. My walk across the bridge was eerily reminiscent of my walk down the beach of the Queen's Lake, and onto the boat, where The Ancient One waited to pull me to face Löwschock. The western end of the bridge, unlike the German side, was heavily armed and fortified. There was a checkpoint where I stood alone, as the only person crossing that bridge into France. The soldiers demanded identification that I could not provide. They turned me away, ordering me back across the bridge, into Germany.

I walked a few steps east, up the ramp, toward Germany, in compliance with their sternly given orders. But I stopped sharp.

"I am the Queen of the Sweeter Realm and the Swan Knight. My duties are beyond the orders of this soldier." I yelled loudly in my head, without disturbing the air around me.

I turned around and took one firm step toward the checkpoint. The soldier who ordered me away walked to within inches of me. He threatened to arrest me if I did not obey his orders. I stood silently. Two more soldiers joined the one. One of them held in front of him a set of plastic wrist restraints. I would not walk away, or even turn around. The soldier with the restraints grabbed my left forearm.

"I am the mother of the feathered boy," I told them in calm, determined German. "Your government has asked for me. Here I am."

The men froze, wide-eyed with gaping mouths. After a few seconds, they looked at each other, each seeming to expect the others to give the next order. Finally, one of them pulled a phone from his vest pocket. He spoke in French into the phone. My mind spun faster than my ears, and I struggled to translate. When he finished talking, he stood in silence, listening for several minutes before returning the phone to his pocket.

Returning to German, he ordered me gently and cordially, "Please, my lady, come with us."

I followed the first soldier, with the other two in step behind me, to a small building just on the other side of the checkpoint. I sat in a cold, white room. A single, small, metal table sat bolted to the middle of the floor. I was escorted to a chair on the far side of the table, facing the door. There was an empty chair opposite of me. All four upper corners of the room had cameras, all aimed at the table.

I knew where this was going, and I knew the role I had to play. They had already written their ideal propaganda script, with my character, the sad German mother, as a central character. I only needed to play that part as they had written it. As I sat alone in the locked room, I began meticulously writing my own lines in the story, creating a back-story — an identity, a name, a home, a career, a good German family, and most importantly, a moving story of how my son had been taken from me.

I was ill-equipped to provide the necessary details. Any story I gave would be subject to scrutiny and verification. The truth is, I had no German address, no German identity or job. There was no police report about my stolen child. In other words, there was no lie I could get away with. Still, I hoped that their desire for their propaganda victory might help them to see past all of that and return the poor "stolen child" to her desperate mother and send them home to Germany. I was prepared to say whatever I must, to thank the good government of the West for their great wisdom and goodness, to curse the East for the inhumane experiments done on my son, to renounce the East on behalf of all German mothers. The loss of German trade would be devastating to the Eastern economy. I was ready to paint the entire incident as an attack by the East against the good people of the German speaking states.

After what felt like an hour or two, a man in a suit, no more than a few years older than me, came into the room and sat in the other chair. A soldier came with him and remained in the room, one I had not seen before. His uniform was different, entirely black. He held a small rifle in his hands, and a handgun and baton hung holstered to his belt.

The man in the suit extended his hand to mine and introduced himself in English, "I am Mr. Lewiston, Samuel Lewiston."

His accent was American. I found it soothing and almost answered in my Colorado English. But I caught myself and broke my English with a forced German accent. I am no actress. I never have been. So I spoke in English, pronouncing the sounds of the letters as they would be pronounced in German. I sounded German to me, and apparently to Mr. Lewiston too.

"So you are Joseph's mother?" he asked me. "What is your name?"

Just like in first year German class with Herr Fischer, I did not need to make up a fake German name. I already had a real one. So I gave him my name.

"And where are you from?"

I crossed the Western border in the south, so I gave a southern city, a large city, where the population made obscurity a possibility, and could delay any attempt to verify my identity.

"I am from Stuttgart."

Two seconds after I said it, I knew that faceless figures beyond the walls of the little room were searching away, trying to find what they could about Verena Kessler from Stuttgart. In every subsequent moment, I expected the soldier in black to point his rifle at my face and demand the truth. But nothing of the sort happened. Mr. Lewiston continued to inquire about my life and about Joseph. His questions were surprisingly vague — what he was like as a baby (before the kidnapping and genetic alterations), his favorite toys, his best subjects in school, and similar questions. All of these I could answer quickly and authentically, with no hint of deception and without giving away the fantastic truths hidden just beneath my answers.

In a snap, the questions focused — what was the name of his school, who is his father, what did his father do for a living. I continued with truths, telling him that Joseph was schooled mostly at home, under the care of a tutor named, Ms. Taufe. Joseph's father was not a human being that I knew very well, and I am not with him now. I constructed each sentence to be thinly truthful while remaining incomplete. I said that I am an administrator at a home for animals. He would see the creatures of the Sweeter Realm as animals, so this too was thinly truthful.

Mr. Lewiston leaned forward and his tone went grave, "Your son killed twenty-two men and women."

Again walking a thin line of truth, I answered, "I assure you, in his mind he did not. Somebody else is to blame for those deaths."

"Yes," he responded, "I think it was forced upon him, along with many other things."

He pulled a hand-held computer from his pocket and faced the screen to me, saying, "I am afraid much more than that was forced on him."

There, on the screen was a picture of Joseph, a sadder, more frightened version of the same feathered child I saw in the palace a few evenings earlier. I cried. That was authentic. But I pretended to be surprised and appalled at his appearance.

I whispered, "My son, my son, what have they done to you?"

This too was in earnest. But my thoughts were not what Mr. Lewiston believed them to be.

"We have never seen anything like it," Mr. Lewiston added after a sympathetic pause. "The feathers are real. They are growing from him. We don't know the point of the feathers. He cannot fly. And the soldiers he killed had wounds as if slashed with a small blade. Yet your son had no weapon, and none was found at the scene of the attack. But he killed twenty-two highly trained soldiers before most of them could fire a single shot in their defense. Your child does not seem capable."

Hesitantly and fearing his answer, I asked, "What did Joseph tell you?"

"The good boy that you raised came through. Your son cried as he carried the bodies of two of his victims onto a military base. He prayed for them and their families. When we asked him what he was doing in France, he spoke in incoherent sentences about his mission. Along with the physical alterations, and the advancements in speed and strength, he clearly suffered extreme psychological trauma at the hands of his Eastern captors."

"What did they do to him?" I asked.

"We believe that he is an experiment, an early phase of a program to create perfect soldiers and assassins. I am afraid his… differences might not be finished. The feathers might continue to grow. He might be able to fly and kill even more efficiently than he already has."

Mr. Lewiston put his hands over mine and pulled them to the center of the table, forcing me to lean forward toward him.

"We want him to see you, to hear your voice, to pull him back."

"So he can tell you the secrets of your enemy?" I asked indignantly.

"No. So you can have your son back."

He was not being honest. Still, I reveled in the idea of seeing my son.

Mr. Lewiston continued, "He will have to stay with our doctors and scientists for a while, so we can try to heal him and return him to you as the normal boy you lost."

I knew why their scientists wanted him. But my paths were few and narrow, so I continued to play my part.

Mr. Lewiston and the soldier in black left the room. I hadn't forgotten the cameras. I was aware that eyes remained on me. So my body remained still while my mind tried to connect to my friends and family at Linderhof. I weakly found the mind of Friedrich, who dreamed of Wühlenvogel land while he slept in the abandoned city beneath the Black Forest. I stretched my thoughts to the Unicorns. My connections with them have always been thicker and more natural than with any other breed. I could not touch the thoughts of Acheriel and Lenelil, or my husband, or any of the others who waited nervously under the Venus Grotto. But I found the thoughts of one creature still in the Sweeter Realm. With my mental fingertips stretched to their limits, I brushed against the thoughts of Senische.

She worried for Joseph and she worried for her Queen. She remained near the Portal Point, in the Nomadic Belt, staring into the thick warm air of the Sweeter Realm, waiting for the circle of nothing to appear in front of her. She strained to connect to her father's mind. But she could

342

not. I backed away from her mind, fearing that any partial thought that might make it through to her could be misunderstood and cause unnecessary distress to my entire queendom. In truth, I would not have known what message to send to them if I had their minds cleanly in my grasp. Nor would I want to burden Felix and The Ancient One with what little I had to share. As I sat alone in the little room, I took comfort in the Holy Eucharist inside of me from the morning mass, and in knowing that Taufe and the sisters of St. Hildegard maintained a constant vigil of prayer.

I could not have guessed how much time I spent waiting alone in the room. My mind moved much faster than time and every second felt like hours. Mr. Lewiston came back into the room with the soldier in black and another man, a thin, young man who looked hardly old enough to be away from his *own* mother. He wore jeans and a t-shirt, with an untucked flannel shirt over it.

Mr. Lewiston looked at me scornfully and said, "We are having trouble finding you, Ms. Kessler, you or your son, or your son's teacher."

I felt like my heart was in my throat, pounding so hard that I was afraid they would see the skin of my neck rise and fall with every terrified pulse.

"There is one part of your story we can clear up now," he added.

The young man in jeans came at me with a glove on one hand.

"Open your mouth, Ms. Kessler," Mr. Lewiston demanded in a firm and authoritative tone.

I obeyed and the young man swabbed the inside of my cheek with a cotton swab. All three men were gone from the room and the door closed and locked behind them before I realized that my mouth still hung open.

I was scared. I was thirsty and hungry, and I spoke looking at one of the cameras, "May I have some water... and I have not eaten today."

A soldier I had not yet seen came into the room with a bottle of water. He loosened the lid, set it on the table in front of me, and left the room without a word. I emptied the bottle down my dry throat in a couple of seconds.

Several minutes later, Mr. Lewiston came into the room, without the soldier in black. He entered alone and stood facing me with his back against the closed door. He stared at me and I stared back. Fear and worry were racing for control of my emotions. I did not cry. That is to say, I did not sob. Tears rolled down my face and I could feel my complexion turning red. Mr. Lewiston just stared at me, neither compassionate nor detached from the display in front of him. Screams and cries, perhaps even violence, clawed at the inside of my skin, trying to break free of the cage of my self-control. But I held them in, and the constant flow of tears was their only release.

Mr. Lewiston jolted forward, pushed by the opening door. The young man entered the room and whispered into Mr. Lewiston's ear, then showed him a piece of paper and left the room. Mr. Lewiston dropped his head and stared fixedly at the floor in front of him, rubbing the edges of his lips with his thumb and index finger. After several seconds like that, he raised his head to me and set his hands on his hips.

"Well, you *are* Joseph's mother," he said, clearly surprised by the report of the young man. "Who are you Ms. Kessler, and what is your real story? And what has happened to your son?"

Again with a truth that veiled more than it revealed, I answered, "I lost my Joseph and I am just trying to get him back."

I spoke with a broken voice that put on bold display the degree of my distress. But in my state, my answer lost its German accent, and I spoke in the shattered voice of an honestly frightened American mother. I didn't realize what I had done for several seconds, until I saw it dawn upon Mr. Lewiston, and his face transformed from a man of genuine feeling to a man of extreme suspicion. This was an intelligent man, an experienced man. I did not bother trying to throw the mask back over my voice.

I took several slow and awkwardly deep breaths, while he gazed penetratingly into my eyes, then begged in my normal Colorado accent, "My son is no weapon. He is no spy. He saves lives. He does not take them. Please give him back to me."

Mr. Lewiston took a hard step toward me, slammed his palm on the table, shocking my breath out of me, and he yelled, "Why was he in France? If he did not kill those soldiers, who did?"

I gasped to replace the breath that was startled out of me. Not fully recovered, but with enough air inside of me to speak, I said, "I don't know why he was in France, but he did not kill the soldiers."

He stepped toward me, placed his palms on the table, and leaned into his arms with locked elbows. He glared menacingly down to me.

He asked in a snide, accusatory tone, "Are your words as fake as your accent?"

Everything we planned before I left Linderhof was falling apart. I no longer fit their narrative, and my discovered deception made me villainous in their eyes. Truth would exonerate Joseph and me from the treachery we were suspected of. But truth was a weapon that had to stay holstered at my hip, no matter how desperately I wanted to wield it.

I answered his question in the choppy pauses between the spasming inhales of my hyperventilating chest, repeating, "He did not kill the soldiers."

Those words used what little was in my lungs, and I gasped frantically to breath. Mr. Lewiston relaxed his posture. He backed away from me slowly, until his back was against the door again, never allowing his eyes to stray from mine. He was obviously aggravated. But a sly compassion peeked at me through his eyes and from behind the subtle twitches of his mouth.

He asked quietly and slowly, "You are not from Stuttgart, not from Germany. Where are you from?"

He did not demand an immediate answer, but waited until I calmed enough to reply, "I am from America. But Joseph has never been there… and he only wanted to find his grandparents."

As I mentioned Joseph's grandparents, I felt my face swell flush. A crippling surge of emotion washed over me as the teenager who frighteningly sought her parents in Linderhof Palace all those years ago made a bold and unannounced appearance on the throne of my identity. I thought about my father. I thought about my mother and brother, and how much they would love Joseph, and Joseph would love them. I knew my father would never feel his grandson's feathers, and I began to doubt that I ever would again. The violent sobs that had held their ground just beneath my skin, but had not advanced, charged through ever pour of my body. I convulsed, shaking uncontrollably, and pressing my face hard against the table. My face slid on the smooth, wet surface. I don't know if it was blood, tears, or snot that I felt. I didn't care. I continued to push my face hard against the table, pull at my hair, and claw at the back of my neck, until I heard the door close. I looked up and saw that I was alone again.

Through all of the emotions, all of the thoughts on my mind, I pitied Mr. Lewiston. He was torn. He did not doubt my love of my son, or the depth of my desire to have him back. He saw before him a truly distraught mother and a tortured human being. But he knew I was American, that my son had feathers growing from him, and that he left a massacre of twenty dead soldiers behind him as the small boy carried the bodies of two full-grown men a great distance, through dense woods, to a military base. A man twice his size could not have carried those soldiers so far.

Mr. Lewiston did not know that Joseph's strength is quite ordinary, a signature trait of his father's people. And he carried those bodies out of love for them and respect for their families. He did not know it, and I could not explain it to him. My son's life and freedom sat behind a thin fictional drop, one that if lifted would expose a secret kept in sacred obscurity since the year 515. Many died to keep that secret. Many were killed and many sacrificed themselves. And there I sat, another Swan Knight placed in that same position. But whose blood would spill to keep that secret during *my* knighthood?

The scientifically altered killing machine remained Mr. Lewiston's most plausible explanation for the feathered enigma, and remained his deepest concern. He was a patriot, as paranoid of Eastern treachery as the rest of the West. Part of him wanted to hand me my son and send us back across that pedestrian bridge into Germany with a compassionate pat on my back. Another part wanted to torture us both until every minute detail of every hidden secret in our heads was upon a Western military table to be anatomized by his government. I believe he was more cut up by his own duality of heart than by any danger he thought Joseph might pose to his precious confederation.

Poor Mr. Lewiston had two aposing truths before him. Joseph was my son, and I his worried mother. But I had not been honest with him and I clearly kept secrets behind my vague answers. He left the room with an inner dispute raging between his seasoned military mind and the deepest portions of his gut.

CHAPTER 26
On Native Soil

A COUPLE OF HOURS MUST HAVE PASSED as I alternated between sitting alone at the table and pacing laps around it. Three soldiers came into the room and positioned themselves around me, as if I was a threat to them.

One of them asked, "Do you need the restroom?"

"Yes please," I answered with my head down, in my softest, humblest, passive voice.

They escorted me out of the room and around a corner to the restroom. When they brought me back, Mr. Lewiston was in the room, standing behind my chair. He pulled the chair back and gestured for me to take a seat. On the table was a plate with a large pile of deli meat and a croissant.

He winked at me and said, "You might as well experience France while you are here."

There was a compassionate light-heartedness in his delivery, not at all suspicious as before. Tremendously relieved by his alteration in mood, I took my seat. He pushed in my chair, and I devoured the meal, in front of him and the three soldiers. When I was finished, Mr. Lewiston gestured for me to stand. I stood and the soldiers positioned themselves strategically around me, as before. One of them pulled plastic zip-restraints from the back of his belt. I looked worriedly to Mr. Lewiston. He simply raised his eyebrows and slightly lifted his shoulders.

The soldier restrained my hands behind my back. I was less scared with Löwschock's fangs dug into my arm than I was at that moment. I felt so captive, like I would never again be free. Mr. Lewiston walked out of the room first. I followed with each arm in the tight grasp of a soldier and the back of my collar wrenched in the clutch of the third. I thought about my palace, about St. Hildegard and the soft Brunnen beds, about the sharp, jagged rocks of the steep Pfeifen Mountains. They all seemed equally soft and beautiful to me, and I would have taken a hundred of Reid's wooden blades into my back and side to be there again, to be there with my son and with my husband.

The soldiers walked me to a helicopter, which flew me to a military base that seemed out of place amid a lush meadow whose spring blooms were just beginning to show their colors. On the base, they transferred me to a plane. It did not look like a military plane, but a fancy private jet. The upholstery was plush and an elegant mahogany wet-bar dominated the rear. The helicopter was loud, too loud to speak and be understood.

But on the plane, once in the air, I asked the soldiers, "Why am I under arrest? What crime have I committed?"

I repeated the question, getting louder and more belligerent with each recitation. I felt a calming hand on my shoulder. When I turned to face it, I saw that it belonged to Mr. Lewiston. I don't really understand why, but seeing him calmed me. And I did not want him to leave my side.

With slower breaths, and in a less confrontational, more plaintive tone, I asked him, "Why am I under arrest? What crime have I committed?"

"You lied to me, but that isn't why you are in this plane, or why you are in restraints. Twenty-two soldiers are dead. They too had mothers who loved them. The only person connected with that crime is your son... a small, strangely feathered boy with extraordinary strength, and maybe, the ability to kill like no trained killer I have ever seen."

Half crying, half scolding, I reminded him, "I told you, Joseph did not kill those soldiers."

In immediate response to my words, he twitched his face quickly to one side and let out a quick exhale. It was followed by a clinching of his fists, rising of his shoulders, and twisting of his back. I waited for a harsh response, but it did not come. I half-expected him to hit me. A great deal of violent frustration revealed itself in his writhing. He drew a slow, deep inhale, followed by an equally slow exhale. During the length of that exhale, all of the tension that contorted his figure melted away.

He squatted down in the aisle, so he was looking up at me, and asked, "Can you tell me who did? You know more than I do about this and it frustrates me. But far more frustrating than that, I'd like to help you, if your son is innocent. You seem like a good woman, with deep and real love for your child. But you continually refuse to help me."

He remained like that, squatting in the aisle beside my seat, staring directly and deeply into my eyes, trying to pull truth from them.

I began to squirm, but still looking him in the eyes, I asked, "Can you remove the restrains now?... My shoulders hurt."

He nodded to the soldiers sitting behind me. They bound my ankles with the same sort of zip-ties. Two of them seized my upper arms with bruising force, while a third stood behind my seat and took control of my head. He wrapped one arm around my forehead and pulled against my chin with his other hand. Their cold hands had me entirely immobilized, like I was embedded in ice. The soldier behind me pushed me to lean forward, and some unknown other pair of hands cut the ties at my wrists. The soldiers at my arms brought my hands to my lap and one of them reapplied restraints to my wrists. Once they were comfortable with my immobility, all of the soldiers backed away from me.

"Is that better?" Mr. Lewiston asked.

I circled my shoulders and arched my back until it popped.

I nodded to Mr. Lewiston, gestured to my bound hands in front of me and leaned forward to look at my bound ankles, then asked, "Is all of this necessary?"

He answered grimly, "Had you seen the bodies, torn and sliced, most of whom did not have time to unholster their guns, you would understand. We don't know what you are capable of, and you have been less than honest."

I wanted to apologize for lying to him. But I wasn't sorry for keeping Brunhilde's secret, or all of the other secrets I was sworn to keep. Ludwig and Ludmilla, Otto and Agnes, Brunhilde's childhood friend Elizabeth, all lived their lives and died, never releasing the secret of Tannhäuser's daughter. I would not be the Swan Knight to betray them all. So I had no response but to lower my eyes from him and stare down at my lap. Except for taking a few sips of water, I remained just like that for hours, as we flew over the ocean, west, to America.

During the flight, I was served the same meal eaten by Mr. Lewiston and the soldiers. With my hands restrained in front of me, I ate and drank easily. Mr. Lewiston served me and cleared my dishes from my lap. He seemed honored to do so. His words were kind and cordial, his movements and facial expressions calm and subtle. Except for the restraints and the stern stares from the soldiers, I felt more like Mr. Lewiston's guest than his prisoner. He worked hard to create that environment. What I did not know was his motivation. I kept in the back of my mind the thought that his every movement was calculated to manipulate me in service to his government. I wanted to like him. I wanted to trust in his apparent goodness. But I had missions divine and personal that forbade such naivety.

The sun was low and the sky turning purple. But through the window of the plane, I saw the coast of my native country. I didn't know where on the East Coast we were. There was an empty beach, pushed against the shore by thick woods. We flew for just a few more minutes before we descended and landed on another military base nestled snuggly in the dense forest.

The soldiers from the American base boarded the plane to take custody of me. They saw that my hands were bound in front of me. They sneered at the soldiers from France and asked them to explain why my hands were bound in front. Mr. Lewiston declared that it was his decision. His authority carried as much weight in America as it did in France.

The soldiers apologized for their tone but reminded Mr. Lewiston of their orders. They ran a chain around the restrains between my wrists, down to wrap around the restrains at my ankles. They pulled it tight, so I was forced in a forward-hunching position, and they locked it with a padlock.

Defiantly, I looked to one of the American soldiers and asked, "Have the laws changed so much in this country, since I called it home?"

He responded by pulling a black, cloth bag from a pocket on his pant leg, and with no expression at all, he placed the bag over my head and pulled it tight around my neck with a drawstring. Before I knew it, I was off of my feet, belly down, and being carried head first off of the plane. My "escorts" bumped my head and shoulders against the seats of the plane."

"Be careful with her, damnit!" Mr. Lewiston scolded them.

In response, they were more careful, but no gentler.

I don't know how long I was carried, or in which direction once we left the plane. I'm not sure how many hands were upon me. But I was comprehensively secured by people who seemed to fear me more than I feared them. I heard a door open. I felt the descent from the plane level out on the ground, and the clop of the soldiers' boots against concrete. Still, they carried me, head-first, belly-down, and blindfolded. The sounds of the breeze and birds disappeared with the click of a closing door behind us. We went through many more doors. And my head and shoulders struck many more implacable items, until I was turned right-side-up and sat upon a chair.

The hood was removed from my head, revealing a grey room with long florescent lights hanging from an unpainted concrete ceiling. In front of me was a metal table, similar to the one in France, also bolted to the floor. Four soldiers were in the room. They removed the chain, cut my wrist restraints, and strapped my forearms to the arms of the chair with Velcro. A low, irritating, grinding sound accompanied my forward movement, as someone pushed my chair forward, with me in it, until my lap was tucked under the table.

Mr. Lewiston was not in the room. But I heard his voice faintly from behind the door. I wanted him in the room, knowing that I was less likely to be abused in his presence. But he did not enter. His voice faded as he walked away. A popping sound drew my attention to a speaker that was mounted to the ceiling against the wall in front of me. The wall was not a wall, but a large, grey glass through which I could not see.

I knew I was being watched through that glass, and I knew they could hear me when I asked, "Do I get a phone call, or a lawyer or something?"

They had me at a terrible disadvantage. With all that I had learned and all that I had accomplished since I rolled

354

down the driveway in Centennial, Colorado with my family all those years ago, I knew little of my own native land. I still had a teenager's understanding of the law, and no idea what sort of changes accompanied the drastic political evolutions that had occurred in my absence.

"Ms. Kessler, you have rights, but so do we." Mr. Lewiston's familiar voice came over the speaker.

After a pause while I strained my mind for something to say, he continued, "I'd like to reunite you with your son. But he is on trial for murder and espionage. The East has denied any knowledge of him, a denial our government doubts."

"But you do not doubt," I loudly and boldly interrupted.

"I don't know what to think," he answered.

"I'm hungry," I begged in a calmer voice.

There was long pause, followed by a faint response of "No" in a stranger's voice.

Mr. Lewiston's voice continued, "You will be fed eventually. But something has happened that has complicated your situation."

The speaker clicked off and remained silent for several minutes.

It clicked back on and another voice, a higher, abrasive and angry voice demanded, "Tell us about the mind-control."

"Mind-control?" I asked, "I don't... know what..."

The voice screamed, nearly blowing out the speaker, "The mind-control your son..."

There were thumping sounds through the speaker, as if people were fighting over the microphone on the other end.

Mr. Lewiston's voice returned, calmer than the last voice, but more irritated that he had been, "Joseph has shown the ability to manipulate people. He makes them think what he wants, say what he wants. He even has controlled their movements."

"Has he hurt anybody?" I asked, more to make a point than in search of an answer.

"No. In fact, it seems he could have, but chose not to. But this will not help him. They are scared of him. He remains in isolation, bound, gagged, and blindfolded, and he goes before a tribunal tomorrow. I fear for his life if you do not talk to me."

"Mr. Lewiston," I implored him, "I will say whatever you want me to say, but there are things happening here that I don't understand."

That was true, and after a long pause, I asked, "Can I attend the trial? Can I at least do that? I have done nothing wrong and I deserve to do that."

The speaker clicked off again and remained off for several minutes. Through the crack under the door, I could hear yelling — Mr. Lewiston yelling.

The speaker clicked on again and Mr. Lewiston spoke, "Yes. This country has not changed that much. We have not entirely lost our way. You have the right to attend the tribunal. But you will not be with your son. He will remain in isolation. He will be seen and heard by the judges through closed-circuit television. You may view the proceedings from a cell in the courtroom."

"Why a cell?" I challenged him. "I am an American! Tell me what law I have broken! What is this? Have I been charged with a crime?"

"You are not in the domestic legal system, Ms. Kessler," he answered sternly. "You are in military custody under extreme and mysterious circumstances of national security. Different rules apply."

Extreme sadness fought against furious anger for control of me. One wanted to swell my teary eyes and blush my face. The other wanted to grind my teeth and growl through my clenched jaw. My reason took control from both and I sat still and silent.

The speaker clicked off, followed by the scuffle of shoes across the floor on the other side of the door. The bustle faded, leaving an eerie stillness in the room, under the oppressive light of the hanging fluorescents. To escape it, I dropped my forehead onto the table in front of me and closed my eyes. The only thing breaking the silence was a low hum coming from behind the wall to my right. I hadn't noticed it before and there was nothing else for my senses to hold on to. It lulled me to sleep. I jerked awake several times, from dreams I don't remember. All I remember is that the dreams were distant enough for me to wake surprised to be bound to a chair, with my head on a cold, metal table, under the relentless thrust of the stabbing bright lights. I dozed off several times, waking with no idea of how long I had slept.

Finally, I slept for what felt like several hours, an estimation that was verified by the intense hunger in my stomach.

I lifted my head and called out, "Can I get something to eat and drink? Mr. Lewiston? Are you there? I am hungry and thirsty… Mr. Lewiston.. please… anybody?"

My back was stiff. My legs were numb. I was in extreme discomfort and would have sacrificed several meals just to be able to stand and stretch. But nobody came. Nobody responded. I slammed my head on the table a few times, just to relieve my other pains. When it only compounded my discomfort, I released all tension and melted into the chair, laying my cheek on the table. In this position, I fell asleep again.

CHAPTER 27
A Crimeless Mother

I AWOKE AGAIN TO THE RATTLING OF CHAINS. Two soldiers had unstrapped my arms from the table and replaced the soft, cloth straps with steel handcuffs. They were running a chain between the cuffs and locking it to the arms of the metal chair. The handcuffs were too tight, and every twisting attempt I made to reposition my wrists within them seemed to tighten them further. The chain was long enough for me to raise my cuffed hands to my face. As soon as the padlock was in place, securing the chain to the chair, I raised my hands and satisfied the dozens of itches on my face, head, and neck, which seemed to land on me like bugs and taunt me while my hands were still strapped to the chair.

Despite the discomfort of the steel handcuffs, I was greatly relieved by my new mobility. The purpose of allowing it became clear when a third soldier stepped up from behind me and placed a piece of flatbread on the table. A fourth stepped around him and set a paper cup of water. I thanked them, wholeheartedly, with sincerity that must have been apparent. The four soldiers walked out of the room, but not before one of them turned his head half-way to face me, and said, "You're welcome."

It was a perfectly baked piece of flatbread, slightly peppered to perfection — or perhaps that was the interpretation of a mind that would have, in its starvation, celebrated a rotten egg. I did not savor it. My hands, obeying the mandates of my stomach, force-fed my mouth almost faster than it could do its job. I was far from satisfied. I had not eaten since the small meal on the plane, and I had no idea how long ago that was or what day of the week I was living in. The bread served only to remind my stomach of just how empty it was.

Just as I was regretting having teased my stomach with the bread, Mr. Lewiston came into the room. He was dressed in a military uniform, but not similar to the soldiers. His shirt looked like an old officer's tunic, with badges and metals covering almost every inch of cloth on his chest.

He looked at me with a most fervent expression of compassion. He handed me a sandwich on a folded paper napkin. It was made with the same flatbread given to me by the soldiers. But between *two* pieces was egg, ham, and cheese. It appeared to be a large half of a very large sandwich, and I assumed it to be the other half of his own breakfast. He gestured to the water in front of me and suggested that I drink it. I drank the water. He took the cup, and replaced it with a similar cup, filled nearly to the brim with orange juice. He smiled at me as I drank the juice and thanked him between each sip.

When I finished the juice, he took the cup from my bound hands and said in a voice so uncharacteristically nurturing that I believe he hardly recognized it as his own, "I truly hope things go well for you today."

I was deeply touched by his compassion, and in need of nurturing of any kind, from any source. As pleased as my body was with the egg sandwich and orange juice, my spirit was equally tortured by his subtle reminder of the day's event. I looked at Mr. Lewiston, and unable to activate a throat seized with emotion, I remained silent.

He placed one hand on my shoulder and continued his thought, "But I fear it will not."

Mr. Lewiston took his hand from my shoulder hesitantly. He grimaced his face, nodded slightly, and turned to walk out of the room.

"Will you be there?" I asked quickly, afraid that my throat might take too long to make the sounds of language and I would miss my opportunity.

Mr. Lewiston turned back to me, lowered his eyes to the floor, shook his head, and said, "No."

"Please!" I begged him, "I don't want to be alone."

"You won't be alone," he responded with a confused expression.

"Yes I will. I will be alone. Please be with me."

"I cannot. I work for the government. I represent the interest of the West. I do not represent you."

"I'm not asking you to represent me, only to be with me."

He shook his head again.

I continued, "If I can't have your company, can I at least have your prayers?"

"You *have* my prayers, Ms. Kessler. You have had them since France."

I could tell that he wanted to come to me, to rub my shoulder, or pat my head. But he fought the instinct and walked out of the room without another word or gesture. He knew his government. He knew how they think, act, and react. And he was fearful for Joseph. As if my own terrors were not heavy enough. They were compounded by what was an obvious lack of faith in a positive outcome in the mind of one who would know.

Mr. Lewiston seemed to take the air from the room with him when he walked out. And I struggled to breathe. I cried and gasped, sobbed and wheezed. I turned to God, who had guided me and protected me through battles, falls, attempted abductions, and a nearly successful assassination. I did not have the mind to construct any semblance of a coherent prayer. I simply thought of God and whispered, "Please."

I was not alone again for long when soldiers came back into the room. Two stood at the doorway while two unfastened me from the chair. They ran the chain from my hands to my feet, forcing a hunch as before. They walked me past the two at the entrance, into the hallway, which was lined on both sides by dozens more. I'm not sure what they thought I could do or would do to them. Bound as I was, a single child could have escorted me safely, despite my training. They took me into a room with tile floors, a drain in the middle, and wooden benches lining the walls. It looked like a gym locker room, but with no lockers.

The soldiers awkwardly crammed themselves into the room and lined the walls. The two that had ahold of me removed my restraints and stripped my clothes from me. With firm grips on my bare arms, they walked me to the far side of the room, to a short hall with shower heads protruding from the tile.

They let go of me and stood at the threshold of the shower hallway. I walked to the far end and pressed the small, round, chrome button beneath the shower head. Ice-cold water responded to the call. It shocked me at first. But I closed my eyes and let the water pound against my scalp. It muted the breaths and other subtle sounds of the soldiers and allowed my thoughts to wander. Perhaps "wander" is the wrong word. My mind went unguided, but quite directly, to Joseph, and the sound of his voice, the touch of his hair and feathers, and the intimate sensation of communicating directly to his mind. I cried, begged out loud for him to connect with me. But the only thing in my mind was my own thoughts.

The water cut off automatically. I wanted to stay longer, and I stood in a lunge, with my forearms resting against the tiled wall, until a throat cleared, and a voice came forward, "Ma'am, ma'am, we need you to come here."

I had almost forgotten about the many soldiers who waited in the room. I walked to them. A towel sat on the floor of the shower. I took it and dried myself. As soon as I stepped from the shower hall to the room, still drying my hair, the same two soldiers took my arms with force. I dropped the towel. Another soldier handed them a lime-green jumpsuit and they dressed me in it and shackled me as before.

From there, we left the showers, back into the hallway that led us there, with four soldiers walking in front of me, one soldier on each arm, and the rest marching loudly behind. I sensed no ill-will from the soldiers. In fact I felt some compassion come to me through their sighs and their sorrowful eyes. But above all, I sensed fear. They *were* afraid of me, mortally afraid that I would do to them what Brunhilde had done to their French colleagues.

They turned me down a new hallway, which went on beyond the length of my vision. We marched it for at least five minutes, until it opened into a large room with benches, similar to the wooden pews at church, but blue and plastic. Against the far wall, on the left side, was a double-door of wood. On the right side was a single-door of metal. The soldiers led me to the single-door. It opened into a cell, with thick glass that looked onto the courtroom. It had three rows of stadium-style bleacher seats. And everything was painted bright white — the walls, the ceiling, the inside of the metal door, and the three rows of seats. The soldiers released me into the room, still shackled. They closed the door behind me and I took a seat.

On the other side of the glass was the courtroom, dominated with wood tones and grand furniture. The walls were lined with rows of seats, like a jury box, but not enclosed. A half-circle of stately chairs sat in the center of the room, with one taller and grander than the rest, situated in the center. A large, flat television, almost floor to ceiling, and at least fifteen feet wide, covered the wall that faced the semi-circle of chairs. My room faced the left side of the semi-circle, giving me a harsh-angled, obscured view of the screen.

The double-doors opened, and the side seats were filled with people, mostly in military uniforms, some in suits, some in lab coats. No sound from their bustling, sometimes clumsy entrance made it into my cell. Once they were seated, another door opened on the other end of the courtroom. An eclectic mix of suits and uniforms took the semi-circle of seats. A clicking sound preceded the rush of all courtroom sounds into my cell. A woman in the center chair pointed to the screen and it lit up. From my harsh angle, I saw my son on that screen, seated in a grey room, hands bound behind him, feet bound beneath him, eyes covered, and gagged by a band of some sort that was wrapped around his head and across his mouth.

His lower jaw was forced unnaturally open by the band, like it had been stretched and broken. His feathers were jaundiced, and his flesh was ashen-grey. His eyes were covered, but the skin above his cheeks were exposed and looked to be swollen. I gasped in horror.

The woman in the center of the tribunal, clearly the chairwoman or head, turned in quick response to my gasp, which she must have heard through a speaker in the courtroom.

"Who is that woman?" she demanded.

A voice I had not heard responded from some unknown mouth, "That is his mother."

364

The chairwoman demanded, "Has she been charged with a crime? Why is she shackled in a cell?"

A man in a military dress-uniform walked to her and whispered in her ear.

"Good God!" she proclaimed. "Have you all gone mad? I want her released at once!"

The same mystery voice called out, "She is here to see the proceedings. She came to see her son."

"She came in a prisoner's jumpsuit and shackles? I don't think so. If she is not charged with a crime, this court has no business with her. There are plenty of seats in this room. If her only crime is being the boy's mother, she should be watching the proceedings from a seat in this room, like the rest of you."

The man whispered in her ear again.

The chairwoman responded loudly, "You have hundreds of armed soldiers on this base. I am confident they can protect me from this mother."

After one more protest whispered in her ear, she proclaimed, "Fine. But after we are done here, she will be released with the apologies of this court. And then you sir, will have to give some answers for these violations of her rights."

The man bowed to her and backed out of the sight of my cell.

The proceedings resumed. Soldiers appeared on the screen with Joseph, along with a man in a suit. The suited man began to describe the scene of the attack on the French soldiers.

"And this little boy is your suspect?" one of the judges asked.

The suited man nodded and continued to describe the scenario, all the way to Joseph's arrival on the base with the bodies of the two slaughtered soldiers. One of the soldiers brought forward a chart, a diagram of the wounds inflicted by Brunhilde's knife.

Descriptions were followed by questions, questions by debates and further descriptions. The chairwoman seemed unimpressed by the merits of the case. That is, until they showed her a video. On the video, Joseph was bound to a chair just like I had been. He told a soldier to unbind him and the soldier obeyed. He told two soldiers to stop arguing, and they stopped. With swaying of his head and slight gestures of his hand, Joseph seemed to direct their movements. The final stroke came when soldiers appeared in the courtroom to testify. They described the loss of their free will, the loss of their own movements. They described Joseph's control of them in ways that made him seem quite sinister.

After the testimony of the soldiers, the suited man described intelligence reports of their agents, of Eastern scientists manipulating genetics to create killers — perfect killers "just like this boy."

The tribunal was convinced. Had I not known my son and all of the surrounding truths, *I* would have been convinced, and made to fear the little feathered boy as they did. Even the chairwoman looked at Joseph like he was a monster, some gruesome weapon designed to destroy their lives.

The whisperer went back to the ear of the chairwoman, to which she responded, "I made my order clear before. The mother is charged with nothing. She will be released to mourn the loss of her son."

With those words, I screamed, "Joseph!"

Everyone in the courtroom turned to my cell, some with looks of pity and some with faces of sheer disgust.

"The loss of her son." Those words wrapped their long, strong fingers around my throat and squeezed with all their might. I choked. I gagged. I fell forward from my seat and smashed my head on the glass. Blood pulled on the floor beneath my face. Medics rushed in — without soldiers — and rapidly tended my wound. While being awkwardly jostled around, I lost consciousness.

I awoke on a medical bed, in a medical clinic, unbound by steel or plastic. My head pounded in pain, and the bandage went low enough for me to see it drop beneath my right eyebrow. I wore the same lime-green jumpsuit, soiled across my shoulder and chest by reddish-brown blood, still damp and sticking the cloth to my skin. I was dizzy. My head pounded. Pain stabbed at me everywhere and I did not know what of it was physical and what was the manifestation of emotional anguish. Only one soldier stood in the room, guarding the entrance.

I sat up, drawing the attention of the medics, who checked my bandage and gauged my pulse.

I shouted to the soldier, "What happened? What did they decide? What is going to happen to my son?"

The soldier spoke into his radio, nodded to me, and returned to his stone-like stillness. A few minutes later, Mr. Lewiston came into the clinic.

"You are free to go," he said to me, "as soon as you are well enough and wish to go."

"I won't go without Joseph," I told him in a low growl.

"Your son is not leaving here. The evidence was strong against him. He has been deemed an immediate and critical threat. He will be executed in two days."

The room went hazy brown and I fell from the bed, striking my newly sewn wound on the floor."

"Mr. Lewiston," I heard a woman's voice say, "is this the time to tell her that?"

"She deserves that much," he replied with sorrow in his cracking voice, "that much and more that I cannot give."

The medics and Mr. Lewiston helped me back to the bed, where I struggled to sit straight.

"Please, Mr. Lewiston," my faltering voice whined, "I beg you to do something. They listen to you. You have influence. Keep him. Lock him up. But don't kill my boy. He's just a boy."

As I said that, I thought, "He's not just a boy. He's an extraordinary boy, one of only two products of a human and a native of Eden. He is here on an errand of God, and I should trust him, God *and* Joseph. It is happening now."

Mr. Lewiston began to respond, but I interrupted, loudly and boldly quoting the Book of Isaiah, precisely as it arrived in my memory, as if it was spoken through me, not by me,

Pass through, pass through the gates!
Prepare the way for the people.
Build up, build up the highway!
Remove the stones.
Raise a banner for the nations.
They will be called the Holy People,
The Redeemed of the Lord

Mr. Lewiston took a few slow and stumbling steps back. He did not buy the narrative presented by the military and believed by the tribunal. He considered what the others had not — that although Joseph commanded his binds removed, he did not escape. His influence over the soldiers could have opened every door between his cell and the fresh air of the American coast. But he stayed. While commanding the movements of the soldiers, he could have made them shoot one another, but he did not.

Mr. Lewiston was a man of deep faith from a family a faith. The compassion he showed me from the beginning was less driven by his inherent goodness than by his sense of the Godly presence in the events that brought me into his life. The eruption of scripture from my mouth,

368

delivered in ghostly reverberation, struck him to the core with a sense of Providential, apocalyptic truth. His face went blank. His lips gestured some words that made no sound.

As much as I had tried to normalize the extraordinary events at hand, everything about my arrival in Mr. Lewiston's life was unearthly. Most involved looked to earthly explanations — military biologists, cruel experiments, science. But *his* heart was open enough by faith to allow other possibilities, mystical, divine possibilities, to tip-toe into the back of his mind. My sudden recitation of the scriptures, and the manner in which I delivered it, cemented in him the notion that the events surrounding Joseph could not be explained by the men in uniforms and lab coats. He turned away from me as if possessed by some power other than his consciousness, and he walked out of the room with slow, stumbling paces, like he walked through a knee-deep pool, his heart and his head stumbling into each other as blindly and clumsily as his body, a shaking body that knocked everything it neared on its way to the clinic door.

CHAPTER 28
Turning to God

I HAD LOST A GREAT DEAL OF BLOOD, and my mind was swirling in a pool that had anger, regret, intense sorrow, yet gratefulness and a gripping sense of holy destiny all mixing inside of it. In this diverse, swirling, saturating substance, I was helped to a room. It was a dorm of sorts, not much larger than a closet, with a cot, a small dresser with two drawers, and a footlocker. There were no windows and I could not tell whether it was day or night. I lay on the cot but could not sleep. My mind must have revisited every memory, every sensation, every thought, wish, and dream it had ever encountered. After perhaps an hour of aimless musings, I fell to the cot and went to sleep.

I awoke with the smell of Joseph's feathers pungently in my nose. I sat up quickly, but my son was not in the room. My dreams and imagination placed the aroma into a nose that was thoroughly fooled. Joseph was not with me, and I could not smell him or feel him. As consciousness pulled me further out of dreaming, the imaginary sensations of Joseph quickly faded. As they did, they were replaced by a weight on my chest and a restriction in my throat. I clawed at the fleeing smell. But it was in my subconscious and I was not. Within a few seconds, the smell was gone from my head. I fought to recall it, but I failed.

I walked the few steps back and forth, from the door to the opposite wall, increasing in speed. My mind wandered as it had. I suppose it probably never stopped since I awoke in the clinic. In this fog I paced the tiny room. But the fog was lifted when I opened the top drawer of the dresser and found a pile of new clothes, in a variety of fashions. They were all black. A hand-written note sat atop the pile. The note read,

> My Dear Ms. Kessler,
>
> I bought you some clothes. I think they will fit. I'm pretty good at that. You are a good woman, and I believe your son to be good too, for "A good tree does not produce bad fruit." Please believe me when I tell you that you and your son are in my prayers and the prayers of my wife and children.
>
> I don't know what you are, or what strange events have brought a boy like Joseph into being. But I suspect God's hand in it. In my sorrow for your circumstances, I must believe that God's hand is in that too. I will never forget you, and I have the feeling I have not heard the last of you.
>
> All of My Prayers and Wishes,
> Samuel Lewiston

I felt the irony of Mr. Lewiston writing the exact quotation that Brunhilde used when describing Joseph. The penmanship and the words themselves were in stark contrast to the man I met in France, to the furious interrogator who slammed his hand on a table and demanded the truth from me. There was a softness in the signature at the bottom of the letter. It spoke of a complex mind and deep spirit, of a man out of place in his career and among his kind. I ran my fingertips over the signature several times, expecting the softness of the curved ink-lines to be experienced by my sense of touch. I returned my eyes to the body of the letter and reread the quotation, over and over again. In my head, Mr. Lewiston's voice mutated slowly into Brunhilde's. They were very similar to each other, not at first glance, but in those deeply hidden characteristics that I doubt many saw in either of them.

I changed from the bloody jumpsuit, into a black pair of slacks and a black blouse. The black was chosen for a reason. These were clothes of mourning. Mr. Lewiston knew that I would be in mourning. And the black fabric forbade me to forget what it stood for and what an atrocious loss I would soon suffer.

There was underwear, socks, and shoes to match. I put them all on and turned the doorknob of the room. I expected it to be locked, and to have to yell to some soldier to let me out. The knob turned and the door opened. I walked down a hallway that had many more rooms like mine. The hallway led to a gathering hall and dining room. Small clusters of men and women, soldiers and civilians, sat at tables, eating, laughing, and carrying on. This day was not extraordinary in their lives. I walked by and among them unnoticed. I was just another faceless inhabitant of the base.

On the side of the gathering hall was a large glass door that opened to a grassy courtyard, enclosed within high, concrete walls. The sun was out and I longed for the warmth that it provided. I went into the courtyard and closed the sliding-glass door behind me. I took two steps from the door and heard it reopen. When I turned around, Mr. Lewiston was there. He closed the door, to give our conversation privacy.

"I was afraid I'd never see you again," he said. "But they have put me in charge of you. That is, they have put me at your disposal, at least through the…"

He caught himself, unable to say the word "execution" to me.

He stumbled for a follow-up word, but I saved him the distress, saying, "Thank you for the clothes, for the letter, and for your prayers."

He nodded to me, and in a breaking voice, he answered, "You're welcome. It looks like they fit. I wasn't sure if you wanted a suit or a dress, so I bought a variety."

"They're perfect. Thank you." And after a short, breathless pause, I added, "Are you sure there is nothing you can do for us."

"I can hold your hand through this. I have been ordered to do so, but I would have *against* orders if that's what it took."

He placed a hand on each of my shoulders and said, "Reuniting you with your son would have been a great propaganda triumph for us. But he reveals another terrifying ability every day. These things don't usually happen so quickly. But he frightens them. I am sorry. I wish the real killer could be found and caught. Maybe things would be different."

I thought about Brunhilde. I wished that Joseph had a remote castle to hide away in, like she did when she was young. But I would not betray her, and in doing so betray all of the hidden truths tied to her existence. Even if I did, I would not be believed. The mystical nature of truth is its best defense against the cynical. The faithless cannot wrap their heads around it, or cram it into their narrow definitions of reality. So they dismiss and leave it to live in peaceful obscurity. That, above any sword or axe or Unicorn horn, was the sharpest weapon of the Swan Knights.

Mr. Lewiston led me back into the dining hall and showed me how to order and receive my meals. He had already eaten. But he ordered a snack so we could eat together.

After a few bites of our shared breakfast, he cleared his throat in preparation for a difficult topic, and followed, "Joseph is permitted a final meal. But we cannot ask him. They keep him gagged and blindfolded, and with sound-eliminating ear guards always on him."

In a disgusted, accusatory tone, I asked, "When was the last time he ate or drank?"

"It's been a full day... at least. But they have hydrated him intravenously."

My jaw clinched in anger, and a furious scowl took control of my face. Mr. Lewiston could see my anger. How could it be otherwise? Maternal fury erupted from my every pore.

His timidity fed my courage and I yelled, awkwardly loud in the emptying dining hall, "He is fourteen. He would not yet be in high school if he was raised here, if he was not... if he... He is only a child!"

He tried to explain, "Joseph controls them with his eyes, with his words, and with the slightest gestures. Our military has never faced such a dangerous threat. You know that I am on your side. But I am on their side as well. Frankly, your son terrifies me too. Honestly, if I did not have such an inexplicable faith in your goodness, I would have insisted as they did. I have no argument in his defense, beyond the deepest whispers of my inner-heart."

He brought us back to the point he began to make, "He is allowed a final meal, but there is no way to ask him what he would like it to be without restoring his senses and endangering the soldiers."

"Your soldiers are in no danger from my son."

"I believe that. But again, I understand their precautions... I want to ask you to speak for him. What would he like for his last... for his last meal?"

I could not bring myself to consider the subject, and I remained on the offensive, asking, "Does he know? Has he been made aware that he is condemned to die?"

Mr. Lewiston considered the question, seemingly for the first time. His eyes rolled to the side as he combed through his memory for an answer to my question.

"I don't know," he answered, returning his eyes to mine. "I don't know if he realizes his fate. That is, I'm not sure anyone has told him directly. You see, they keep him blindfolded and..."

I interrupted, "Yes, yes, and gagged with earphones. You already told me that. And I saw him on the screen from my cell in the courtroom. Doesn't he have a right to know?"

Mr. Lewiston was visibly aggravated, more I believe from the legitimacy of my complaints. But there was something else. He did his job well, and his loyalty began to outweigh his compassion.

He brought the conversation back, saying in a demanding tone, "He has a *right* to a last meal. What would you like it to be?"

With a sneer, and in a lofty, flippant tone, I responded, "By this point, Joseph will have fully escaped the desires of his senses. One thing would be just like any other to him. Don't bother *risking your soldiers* for his pleasure. He is beyond them, beyond you, beyond any of us."

We ate a few more bites in silence, not daring to raise eyes to each other.

In that silence, I thought. Joseph was formidable, to be sure, with powers beyond mine. But his powers were not for destruction. They were healing, constructive abilities. I on the other hand, was an experienced warrior and a trained knight. The soldiers of the base had nothing to fear from the little feathered boy, not because he could not harm them, because he *would* not. But I had the fury of a protective mother, united with the intense training I had undergone in recent years. It was probably right that the soldiers feared me. And as I snarled at the food on my plate, I began plotting my destruction of the base and rescue of my son. The swan had prepared me to face an army, to battle under circumstances far more desperate than any I faced during the war with the Deep.

I thought to myself, "They were foolish to unshackle me."

The tray, the plate, my fork and knife, these were more than I would need to free my son. In an open field, maybe even a forest, the soldiers of the base would be more than I could handle. But the narrow halls and rooms of the complex would give me an advantage. But then what? Even if I killed every soldier on the base, how would we escape? I did not know the layout of the building. I did not know how many buildings made up the base or how many soldiers were stationed there. Would I kill everyone, even the civilians? How many human lives was Joseph worth? These questions plunged their daggers into me one at a time. I could not wage war on the West, defeat them all, and take my son home.

In my renewed despair, my thought fell hard and clear to Joseph, or so I thought. In fact, he found me. His thoughts brushed my mind briefly. The moment we connected, I could not help but pass to him all that I knew, all that I feared, and the violent scenerios running through my head. There is so much else I would have preferred to

377

tell him. But the connection surprised me, and my mind simply dumped onto him that which it currently held. He left my mind as quickly as he came into it, but with a clear thought of determination. It was a thought of resolve without fear. It was almost a happy thought. After the connection was lost, and I had taken a few seconds to dissect what I just experienced, I realized that it was excitement that I felt from him.

But why did he connect with me? Was there something he was instructing me to do? He was confident, perhaps in my ability to save him. My confidence in myself sat miles beneath his. I saw nothing that I could do. But the connection electrified me, and my thoughts flew at hyper-speeds around my head.

A thought came to mind, springing from the flying, darting, bouncing chaos between my ears, and I spoke to Mr. Lewiston with a full mouth of food, "Are there still religious freedoms in this country, or have those been dissolved as well?"

"Of course there are," he replied with more introspection than defensiveness. "Joseph has a right to religious services."

He seemed delighted to offer them, in light of all that was not allowed.

"Good," I went on firmly, "We are Catholic, and he must receive confession and the Holy Eucharist before he dies."

"Done!" he snapped back with alacrity. "He will have it, I promise. Would you like to use the base chaplain or do you have a priest of your own?"

"Your chaplain is fine, so long as he is a Catholic priest."

"He is, and I will send him to your room within the hour."

A plan, not one certain of success, but at least a plan, budded in my brain. I remained deep in contemplation of that plan while we finished our food. Mr. Lewiston looked deeply into my face, snapping his gaze from me when I raised my eyes to him. My mind was hard at work and I suspect he could see it. But my shifting eyes and quickened breaths spoke for a mind that would not tolerate interruption. So we finished our meals without another word spoken between us.

When we rose from the table, he took my plate and said, "I will send the priest to you. He is a good man." And he turned from me to dispose of our dishes.

Back in my room, I had one difficult goal — to find the mind of a creature, any creature of the Sweeter Realm, on either side of the portal. I dwelled intensely on my son's fate, a fate brought about by the actions of Brunhilde. I admired her. I always had. But as my son's demise approached, I could not hold back my anger for her. The intensity of my emotions magnified my thoughts, and I found her. It was a slight and subtle connection. Free and expansive thoughts could not flow through the tiny cord of connection between us. But I beckoned her with an imperative I was sure she would not defy.

"Come. Find me... immediately." That was all I repeated, bombarding her thoughts with that simple message.

The priest came as promised, interrupting my connection to Brunhilde with his knock on my door. I asked him to perform the duties of his ordination, to provide Joseph with the rites of the condemned. He asked if I wanted any particular readings from scripture. The Conspicuous Scriptures were out of the questions.

"Luke, Chapter Twenty-Two," I snapped in response. "The Last Supper."

The priest nodded, believing he understood the significance of the choice. He did not. I did not choose the passage to prepare Joseph for death, but to save his life. The Grail. The passage is about the Grail. I told the priest that I would like the wine served to him in a special cup, a family heirloom of sorts. He agreed and asked for it.

"Soon," I told him. "I will get it to you soon."

As the rest of the day went by, I grew increasingly excited. The Grail had saved Parsifal. It saved me in the lake. It could save Joseph. Those were the thoughts that dragged me reluctantly through the slow movements of the lethargic clock — until sundown, when I finally left my room and made my way to the courtyard adjacent to the gathering hall. The yard was empty and the sky was clear and dark. The moon had not risen and the light of the stars had full reign of the night.

I gazed into the clear night sky, begging God for help, "You created the universe and all that exists. You can fix this. Please, help me now. Please."

I focused on a small group of stars and imagined the mysteries they held. My small cluster of lights fluttered and distorted. They waved, disappeared and reappeared. The distortions revealed themselves as Brunhilde, as soon as she entered the halo of courtyard lights. She shone silvery, as if clad in polished steel.

She landed at my feet, stood tall, looked downward into my eyes and declared, "I will not kill these people. They are not evil, only scared. They are losing their faith, but the Holy Spirit still lives in them. I will not kill them for you."

"I agree with you. They are good. And I would not ask you to kill anyone."

She tilted her head slightly and raised an eyebrow.

She parted her lips to speak but I continued before her thoughts mounted her breath, "No, I called you for a different errand. I need you to open the portal."

Her shoulders slouched and she took one step backward, saying humbly, "I am not the Swan Knight. The portal is not mine to open."

"No it is not. I am the Swan Knight. You were raised in that valley. And this is not the first time a Swan Knight has asked you to open the portal, is it?"

She recovered her posture and turned her head to the side in thoughtful reminiscence, turned back to me, and said in a softer, childlike voice, "I have opened it many times, for Ludmilla and Agnes."

"Yes. And now the Swan Knight asks you to do it again. Open the portal. Send Acheriel and the teacher through. Tell them to bring the Grail."

She looked doubtful, drawing her chin back and subtly shaking her head.

I continued, "Tell them to give it to Friedrich. He must fly it to me immediately. Speed is more important than stealth. I don't care who sees him. I need the Grail as soon as possible."

She continued her signs of disapproval during a few seconds pause, then surprised me by challenging my request, "Do you want the Holy Grail for God's purposes or yours?"

I stepped to her, recovering the space that had been lost when she walked back. Despite the magnificent beauty glowing in front of me from the courtyard lights, I remained locked in a stare into her eyes.

"The portal is in the care of the Swan Knight. I am the Swan Knight and I ask you to open it. The Grail is in the care of the Queen. I am the Queen and I ask you to fetch it. I am the heir of Ludmilla and Agnes, of Ludwig and Otto. And I am the Queen of your homeland, the Queen of your

Brunnen cousins. I tell you this, The Ancient One would obey me. Would you defy him?"

As I spoke, Brunhilde transitioned from the silvery polish of the Valkyrie to the pale flesh color of Elizabeth's childhood friend and the daughter of a human poet.

She dropped to one knee, laid her chest across her thigh, lowered her eyes to the ground beneath her, and begged, "Forgive me, my Queen. I have been alone for so long, with nobody to obey, nobody to guide me. If you will please forgive me, I will obey you."

I cupped her cheek in my hand and pulled her gaze to me, saying, "There is nothing to forgive. You have seen much more, known more and done more, and you received the Swan Knight training. I would yield to you on all matters but this. Please go quickly and do as I ask."

She took my hand from her cheek with both of her hands. She turned my palm down and kissed my knuckles, then turned my palm up and kissed my fingertips. She released my hands and ran her fingertips across my closed mouth whispering, "These... lips... drank from... the Cup... of Christ."

After speaking those words, she sank my left cheek bone into her lips and held it there with the slight suction of a sustained kiss, for several long seconds. As she pulled from me, the almost silent smack of her kiss seemed to echo back and forth across the small courtyard, bouncing off the concrete walls. She looked up — but not to me. She looked to the night sky above us and whispered something in a human language I did not recognize. Her flesh began to ripple upward, which turned to furious waves, like rapids on a rushing mountain river. Her skin transitioned through a series of pale florescent colors. She pushed off of the ground and was out of my sight before my eyes could translate her departure to my brain.

A deep chill followed the realization that she was gone. She was as fast as the wind, on an errand I desperately desired. Yet, her beauty was out of the reach of my senses, and my senses mourned the loss. She is the most affluently beautiful and hauntingly powerful figure I have ever met. The Ancient One has often compared the air around her like that which constantly surrounded the Queen Kandake. I wish I could have met her and allowed my eyes to dance freely across her shimmering scales.

CHAPTER 29
The Family Heirloom

MY ENCOUNTER WITH BRUNHILDE did much to remind me of home, of the Brunnens I lived with during my training, and of my beloved Taufe. She also made me think of The Ancient One and all of their shared stories in the Swan Knights History. Although I slept, my spinning mind never rested that night. Each tiny cabinet of my memory was filled with dangers and joys, love and loss, creatures and wonderful places from my time in the Sweeter Realm. My dreams that night seemed to open each one of them, pull out their contents, and play with them in a fit of nostalgia. I had only been away for a week, but it felt like a year.

When I awoke in the morning, all of my existing anxieties were coated with a thick, cumbersome film of homesickness. I thought about how stressed I had been over the coronation gifts, and how infinitely more monumental my problems had become since. No Swan Knight had ever demanded the Grail, intentionally exposing it to a perilous and greedy world. I doubted my decisions and I doubted my motives. I desired the advice of those who had guided me before — the swan, Taufe, my husband. I would have weighed *Cort's* judgment above my own, were I only able to extract it from him.

I thought about recalling Brunhilde from her commission, but changed my mind, only to change again and back again. It was in this state of internal conflict that

Mr. Lewiston found me when he offered to escort me to breakfast. I was in no mood for the daily buzz of the base, in no mood for soldiers or food, or the kindness of Mr. Lewiston.

I declined, to which Mr. Lewiston simply responded, "I understand. If you change your mind, I'll be in the dining room."

He looked into my eyes, trying to gauge my mental state. He must have seen something that concerned him. He took one step away from me, turned back, and said, "I will check on you soon."

I did not join him in the dining room, as he had hoped. I sat until my legs convulsed, paced until my head pounded, and repeated that cycle for half an hour, when, true to his word, Mr. Lewiston knocked on my door again. He asked if he could bring me anything. Something for my headache was all I requested of him. I think he wanted to be of greater use to me, to be put to some toilsome employment that would ease his mind of the dreadful compassion he felt for me and for my son. I had nothing to give him beyond the small errand I requested. He left my room and returned within seconds with pills for my pain.

"You really ought to take these with food," he suggested.

I felt almost as much compassion for his uneasiness as he felt for mine. To help alleviate it, I asked him to bring me something from the breakfast kitchen before it closed. The errand put a spring in his step. I watched him from my doorway as he bounded down the hall, alternating between a fast walk and a slow run. He returned quickly with a selection of everything offered by the kitchen that morning. It was much more than I could have eaten in my most famished, ravenous state. I accepted the food with sincere gratitude, not for the objects I knew I would not eat, but for the eager care with which it was given.

Mr. Lewiston, being a perceptive man, took notice of my desire for solitude. He fought his instincts (and his orders), and he left me alone for the rest of the morning. I took the food he brought me into the bathroom and flushed it, piece by piece, in a cursing fit of protest against some unknown assailant, against fate and time, greed and evil, against God and mystery, and against my own Grail Blood. I cursed anything to which I could portion out some blame for my son's circumstances, and I exacted my revenge by violently breaking apart my breakfast and flushing it down the toilette. It was a childish display, but one I don't regret. It relieved my anger and allowed me to think more clearly.

I was in a strange conflict with time. I wanted it to pass, to bring me to Friedrich and the Grail. But I was keenly aware that each passing second could push me nearer Joseph's death, if things did not go as I planned. I wondered how many heartbeats remain in his chest, hundreds, thousands, or infinitely more. The obscure image of him on the courtroom monitor put an aching itch into each one of my ribs.

I washed my hands after the brutal mutilation of my breakfast. While I dried them, another knock came at my door. It was the base chaplain. He asked if I had the heirloom to give him. Of course I did not. But I invited him in to pray with me. My tirade had cleared my head and calmed me enough for prayer.

We sat on the cot together and he asked, "Would you like to say a prayer or would you like me to say one?"

"Just hold my hands while I talk to God."

He did just that. He held both of my hands in his and closed his eyes. Through the connection of that man's hands, I felt closer to God — perhaps not closer, but more connected, as if the chaplain served as an antenna for the broadcast of my prayers and the reception of God's response. Through my conversation with God, I squeezed his hands tightly and relaxed them again, repeatedly, as my deepest thoughts and prayers traveled from my heart and through the chaplain. He responded to each twitch of my fingers with a return squeeze, reminding me that he was still there, unaware of the exact nature of my prayers, but nevertheless concentrating on reflecting them to God through him.

I had no doubt at all that I was heard, most intimately, as though I stood on Christ's shoulder and spoke directly into his ear. But when I sat silent of mind, waiting for a response, for some small whisper of guidance to graze the back of my brain like the very slightest of breezes, I felt nothing. I heard nothing — nothing to tell me that I was on the right track, that all of this turmoil would bear some fruit somehow, that I would be all right and Joseph would be all right, that I did not destroy a plan infinity in the making by ordering the Holy Grail to be brought to me and handed over to this stranger sitting on a military cot with me.

I finished my prayers, gave the chaplain a tight, filial hug, and walked him to the door. I told him that I hoped the heirloom would arrive at the base that evening.

"Well," he said, "I am either in my office, the chapel, or my bedroom. If I am not in one of those places, I am probably nowhere at all."

"I will find you, thank you."

He stepped backward from the threshold of the doorway, still looking at me, and I closed the door.

I reopened the door just as he was turning away, and I pleaded, "May I receive the Eucharist? I thirst desperately for it."

"Of course. Give me a few hours. My schedule is tight. I will call you to the chapel."

I thanked him again and closed the door. My prayers with the chaplain revealed little of God's will. I was still not sure of anything I had done, decided, or planned, especially of my most questionable decision, to summon the Grail from the safety of the Sweeter Realm. I wanted Christ himself to tell me I was doing right, and I hoped that my visit to the chapel and my reception of the Eucharist would provide me direction.

I skipped lunch. Mr. Lewiston was not surprised, in light of the amount of food he brought me at breakfast. When he came to offer me lunch, I asked only for paper to write letters. He did as I requested and lingered uncomfortably until I asked him for privacy. I sat at the small, concrete desk that protruded from the wall. I wrote letters. I wrote to Felix with raw, sincere effusions of love that had been long overdue in their telling. I felt cold — very cold, in a warm room. Goosebumps covered my skin and every hair on my body rose. They rose in search of the feathers that had warmed them to such blissful comfort before.

I wrote to The Ancient One and Taufe, to Lina and Senische, to all of the figures whose loyalty and affection I depended on the most, and whose company had seen me through my most difficult times. I even wrote to Rüdiger and Prische. They felt dearer to me than when he slept on my lap and when she carried me on her shoulders. I knew as I wrote that Rüdiger and Prische would not be the only ones never to receive their letters. None of them would. But I hoped that while writing them, the strength of my affection might find its way to Linderhof, and through the portal to gently stroke the thoughts of my dearest ones. I also hoped, that in the absence of their counsel, I might at least be advised by my *memory* of their wisdom.

I did not leave my room that day until I joined Mr. Lewiston for dinner. I expected a visitor in the courtyard that night, and my anxiousness propelled me. After a day of deep, secluded introspection and prayer, Mr. Lewiston was pleased to see my energy so high. It was a nervous energy, not a happy one. But I was out of my room, in the gathering hall, eating and partaking in conversation.

There was little Mr. Lewiston could speak of or ask me about that would not connect painfully to a tender subject. His years of experience in his field were put on glorious display. Somehow, he led me in a conversational dance, drifting freely, yet avoiding any topic that was raw and stinging to the touch. I had not passed so many words to such an eager pair of ears since I regaled the Friends of the Scheriers with stories of my childhood. Mr. Lewiston truly delighted in my smile and the flashes of lightness my heart demonstrated during our conversation. He knew what sort of day awaited me with the following sunrise.

But there was something that Mr. Lewiston and the following day did not know. They did not know about Brunhilde's errand and the precious "family heirloom" I hoped to reunite with my fingertips that night. It had to be that night. The following night would be too late. Joseph's sentence would be carried out before the next sunset would open the doors to a stealthy passage for a Wühlenvogel from Linderhof to the East Coast of the United States. At that point, I didn't care about stealth. I would have welcomed Friedrich through the front gates of the base at high-noon, pulling the Grail behind him in a decorated wagon, on grand display.

I was not certain how fast Friedrich could fly. I had no way to compare the distances I had traveled in my queendom with the flights I had taken across the Atlantic Ocean. I had moved in the grasp of a Wühlenvogel too fast to make sense of the blurred images beneath me. Friedrich had flown me from Linderhof to the Rhine in what seemed like minutes. But I could not gauge any comparison, and the idea that Friedrich could fly at top speed and still not arrive in time with the Grail pumped acid into my veins.

Through these considerations, which buzzed in busy chaos just beneath my surface, I maintain conversation with Mr. Lewiston and passed simple pleasantries with the others in the dining room. While we ate and talked, my eyes darted continuously to the glass door and the courtyard behind it. Meal time ended and the crowd in the gathering hall thinned to a few straggling pairs and threesomes. Mr. Lewiston was too pleased by his success in caring for me to notice anything that passed around him. The sun was setting, and I wanted to be alone in the courtyard. I excused myself from the table. Again he cleared my dishes and escorted me to my room.

I waited just one minute after the door closed behind Mr. Lewiston before slipping out of my room, down the hallway, and back to the gathering hall. The staff was still clanging away in the kitchen and porters cleaned the dining tables. I ignored them all and went into the courtyard. Three soldiers were there, telling jokes and reminiscing of their homes and families. I stood on the opposite end of the courtyard, staring at them silently and without expression. This caused enough awkwardness to serve its purpose. The soldiers left me alone and my eyes went to the sky.

Friedrich must have been waiting for that exact moment. Not fifteen seconds after the soldiers left, he landed in the darkened corner of the yard. He used his tail and one claw to land. In the other claw was the Holy Grail. All fears of exposing the Grail to evil evaporated with the sight of it. It seemed right that I should have it, that it should be in my possession at that time. Friedrich, out of breath and slouching with exhaustion, handed me the Grail.

"There is much concern and debate, both at Linderhof and in the Sweeter Realm. My Queen, you must give me some news to pass to them, some explanation for you demanding the Grail, some update on your welfare and

Joseph's. Your entire queendom has not rested easily since you left them on Holy Thursday."

"There is no time for that now. Pray that all will go well enough that these stories and better ones can be shared with you all soon."

"I have been in a constant state of prayer for your success. We all have."

I pulled him from his darkened corner and squeezed him tightly, thanking him in Wühlenvogel for his service to the Portal Valley, to its Swan Knight, and to his Queen. He jerked away from me abruptly and stared with a low growl at the glass door to the gathering hall through his bushy eyebrows. I followed his gaze and saw Mr. Lewiston, standing in the courtyard behind me, not six full feet from a Wühlenvogel.

"Go now," I ordered Friedrich in his native language. "And tell the others to continue their prayers, and I hope they may hear from me soon."

Friedrich turned his eyes to me, back to Mr. Lewiston, and to me again. He bowed low and flew directly upward. In less than a second, the sky showed no signs that a Wühlenvogel had been there. I turned to Mr. Lewiston, whose neck contorted awkwardly upward to where Friedrich had flown away.

"How much of that did you see and hear?" I asked him with the command of a Queen's voice.

He dropped his attention to me, tilted his head, and leaned away from me, biting at the inside of his cheeks and lips.

"How much?" I repeated more forcefully.

His knees shook and looked like they might buckle beneath him as he answered, "All of it... I think."

I stared at him, daring him to say something I did not care to hear. I stood fiercely, like a Queen in battle, like a Swan Knight trained by The Ancient One, like a warrior of the Sweeter Realm trained by Georg. Mr. Lewiston was timidly curious, and clearly taken aback as much by the drastic alteration in my tone and presence as he was by the strange creature he just saw and heard. There was not the frightened mother in front of him. There was certainly no sign of the timid woman he met in France. A knight and Queen stood erect. And despite his height, I towered over him. My low eyes seemed to look down on him, as his looked up at me. The hints in the back of his heart, that there was more to me than he knew, stood at attention and screamed their presence into his mesmerized head.

He studdered, "That thing spoke to you in German."

I nodded.

"And in another language… and you spoke back."

My harsh eyes refused to release his. But he peeled his away long enough to dart to my hand for a quick glance at the Grail before returning where I demanded them to be.

His eyes went one more time to the Grail and back before he asked me, "Ms. Kessler, what is happening here?"

"Nothing sinister, I assure you. But nothing you need ever speak of."

"That was not the product of some Chinese or Russian military scientist, was it?"

"No! And neither is my son. Ferocious as that creature must have looked to you, his heart is the tenderest you will ever meet."

"But its claws, and its…"

"You have nothing to fear from him, and nothing to fear from Joseph. Mr. Lewiston, there are times we have to just accept mystery, without fear, judgment, or prejudice."

He looked at the Grail in my hand and pointed to it.

I did not give him the chance to comment or question. I simply continued, "And that is what you must do now, unless you wish to interfere with your own salvation.

Nothing you have seen tonight requires your action. There is nothing you can do or say that would result in good. Go home. Pray. And go to bed, sir. Tomorrow will be a long day for all of us."

He stumbled to put his thoughts into language, and his words fell clumsily from his mouth, shoved from behind by the next confused thought, "A queen… a swan knight… a portal valley… the Grail… who are… what are…"

I silenced him with a stern gaze and a finger pointed directly between his eyes.

"Go to bed, Samuel Lewiston, and pray to God that you are worthy to be a part of the things that are happening around you."

His shoulders slouched timidly, and he stepped slowly away from me, like he was afraid that lightening would shoot from my pointed fingertip.

I stepped toward him, keeping my finger aimed at his face, saying, "Go… go to bed. Pray. This is in my hands now. Evil will act and I will act against it. All you need to do is nothing."

He opened his mouth to respond but closed it before a breath escaped. He swayed back and forth, rubbing the bridge of his nose hard, as if trying to remove some deep, sticky smudge. He stopped his swaying after a few seconds, stopped rubbing his nose and placed his fingers across his lips and his thumb under his chin. He stared at me like that for several awkward seconds.

Then he looked to the sky again, back at me, and said reverently, with a subtle drop of his head, "I will obey you."

He turned, shaking violently, and walked through the glass doorway, back into the gathering hall, and out my sight, closing the courtyard door behind him. He moved slowly, like a man in deep contemplation, not quickly and shiftily, like a man scrambling to tell what he just witnessed. He shook as he walked. Chills waved over his entire body in relentless rhythm.

Only when he was gone from my senses did I notice that my heart pounded inside of me. I could feel my pulse in every inch of my body. I waited in the courtyard until the bright lights of the kitchen stopped splashing across the gathering hall floor. I walked briskly and quietly through the tables and chairs, down the hallway, and to my room. Only then did I allow my eyes and fingers to relish possession of the Grail.

I was eager to get the Grail to the chaplain, so he could take it to Joseph in the morning, before the execution. But I found myself savoring every moment with it, in a strange, esoteric reluctance to let it go, like I would never see it again. I looked for the lip print of Parsifal. But it had faded under the lake and my eyes were too tired to strain. I was tempted to fill it with water and drink from it.

"I do not need saving," I lectured myself. "Joseph does."

With that grim reminder, I snapped myself from my covetous grip on the Grail and hurried it to the chaplain's office. He was not there, so I sought him in the chapel. I found him there, alone as I hoped he would be, praying softly in a low, half-vocalized murmur.

"Father?" I interrupted. "I have the... cup... the heirloom I told you about."

I had almost said "the Grail", and my heart raced at my near folly. The chaplain took it from me. It seemed to affect him at first touch. He inhaled quickly and let it out slowly though a tight, circular pair of lips. I doubt he suspected it was the Holy Grail, the Cup of the Messiah. But he undoubtedly revered it as some holy relic or another.

He held the cup against his chest and said, "Joseph will receive the sacrament from this cup."

I thanked him, patted his upper arm a few times, and turned to walk away. I was stopped by his voice asking, "What is this? Where is it from? Where did your family get it?"

I answered honestly, "It has been in my family for a long, long time."

I was surprisingly at-ease having just handed the Holy Grail to another human, particularly in light of the lingering sensation that I would never see it again.

I went to bed and dreamed of my flight with The Ancient One, after the battle in the Achima Canyon. But in it, we also flew over my old neighborhood in Centennial. My neighbors stood on their lawns and waved at us. We flew over my middle school. I saw Birgit, Herr Fischer, and many of my other friends and teachers. They were on the roof and lawn of the school, all jumping and waving excitedly. Next, my mother, Karl, Birgit, and a few of my childhood friends were sailing through the air beside me, all in the grasp of Wühlenvogels.

I awoke from this dream well before dawn and was unable to return to sleep. So I prayed. I wondered where Joseph was and how he felt. Was he frightened? I wanted so badly to hold him and sing him to sleep. I took some comfort knowing that the Holy Grail would soon be in his hands. He would recognize it immediately, and he would know that I brought it for him. It felt right to have retrieved the Grail and given it to the chaplain for Joseph's use. Yet I felt no confidence in Joseph's survival. I could not reconcile the conflicting premonitions. I held my pillow to my chest, kissed it, and spoke to it the things I wanted to say to my son. I wet it thoroughly with my tears.

I dropped the pillow as everything cleared from my mind in an instant — everything but one thought.

"The Grail!" I spoke aloud. "It holds the consecrated Blood of Christ."

The Grail spoke to me, or Joseph did. In either case I knew that the chaplain held the Grail in his hands at that moment, and for the first time since the Last Supper, it held the Blood of the Lord.

"Joseph is drinking from the Grail... Thank you Lord." That was my only prayer and all that needed to be said.

The sensation that the full Grail gave to me filled me with a sense of righteous purpose, with the confidence of Divine direction. I sat in prayer, but had nothing to request. I simply listened. I feared the day ahead of me. Of course, I did. But I trusted in God and, as the Queen and Swan Knight, I suspected my role in the day's events would not be that of a simple spectator. I would have to act. Of that I was certain. So I listened in open-hearted silence to God. I received no instructions. But I was filled with a strong sense of duty, which took some of the edge off of my maternal fears. I sat as rigid as a knight in full armor while the wee hours of the early morning passed slowly.

CHAPTER 30
Joseph's Portal

BEFORE THE SUN ROSE, Mr. Lewiston knocked on my door. He was dressed, shaven, and alert, as if it was well into the day. I knew the kitchen wasn't open and I wandered why he would be at my room so early. He wasted no time in telling me.

Before I finished opening the door, he said in a low, somber voice, "Get yourself ready, Ms. Kessler. It's time."

All of the confidence gained in prayer, every sensation of Divine Providence sent to me by the Grail, disappeared in a flash. My entire body seemed to hollow out and cram all of my organs into my neck, cutting off my air. I punched myself in the chest, clawed at my throat, and dropped to my knees.

"Easy, easy," Mr. Lewiston begged, "breathe. Take your time. Breathe slowly."

But I cared nothing for the air around me, nothing for the workings of my body. I cared only for my sweet boy, and I would have given anything to reverse the course of our lives. My mind raced from one moment of my past to the next, seeking moments when a single altered decision, a different word or action, would have placed us all back in the Sweeter Realm, with me performing some mundane ritual and Joseph gallivanting through the woods of the Nomadic Belt on the shoulders of Senische. I must have compiled thousands of such moments in only a few seconds, and each added to the restriction of my airway.

I fell to my side and gave up the heaving, futile attempts to draw breath into my lungs. Such a condition, I'm sure, would have been quite painful. But my pain was concentrated in another area. Mr. Lewiston yelled many things to me. He jostled me around and struck me on the back. It was all as if watching it on a television. My physical senses were numbed. I heard Mr. Lewiston scream for a medic. Two nurses arrived. But by the time they did, I had returned to breathing, slow and shallow as it was. They helped me to sit up on the floor, against the wall of the hallway, just outside my room. As my breath became normal, I began to cry — tears, followed by a moan, followed by full-throated sobbing.

"Is she going to be all right?" Mr. Lewiston asked the nurses.

They told him that I had a panic attack and made him promise to call them if it happens again. He assured them that he would, and he sent them away.

Mr. Lewiston stood in front of me. All I could see in my position was his legs from the knees down. I waited. I wanted him to sit beside me, to throw his arm around me and speak comforting words. I expected that to happen, but it did not. He just stood there, waiting for me to recover.

"My dear, we really have to go now," he said.

I stood quickly, as quickly as my weakened legs would permit, and looked him in the face. His eyes and cheeks were as red as they were wet from his tears.

"The Ancient One calls me that," I informed him in a rather matter-of-fact tone.

"The Ancient One?"

"He's my teacher," I said, sniffing and wiping the tears from my cheeks.

He looked at me. A resurgence of fluid rolled from his eyes.

Somehow, in simply speaking openly about The Ancient One, the faith of a Swan Knight began to pulse through my veins.

Mr. Lewiston cleared his throat and said, "We really must go now."

"Now? Before breakfast? Why so early? Why right now?"

He took in a deep breath, held it for a few seconds and released it sharply, following it with the words, "Four more soldiers left the base last night. That makes nine in total. They just dropped their weapons and walked off the base. They cannot do that. It's illegal. When they have been arrested and questioned, they praise your son for reaching their hearts, speaking of him like they know him well. Joseph is in complete isolation. He cannot see or hear anything. And he has never met the soldiers who left this morning. We don't know how he gets to them… gets inside of them."

He drifted his gaze from my face to some corner of the hallway. But I suspect he looked far beyond our physical walls, as he continued choppily, "I think I might… I mean I'm beginning to believe… that your son, that you and your son are… are…"

The next thought seemed too big to fit through his gaping mouth.

I asked rhetorically, "And are they hurt, harmed in any way? Or do they seem happier, freer, lighter and less burdened?"

He pondered this point for a second, less scared like before, and more curious.

He continued, "Some of these soldiers worked across the base and never encountered your son. Yet somehow, he got through to them. Some were new here and some had been here for years. The last soldier was questioned less than an hour ago. Like the others, he praised Joseph for his liberation. They fear that they will lose the whole base, themselves, or the entire country to Joseph's influence."

I looked at him as if to ask, "Do you believe that to be a bad thing?"

His face transitioned quickly from an almost delighted perplexity to one of grave sorrow, as he remembered why he came for me so early, "They gave him one hour. They said he must be dead in one hour. They woke me and ordered me to bring you."

Mr. Lewiston's voice broke several times as he spoke. His compassionate distress was authentic.

"I'm sorry you had to be a part of this," I told him. "I'm sorry we brought this into your life."

"No, no, no. I'm so sorry for *you*, and for your little boy."

I looked at him confidently. I *was* confident. Hearing tell of Joseph's power over the minds of the soldiers bulstered my spirit. I repeated the thought in my head, as I stared into Mr. Lewiston's eyes, "Joseph drank the concecrated Blood of Christ from the Holy Grail. His blood is holier than mine or Parsifal's."

I reached my hand toward him and he took it in his. He nodded to me and led me down the hallway.

As we made our way to the far side of the complex, still hand-in-hand, I commented, "I wish my husband were here. He'd want to be here, for me and for Joseph."

"So, you *are* married," he spoke with no judgment or suspicion in his voice.

"Yes. His name is Felix and he loves us very much. He deserves to be here."

My thoughts were happy. I meant that Felix deserved to see the miracle of the Grail, not that he deserved to watch his son's death. My words spoke one idea to my hallway companion, while speaking very differently to my own heart.

Mr. Lewiston began the word "Where…," but cleared his throat and discarded the question that would have followed. He wanted to ask about Felix. I watched him evolve over those few days. The man I met in France would have asked the question. He would have demanded an answer. But it seems that I had done to Samuel Lewiston a slower, subtler version of what Joseph had done to nine soldiers of the base. He was liberated from his previous self and the rigid confines of his paranoid patriotism.

He led me to a glass door that glowed pink with the light of the rising sun. On the other side of it was a concrete courtyard, surrounded by walls that were topped with barbed wire. Rows of high posted lights, like those at a stadium, were mounted on poles along the walls. The lights flashed on, flooding the courtyard and reflecting off the concrete floor. All loveliness of the sunrise was lost. The bright lights revealed four soldiers pushing a large, black, square block. It was taller than the men and appeared substantially heavy. They positioned it against the center of one of the walls.

I looked at Mr. Lewiston, and was about to ask him to explain the block. But he squeezed my hand before I could speak. In that squeeze, I figured it out. It was the block Joseph would stand against to be shot.

Mr. Lewiston led me to some bleachers, three rows deep, against the adjacent wall, left of the black square. Nobody joined us. We sat there alone in the center of the first row. Four soldiers came through a wide door that slid open on rails at the top and bottom. They had Joseph in their grasp. I cannot describe what I felt when I saw him. To this day, I cannot put that moment into words. It was both wretched and wonderful in the extreme. He was as Mr. Lewiston had described, bound not only by hands and feet.

403

His eyes were covered. He wore earphones. He was gagged. He could not see, hear, or speak, and he could hardly move any part of him.

Other than the binds, the blindfold, the gag that forced his mouth unnaturally open, and the earphones, he wore nothing but his own feathers. They were scarcer. Many had been pulled out, no doubt to be tested. But there were no wounds. The skin where his feathers had been was fresh and vibrant, healed entirely by the Holy Grail. Other feathers held lightly to him, ready to be taken from him by the first heavy breeze. He was thin, deathly thin. But he shined. He had never been brighter. Evidence of the Grail's influence was on every inch of him.

Chills ran through me, chills of excitement and fear. But the excitement dominated. I awaited a miracle but feared the pain that might precede it. Suddenly, I began to doubt my miracle. I was no more qualified to proclaim God's will than the soldiers who gripped my son. The idea that Joseph would die that morning, that he would be taken from me forever, dropped on me and cracked my skull. I wrapped both arms over my head in reaction to the abrupt pain. When the headache subsided enough, and I released my arms to my side, I looked at Joseph and saw him very differently. He looked doomed to me, condemned and broken.

As much as I would have loved to shout my love to him, I was glad he could not hear me. The thought of bullets flying through him pulled a mortified gasp from my throat, which unplugged the cap of my emotions, allowing the screaming cries that followed the gasp to erupt from me freely. Mr. Lewiston scooted against my right hip and put his arm around me. He alternated squeezes, pats, and rubs of my shoulder and upper arm.

The four soldiers positioned Joseph against the center of the black square and backed away. Still, nobody joined us on the bleachers. A row of marching soldiers came through the same sliding door, each carrying a rifle. They wore earphones similar to the ones on Joseph. They marched into their place, a single line about thirty or forty feet from Joseph. Directions must have come to them through the earphones. They moved in unison, as if hearing identical orders at the same time, but the courtyard remained eerily quiet. Not even the sounds of nature penetrated the blinding dome of white lights that sat over us, accentuating the frightened and mournful sounds coming from me, which, other than the scuffling of boots, were the only sounds to be heard.

I continued crying until the line of soldiers turned to face Joseph. At that point, my faith left me entirely. The sight silenced me and utterly froze my breath. I stared at my son. A breeze picked up, ruffling Joseph's feathers into an exquisite and expressive dance. They seemed to speak the things he could not. It was not a mournful dance, nor was it celebratory. It was a dance of preparation, one that sang of grand things to come. My eyes were captured by the only feathers on his body not dazzlingly white. I focused on his right arm, on the Mark of Sacrifice, first smeared on him by Felix. He was a member of my Royal Guard, sworn to protect me. Who was he protecting now, and who was protecting him? I asked myself these questions, unintentionally and unknowingly aloud, until Mr. Lewiston responded.

He turned his face to me, squeezed me more tightly, and asked, "What did you say?"

Joseph drank from the Grail. Not only did he drink, but he drank the consecrated Blood of Christ from the Cup of the Messiah. I had every reason to expect something miraculous to occur before us. And like it or not, Mr. Lewiston would be witness to it.

So I fearlessly answered him, "Joseph has his own Grail Blood now, not just mine and Parsifal's. Christ is *his* Royal Guard. God will keep him safe."

It was spoken to Mr. Lewiston. But it was spoken *for* me. I reminded myself of the fact, hoping to revive my faith.

I kept my gaze forward, toward Joseph. But I could see through the corners of my eyes that Mr. Lewiston continued to look at me, undoubtedly pondering the meaning of my words and suspecting something more mystically wonderful than just the ramblings of a distressed mother. He remained that way until distracted by the repositioning of the soldiers. They all dropped one foot back and assumed a shooting position. They raised their rifles in perfect cadence. I had nothing left to cry, neither in tears nor breath. I bit the inside of my mouth and thought the most loving and supportive thoughts to my son, praying he perceived them.

He lifted his head and drew a deep breath in response to my thoughts. I had seconds at most to delight in the evidence of my thin connection to him, before the guns would fire. I frantically scanned the courtyard for the chaplain. I was desperate to verify that Joseph took from the Grail. My eyes were drawn back by the deafening, shocking, painful sound of the rifles. I turned to my son and saw feathers falling. Some floated in the air around him. Others were bloody and fell quickly. He did not fall to the ground. He stood there with bleeding holes all over his body, but he remained standing tall. I stared with held breath, waiting to see the miraculous effects of the Grail, to see his wounds close as Parsifal's had, as mine had. I was startled by another round of shots.

Joseph's body was pushed around by the bullets. Blood flew everywhere. His earphone where shot off, taking with it Joseph's ear and a portion of his head. He fell to his side, limp on the ground. I stood from the bleachers and screamed. The guns fired again, pushing Joseph's limp body in convulsions, as more feathers flew, and more blood scattered. One of his arms barely held to his shoulder by the thinnest string of flesh. What was left of his head was misshaped, and barely larger than a fist. A final round of shots left a pile of bloody flesh and feathers hardly recognizable as something that once lived. Where was the Grail? Where was my miracle?

The sight before me was so unlike any horror I could ever have imagined. Of all of the things I describe in these pages, it is that image that has embroidered itself most vividly, perpetually, and constantly to my mind's eye. The clawing, scraping, ripping feeling in my chest was so far beyond any pain I could have believed possible. I could make no sound. I only stared at what was once my son and I waited. I waited for that pile of mutilated flesh to again resume the appearance of the bright, wise, compassionate feathered boy I loved. Although long gone from the courtyard, the echoes of the guns clung to my ears. I prepared myself for another round of shots, but it did not come. The thundering violence settled into silence, and I waited.

The soldiers lowered their guns, turned in unison toward the sliding door, but did not march. They stood there, frozen. Everything was frozen in stillness and silence.

I saw nothing at first. It was the sound that changed the scene. A familiar crackling sound harmonized with another, and then another. From every drop of Joseph's blood that fell to the ground with him, or flew across the courtyard, a Grail Portal opened. Dozens of portals, then hundreds filled the space around us. The soldiers ran in terror. Some shot their rifles at the growing and multiplying circles of nothing. The crackling sound was intense, and it

407

grew with the opening of each new portal. I could still see Joseph, and I knew he was gone. His body was not being reassembled into the darling, dazzling child I knew. It remained a mangled mess on the floor. But as his body bled, portals opened.

Still looking at his body, I heard Joseph's voice — not in my ears, but in my mind. It was not a memory, nor was it imagination. It was Joseph, and he spoke directly into my mind as he used to do, reciting excerpts from familiar passages.

> Pass through, pass through the gates!
> Raise a banner for the nations.
> They will be called the Holy People,
> The Redeemed of the Lord
> Revive us now, God, our helper!
> Put an end to your grievance against us.

His voice was in my head alone, and it reminded me of the private and intimate connection we shared when he was in the womb. I understood my instructions. I looked at the portals around me, closed my eyes, pictured my son, reopened my eyes and took control of the portals. I enlarged them, all of them. I grew them until they consumed the base and the forest around it, the nearest roads and towns, the cities. I continued to enlarge them connecting them together and expanding them until they were one portal that swallowed the continent and crossed the oceans. I grew it until it covered the Earth.

In that moment, when every human stood in Joseph's Portal, we were given our final judgment — our final chance to make good judgment. In that instant, we each decided. Those who were inclined toward God chose to pass into Eden. Those who were not remained. It was a warm and welcoming sensation, and it lasted for just a flash of a moment. It was an invitation to return to our origins, to live with God in the garden that I had called home for nearly two decades. I was scarred deeply by the death of my son, from having witnessed it as I did. My duality of spirit was extreme as I made my choice — to pass through Joseph's Portal and join God in his garden, in my queendom.

Each rifle shot tore as violently though my spirit as it tore through Joseph's body. But inside of the crackling portal — Joseph's Portal, that which would be the salvation of mankind, I was also proud. I was relieved. Every lesson with Taufe, every cryptic word from Hüter, every word of Christ in the Conspicuous Scriptures spoke of that moment. Joseph's gruesome death was not my fault. It could not be prevented by anything I could have done differently, or could have done better. It was the work of God and it threw open the gates of Eden. I would never again touch my son, never touch his feathers or hear his voice in my physical ears. But the Sweeter Realm was again God's kingdom. It was again the sacred garden it was made to be, again serving the purpose of its creation — to be paradise, where God and God's children live together in constant, intimate connection.

I was inside of Joseph's Portal for only an infinitesimally minute moment. But it was long enough for me to savor the sensation and the understanding that it *was* Joseph's portal. His portal bore his signature spirit. And that spirit kissed me quickly but assuredly as I passed through, and it did the same to everyone else who chose to take that doorway to God. Again, no combination of words from any or all languages could capture the diversity of my feelings, simultaneously lower and higher than I had ever been. I relished my moment in Joseph's Portal, knowing it would never open again, and I turned my thoughts to my queendom and the challenges that awaited me there.

CHAPTER 31
Introductions and Reunions

I WAS EXCITED TO RETURN HOME, and excited to see what Eden would become, now that it is cleansed and the gates have been opened. Each time mankind mixed with Eden, miracles happened. Now God's chosen would be returning to Eden in mass. I was excited to see who would pass through, who from my past I would be welcoming into my queendom, and how Eden would be changed by their return home. But all of that excitement was run through a dark filter, the filter of the things I had just witnessed. It *was* excitement. But it was a heavy excitement, as burdensome as uplifting, as hollowing as fulfilling.

I understood the prophesies and I knew what was happening. I knew that Earth would be inhabited entirely by the ungodly and the righteous would leave it behind. I bid a quick farewell to the Earth I had once called home, not expecting and not desiring to ever see it again.

Joseph's Portal closed and deposited me in a sparsely wooded field. I did not recognize the area. But the trees, the thickness and sweetness of the warm air, the way the breezes greeted me like an old friend, all told me that I was home. A scan of the area showed me nothing that told me exactly where I was. I knew well the areas depicted by the centerfold of Rudolf's Map. I traveled many of the areas on the outer folds of the map. I was beyond anything drawn by Rudolf. But the trees were Sweeter Realm trees, and they recognized their Queen. I was still wearing the complete outfit given to me by Mr. Lewiston. I popped off my shoes and allowed the soft grass to embrace my feet. The sandy dirt beneath it rose from beneath the roots and blades. I felt a slight squeeze. I knelt down and ran my fingers through the soil.

I whispered into the breeze, "I'm home."

The breeze passed word to all in its path.

No people or creatures were there, not yet. I was the first to pass through Joseph's Portal. I heard a voice. It was not taken in by my ears, but placed directly into my thoughts. It was Christ.

I knew him the moment the words came to me, "At an acceptable time I have listened to you. And on a day of salvation I have helped you."

I dropped to one knee, looked to the ground in front of me, made the Sign of the Cross, and whispered back to my Lord, "Your will be done."

I stood again, but not by my own power. I found myself on my feet, lifted by God.

This was not like the prayers of my past. This was an intimate connection, one consciousness to another. God was no longer some theoretical figure, bound to me only by the strength of my faith. God was in the air around me, and infiltrated every part of me with each inhale, as real and tangible as the grass and soil still hugging my bare feet.

Another consciousness came clear to me. It was Joseph, my son. He was with God, and as my thoughts touched God, they also touched him. I did not have to form sentences. The comprehensive whole of my love for him, so much deeper and wider than could ever be corralled by language, transferred directly to him. I knew at that moment that I had not lost my son. Oh, I had lost the ability to touch and hold his body. His body was a bloody carcass left behind in a world that had nothing to do with me and my future. But his mind was with me, communicating with me like it did in the womb, only richer and wiser, and filled with a thousand times more love.

I heard his voice ringing in my head, and it seemed to echo in the air around me, "Death, where is your victory? Death, where is your sting?"

There, intertwined with the consciousness of God and Joseph, was Rüdiger. I said to him all the things I had wished I could say since he dove into the lake to rescue the swan. He told me that he had been with me all along, through the fall and my recovery, my training in St. Hildegard, my discovery of the Grail, the war, my victory and marriage, the birth of Joseph and everything I experienced until I passed through my portal in the lake.

Prische was there too, in the air around me. I spoke to her, then heard many voices that should have been unknown to me, but I knew them. Parsifal and Lohengrin, Elsa, Bechtold, Hildemar, and Ermenrich spoke to me, in their own voices, in their own words. Veronika, the Ottos and the Ludwigs, Rudolf, Adolf and Irmengard, and my own dear King Ludwig II spoke to me, not in some hazy whisper from a paper poster in a classroom. They spoke to me more plainly than the clearest mental connection I had ever made.

My mind perceived the tight embrace of fleshy, human arms around my shoulders and back, though nobody touched me. I knew those arms well. It was the embrace of my father. He too was with God and the others, and his mind also had ready access to me, and mine to him.

After sharing the depth of my love for him, I asked him, "Daddy, how is this possible? Why now can I touch my thoughts to my dead loved ones?"

He answered me, "The Sweeter Realm is God's Garden again. And we are again God's children. Eden was not God's garden without the people. But now we are home. We have regained our divinity. You are one with Christ, and your blood is also holy."

"The other people?" I inquired.

"They are coming, and they will need you to guide them."

I felt his embrace again, as he added, "This is all brought about by you. I was devastated when I lost you. But I was always proud of you and I knew I would be with you again. We are all with you. We are all together... forever, my sweet girl."

People began to appear around me, materializing from thin air, some standing, some lying down. They had nothing — no clothes, no jewelry. They came without any of the things they had known. They were disoriented, confused, and frightened. I had passed through Grail portals twice before. I anticipated my passage as I enlarged and connected the portals that opened by Joseph's blood. I controlled the menacing crackle that consumed us. I knew its origin, its purpose, and I knew where it would bring me. The lessons and prognostications from my years of education and training all came to me in that moment, and I understood them. The people did not. They were swept in an instant from their lives. Suddenly there were no houses, no cars or roads, none of the possessions they had so painstakingly acquired over their years. There were no status symbols, nothing to distinguish one from another but the things given to them by God at their birth. They were aware of their nakedness, and shame added to their confusion.

My "indispensable skill", as The Ancient One called it many years earlier, was not only given to me to coordinate attacks against Löwschock and his army of serpents. Oh no. It had a much grander purpose. As each human entered the Sweeter Realm, they entered my mind, each and every one of them. I felt their thoughts and they could feel mine.

I seized their thoughts, instantly suspending their fears. I explained the wonderful truth to them — at the moment of judgement, they chose a life with God over a world of human construction. I soothed them, then connected their minds to each other, to God, and to their departed loved ones.

Laughter and crying echoed off of every hill and every tree, as the people's minds were reunited with the spirits of those they had lost. I remained with them and felt the joy of the reunions as they did. People continued to appear, across the Sweeter Realm. I performed the same service for each, welcoming and explaining, connecting and reuniting. I found my mother and brother as they chose God and crossed through Joseph's Portal, and I connected them to my father, and to my grandparents, and every lost relative, known and unknown.

I was delighted — delighted but not surprised to find Samuel Lewiston. He was less frightened than most, less confused. His encounters with Joseph and me, and with Friedrich, prepared his spirit for something extraordinary. He appeared mere feet from me, and my eyes perceived him before my mind did. He smiled at me, before I made any attempt to soothe his mind and connect him with Christ. He smiled with a face that knew everything was right and as it was meant to be. He was aware of his nakedness, but not ashamed of it, as he gestured with one hand to the clothes that I still wore, the clothes *he* bought for me. I smiled back, gave him a gentle kiss on the cheek, closed my eyes, and connected him to his frightened family, who had also chosen God.

My mind was swelling with more thoughts, more people, alive and dead. But it did not fatigue me. I wanted more. I reached for the native creatures of Eden and found their minds easily. I connected them to the people, and invited them to approach and embrace their new neighbors.

Scheriers, Unicorns, and Brunnens joined the growing ocean of people crossing into their homelands. Each breed of the Land witnessed the appearance of humans in their ancient homes. And they all received orders from their Queen to seek and comfort God's children as they crossed. They too communed with *their* departed friends and family. Taufe connected with Archbishop Conrad and with Hildegard. Acheriel and Prische connected their thoughts as if she still lived and their horns wrapped around each other.

The air of Eden was made divine again by the return of God's children. And every living thing became fully divine offspring of the one God. With the appearance of each human choosing intimacy with God over the seductions of their previous lives, the Sweeter Realm grew Godlier. God and the spirits of our loved ones were everywhere, in the grass and the water, the sand and the air. And we were in constant contact with them, brushing against them with every leaf we touched, smelling them in the air and receiving them into our lungs with every breath.

My friends, my subjects, those dear creatures who elected me their Queen were perfect hosts. They greeted the humans. They loved them and welcomed them into their homelands and cities. Scheriers dug them caves and Unicorns built them huts. Friends of the Scheriers fed them and Brunnens bathed them. Eulesängers sang for them and Zweigwesens tended to every bruise, scrape, and sickness. Wherever they landed when they passed through Joseph's Portal, they made it their home and became part of the creature communities.

My thoughts were flying through the thoughts of the people, as quickly as a Wühlenvogel flies through the crisp night air. I was interrupted by the voice of Joseph in my head.

"Turn around," he told me.

I obeyed my son and turned to see Felix, trotting toward me on the shoulders of Acheriel. Behind them was Lenelil carrying The Ancient One. I ran to them, mounted Acheriel behind Felix, wrapped my arms around my husband and focused my mind on Joseph. I blocked all others out, and Felix and I held the spirit of our son, as tightly and tangibly as we did when he was a baby.

Senische came sprinting up along her father's path, with her surrogate mother clinging tightly to her mane. She was laughing as she always did when she and Joseph rode together. They rode together again, with Joseph in her mind instead of on her shoulders.

Lina leaped from her daughter onto my lap, and Senische turned around and ran back toward the lake, springing and bouncing and relishing her reunion with her childhood friend. Acheriel carried the three of us on his shoulders and back, from the distant reaches of the queendom, where Joseph's Portal set me down, to my palace and home on the shore of the Queen's Lake.

Along the way we stopped at every camp, town, shrine, and city, visiting with the people and the creatures. It was a simple tour, with only a Unicorn, a Scherier, a Federman, and a Queen, with no grand procession and no Royal Guard. But in its way, it was the grandest of tours. On that slow, meandering trip home, weaving in and out of the various communities, we were the thread that sewed them all together. We stayed with some for hours and some for weeks. It took us seven months to get home. Our longest stay was in Gralkirsche, with the Hüter and the Boots of Lohengrin. God's reunion with mankind would have faced a much narrower path if not for their dedication and efforts over the centuries of the Swan Knights.

When we arrived in the throne room of the palace, there surrounded by my Guard, was my mother. My brother Karl was there with his wife, and their children splashed in the shallow water of the palace opening, playing with Vogelkrötes while Cort laughed and accompanied their movements with waving arms that made him look like he was caressing some invisible creature in front of him.

I could connect my mind to my father whenever I wanted. But I could not touch him. I could not smell his hair or rub his earlobe between my thumb and index finger, like I did as a child. My mother was not dead. She stood, body and spirit, in front of my throne. I savored that physical reunion, wrapping my arms around her and inhaling her scent. I kissed her and received her kisses. I introduced my family to The Ancient One. In connecting their minds, they knew him in an instant as I knew him. They saw every memory we shared since my Swimmers pulled him from the Queen's Jail all those years earlier. They knew what was owed to him on my behalf, and they honored him as I do.

I set them up with rooms in the palace — my mother and Karl's family. They enjoyed the perks of being the family of the Queen. Taufe joined us that evening. Before we went to bed that night, we gathered around the table with the living and with the spirits of the departed, together as a family. My husband, my teachers, my mother and brother, my nephew and nieces, my father and my son, and my dear friends conversed late into the night. Afterward, I went to bed alone with my Felix — all alone. In our bed together, I had only him in my mind and only him with my body. Just as I was falling asleep in his warm, feathered arms, he kissed me. My definition of the word "Bliss" is based on that moment.

The next few weeks were the hardest I had ever worked. My mind jumped from groups of people to individuals and on to other groups, comforting them, connecting them, and teaching them how to live in their new home. I was not concerned with the practical logistics of everyday life. I left that to the kind creatures to teach. I concentrated my efforts on their spiritual adjustments. God and their ancestors were in every breath of air. I had to show them how to grab them and how to let them go, how to connect with the mind of God and see the infinite, and how to reduce their thoughts to the mundane. I had to show them how to reach for me when they needed me. It was an almost constant endeavor. I had to rehearse my own lessons and focus briefly on my own surroundings, my own husband and friends, my own departed love ones. Joseph rarely left me in those weeks. He spoke to me, and I to him, almost every minute of every day. My evenings, before bed, belonged to God. Those were some of the only moments I seemed able to completely release the billions of minds reaching to me for help and understanding.

In my fourth week back in the palace, I received a delightful visit that served as quite a distraction. Birgit came to the palace. On the first day in Eden, when so many confused minds clawed at my attention, I found Birgit. I continued to call her Birgit, though it is a name she stopped using when I disappeared from her world that summer after eighth grade. With the help of my faithful Unicorns, I set her up in a wooded field near Gemeinsam, not far from the home of Acheriel, Lina, and Senische.

When we met in the palace, she seemed fourteen years old again. We both did. We sang our old songs and danced our old dances, but with the depth of spirit of two old friends who lived full lives and shared paradise with an ever-present God. She had been in and out of relationships, having never recovered from my disappearance. She was single and had no children. I introduced her to Lina and taught them how to connect their thoughts, intimately and exclusively to each other. In time, I taught them all, humans

419

and creatures alike, how to connect their thoughts. We all had Grail Blood. That is to say, we all had God's blood.

We were again, for the first time since Abel's Portal tore us from Eden, fully-divine children of God. They all became one with Eden. The first generation of human children born in Eden began to quickly display signs of their divinity. They communicated with the winds and the trees. The sands obeyed their wishes. The humans that came to Eden lived as God created us to live — one with God, one with each other, and one with our surroundings.

I continued as the Queen, even after I had nothing extraordinary to offer. Another election was held, but there was no basin filled with ballots. Every inhabitant of Eden, human and creature, living and departed, connected minds to make the decision. I accepted with honor, and with the humility of someone who understands her own minuteness. All sense of individuality has been put into perspective, once one has swam in the comprehensive pool of universal thought.

It is amazing how quickly humans adjusted to Eden. Somehow, Eden remained a part of them, for all those countless generations, as they lived away from God. It did not take long for its familiarity to strike their hearts. They all found a place in my queendom, a realm with no armies, no soldiers, no police, no weapons. There are no banks, no money, no rich, no poor, and no hungry. I wear no gold crown. The thoughts of every soul in Eden, all who live here and those who have died, encircle *my* head. They are my crown, adorning me, bejeweling me more resplendently than any trinket worn on Earth.

Almost everyone who crossed left loved ones behind. More than two-thirds of mankind chose to cross through Joseph's Portal. The rest chose to remain with the things they knew. Maybe someday they or their descendants will find the will and a way to join us. Maybe a new Swan

Knight will surface among them, like a vein on the back of the hand, and lead them through Parsifal's Portal. The Grail did not come with us. Who knows what part it will play in the lives and fate of those who remained? I know this. We are not yet whole. With all of the united spirits filling our days, there is still an emptiness that can only be filled by a fully united mankind. I have faith that it will happen. I'm sure that Earth will continue to be the stage for love and loss, warriors and villains, teachers and students, perhaps even a teenage girl, called from her life by a classroom poster. I doubt that those heroics will have anything to do with Verena Elizabeth Kessler. My place is here. My battles have all been fought.

Brunhilde did not join us. She stayed — not in a refusal of God, but rather in an embrace of her centuries-old duty to protect the innocent and persecute the vile. She is the greatest hope I have for those who remain divided from God. She deserves paradise. She has earned a life in Eden. But she has chosen to fight for God from within the Lion's Den. Perhaps she holds the Holy Grail in her hand as I write this. She is the perfect hero for the new Earth, an Earth suddenly bereft of all who were inclined toward God. She is far more suited to deal with that world than I am or ever was.

The Ancient One weeps daily for her. Although his new-found divinity has allowed reunions he relishes, reunions with Parsifal, Lohengrin, Elsa, and all of the Swan Knights he raised, taught, loved, and buried, he lost his Brunhilde. But he knows why she remained. He knows what she has sacrificed. She is the only remaining paladin of God in a world that has lost its population of righteous. She has always been unique. Since the return of the righteous to Eden, she is all the more extraordinary, all the more important to her world.

Parsifal's Portal is now hers to protect. The Grail is her concern, making her, not me, the Swan Knight. Although I still carry the title, here in Eden, where it has no practical purpose, we all know that Brunhilde is really the Swan Knight now, not only for the protection of the portal and Grail, but for the salvation of the rest of humanity. This understanding is the only tonic that takes away some of the sting of The Ancient One's lost love — well, not the only tonic. In the pool of divine thought, he is revered above all that have walked the Earth or Eden, save Christ himself. We have all shared his mind. We all know what he has done. We all know that our place in paradise has been purchased by his diligence and loyalty over his many centuries, by his blood and tears, and by his wing. He is honored above all, as he should be.

The swan has become the symbol of goodness and dedication in Eden. His image adorns every household, as it adorned the homes, lodges, and palaces of the Wittelsbach. My mind is still the nexus of connection between billions. But his image, his spirit is the reminder of all that he and the Swan Knights did to protect the Grail and the Sweeter Realm until the gates to Paradise reopened. Every lesson he taught from Lohengrin to Joseph, every time he threw his body in front of the sword of an invading knight, every friend and student he buried, and every pain he suffered in captivity is celebrated by all. Each chapter in the story of salvation, from the moment he met Parsifal, is his story, and told at every campfire and at every bedside in Eden. The story I have written here is his much more than mine. I write myself into *his* history with unspeakable pride and gratitude.

And now I will retire my pen. I exchange it gladly for the breath of God that is in my lungs, the touch of my husband's feathers against my skin, the smiles and caresses of my friends and family, and the sense of oneness I share with my beloved departed. I have written this account, documented these stories with the thought that someday I might swim to the bottom of the lake, cross through my portal, and deliver it into the hands of those who could most benefit from the lessons within these pages. And I leave this story behind with the hope that, if we should ever again choose greed, hate, and violence over life in the presence of God, this tale might serve as a roadmap home. God bless the many marvelous figures who shared these pages with me. God bless the Swan Knights, the native creatures of Eden, and my husband and son. God bless The Ancient One. And God bless humanity.

GLOSSARY

(Warning: Plot points revealed in definitions)

Sweeter Realm Creatures and Breeds

Acheriel [a x e: r i: ɛ l] – A Unicorn, light-grey with a salt-and-pepper mane and beard. His horn is brilliant white with blue-grey hints in the depths of the recesses of the spirals. He is the husband of Prische and the first Unicorn Verena meets in the Sweeter Realm. He knew many of the Swan Knights well. He also served as a teacher to the young Unicorn warriors. He is one of the fastest, strongest, and wisest of the Unicorns. He is the best friend of the Federman, Felix, who married Queen Verena. He is the father of Senische.

Agnes, the Scherier - A Scherier and Portal Steward who was trapped in Linderhof after the death of Ludwig II. She lived in a Wühlenvogel cave beneath Linderhof with the other creatures who happened to be in the valley when Ludwig died. She is the oldest of the Stewards trapped in the valley. She was a childhood friend of Brunhilde and Elizabeth.

Bechtold and Hildemar – Two Schildbüffels that Rüdiger called from a shallow lake. They joined Verena's effort to free The Ancient One from the Queen's Jail. They also responded to Verena's call and retrieved Joseph from the jail and brought him to the surface under an old discarded Schildbüffel shell.

Brunhilde [b r ʊ n h ɪ l d ə] – The daughter of Tannhäuser and his Brunnen lover, born deep in the Brunnen wilderness and raised alone with her parents until her mother died and her father abandoned her. She was adopted by the Swan Knight family and raised by The Ancient One. Among her amazing talents is the ability to jump high into the air and float weightless, and to sense the nature of human hearts. Duke Ludwig I built the castle for her, over the ruins of which King Ludwig II built Neuschwanstein Castle. When her father died, she left the castle and traveled north to fight cruelty.

Brunnens [b r ʊ n ə n s] – Creatures of the Sweeter Realm, with tall, feminine figures, and almost clear bodies that ripple like water when they move. They have two throats through which they speak in sweet melodic tones. They are a unisex breed generally referred to as female. They are highly spiritual with a strict sense of decorum and pride.

Cort – A Friend of the Scheriers, a nomadic breed and Verena's first acquaintances in the Sweeter Realm. It is Cort who first declares Verena to be Queen. He traveled the Land and Shallow Waters during Verena's training, preparing the creatures to rally behind the Queen. After the war, he served as master of palace Ceremonies. He is the most famous and revered Friend of the Scheriers.

Eichengeist – A young Zweigwesen and goddaughter of Verena. When she came into her sap, her family chose Verena to receive her first controlled sapping from her fingertips. The bond is eternal and is the greatest honor a Zweigwesen can give. Eichengeist received her name from

Verena. As young as she was during the war, she wanted to fight, to stand beside Verena and protect her. This earned her the name that translates to "Oaken Spirit".

Eulesängers [ɔʏ l ə s ɛ ŋ ɐ s] – Creatures of the Sweeter Realm, brown, ankle-high birds, with awkwardly large wings, a bushy tail, and a hooked beak like an owl's. They communicate in high-pitched, high-spirited whistles. They are the favorite breed of Rudolf I. Their cities consist of small huts set on giant grassy nests. Those who live outside of the cities usually live in trees, in small social and family groups.

Federmensch [f e: d ɐ m ə n ʃ] – A nomadic breed of feathered men and women. They live mostly on the northwestern side of the Queen's Lake. They are slightly shorter than the average human, but renowned for amazing physical strength. They have an unwritten, but rigidly maintained oral history. A male is called a Federman. A female is called a Federfrau. A child is called a Federkind.

Felix [f e: l ɪ k s] – A Federman, the first of his kind to meet Verena. He is an old friend of the Unicorn Acheriel and spends more time roaming the Land and Shallow Waters with Unicorns than roaming the Nomadic Belt with his own kind. He tore out his own feathers to make a prosthetic wing for The Ancient One. He sacrificed himself to save Verena from a fall that would have killed her. In doing so, he suffered breaks of every bone in his body. These and many other heroic acts endeared him to Verena. They fell in love and married.

Flaumig [f l aʊ m ɪ ç] – A Federman and cousin of Felix. He fell from a tree and was rescued by Joseph. New abilities sprang from Joseph as he manipulated the trees to catch Flaumig and commanded the sand to receive him gently to the ground. He also communicated with Flaumig's bones and commanded them to heal. This was the first sign of Joseph's expanding abilities beyond his telepathy.

Friends of the Scheriers – A nomadic breed that lives near the shore of the Queen's Lake. They have no names for their breed or their individuals, until Cort, the Friend of the Scheriers who befriended Verena on her first day in the Sweeter Realm. He remains the only of his kind to have a name. They are very service oriented and are happiest when gathering and presenting food to their friends and guests. They sleep in circular clearings in the thickest woods around the lake.

Friedrich, the Wühlenvogel [f r i: d r ɪ ç] - A Portal Steward who was trapped in Linderhof after the death of Ludwig II. He took Verena with his tail and brought her into the cave of his own construction, beneath Linderhof. He is the fastest Wühlenvogel in memory. Verena put that speed to use.

Gaier [g aɪ ɐ] – A Vogelkröte who was trapped and injured in an abandoned passageway of the old Deep Waters. From the throne room of the palace, Joseph controlled the sand to free him and commanded his body to heal. Gaier's mind found Joseph in song while Joseph slept.

Georg [g e: ɔ r k] – The Unicorn chosen to train Verena in riding and combat during her Swan Knight training in St. Hildegard. Georg became the Captain of the Royal Guard, wearing the "Mark of Sacrifice", the smudge across the arm in imitation of Felix's stained feathers.

Glühenchor [g l y: ə n ʃ o: r] – A breed of Shallow Waters creatures native to a particular pond. Each evening, they produce a glow from their bodies and an accompanying musical tone. The corps of them unite in lights and harmony to the delight of visitors from across the Land and Shallow Waters. Many of them were wiped out during the war. Some joined Verena's quest to free the swan.

Helsie [h ɛ l z i:] – A Zweigwesen, full name is Heilungslied. She is one of the oldest living Zweigwesens when she meets Joseph. Her encounter with him in the Zweigwesen village of Wurzelstadt leads to Joseph falling in love with her. He was only six years old.

Hüter [h y: t ɐ] – Member of the Scherier religious order, the *Stiefel von Lohengrin* (The Boots of Lohengrin), the only monk of the order to survive the war with the Deep. Verena found him in the steeple of the holy temple in Gralkirsche. After the order was revived and replenished, he ran the order as Grand Master.

Kandake [k a n d a k ə] – The Queen of the Land and Shallow Waters before being killed by Löwschock. She followed the Unicorn Achima as Queen and was succeeded by The Ancient One. She is a creature of the Shallow Waters of the breed of Wassermönche.

Knobby-headed Serpent – A creature of the Deep Waters. It has a large, knobby, scaled head. Each scale on its head is larger than a human hand. Its mouth is wide, with its lips wrapping around to nearly meet at the back of its enormous head. It has a bulky, rounded body with no arms or fins and a long, wrapping tail, which begins fat at the base of its bulky torso, and narrows as it winds and wraps, until it comes to a fine point at the tip of a crusty appendage that looks like an arrowhead. It is commanded by the King of the Deep Waters. It has a strong affinity for Scherier meat. The only three known to exist were killed on the shore of the Queen's Lake by the Scheriers in Verena's army.

Krummzahn [k r ʊ m ts a: n] – Old Wühlenvogel leader, known well by The Ancient One. She meets Verena after the battle at the Achima River. She joins the committee to determine the fate of Reid and serves on the panel of judges during his trial.

Lenelil [l e: n e: l ɪ l] – A Unicorn and Portal Steward. He was trapped in Linderhof when Ludwig II was killed and remained there until Verena returned to Linderhof and opened the portal. He recognized Verena as a Wittlesbach the moment she entered the Linderhof grounds as a teenager, through the perceptions of his horn. He is an old friend of Acheriel and Felix.

Lina [l i: n a] – A Scherier, dear friend of Verena, wife of Rüdiger, niece of the Old Digger. After the death of Prische, she is chosen to be the surrogate mother of Senische, Prische and Acheriel's goat. She has the honor of naming the goat's horn.

Lizzie, the Wühlenvogel – A member of Verena's Royal Guard. She was named Elizabeth after the daughter of Swan Knight, Duke Otto II of Bavaria. She carried Verena to the Portal Point when Reid came through. She fought Reid in the throne room and held him while Georg delivered the fatal strike.

Löwschock [l œ v ʃ ɔ k]– King of the Deep Waters, a large, clawed, horned water creature with the face of a lion, muscular arms and shoulders, a scaled tail with short, knobby legs and webbed feet. He crossed the portal into Linderhof, pursued, and eventually killed King Ludwig II. He returned to the Sweeter Realm years later to resume his war with the Land and Shallow Waters. He was killed by Verena, cut in half by Verena's Portal on the floor of the Queen's Lake.

Pfützeschilfs [pf ʏ ts ə ʃ ɪ l f s] – Creatures of the Shallow Waters of the Sweeter Realm. They are narrow and tubular, one to two inches long, with wings and one single, bulgy eye. They speak in high-pitched squeals. After the war with the Deep, they lived mostly in small puddles on the Land. They are the first wet creatures to join Verena in the quest to free The Ancient One.

Prische [p r ɪ ʃ ə] – A pure white Unicorn, the most beautiful in a thousand years. She was the wife of Acheriel. She was chosen to carry Verena during the procession to find swimmers to rescue The Ancient One. She left Verena to have her baby and rejoined the army for the Battle in the Achima Mountains, where she was killed by the serpents of the Deep. She is the mother of Senische, the horn named by Lina.

Queen/King of the Land and Shallow Waters – the ruler elected by the creatures of the Sweeter Realm to rule the known region on the other side of the portal, excluding the Deep Waters. The Queen from the Shallow Waters, who ruled during the lives of the Swan Knights was named Kandake. When she was killed by Löwschock, The Ancient One was elected King. After the presumed death of The Ancient One, the Kingship fell to Swan Knight, Ludwig II. When Ludwig died, the Land and Shallow Waters was without a Queen. When Verena came through the portal and resumed the line of Swan Knights, she inherited the title as the presumed heir of Ludwig. After the death of Löwschock, the border between the Deep and Shallow Waters was erased and the Deep was taken into the united queendom of the Sweeter Realm. An election was held after the war, in which Verena was elected to remain Queen.

Royal Guard – A group of exceptional creature-soldiers from the Sweeter Realm, selected by Georg. They were initially chosen as a special guard for Verena during the march to face the army of Löwschock. After the war, Verena requested that Georg reassemble the Guard and lead them as Captain. She did this primarily to satiate Georg's zealous commitment to Verena. The Move proved fortunate when the Royal Guard saved Verena's life.

Rüdiger [r y: d ɪ g ɐ] – A Scherier, dear friend of Verena, husband of Lina. He and Lina were the first Scheriers to meet Verena. He was spirited, even for a Scherier, with unlimited faith in the God, the Queen, and the Swan Knights. He was bound more by love than tradition and was remarkably brave. It was he who convinced Verena to free the swan. He died during The Ancient One's rescue from imprisonment in the Queen's Jail.

Rupert, the Scherier – A Portal Steward who was trapped in Linderhof after the death of Ludwig II. He lived in a Wühlenvogel cave beneath Linderhof with the other creatures who happened to be in the valley when Ludwig died.

Scheriers [ʃ e: r i: r s] – Creatures of the Sweeter Realm, with white hair and short, flat bodies. They are social creatures who love to wrestle. After The Ancient One, they were the first breed to meet the Swan Knights. They gifted a boulder of ore from their homeland to Elsa. Lohengrin forged it into Elsa's armor. Verena found the armor on her first day in the Sweeter Realm. The Scheriers are burrowers. They live mostly in caves of their own construction. They are avidly loyal to the Swan Knights and to the Queen of the Land and Shallow Waters.

Schildbüffels [ʃ ɪ l t b ʏ f ə l s] – Creatures of the Shallow Waters, large, with deep shells like turtles. They have wide heads like a buffalo, but with two tightly curled horns, like a ram.

Schwerthorn [ʃ v ɛ r t ɔ r n] – Large Unicorn Verena met in the Wendel Marsh, a retired Unicorn warrior who served Linderhof during Veronika's knighthood.

Senische [z eː n ɪ ʃ ə] – A Unicorn from before recorded history. According to legend, she was the first to use the horn to communicate. She held the spirits of all Unicorns in her horn, protecting them with her own goodness from the chaos that plagued the Unicorns. Once order was restored, she returned the spirits by touching horns with each living Unicorn. It is said that the horn-shaped obelisk that stood in Gemeinsam was a replica of her horn. She is known as the founder of the Unicorn collective.

Senische [z eː n ɪ ʃ ə] – Unicorn daughter of Acheriel and Prische. After Prische's death the Scherier Lina assumed motherhood of Senische and named her horn. Senische became closest friend to Joseph, the son of Verena and Felix.

Stiefel von Lohengrin [ʃ t iː f ə l f ɔ n l oː ə n ŋ r ɪ n] – Literally *The Boots of Lohengrin*, an order of ordained Scheriers living in Gralkirche. The order was established shortly after Lohengrin's death. The monks of the order school every Scherier born to the Sweeter Realm. Their primary purpose is to maintain Scherier devotion to the Swan Knights.

Syllia [z ʏ l iː a] – A Scherier and Portal Steward who was trapped in Linderhof after the death of Ludwig II. She lived in a Wühlenvogel cave beneath Linderhof with the other creatures who happened to be in the valley when Ludwig died.

Taufe [t aʊ f ə] – A Brunnen who lived for many years with Conrad of Wittelsbach, Archbishop of Mainz and Second-in-Training under Otto I. While with Conrad, she met Hildegard of Bingen, the Benedictine nun who received messages from God that related to the Sweeter Realm. When Conrad died, Taufe lived in the wild near Aischquelle, at the source of the river Aisch. When she returned to the Sweeter Realm, she was eventually granted the title of Abbess at a holy site dedicated to St. Hildegard. She was chosen to be Verena's moral tutor during her training and after the war.

The Ancient One – Creature of the Sweeter Realm, a giant swan, the first creature to meet Parsifal. He took the Grail from Parsifal and gave it to the Queen. He is the teacher of the Swan Knight children and the keeper of the Grail Blood history. He taught German to the Queen and the other creatures of the Land and Shallow Waters. He was elected King of the Land and Shallow Waters after the death of Kandake. He was abducted by Löwschock and imprisoned in an underwater jail. Upon his abduction, Ludwig II became King. While imprisoned, his left wing was brutally torn from him. He was rescued from the jail by Verena. He resumed his old duties and became teacher to Verena and eventually to Verena's son, Joseph.

Tinyn [t ɪ n i: n] – A Brunnen and Portal Steward. She was trapped in Linderhof after Ludwig II's death. It was she who received the journal from Ludwig and she who placed it in the boat in the Venus Grotto for Verena to discover. It was her voice that Verena heard echoing back to her when she first entered the Venus Grotto. She watched as Verena read the journal, and watched as Verena was pulled through the portal.

Unicorns/ Die Einhörner [d i: aɪ n h œ r n ɐ] – Creatures of the Sweeter Realm, single-horned goat-like creatures, with shaggy, bearded faces, the height of a horse, but with a slightly sloping back and narrow hips. They can communicate with each other and others through a touch of their horns. For many hundreds of years, they were the primary sentries of the portal valley. In their capital is an obelisk altar in the shape of a horn. Through it, they can communicate with their ancestors.

Vogelkrötes [f o: g ɛ l k r ø: t ə s] – Creatures of the Sweeter Realm, literally Bird Toad. They live in the Shallow Waters. They are the first wet creatures encountered by Conrad Gessner. Several of them joined Verena in her efforts to free The Ancient One. After the war, when Verena took residence in the lakeside palace, they were regular visitors and enjoyed playing in the shallow pool of the palace entrance.

Weichkern [v aɪ ç k ɐ n] – A young Zweigwesen and great-great nephew of Helsie. He injures himself when a playhouse he contructed in the wilderness collapses on him. He is as near to death as a living thing can be, beyond the help of the zweigwesens, when Helsie uses Joseph's love for her to enter his dreams and direct his powers to heal Weichkern. It is this event that adheres Joseph's spirit so tightly to music.

Wühlenvogels [v y: l ə n f o: g ə l s] – Sweeter Realm creatures. They are birds, with long necks and the snouts of wolves and jaws just as powerful, teeth just as sharp. They stand just shorter than The Ancient One. They have two hard, curled horns on their heads, which they use, with the powerful swing of their long necks, to smash the skulls of their enemies. They have large, clawed feet, which they use to burrow into the homes and hideaways they make underground. They have long powerful tails that can wrap and squeeze, with amazing dexterity and strength, whatever they choose to grab. They live in large underground cities, which they burrow with their collective efforts in a few days' time. They are hunters, predators. They built Einigkeitstadt, the city beneath the Black Forest. Their laws demand a fierce oath of loyalty to the Queen/King of the Land and Shallow Waters. Upon the presumed death of The Ancient One and the death of Ludwig II, their oath transferred to the only remaining King in the Sweeter Realm — Löwschock. Verena reclaimed their loyalty during the Battle in the Achima Mountains. They turned on Löwschock and have served the Queen ever since.

Zweigwesens [ts v aɪ g v e: z ə n s] – Creatures of the Sweeter Realm, branch-thin, chest-high, covered from head to toe in soft, almost glowing, coarse, brownish-orange hair. Their hair looks like tree bark on their thin bodies. They have the ability to seamlessly connect to one another and form balances in intricate geometric shapes. When many connect together, they can form into the shape of a tree that nobody could distinguish from a real tree. They are master botanists and they use their knowledge to concoct botanical medicines. For this reason and the medicinal value of the sap-like substance they secrete from their fingertips, they are the Sweeter Realm's most reliable medics. They enter adulthood when the first sap secretes from their fingers. It is recognized in an ancient ceremony that chooses an adult to serve as the young Zweigwesen's spiritual guide for life. Verena is chosen for the honor and serves as a sort of godmother to the young Zweigwesen.

Sweeter Realm Locations

Achima Mountains – A mountain range east of the Queen's Lake. It is named after Achima, a Unicorn and the Queen responsible for uniting the Land with the Shallow Waters. A canyon, cut by the Achima River, it the easiest passage from the Queen's Lake to Gemeinsam, the Unicorn capital.

Achima River – A river that runs from the Wendel Marsh to the Queen's Lake. It cuts a canyon through the Achima Mountains. The canyon hosted the first battle between Verena's Army and Löwschock.

Circle Clearing – A circular clearing in a densely forested part of the Nomadic Belt, on the east side of the Queen's Lake. It is about ten yards in diameterand warmly lit day and night. It is covered in short, bright grass. No sound or light escapes the circle of trees that make the clearing perimeter. Verena spent her first two night in the Sweeter Realm there, with Cort and the Friends of the Scheriers.

Deep Waters – A kingdom of the Sweeter Realm consisting of the deep parts of all bodies of water. It was ruled by Löwschock, whose throne was in the deep center of the Queen's Lake. There was a tangible border between the dark, cold waters of the Deep and the bright, warm waters of the Shallow, until Verena Killed Löwschock and united the Deep Waters with the Land and Shallow Waters. It was in the Deep Waters, near the throne of Löwschock, where Verena's blood opened her portal. It is there that she lost the Holy Grail.

Eierheim [aɪ r h aɪ m] – The Eulesänger capital, a large nest atop a plateau, covered with tiny, Eulesänger huts and houses.

Eineklaue [aɪ n ɛ k l aʊ ə] – Scherier capital city. It is a massave web of hollow mounds, tunnels, roads and arenas. Every Scherier is born in the capital before being taken to the holy site of Gralkirche to be baptized and schooled.

Erstersappe [ɛ r s t ɛ r z a: p p ə] – A town in the heart of Zweigwesen land. I has only one building — a gathering hall designed and commissioned by Verena to serve as a central gathering place for sapping ceremonies. It was her coronation gift to the Zweigwesens. Prior to Erstersappe, there was no central location for sapping ceremonies. They occurred at random places that were often out of reach for distant family and friends. The gift was particularly fitting in light of the one deepest connection between the Zweigwesens and Verena, the "First Sapping" Verena received from her Zweigwesen goddaughter, Eichengeist.

Gemeinsam [g ə m aɪ n z a m] - The Unicorn capital city. The Holy Grail was hidden there by Queen kandake, in a shallow pit beneath the sacred Unicorn Altar in the city's center.

Gralkirche [g r a l k ɪ r ç ə] – A sacred Scherier site, home of the Boots of Lohengrin. All Scheriers are brought there shortly after birth to be baptized, raised, and schooled by the Boots.

Land and Shallow Waters – The known region of the Sweeter Realm, excluding the Deep Waters. It is the jurisdiction of the Queen. It includes in its citizenry all breeds except for the creatures of the Deep. In the earliest days of the Sweeter Realm, the Lands and Waters were divided and the creatures within each had no interaction with the other. A slow-moving movement began to unite the Land and Waters, beginning with the shallow water creatures near the shore and the namads that roamed the Nomadic Belt. The sentiments grew as trust and frindships developed. Under the Queen of the Land, a Unicorn named Achima, a treaty was made to unite the Land and Waters. The creatures of the Deep Waters resisted the treaty. They isolated themselves from the Shallow Waters. The land and Shallow Waters united without the Deep. They elected Achima as the first Queen of the Land and Shallow Waters.

Pfeifen Mountains [pf aɪ f ə n] – Mountain range on the eastern side of the Eulesänger homeland. It has remained untraveled for centuries because of its sharp, jagged rocks and sudden drops.

Der Mutterleib des Flusses [d e: ɐ m ʊ t t ɐ l aɪ p d ɛ s f l ʊ s ə s] – Literally "The River's Womb". It is an island at the mouth of the Achima River. For countless generations it served as a meeting place between creatures of the Land and creatures of the Shallow Waters. After the union of the Land and Shallow Waters, the island served as the symbol of the union, and was the site of celebrations in honor of the union.

Nomadic Belt/Der Nomadengürtel [d e: r n o: m a: d ə
ŋ ʏ r t ə l] – A strip of land in the Sweeter Realm, which
wraps around the Queen's Lake. It is where the Nomadic
Breeds roam. Parsifal's Portal is in the southeast corner of
the belt.

Parsifal's Portal – Also known generally as "the Portal",
it is a passage into the Sweeter Realm from Linderhof
valley, opened for the first time when Parsifal's Holy Grail
enchanted blood fell to the earth. It opens at the approach
of all with Grail Blood —all descendants of Parsifal. It is
located at the southeast end of the Nomadic Belt, near
Zweigwesen land.

Queen's Lakeside Palace – A palace built for Kandake,
Queen of the Land and Shallow Waters. It sits with its
entrance dipping into the Queen's Lake, so that the main
floor is submerged in a few inches of water. It served as a
beacon for the united good-will of the Land Creatures and
the Shallow Waters creatures. It becomes the home of
Verena and Felix after the war. It is cone-shaped with a
large triangular entrance. The only entrance opened to the
throne room. A spiraling hallway ramps upward from the
throne room, with several smaller rooms, like grapes on a
spiraling vine. The ramp is topped with a single room, the
highest room in the palace. Nobody know how it was used
by Kandake, but Verena and Felix claimed it as their
sleeping chamber.

Saint Hildegard of Bingen [z ɛ: n t h ɪ l d ə g a r t f ɔ n b
ɪ ŋ ə n] – A twelfth century nun who received visions from
God of the Sweeter Realm. She befriended Archbishop
Conrad and Taufe, communicating with them in the

Brunnen language. Taufe dedicated to her the city and cathedral that bear her name.

Saint Hildegard (city) [z ɛ: n t h ɪ l d ə g a r t] – Religious center of the Brunnen homeland, named after its patron saint, Hildegard of Bingen, friend of Taufe and Conrad Wittelsbach. The site is a cloister, the sisters of which are rarely allowed to leave the city. After Verena is elected Queen, she venerates the site and it becomes a place of pilgrimage for the creatures, and eventually the people, of the Sweeter Realm.

Saint Hildegard Cathedral – Primary place of Brunnen worship, a place of religious pilgrimage for all creatures of the Land and Shallow Waters. Its side chambers served as classrooms for Verena's moral schooling during her Swan Knight training.

Sicherheit Marsh [z ɪ ç ɐ h aɪ t] – A large marsh divided in half by the Scherier/Eulesänger border. It runs east-west across the border. Its western edge abuts Eineklaue, the Scherier capital. Many Scheriers hid there after Löwschock ran them from their cities and shrines.

Steinhörner [ʃ t aɪ n h œ r n ɐ] – The Wühlenvogel capital, a tremendous underground cavern, large enough to hold, albeit snuggly, the entire Wühlenvogel population at once. Seven Wühlenvogel holidays throughout the year require the entire breed to meet in one cave. Steinhörner is the only place that will accommodate them all. The city flooded during the war with the Scheriers, killing more than a third of the breed. They blamed the war for the flood, leading them to take a strong stance against war and killing. The city holds a sacred reverence connected to those events, and meetings in Steinhörner often include songs about the flood and about Queen Kandake's role in saving them.

Sweeter Realm – The known world on the other side of the portal. Prior to Verena's victory over the Deep, it consisted of two kingdoms, the Land and Shallow Waters, ruled by the Queen, and the Deep Waters, ruled by Löwschock. It was the Garden of Eden before the expulsion of humanity. When God's children left Eden, it was left to its own devices. Species sprang up naturally and individual societies came from those species. The different species of the Sweeter Realm remained entirely isolated from one another until the Land united. Later, under the Queen of the Land, a Unicorn named Achima, the land and the Shallow Waters united, to the exclusion of the Deep Waters. After the death of Löwschock, the border between the Deep Waters and the land and Shallow Waters dissolved, and the Sweeter Realm was whole and united for the first time since mankind left Eden.

Unicorn Altar – A monument in the heart of the Unicorn capital of Gemeinsam, in the Sweeter Realm. It is a tall obelisk, in the shape of the horn of the greatest hero in Unicorn history. Around it are several stones, each with a single hole facing outward from the altar. The Unicorns insert their horns into the holes to connect with each other and their ancestors. A replica was built in Einigkeitstadt, the hidden city beneath the Black Forest. It was under this altar that Queen Kandake hid the Holy Grail. It was destroyed to retrieve the Grail and later rebuilt.

Unicorn Warrior Training Ground – A grassy field with low rolling hills, in a narrow strip of Unicorn land between the Brunnen and Eulesänger homelands where the

Unicorns who defended the Portal Valley and the Unicorn homeland were trained.

Wendel Marsh [v ɛ n d ə l] – A wide, deep, and sticky marsh, with sharp, hard reeds protruding through the muddy waters. It runs from Scherier land, south of Gralkirche, south into Unicorn land.

Wurzelstadt [v ʊ r ts ə l ʃ t a t] – A town in Zweigwesen land, southeast of the Portal Point. It was in this town that Joseph addressed a congregation and fell in love with Helsie.

Humans

Adolf of Wittelsbach, Count Palatine [a: d ɔ l f v ɪ t ə l s b a x] – Swan Knight and ruler of Einigkeitstadt during the Schism. He is the second son of Duke Rudolf I, the Rightful Swan Knight and Mechtild of Nassau. He married Irmengard of Öttingen, one of the most beloved and respected Swan Knight's spouses. He was assassinated in the Black Forest while celebrating the birth of his daughter.

Albert V, Duke of Bavaria – The Swan Knight who sealed the schism. His mother is descendant from Duke Rudolf I and his father from Emperor Ludwig. He is the first descendent of Rudolf I to serve as the Swan Knight in the portal valley. He exposed the portal to his friend, Conrad Gessner, who entered the Sweeter Realm and drew the attention of Löwschock.

Birgit (Hope) – Verena Kessler's best friend in middle school. She took German class with Verena and bonded with her over her obsession with Bavaria and King Ludwig II.

Conrad of Wittelsbach, Archbishop of Mainz – Brother and Second-in-Training behind Otto I, the Redhead. He was appointed Archbishop by Emperor Friedrich Barbarossa as a reward to Conrad's brother. Conrad was the first to take a Sweeter Realm creature from the valley. He kept a Brunnen as a personal friend when he left Linderhof.

Elsa – The greatest Swan Knightto live in the Portal Valley. She was the third Swan Knight, the daughter of Lohengrin and Nethe. She is the only Swan Knight to fully control the behavior of the portal with her mind. She developed telepathic communication with the Unicorns without having to make contact with the horns.

First-in-Training/Second-in-Training – The oldest and second oldest children of the reigning Swan Knight, the only two children who may know of the portal and train with The Ancient One, according to the Laws of Ermenrich.

Herr Fischer – Verena's German teacher in sixth, seventh, and eighth grade. He is a young man of German Heritage. He has a powerful passion for Germany, the German language, and the culture.

Gessner, Conrad – Friend of Duke Albert V, Swan Knight. He is a biologist and naturalist. Albert V opened the portal for him and he ran through it. He published *Historia Animalium* in 1551, with sketches and descriptions of Sweeter Realm creatures.

Irmengard of Öttingen [ɪrmənart fɔn œtɪŋən] – Swan Knight's wife of Adolf, the Rightful Swan Knight during the Schism. She had an instant connection with the

Unicorns and was the first human to share in their collective connection ritual. It was often assumed that she had Grail Blood, but her husband's banishment from the Portal Valley forbade the truth from ever being known.

Karl Kessler – Verena's younger brother.

Lewiston, Samuel – An American Intelligence officer who was stationed in France when Verena crossed over the Rhine. He was in charge of the incident with Joseph and the slaughtered soldiers. He is a good-hearted, compassionate man, but one with a strong sense of duty.

Lohengrin [l o: ə n ŋ r ɪ n] – Second Swan Knight and only child of Parsifal and Gütel. He married Nethe and was father to Elsa, the greatest Swan Knight. He was the first Swan Knight to train under The Ancient One.

Ludwig I (the Crusader), Duke of Bavaria – Swan Knight and youngest child of Swan Knight Otto I, Duke of Bavaria and his wife Agnes of Loon. Ludwig became Duke at ten years old, when his father died. His mother served as regent until Ludwig came of age. His sister Agnes yielded the Swan Knighthood to Ludwig when he grew strong enough. Ludwig served in the Fifth Crusade as Commander of Imperial Forces.

Ludwig II, King of Bavaria – Swan Knight who faced Löwschock on the banks of Lake Starnberg. He was killed by Löwschock and his body was found in the lake the next day beside that of his friend and psychiatrist, Dr. Bernhard von Gudden. Ludwig constructed Castle Neuschwanstein to be a home and refuge for his friend and teacher, The Ancient One. He built Herrenchiemsee Palace to serve as a hospital for creatures wounded in the war with Löwschock.

He recorded the Swan Knight history in a journal left for Verena Elizabeth Kessler, Swan Knight, to find.

Nethe [n ɛ t ə] – Second wife of Lohengrin and mother of Elsa, the greatest Swan Knight. She died in the house fire with Lohenfrin and their grand-daughter, Birgit.

Otto I (The Redhead), Duke of Bavaria - Swan Knight, first Wittelsbach Duke of Bavaria, known as The Red-Head. He was the hero of the battle of Verona, where enemies attacked the caravan of Emperor Fredrich Barbarosa. He inherited his Grail Blood from his paternal great-great-great grandmother, Elika van Walbeck, who married Berthold of Wittelsbach and attached the Swan Knighthood to the Wittlesbach. Otto's brother was Conrad, who became the Archbishop of Mainz and later of Salzburg.

Otto II, Duke of Bavaria – Swan Knight and only child of Duke Ludwig I and Ludmilla of Bohemia. He married Agnes, daughter of Count Heinrich of the Palatinate on the Rhine. The marriage gave Otto's father, and later Otto, the electorship of the Count Palatine.

Parsifal [p a r z i: f a l] – The First Swan Knight and a keeper of the Holy Grail. His spilled blood created the portal after he drank from the Grail. He and his wife Gütel founded the portal valley. He was father to Lohengrin. He was the first person to enter the portal and the only one to open the portal from the Sweeter Realm and return to the portal valley. He was the first to meet The Ancient One.

Reid – An American descended from Parsifal. His exact connection to the line of Swan Knights is unknown. He came through Parsifal's Portal while trying to vandalize the

Tannhäuser mural with spray paint. After a tour of the Sweeter Realm, he became intensely covetous of Verena's influence and misinterpreted her power. He tried to kill her in the throne room, assuming that with her death, his Grail Blood would elevate him to the position of Swan Knight and King. He was killed by Georg and the Royal Guard. His body was put on trial and sentenced to be spread in pieces across the Sweeter Realm.

Rudolf I, Duke of Bavaria – Swan Knight known during the Schism as the Rightful Swan Knight. He was deposed of the knighthood and the dukedom by his younger brother, Ludwig. He maintained his other hereditary title, Count Palatine of the Rhine, until he yielded that to Ludwig. He was the first to rule Einigkeitstadt, the Wühlenvogel city beneath the Black Forest. He died in England, in a desperate search for the mythical sword Excalibur.

Saint Hildegard of Bingen [z ɛː n t h ɪ l d ə g a r t f ɔ n b ɪ ŋ ə n] – A twelfth century nun who received visions from God of the Sweeter Realm. She befriended Archbishop Conrad and Taufe, communicating with them in the Brunnen language. Taufe dedicated to her the city and cathedral that bear her name.

Simon of Cyrene – A Jew from the Greek settlement in Cyrene, in Eastern Libya. He was forced by the Romans to carry the cross of Jesus' crucifixion, expediting the death of Christ. Simon served Jesus, while ushering his death. Simon is referenced by Verena in comparison to The Ancient One's service in paddling Verena to the center of the Queen's Lake to face Löwschock. Nobody believed that Verena would survivce the encounter. The Ancient One felt the duality of the situation, much as Simon must have.

Swan Knights – The line of the descendants of Parsifal, knighted by The Ancient One, whose Grail enchanted blood opens the portal. They are sworn to the protection of the portal and to the service of the Queen of the Land and Shallow Waters.

Tannhäuser [t a n h ɔʏ z ɐ] – A Teutonic Knight with Grail Blood. His name means that he comes from the house of the Lords of Tannhausen. He fought with Duke Ludwig I in the Fifth Crusade. He met Duke Ludwig in the Egyptian prison where the captured crusaders were held. He was unaware of his Grail Blood until he accidentally opened the portal.

Veronika of Welf [f ɛ r oː n ɪ k a   f ɔ n   v ɛ l f] – Swan Knight and great-granddaughter of Swan Knight Ermenrich. She had an adventurous youth before taking the Swan Knight oath. It was from her adventures that the legend of Tristan and Isolde was born.

Objects

Albert's Sword/Verena's Sword – A Unicorn-horned sword fashioned by Duke Alvert V of Bavaria, Swan Knight. The horn was lost during Albert's Battle and gifted to Albert by the Unicorn. Scared of the curious eyes it drew, Albert sent it through the portal. The Ancient One hid it there until he sent Felix to fetch it for Verena. Although detached from its Unicorn, it still hold its mystic properties. It can still connect to the collective and it hold the memories of its Unicorn.

The Conspicuous Scriptures – Books of Christian and pre-Cristian scripture not included in the Bible. These include writings of the early Hebrew prophets and Gospels of the life and teachings of Christ. Many of them speak clearly to the ultimate fate of mankind. They spell much more clearly those events and sacrifices required to bring about the Final Judgment. Taufe kept a large manuscript of the Conspicuous Scriptures and presented it to Verena in preparation for the coming of God's Will.

Coronation Gifts – It is a tradition older than time that a newly elected Queen or King of the Sweeter Realm present a gift to each breed. The gift is entirely of the Queen's choosing and is generally symbolic of her relationship and experiences with each breed.

Elsa's Armor/Verena's Armor – The armor of the third Swan Knight, Elsa, made for her by her father, second Swan Knight Lohengrin. The armor was made from an ancient Scherier ore with the magical ability to bring a sense of well-being when touched. It consists of a breast plate with attached shoulder plates, upper and lower leg coverings, arm coverings, and a helmet. Small swan figures are on the shoulders and swan wings extend out from the sides of the helmet. Elsa's son gave the armor to The Ancient One to hide it from Elsa. It remained unused until Verena found it on her first day in the Sweeter Realm.

Eulesänger Eggs – Stone replicas of the eggs of the Eulesängers, gifted to Nethe at Elsa's birth, with a hole on one end. When blowing through the hole, the eggs replicate the song of the Eulesängers.

Rudolf's Map – A map of the Sweeter Realm drawn from the descriptions of his Eulesänger friends by Duke Rudolf I when he was a boy. King Ludwig II wedged it into his journal to be found by Verena.

Unicorn Nectar - A thick nectar, the consistency of honey, but salty and bitter. It gives instant clarity of mind when eaten. It reveals no secrets that are not already known, but it clears away peripheral distractions from the subject at hand. The Unicorns consume it when important decisions need to be made.

Vambrace – The forearm guard of set of armor. The vambrace of Verena's armor still demonstrates the holes made by Löwschock's fangs, from when he bit her and spilled her blood that initiated Verena's Portal. When gifting her armor to the Scheriers at her coronation, Verena kept the vambrace with Löwschock's fang-holes. She kept it as a reminder of her mortality and of how God and the Grail saved her in the lake.

The Zweigwesen Medical Manuscript – A book of Zweigwesen medicinal plants and recipes, written collaboratively with Swan Knight Maximiliana "Milli" Maria, daughter of Albert V. The plants are all native to the Sweeter Realm. The book is written in Zweigwesen. It has been passed through many owners throughout the centuries. The Swan Knights are the only humans who know the origin language. It has baffled linguists since it left the hands of the Swan Knights. The manuscript was acquired in 1912 by Wilfrid Voynich and is now known as the "Voynich Manuscript". The manuscript has illustrations and descriptions, with specific details, from the collection and storage of the plants to the preparing of the ingredients to the application and dosage of the medicines.

Miscellaneous

Ash Wednesday – A Catholic holy day signifying the beginning of the Lenten Season. Observers of the day are reminded of their mortality and the brevity of their physical form with blessed ashes that are smeared upon the forehead in the Sign of the Cross.

Auenheim, Baden-Württemberg, Germany [aʊ ə n h aɪ m] – A small German town on the banks of the Rhine River, near the French border. It is where Friedrich takes Verena when she travels to France to find Joseph.

Battle of Einigkeitstadt – An invasion of the underground city in the Black Forest by the forces of Duke Ludwig IV of Bavaria against the children of his brother, Duke Rudolf, the Rightful Swan Knight. The invaders breached the underground city. Many creatures were killed, including the young twins of Adolf and Irmengard, Rupert and Friedrich. The battle saw the return of Brunhilde, who arrived just in time to save the line of Rudolf I.

Benedictine Order – "The Order of Saint Benedict" is a Catholic order of monks and sisters. They follow the monastic "Rules of St. Benedict". The Brunnen sisters of St. Hildegard are Benedictines, cloistered in the city named after its patron saint, a Benedictine nun who befriended Taufe and Archbishop Conrad Wittelsbach. The Benedictines do not have the tight hierarchy of other Catholic monastic orders. Each monastery operates independently, making the St. Hildegard cloister in the Sweeter Realm not much different from the Benedictine monasteries in the human world.

Black Forest – A thick forest in southwest Germany, south of Heidelberg. It was under this forest that the Rightful Swan Knight, Rudolf commissioned the construction of Einigkeitstadt, a Wühlenvogel city. The city was built for the children of Rudolf to train and hide until they could return to Linderhof and resume the Swan Knighthood. The Black Forest received its name from Roman soldiers, who noted that the canopy of the forest was so thick above head that no sun penetrated to light the forest floor below. This, and its proximity to Heidelberg, made the forest ideal for the Rightful Swan Knights.

Centennial, Colorado – A new and growing suburb of Denver, Colorado, in the U.S.A.

The Conspicuous Scriptures – Christian scriptures that were left out of the Holy Bible. They include the Gosepls of Thomas and Philip. Taufe maintains a bound book of all of the Conspicuous Scriptures. They have the name because the truths and prophesies surrounding the Sweeter Realm, Verena, and the Holy Grail that are hidden between the lines of traditional Christian scriptures are spelled out conspicuously in the Conspicuous Scriptures. After the coronation, and Joseph's conception, Taufe includes the C.S. as a daily part of Verena's spiritual schooling.

The Coronation – After the election, Verena's coronation was held in Gralkirsche, the sacred home of the Boots of Lohengrin. The city and the order exist primarily to instill in young Scheriers a strong dedication to the Swan Knights. The rites of the coronation were performed by Höter, the Grand Master of the order of The Boots of Lohengrin.

The Coronation Procession – Verena's procession with many of the creatures who attended the coronation. Organized by Felix, it began at the Portal Point, in the Nomadic Belt, near Zweigwesen land. It ran to the Queen's Lake and around the shore to the mouth of the Achima River. It moved up the river canyon to Gemeinsam and through the Wendel Marsh to Gralkirsche, where the coronation was held.

Easter Sunday – The holiest holiday in the Christian Calendar. It commemorates the Resurrection of Christ from the dead. The glory of the Ressurection is the foundational belief of Christianity. The entire Lenten Season proceeds it in order to prepare Christains to celebrate the Resurrection as purely and profoundly as possible.

Einigkeitstadt [aɪ n ɪ ç k aɪ ts t a t] – Literally "Unity City", an underground city, beneath the northern part of the Black Forest, built during the Schism by the Wühlenvogels for Rudolf I, ruled by the Rightful Swan Knights until the schism sealed with Albert V.

Eucharist, The Holy – A sacrament in the Catholic Church, when consecrated bread and wine, in remembrance of the Last Supper, are transformed into the Body and Blood of Jesus Christ. Jesus performed the first consecration of the Holy Eucharist with his Apostles, on the night before his crucifixion in an effort to maintain the influence of his Divinity on Earth and incline practitioners toward God.

The Final Judgment – Misunderstood by general Christendom as the moment Jesus returns to judge the sins of mankind. It actually refers to mankind's final chance to make good judgment — to choose between life with God in the garden of his making, and life away from God in a world of their own making.

Grail/The Holy Grail – The cup Jesus Christ used at the Last Supper to hold and distribute to the Apostles the first consecration of wine into the Blood of Christ. It was in the possession of Parsifal, who traveled the world to keep it safe from attack and out of evil hands. By the power of the Grail, Parsifal opened the portal at Linderhof. He gave the Grail to The Ancient One, who gave it to Kandake, Queen of the Land and Shallow Waters. It remained in Kandake's possession until the war with Löwschock, King of the Deep Waters. Fearing for her life and the safety of the Grail, Kandake hid it under the ancient Unicorn altar, and obelisk in the likeness of the horn of Senische. The Grail remained under the obelisk until it was discovered by Verena. Verena drank from the Grail at the bottom of the Queen's Lake, while battling Löwschock. It opened Verena's Portal and healed her wounds, as it did Parsifal's. These miracles are the only discovered and documented powers of the Grail. But nobody knows the extent of its powers, nor the ultimate part it will play in the Will of God.

Grossostheim, Bavaria, Germany [g r o: s s ɔ s t h aɪ m] – A town in northwest Bavaria, in the district of Aschaffenburg. Verena's Portal opens in a museum southeast of the town.

Joseph's Portal – The portal to the Sweeter Realm opened by the spilling of Joseph's blood, after he drank from the Holy Grail.

Kehl, Baden-Württemberg, Germany [k e: l] – The German town on the French border where Verena crossed the Rhine into France to find Joseph. There is a pedestrian walkway across the river, guarded on the French side by a military outpost.

Last Supper – A Passover meal shared between Jesus Christ and his Apostles on the night before Jesus was crucified. At this meal, Jesus broke bread and poured wine, consecrating them into his Divine Body and Blood, the first Holy Eucharist.

Lent – A season in the Christian Liturgical Calendar. It begins on Ash Wednesday and ends on Holy Saturday, the day before Easter. The season is used to prepare for the celebration of Easter and to recognize the suffering of Christ. Fasting and other forms of self-denial and sacrifice are combined with alms-giving and and penance to direct the eyes away from the seductive pleasures of society and toward Christian obligations.

Linderhof [l ɪ n d ɐ h oː f] – The name of the portal valley, given by Duke Ludwig II when he was very young. He was trying to say that it was a soft and gentle courtyard compared to the palace at Landshut. The name stuck and it was called Linderhof ever since. By the swan Knight family and the Sweeter Realm creatures, it is also called the Portal Valley, the Grail Valley, Parsifal's Valley, or simply the Valley.

Linderhof Palace – The palace at Linderhof valley that King Ludwig II built where the old lodge stood. He built it so that he could rule Bavaria without leaving the portal valley.

Main, River [m aɪ n] – A river in Germany. A tributary of the Rhine. It runs through the Franconia region.

Mark of Sacrifice – A black smudge across the right upper-arm, front leg, or fin, depending upon the breed. It denotes membership in the Queen's Royal Guard, an elite group of warriors chosen to protect Verena. The mark is in imitation of the stained feathers on Felix's arm, made black when he wiped Verena's armor with his own feathers before her initial procession to find swimmers to rescue The Ancient One. The stains on Felix's arm never faded, which is not usual for that sort of stain on a Federman's feathers. Verena always said that it was not the dirt that marked the feathers, but the love and sacrifice, which is why it never faded.

Mural of Tannhäuser – A painting of the legendary poet as portrayed inaccurately by Germanic folklore. Rather than the Brunnen lover and mother of Brunhilde, the mural depicts the goddess Venus as Tannhäuser's romantic obsession. Swan Knight, King Ludwig II commissioned the painting to be placed at the Portal Point, inside of his artificial cave, the Venus Grotto. The symbolism of Tannhäuser's breach of the portal in search of his Brunnen lover, portrayed by the poet in Venus' lair, served as a code to those who knew the Swan Knights history as the Portal Point into the Sweeter Realm.

Niemitz Skeletons [n iː m ɪ ts] – The skeletal remains of Löwschock's lower half and the serpents banished by Verena through her portal. The portal deposited the creatures beneath the ground, where they died embedded in earth. Construction crews discovered the unique bones and turned the discovery over to a team of scientist, led by zoologist and bioscientist Nicholas Niemitz. The skeletons were named after Niemitz, as was the museum that was erected on the site where the bones were found.

Oberammergau, Bavaria, Germany [oː b r a m ə r g aʊ] – A town in southern Bavaria, near Linderhof. Verena took the train from Grossostheim to Oberammergau. From there, she took a bus to Linderhof to meet the Portal Stewards. Oberammergau is a quaint, medieval town, with half-timbered buildings with painted murals of German folk tales.

Ohhl Ginshass Wahuff [o h j l g e n s h a s v a h ɔ f f] – An ancient Unicorn slogan, roughly meaning "From the scattered to a united mind". Legends say that it was first spoken by the Unicorn prophet Senische. She spoke it to each Unicorn as she returned their souls to them after the Age of Chaos.

Palm Sunday – A holy day in the Christian Liturgical Calendar. One week before Easter, the holiest Christian holiday, observers recognize Christ's entrance into Jeruselem. Services on Palm Sunday feature blessed palms in remembrance of those laid before Jesus' feet as he entered the city.

Portal Point – The spot in Linderhof Valley where Parsifal's blood hit the ground and the portal opened. In the Sweeter Realm, the Portal Point sits on the southern end of the Nomadic Belt, near the Queen's Lake.

Portal Steward – Any creature or human who lives in the Portal Valley and commits to the protection of the portal and the Grail.

St. Johannes Church – A Roman Catholic Church in Kehl Germany. Verena attended mass at the church before crossing into France.

Sapping Ceremony – A Zweigwesen "coming of age" ceremony, performed when a young Zweigwesen's sap glands come into maturity. During puberty, sap begins to flow from a young Zweigwesen's fingertips. Although the sap flows uncontrolled at first, for the first several days, the Zweigwesen soon learns how to control the flow. At the first sign of sapping, the ceremony is planned. By the time the community has gathered, the celebrant has control of the sap and can distribute it at will. A godparent is chosen by the family. In the sapping ceremony, the young Zweigwesen saps the godparent's forehead, lips, and chest. The godparent serves as a moral guide for life. Verena was the first non-Zweigwesen ever chosen for the honor. She became the godparent of a Zweigwesen she affectionately calls Eichengeist (Oaken Spirit).

Schism, the – The split in the Swan Knighthood after the children of Duke Ludwig II, Rudolf and Ludwig, fought over the dukedom and the knighthood. During the schism, the line of Ludwig remained in the portal valley as Swan Knights there, while the line of Rudolf maintained a simultaneous Swan Knighthood in Einigkeitstadt, a secret city beneath the Black Forest. For most of the Schism, the Rightful Swan Knights in the Black Forest held the title of Counts Palatine on the Rhine.

Venus Grotto – An artificial cave built by King Ludwig II to hide and protect the portal. A mural depicting Tannhäuser and the goddess Venus sits precisely on the Portal Point. The grotto holds an artificial lake and a boat built to replicate Lohengrin's boat pulled by The Ancient One. The grotto was one of the first places in Bavaria to be lit with electric lights and powered by an electric generator.

www.ingramcontent.com/pod-product-compliance
Lightning Source LLC
Chambersburg PA
CBHW071340020726
47502CB00001B/184